Bath Tangle

Georgette Heyer

Published by Sourcebooks Casablanca, an imprint of Sourcebooks, Inc.
P.O. Box 4410, Naperville, Illinois 60567-4410
(630) 961-3900
Fax: (630) 961-2168
www.sourcebooks.com

Library of Congress Cataloging-in-Publication Data

Heyer, Georgette.
Bath tangle / by Georgette Heyer.
p. cm.
1. Stepdaughters—Fiction. 2. Bath (England)—Fiction. I. Title.
PR6015.E795B38 2011
823'.912—dc22

2011015762

Printed and bound in the United States of America
POD 10 9 8 7 6 5 4

Also by Georgette Heyer

Romance

The Black Moth
These Old Shades
The Masqueraders
Beauvallet
Powder and Patch
Devil's Cub
The Convenient Marriage
Regency Buck
The Talisman Ring
The Corinthian
Faro's Daughter
Friday's Child
The Reluctant Widow
The Foundling
Arabella
The Grand Sophy
The Quiet Gentleman
Cotillion
The Toll-Gate
Bath Tangle
Sprig Muslin
April Lady
Sylvester
Venetia
The Unknown Ajax
Pistols for Two
A Civil Contract
The Nonesuch
False Colours
Frederica
Black Sheep
Cousin Kate
Charity Girl
Lady of Quality

Historical Fiction

Simon the Coldheart
The Conqueror
An Infamous Army
Royal Escape
The Spanish Bride
My Lord John

Mystery

Footsteps in the Dark
Why Shoot a Butler?
The Unfinished Clue
Death in the Stocks
Behold, Here's Poison
They Found Him Dead
A Blunt Instrument
No Wind of Blame
Envious Casca
Penhallow
Duplicate Death
Detection Unlimited

One

Two ladies were seated in the library at Milverley Park, the younger, whose cap and superabundance of crape proclaimed the widow, beside a table upon which reposed a Prayer Book; the elder, a Titian-haired beauty of some twenty-five summers, in one of the deep window-embrasures that overlooked the park. The Funeral Service had been read aloud, in a pretty, reverent voice, by the widow; but the Prayer Book had been closed and laid aside for some time, the silence being broken only by desultory remarks, uttered by one or other of the ladies, and the ticking of the clock upon the mantelpiece.

The library, whose curiously carved bookshelves and gilded and painted ceiling had earned it honourable mention in every Guide Book to Gloucestershire, was a handsome apartment, situated upon the ground floor of the mansion, and furnished with sombre elegance. It had been used, until so short a time previously, almost exclusively by the late Earl of Spenborough: a faint aroma of cigars hung about it, and every now and then the widow's blue eyes rested on the big mahogany desk, as though she expected to see the Earl seated behind it. An air of gentle sorrow clung about her, and there was a bewildered expression on her charming countenance, as though she could scarcely realize her loss.

It had indeed been as sudden as it was unexpected. No one, least of all himself, could have supposed that the Earl, a fine, robust man in his fiftieth year, would owe his death to so paltry a cause as a chill, contracted when salmon fishing on the Wye. Not all the solicitations of his host and hostess had prevailed upon him to cosset this trifling ailment; he had enjoyed another day's fishing; and had returned to Milverley, testily making light of his condition, but so very far from well that his daughter had had no hesitation in overriding his prohibition, and had sent immediately for a physician. A severe inflammation of both lungs was diagnosed, and within a week he was dead, leaving a wife and a daughter to mourn him, and a cousin, some fifteen years his junior, to succeed to his dignities. He had no other child, a circumstance generally held to account for his startling marriage, three years earlier, to the pretty girl who had not then attained the dignity of her twentieth year. Only the most forbearing of his friends could think the match allowable. Neither his splendid physique nor his handsome face could disguise the fact that he was older than his bride's father, for his birth-date could be read in any *Peerage*, and his daughter had been the mistress of his establishment for four years. When no heir to the Earldom resulted from the unequal match, those who most deprecated the Earl's many eccentricities pronounced it to be a judgment upon him, his sister, Lady Theresa Eaglesham, adding obscurely, but with conviction, that it would teach Serena a lesson. Any girl who dismissed her chaperon at the age of twenty-one, refused two flattering offers of marriage, and cried off from an engagement to the most brilliant prize in the Marriage Mart was well served when her father brought home a young bride to supplant her, said Lady Theresa. And all to no purpose, as she for one had foretold from the outset!

Some such reflection seemed to be in the widow's mind. She

said mournfully: 'If I could have been more dutiful! I have been so very conscious of it, and *now* the thought quite oppresses me!'

Her stepdaughter, who had been leaning her chin on her hand, and gazing out at the trees in the park, just touched with autumn gold, turned her head at this, and said bracingly: 'Nonsense!'

'Your Aunt Theresa –'

'Let us be thankful that my Aunt Theresa's dislike of me has kept her away from us at this moment!' interrupted Serena.

'Oh, don't say so! If she had not been indisposed –'

'She was never so in her life. Wretched work my Uncle Eaglesham made of her excuses. He is a poor creature.'

'Perhaps she has stayed away, then, because she does not like me,' said the widow unhappily.

'No such thing! Now, Fanny, don't be absurd! As though anyone could help liking you! For my part, I am excessively obliged to her for remaining in Sussex. We can never meet without rubbing one another, and although I think her the most Gothic woman alive, I own she had something to bear when I spent my first Season under her roof. Poor woman! She brought two eligible suitors up to scratch, and I liked neither. My character was retrieved only when I was stupid enough to become engaged to Ivo Rotherham, and lost beyond recovery when I put an end to that most abominable episode of my life!'

'How dreadful it must have been for you! Within a month of the wedding!'

'Not in the least! We quarrelled more royally than ever before, and I positively enjoyed crying-off. You will allow, too, that there is a distinction in having given the odious Marquis a set-down!'

'I should never have dared to do so. His manners are so – so very unconciliating, and he looks at one as though he held one in contempt, which throws me into confusion, try as I will to overcome such folly.'

'Detestable man!'

'Oh, Serena, hush! You cannot always have thought so!'

Her stepdaughter threw her a quizzing glance. 'Are you in one of your romantical flights? Goose! I became engaged to Ivo because I thought it would suit me to be a Marchioness, because Papa made the match, because I have known him for ever, because we have some tastes in common, because – oh, for a number of excellent reasons! Or so they seemed, until I discovered him to be unendurable.'

'Indeed, I don't wonder at it that you could not love him, but have you never – have you never met anyone for whom you felt a – a decided partiality, Serena?' asked Fanny, with a wondering look.

'Yes, indeed! Does that set me up in your esteem!' Serena replied, laughing. 'I fancied myself very much in love when I was just nineteen years old. The most handsome creature, and with such engaging manners! You would have been in raptures! Alas, he had no fortune, and Papa would not countenance the match. I believe I cried for a week, but at this length of time I cannot be sure.'

'Oh, you are funning!' Fanny said reproachfully.

'No, upon my honour! I did like him very much, but I have not laid eyes on him in six years, my dear, and the melancholy truth is that Papa was quite right when he assured me that I should recover from the disappointment.'

The widow looked as if she thought this melancholy indeed. 'Who was he, Serena if you don't dislike telling me?'

'Not in the least. His name was Hector Kirkby.'

'And you have never met him again?'

'Never! But he was a soldier, and his regiment had just been ordered to Portugal, so that that cannot be considered wonderful.'

'But now that the War is over –'

'Fanny, you are incorrigible!' exclaimed Serena, a good deal of affectionate amusement in her face. 'Now that the War is over, I am no longer a green girl, and Hector if he is alive, which I am sure I hope he may be – is in all likelihood married, and the father of a hopeful family, and would be hard put to it to recall my name!'

'Oh, no! *You* have not forgotten!'

'Well, no,' acknowledged Serena, 'but, to own the truth, until you put me in mind of him I had not thought of him for years! I am afraid I am a coldhearted sort of a female after all!'

Fanny, who had seen her flirt with and rebuff several eligible suitors, was almost inclined to believe that it must be so. But no one could look upon that beautiful face, with its lovely, wilful mouth, its lustrous eyes, brilliant under rather heavy, smiling lids, and think its owner coldhearted. In fact, it was quite the last epithet anyone could have found to bestow upon such a vital, passionate creature as Serena, thought Fanny. She was headstrong, and obstinate, sometimes quite dreadfully mannish, as eccentric as her father, quick-tempered, impulsive, impatient of restraint, and careless of appearances; but with all these faults, and a great many more, she had a wealth of kindness and of generosity, and a chivalry which made her beloved amongst her father's dependants.

'You are putting me out of countenance! Why do you stare so?'

Recalled by the sound of that low-pitched, musical voice, Fanny gave a little start, coloured up, and said: 'As though anything could! I beg your pardon: my wits were wandering! Oh, Serena, how *very* kind you have been to me!'

'Good gracious!' The brows which Serena did not scruple to darken, shot up; the eyes, gleaming more green than hazel, mocked, but gently. 'My poor dear! This dismal occasion has put the most sickly thoughts into your head! Or is it rather my cousin Hartley? I am sure I do not blame you, if that is the case!'

Diverted, the widow exclaimed involuntarily: 'How much *you* must blame *me* for having disappointed all your hopes of keeping him out of the succession!'

'Fudge! I never had any! No, indeed! I am much in your debt, for not having given me a half-brother young enough to have been my son. How ridiculous I must then have appeared! It does not bear thinking of.'

'Too generous!' Fanny said into the folds of a black-bordered handkerchief. 'And your Papa – ! Never one word of reproach to me, but I know how much he disliked the thought of Hartley's succeeding him!'

'Dear Fanny, pray don't cry! We shall have my uncles, and your father, and Mr Perrott upon us at any moment, to say nothing of Hartley himself! To be sure, one would not have *wished* him to have stepped into Papa's shoes, but it is no such great matter, after all! If you know any harm of him, it is more than I do.'

'Your Papa said that he would have liked him better if he *had* known any harm of him,' said Fanny dolefully.

This made Serena laugh, but she said: 'Very true! He is virtuous and a dead bore! I am sure, the first Carlow to be so. However, my father had known it any time these dozen years, and might, had the matter seriously troubled him, have married again long before you were out of the schoolroom. To suppose that he married you only for the sake of an heir shows you to be a great simpleton. Heavens, will they never bring this carouse to an end? It is a full hour since the carriages returned!'

'Serena! Not a *carouse*!' Fanny protested. 'How can you talk so?'

'To hold a feast over the remains of the departed is a custom that can only disgust any person of sensibility!'

'But, indeed it is only a cold collation!' Fanny said anxiously.

The doors at one end of the room opened softly, and the butler came in, with the intelligence that the funeral party was breaking up, carriages being called for, and Mr Perrott, his late lordship's attorney, desiring him to carry his respects to my lady, and to ask if it would be convenient to her to receive him presently. Addressing himself to Serena, he volunteered the information that the funeral had been so well attended that several of the humbler mourners had found it impossible to force their way into the church, a circumstance which appeared to afford him consolation. Receiving from Fanny an assurance that she was ready to see Mr Perrott, he withdrew again.

The minutes lagged past. Fanny said faintly: 'I don't know why it should affect one so. The Will must be read, I know, but I wish it were over!'

'For my part, I think it a great piece of work to make!' said Serena. 'Such a parade, such stupid formality, which there is not the least occasion for! The only persons who might wish to hear it read are those to whom my father has left private bequests, and they are not invited to be present! It can contain no surprises for you, or for me, or, indeed, for my cousin.'

'Oh, no! It is all my folly – and fearing to vex Papa! From what he said to me, I collect that he and Mama expect me to return home – to Hartland, I mean. He spoke as though it were certain. I said nothing, for there was no time – or perhaps I had not the courage,' she added, with a pitiful little smile.

'Tell me what you wish to do!'

'If it were my duty to return, I would do so,' the widow faltered.

'*That* does not answer my question! At Hartland, your wishes are of no account; *here*, surely, it has been otherwise!'

'Yes, indeed it has!' Fanny said, her eyes filling with tears. 'It is that which makes me wonder whether it is perhaps naughtiness and self-will which prompts me to think that my first duty *now* is to you, and not to Papa!'

'If you can't be comfortable without the assurance that you are doing your duty, let me tell you that my whole dependance is upon you – Mama!' Serena said, her voice prim, but irrepressible humour gleaming in her eyes. 'If you are not to take me in charge, what is to become of me? I give you fair warning I won't live with my Aunt Theresa, or with my Aunt Susan! And even I should hesitate to set up my own establishment without a respectable female to bear me company. Depend upon it, *that* would mean Cousin Florence! The Carlows and the Dorringtons would be as one in agreeing that the poor creature must be sacrificed.'

Fanny smiled, but said in a serious tone: 'I can't take you in charge, but I *can* be your chaperon, and although I am very silly I do think it would answer better than for you to be obliged to live with Lady Theresa, or even with Lady Dorrington. And if it is what *you* would like, dearest Serena, I cannot doubt that it is what your Papa would desire me to do, for he was fonder of you than of anyone.'

'Fanny, *no*!' Serena said, stretching out her hand impulsively.

'But it is not at all to be wondered at! You are so very like him. So I have quite made up my mind what I ought to do. Only I do hope that Papa will not order me, for it would be so very shocking to be obliged to disobey him!'

'He won't do so. *He* must realize, though you do not, that you are Lady Spenborough, not Miss Claypole! Moreover –' She stopped, but, upon receiving a look of enquiry, continued bluntly: 'Forgive me, but I am persuaded neither he nor Lady Claypole will press you to return to them! With such a numerous family, and your elder sister still unwed – oh, no, they cannot wish for your return!'

'No! Oh, how very right you are!' exclaimed Fanny, her brow clearing. 'Agnes, too, would so particularly dislike it, I daresay!'

There was no time for more. The doors were again opened, and a number of funereally clad gentlemen were ushered into the room.

The procession was led by the eldest, and certainly the most impressive of these. Lord Dorrington, whose girth had upon more than one occasion caused him to be mistaken for the Duke of York, was brother to the first Lady Spenborough and from having a great notion of his own importance, and a strong disposition to meddle in other persons' affairs, had appointed himself to the position of doyen to the party. He came ponderously into the room, his corsets slightly creaking, his massive jowl supported by swathe upon swathe of neckcloth, and, having bowed to the widow, uttering a few words of condolence in a wheezing voice, at once assumed the task of directing the company to various chairs. 'I shall desire our good Mr Perrott to seat himself at the desk. Serena, my love, I fancy you and Lady Spenborough will be comfortable upon the sofa. Spenborough, will you take this place? Eaglesham, my dear fellow, if you, and ah – Sir – William, will sit here, I shall invite Rotherham to take the wing-chair.'

Since only Mr Eaglesham attended to this speech, only he was irritated by it. Precedency having been cast overboard, he had entered the library in Lord Dorrington's ample wake. He was as spare as his lordship was corpulent, and wore the harassed expression which, the unkind asserted, was natural to Lady Theresa Carlow's consort. Having married the late Earl's sister, he considered that he had a better right than Dorrington to assume the direction of affairs, but he knew no way of asserting it, and was obliged to content himself with moving towards a chair as far distant as possible to that one indicated by Dorrington, and by muttering animadversions against pretentious and encroaching old popinjays, which were as soothing to himself as they were inaudible to everyone else.

The first in consequence was the last to enter the room, the Marquis of Rotherham, saying: 'Oh, go on, man, go on!' thrusting the attorney before him, and strolling into the library behind him.

His entrance might have been said to have banished constraint. The Lady Serena, never remarkable for propriety, stared incredulously, and exclaimed: 'What in the world brings *you* here, I should like to know?'

'So should I!' retorted his lordship. 'How well we should have suited, Serena! So many ideas as we have in common!'

Fanny, well accustomed to such exchanges, merely cast an imploring look at Serena; Mr Eaglesham uttered a short laugh; Sir William Claypole was plainly startled; Mr Perrott, who had drawn up the original marriage settlements, seemed to be suddenly afflicted with deafness; and Lord Dorrington, perceiving an opportunity for further meddling, said, in what was meant to be an authoritative tone: 'Now, now! We must not forget upon what a sad occasion we are gathered together! No doubt there is a little awkwardness attached to Rotherham's unavoidable presence here. Indeed, when I learned from our good Perrott –'

'*Awkwardness?*' cried Serena, her colour heightened, and her eyes flashing. 'I promise you, I feel none, my dear sir! If Rotherham is conscious of it, I can only say that I am astonished he should choose to intrude upon a matter which can only concern the family!'

'No, I am not conscious of it,' responded the Marquis. 'Only of intolerable boredom!'

Several pairs of eyes turned apprehensively towards Serena, but she was never a fighter who resented a knock in exchange. This one seemed rather to assuage than to exacerbate her wrath. She smiled reluctantly, and said in a milder tone: 'Well! But what made you come, then?'

Mr Perrott, who had been engaged in spreading some documents over the desk, gave a little, dry cough, and said: 'Your ladyship must know that the late Earl appointed my Lord Rotherham to be one of the Executors of his Will.'

That this intelligence was as unexpected as it was unwelcome was made plain by the widening of Serena's eyes, as she turned them, in a look compound of doubt and disgust, from Rotherham to the attorney. 'I might have guessed that that was how it would be!' she said, turning aside in mortification, and walking back to her seat in the window embrasure.

'Then it is a great pity you did not guess!' said Rotherham acidly. 'I might then have been warned in time to have declined the office, for which I daresay there could be no one more unsuited!'

She deigned no reply, but averted her face, fixing her gaze once more upon the prospect outside. Her cousin, wearing his new dignities uneasily, was inspired by his evil genius to assume an air of authority, saying in a tone of reproof: 'Such conduct as this is quite unbecoming, Serena! Now that the late unhappy event has made me head of the family I do not scruple to say so. I am sure I do not know what Lord Rotherham must be thinking of such manners.'

He brought himself under the fire of two pairs of eyes, the one filled with wrathful astonishment, the other with cruel mockery. 'Well, you can certainly be sure of that!' said Rotherham.

'For my part,' said Dorrington, in a peevish voice, 'I consider it very odd in my poor brother, very odd indeed! One would have supposed – however, so it has always been! Eccentric! I can find no other word for it.'

This provoked Mr Eaglesham, swelling with annoyance, to point out to his lordship the very remote nature of his connection with the late Earl. There were others, he took leave to tell him, whose claims to have been appointed Executor of the Will were very much nearer than his. Lord Dorrington's empurpled cheeks then became so alarmingly suffused that Spenborough said hastily that the appointment of Lord Rotherham was perfectly agreeable to him, whatever it might be to others.

'Obliging of you!' said Rotherham, over his shoulder, as he crossed the room to where Fanny was still standing nervously beside her chair. 'Come! Why do you not sit down?' he said in his abrupt, rather rough way. 'You must be as anxious as any of us, I daresay, to be done with this business!'

'Oh, yes! Thank you!' she murmured. She glanced fleetingly up at him, as she seated herself, faltering: 'I am very sorry, if you dislike it. Indeed, I am afraid it may be troublesome to you!'

'Unlikely: Perrott will no doubt attend to everything.' He hesitated, and then added, in a still brusquer manner: 'I should be making you speeches of condolence. Excuse me on that head, if you please! I am no great hand at polite insincerities, and give you credit for believing you cannot wish to figure as inconsolable.'

She was left feeling crushed; he walked away to a chair near the window in which Serena sat, and she, taking advantage of Sir William Claypole's claiming his daughter's attention at that moment, said: 'You might give her credit for some natural sorrow!'

'Dutiful!'

'She was most sincerely attached to my father.'

'Very well: I give her credit for it. She will soon recover from such sentiments, and must be less than honest if she does not feel herself to have been released from a most unnatural tie.' He looked at her from under the heavy bar of his black brows, a satirical gleam in his eyes. 'Yes, you find yourself in agreement with me, and don't mean to admit it. If sympathizing speeches are expected of me, I will address mine to you. I am sorry for you, Serena: this bears hard on you.'

There was no softening either in voice or expression, but she knew him well enough to believe that he meant what he said.

'Thank you. I expect I shall go along very tolerably when I have become – a little more accustomed.'

'Yes, if you don't commit some folly. On that chance, however, I would not wager a groat. Don't shoot daggerlooks at me! I'm impervious to 'em.'

'On this occasion at least you might spare me your taunts!' she said, in a low, indignant voice.

'Not at all. To spar with me will save you from falling into a green melancholy.'

She disdained to answer this, but turned again to look out of the window; and he, as indifferent to the snub as to her anger, took up a lounging position in his chair, and sardonically surveyed the rest of the company.

Of the six men present he gave the least impression of being a mourner at a funeral. His black coat, which he wore buttoned high across his chest, was at odd variance with a neckcloth tied in a sporting fashion peculiarly his own; and his demeanour lacked the solemnity which characterized the elder members of the party. From his appearance, he might have been almost any age, and was, in fact, in the late thirties. Of medium height only, he was very powerfully built, with big shoulders, a deep chest, and thighs by far too muscular to appear to advantage in the prevailing fashion of skin tight pantaloons. He was seldom seen in such attire, but generally wore top-boots and breeches. His coats were well-cut, but made so that he could shrug himself into them without assistance; and he wore no other jewellery than his heavy gold signet-ring. He had few graces, his manners being blunt to a fault, made as many enemies as friends, and, had he not been endowed with birth, rank, and fortune, would possibly have been ostracized from polite circles. But these magical attributes were his, and they acted like a talisman upon his world. His Belcher neckties and his unconventional manners might be deplored but must be accepted: he was Rotherham.

He was not a handsome man, but his countenance was a striking one, his eyes, which were of a curiously light gray, having a great deal of hard brilliance, and being set under straight brows which almost met. His hair was as black as a crow's wing, his complexion swarthy; and the lines of his face were harsh, the brow a little craggy, the chin deeply cleft, and the masterful nose jutting between lean cheeks. His hands were his only beauty, for they combined strength with shapeliness. Any of the dandy set would have used all manner of arts to show them off: my Lord Rotherham dug them into his pockets.

Since Lord Dorrington and Mr Eaglesham showed no disposition to bring their acrimonious dialogue to an end, and Lord Spenborough's polite attempts to recall them to a sense of their surroundings were not attended to, Rotherham intervened, saying impatiently: 'Do you mean to continue arguing all day, or are we to hear the Will read?'

Both gentlemen glared at him; and Mr Perrott, taking advantage of the sudden silence, spread open a crackling document, and in severe accents announced it to be the last Will and Testament of George Henry Vernon Carlow, Fifth Earl of Spenborough.

As Serena had foretold, it contained little of interest to its auditors. Neither Rotherham nor Dorrington had expectations; Sir William Claypole knew his daughter's jointure to be secure: and once Mr Eaglesham was satisfied that the various keepsakes promised to his wife had been duly bequeathed to her he too lost interest in the reading, and occupied himself in thinking of some pretty cutting things to say to Lord Dorrington.

Serena herself still sat with her face turned away, and her eyes on the prospect outside. Shock had at first left no room for any other emotion than grief for the loss of her father, but with the arrival of his successor the evils of her present situation were more thoroughly brought to her mind. Milverley, which had been her home for the twenty-five years of her life, was hers no longer. She who had been its mistress would henceforth visit it only as a guest. She was not much given to sentimental reflection, nor, during her father's lifetime, had she been conscious of any deep attachment to the place. She had taken it for granted, serving it as a matter of duty and tradition. Only now, when it was passing from her, did she realize her double loss.

Her spirits sank; it was an effort to keep her countenance, and impossible to chain her attention to the attorney, reciting in a toneless voice and with a wealth of incomprehensible legalities a long list of small personal bequests. All were known to her, many had been discussed with her. She knew the sources of Fanny's jointure, and which of the estates would furnish her own portion: there could be no surprises, nothing to divert her mind from its melancholy reflections.

She was mistaken. Mr Perrott paused, and cleared his throat. After a moment, he resumed his reading, his dry voice more expressionless than before. The words: '...all my estates at Hernesley and at Ibshaw' intruded upon Serena's wandering thoughts, and informed her that her share of the bequests had been reached at last. The next words brought her head round with a jerk.

'...to the use of Ivo Spencer Barrasford, the Most Noble the Marquis of Rotherham –'

'*What?*' gasped Serena.

'...in trust for my daughter, Serena Mary,' continued Mr Perrott, slightly raising his voice, 'to the intent that he shall allow her during her spinsterhood such sums of money by way of pin-money as she has heretofore enjoyed, and upon her marriage, conditional upon such marriage being with his consent and approval, to her use absolutely.'

An astonished silence succeeded these words. Fanny was looking bewildered, and Serena stunned. Suddenly the silence was shattered. The Most Noble the Marquis of Rotherham had succumbed to uncontrollable laughter.

Two

Serena was on her feet. 'Was my father out of his senses?' she cried. '*Rotherham* to allow – ! *Rotherham* to consent to my marriage! Oh, *infamous*, abominable!'

Her feelings choked her; she began to stride about the room, panting for breath, striking her clenched fist into the palm of her other hand, fiercely thrusting her uncle Dorrington aside when he attempted ponderously to check her.

'Pray, Serena – ! Pray, my dear child, be calm! Abominable indeed, but try to compose yourself!' he besought her. 'Upon my word! To appoint a trustee outside the family! It passes the bounds of belief! I suppose I am not nobody! Your uncle! What more proper person could have been found to appoint? God bless my soul, I was never more provoked!'

'Certainly one may say that eccentricity has been carried pretty far!' observed Mr Eaglesham. 'Very improper! I venture to say that Theresa will most strongly disapprove of it.'

'It must be shocking to any person of sensibility!' declared Spenborough. 'My dear cousin, everyone must enter into your feelings upon this occasion! No one can wonder at your very just displeasure, but, depend upon it, there can be found a remedy! Such a whimsical clause might, I daresay, be upset: Perrott will advise us!' He paused, looking towards the attorney, who, however, preserved an unencouraging silence. 'Well, we shall see! At all events, the Will cannot be binding to Rotherham. It must be within his power to refuse such a Trusteeship, surely!'

'*He!*' The word burst from Serena's lips. She swept round, and bore down upon the Marquis, as lithe as a wild cat, and as dangerous. 'Was it your doing? *Was* it?'

'Good God, no!' he said contemptuously. 'A pretty charge to saddle myself with!'

'How could he do such a thing? How *could* he?' she demanded. 'And without your knowledge and consent? No! No! I don't believe it!'

'When you have come to the end of all this fretting and fuming, perhaps you may! Your father desired nothing so much as our marriage, and this is his way of bringing it about. It's a cock that won't fight, however!'

'No!' she said, cheeks and eyes flaming. 'I will never be so enforced!'

'Nor I!' he said brutally. 'Why, you featherheaded termagant, do you imagine that I wish for a wife upon such terms? You mistake the matter, my girl, believe me!'

'Then release me from so intolerable a situation! To be obliged to beg *your* consent – ! *Something* must be done! It must be possible! My whole fortune tied up – pin-money – Good God, how could Papa treat me so? Will you assign the Trust to my cousin? Will you do that?'

'Poor devil, no! If I could, I would not! You would bully him into giving his consent to your marriage to the first wastrel that offered, only to break the Trust! Well, you won't bully me, so make up your mind to that, Serena!'

She flung away from him, and resumed her restless pacing, tears of rage running down her face. Fanny went to her, laying a hand on her arm, saying, in a beseeching tone: 'Serena! Dearest Serena!'

She stood rigidly, her throat working. 'Fanny, don't touch me! I am not *safe*!'

Fanny found herself being pushed unceremoniously aside. Rotherham, who had come up behind her, seized Serena's wrists, and held them in a hard grasp. 'You have edified us enough!' he said harshly. 'A little more conduct would be becoming in you! No, you will neither hit me, nor claw my eyes out! Be still, Serena, and think what a figure you make of yourself!'

There was a pause. Fanny trembled for the issue, herself a good deal distressed. The stormy eyes, shifting from Rotherham's dark face, found hers. The glare went out of them. A shuddering sigh broke from Serena; she said: 'Oh, Fanny, I beg your pardon! I didn't hurt you, did I?'

'No, no, never!' Fanny cried.

Serena began unconsciously to rub the wrists which Rotherham had released. She glanced round the room, and gave a rather hysterical little laugh. 'Indeed, I am very sorry! I am behaving so badly, and have thrown you all into embarrassment. Pray excuse me! Rotherham, I must see you before you leave Milverley: will you come to me, if you please, in the Little Drawing-room?'

'At once, if you wish it.'

'Oh, no! My senses are quite disordered still. You must give me time to mend my temper if I am not to be betrayed again into unbecoming warmth!'

She hurried out of the room, repulsing Fanny, who would have accompanied her, with a gesture, and a quick shake of her head.

Her departure unleashed the tongues of her relations, Mr Eaglesham deploring so passionate a disposition, and recalling his wife's various pronouncements on the subject; Fanny firing up in defence; Dorrington ascribing the outbreak to Rotherham's provoking manners; and Spenborough reiterating his determination to overset the clause. This at once led to further disputation, for Dorrington, while agreeing that the clause should be overset, resented Spenborough's assumption of authority; and Mr Eaglesham, on general grounds, was opposed to any scheme of Dorrington's. Even Claypole was drawn, though reluctantly, into expressing an opinion; but Mr Perrott, waiting with gelid calm for the discussion to end, met all appeals with noncommittal repressiveness; and Rotherham, his shoulders to the door, his arms folded across his chest, and one leg crossed negligently over the other, appeared to consider himself the audience to a farce which at once bored and slightly diverted him. It lasted too long for his patience, however, and he put a ruthless end to it, interrupting Dorrington to say: 'You will none of you overset it, and you are none of you concerned in it, so you may as well stop making gudgeons of yourselves!'

'Sir, you are offensive!' declared Mr Eaglesham, glaring at him. 'I do not hesitate to tell you so!'

'Why should you? I don't hesitate to tell you that you're a muttonhead! I collect that you think her aunt the properest person to control Serena's hand and fortune. You'd look mighty blue if you could succeed in foisting that charge on to Lady Theresa! What a trimming she would give you, by God!'

Lord Dorrington burst into a rumbling laugh which immediately set him coughing and wheezing. Mr Eaglesham, much incensed, opened his mouth to retaliate, and then, as the appalling truth of Rotherham's words came home to him, shut it again, and seethed in silence. After regarding him sardonically for a moment or two, Rotherham nodded at the attorney, and said: 'You may now read us the rest of this original document!'

Mr Perrott bowed, and replaced the spectacles on his nose. The Will contained no further surprises, and was listened to without comment. Only at the end of the reading did

Rotherham unfold his arms, and stroll over to the desk, holding out an imperative hand. Mr Perrott put the Will into it; the stiff sheets were flicked over; in frowning silence the Marquis studied the fatal clause. He then tossed the document on to the desk, saying: 'Ramshackle!' and walked out of the room.

His departure was the signal for the break-up of the party. Mr Perrott, declining Fanny's civil offer of hospitality, was the first to take leave. He was accompanied out of the library by the new Earl, who desired information on several points, and followed almost immediately by Mr Eaglesham, who was engaged to spend the night with friends in Gloucester; and by Lord Dorrington, who had had the forethought to bespeak dinner at one of his favourite posting-houses, and was anxious lest it should spoil. Fanny soon found herself alone with her father, who, with Spenborough, was remaining at Milverley until the morrow.

She awaited his first words with a fast-beating heart, but these, not surprisingly, were devoted not to her affairs but to Serena's. 'An awkward business!' Sir William said. 'Quite unaccountable! A strange man, Spenborough!'

She agreed to it, but faintly.

'One cannot wonder at your daughter-in-law's vexation, but I should be sorry to see any daughter of mine in such a passion!'

'Oh, pray do not regard it, Papa! In general, she is so good! But this, coming as it does at *such* a moment, when she is in so much affliction and behaving so beautifully – ! The distressing circumstances, too – her previous connection with Rotherham – the most ungentlemanly language he used. She must be pardoned! She is so good!'

'You astonish me! Your Mama was much inclined to think her not at all the thing. She has some odd ways! But there, these great ladies think they may behave as they please! I daresay she would tie her garter in public, as the saying goes!'

'Oh, no, no! Indeed, you misjudge her, Papa! If she is an unusual girl, recollect that to dear Lord Spenborough she was more a son than a daughter!'

'Ay! It is an unhappy thing for a girl to lose her mother! No more than twelve years of age, was she? Well, well! You are very right, my dear: allowances must be made for her. I am very sensible to it, particularly now, when I should have wished above all things that I could have brought your mother to you!'

Fanny was too much astonished at having her opinion deferred to by him to do more than murmur a confused assent.

'It is an unfortunate circumstance that she should be lying-in when her presence must have been a comfort to you.'

'Oh, yes! I mean – that is, it was so kind of her to have spared you to me!'

'No question of that! I never knew your Mama to give way to crotchets of that kind. Besides, you know, a tenth lying-in is by no means the same thing as a first. One does not make a piece of work over it! She will be sadly disappointed, however, not to receive better news of you than I can carry to her. Not that my hopes were high. After three years, it was scarcely to be expected. A sad pity, upon all counts!' She hung her head, blushing deeply, and he made haste to add: 'I don't mean to reproach you, my dear, however much I must wish it had been otherwise. I daresay Spenborough felt it?'

She replied in so suffocated a voice that only the words 'always so considerate' could be distinguished.

'I am glad to hear you say so. It is no very pleasant thing to know that one's possessions must pass into the hands of some trumpery cousin – no great thing, the new Earl, is he? – but I hold him to be as much to blame as you. What a freak, to contract inflammation of the lungs while the succession was still unsure! I never knew such improvidence!' He sounded indignant, but recollected immediately to whom he spoke, and begged pardon.

'There is no sense in dwelling upon the matter, to be sure. For *your* sake, it is a great deal to be regretted. Your rank must always command respect, but had you been the mother of a son your consequence would have been enhanced beyond anything, and your future decided. As things have fallen out, it is otherwise. I don't know, Fanny, if you have any thoughts on this head?'

She gathered her forces together, and replied with tolerable firmness: 'Yes, Papa. I have the intention of removing to the Dower House, with dear Serena.'

He was taken aback. 'With Lady Serena!'

'I am persuaded it is what Lord Spenborough would have desired me to do. She must not be deserted!'

'I imagine there can be no question of that! She has her uncle, and that aunt who brought her out, after all! Spenborough, too, was saying to me this morning that he and my lady hoped she would continue to make this her home. I own, I thought it handsome of him. To be taking a firebrand into one's family is not what *I* should choose!'

'Hartley and Jane – Lord and Lady Spenborough, I mean, have been everything that is kind: Serena is fully conscious of it, but she knows it would not do. If you please, Papa, I believe it to be my duty to take care of Serena!'

'*You* take care of *her*!' he ejaculated, laughing. 'I wish I may see it!'

She coloured, but said: 'Indeed, it is she who has taken care of me, but I am her mother-in-law, and the most proper person to act as her chaperon, sir.'

He considered this, and yielded a reluctant assent. 'It might be thought so indeed, but at your age – I don't know what your Mama will say to it! Besides, the young lady, with that fortune at her back, will very soon be snapped up, temper and all!'

'She has too strong a mind to be taken-in. I don't fancy she will be married for a little while yet, Papa.'

'Very true! Nothing of that nature can be contemplated for a year at least. You will keep strict mourning, of course. Your Mama was inclined to think that you should return to Hartland for that period, for however much you may be known as the Dowager Countess, my dear, it cannot be denied that you are by far too young to live alone. We had some notion that when you put off your mourning, and will no doubt be thinking of setting up an establishment of your own, you might take one of your sisters to live with you. But that is to look some way ahead, and I don't mean to dictate to you! There is something to be said for this scheme of yours, after all. You have been used to be the mistress of a great house, my dear, and you would not like to be living at Hartland again, in the old way. No, I am much disposed to think that you have hit upon the very thing to make all straight! That is, if you believe that you can be comfortable with Lady Serena?'

'Oh, yes! So *very* comfortable!'

'Well, I should never have thought it! I only hope she may not get into a scrape. You will be blamed for it, if she does! Her character is unsteady: *that* was plain when she made herself the talk of the town by jilting Rotherham! You were still in the schoolroom, but I well remember what an uproar it caused! I believe the wedding-cards had actually been sent out!'

'It was very bad, but, indeed, Papa, I honour her for her resolution in drawing back before it was too late! Dear Lord Spenborough wished the match to take place, but nothing, I am persuaded, could have been more ineligible! *He* liked Rotherham because he is such a great sportsman, and such a splendid rider to hounds, and he could never be brought to see that he would be a dreadfully harsh and disagreeable husband! He would have made Serena so unhappy! He is the most hateful man, and takes a delight in vexing her! You must have heard the way he speaks to her – the things he doesn't scruple to say!'

'Ay! And I heard her too! A very improper style she uses towards him! Let me tell you, Fanny, that there is something very displeasing in that bold manner of hers! She expresses herself with a freedom I would not tolerate in one of *my* daughters.'

'She has known him since she was a child – has never stood upon ceremony with him! If she is sometimes betrayed into unbecoming warmth, it is his fault, for so unkindly provoking her! And as for temper, I am sure he has a worse one than hers could ever be!'

'Well, it's plain you have a fondness for her, my dear,' he said indulgently. 'For my part, I would not be in Rotherham's shoes at this moment for something! He may think himself fortunate if he comes off without a scratched face, I daresay!'

But when he joined her in the Little Drawing-room, Rotherham found Serena quite composed. He said, as he closed the door: 'What now? Am I here to be entreated, or abused?'

She bit her lip, but said: 'You would not be moved by either, I suppose.'

'Not in the least, but I am quite at your disposal if you wish to continue quarrelling with me.'

'I am determined not to do so.'

He smiled. '*That* resolution will be broken soon enough! What *do* you want, Serena?'

'I wish you will sit down! Ivo, what is to be done?'

'Nothing.'

'You cannot mean to accept the Trust!'

'Why not?'

'Good God, one moment's reflection must be enough to make you see how intolerable it would be! For both of us!'

'I can see why you should think it intolerable, but why should I find it so?'

'You don't want for sense, so I suppose you are trying to provoke me! Can you doubt that the story will be one of the

on-dits of the town within a week? My Uncle Dorrington will take care of that! Everyone will be talking about it, and laughing at it!'

'This is a new come-out for you, Serena!' he said admiringly. 'You were never used to give a straw for what anyone might say of you!'

She flushed, and looked away. 'You are mistaken. In any event, to have everyone watching us would be detestable!'

'Let 'em watch! They will be tired of it by the time you are out of black gloves, and in the meanwhile it won't worry me.'

'To have everyone conjecturing?'

'Lord, Serena, I've been food for conjecture any time these dozen years! There have been some very good stories made up about me, too.'

She looked despairingly at him. 'I know this humour too well to suppose it is of the least use to continue talking. You mean to fob me off by pretending not to understand me.'

'No, I don't. I understand you very well, but you're refining too much upon it. There's nothing remarkable in my being appointed to be your Trustee: everyone knows I was one of your father's closest friends, and no one will be surprised that he chose to name me rather than that old fool, Dorrington, or the rasher of wind your aunt married!'

'No – if it had not been for that wretched engagement!' she said frankly. '*That* is what makes it so intolerable! Papa's intention is – is *blatant*!'

'You can console yourself with the reflection that it is I, and not you, who will be a laughing-stock for the vulgar,' he said grimly.

'How can you talk so? I promise you, I don't wish you to be put into such a position!'

'Don't waste a thought on it! I'm inured!'

'Oh, how *odious* you are!' she exclaimed, with suppressed violence.

'*That* sounds more like you!' he said cordially. 'I thought it would not be long!'

She controlled herself with a strong effort, not lost on him, tightly gripping her hands together in her lap, and clenching her teeth on her lower lip.

'Take care, Serena! you will go into strong convulsions if you bottle up so much spleen!'

She was always quick to perceive the ridiculous, and gave a gasp. Her eyes did indeed flash a challenge, but her sense of humour got the better of her temper, and she burst out laughing. 'Oh – ! At least own that you would provoke a saint!'

'I never tried to. *You* are no saint!'

'No, alas!' she sighed. 'Come! don't tease me, Ivo, *pray*! Is there *no* way of upsetting that infamous Will?'

'I should imagine not. I'm no lawyer, however. Consult your father's attorney! I warn you, he returned no very encouraging answers to your uncles, when they appealed to him. I daresay it might be upset if I were to contravene the Trust, but I shan't.'

'If you were to refuse to act – ?'

'I shan't do that either. You wouldn't get control of your fortune if I did, and that's what you chiefly want, isn't it?'

'Of course it is! My father gave me £250 pounds a year for pin-money, and that was very well while he lived, but how the *deuce* am I to support myself on such a sum?'

'Don't try to bamboozle me, my girl! Your mother's fortune was settled on you.'

'Ten thousand pounds, invested in the Funds! The whole of my income will be less than £700! Good God, Ivo, I daresay Papa must have spent as much on my hunters alone!'

'Oh, more! He gave a thousand guineas for that flea-bitten gray which carried you so well last season. But you will hardly hunt this year!'

'This year! No! But am I to be reduced to penury all the days of my life?' she demanded. 'What if I should remain a spinster? Has any provision been made for that contingency?'

'No, none. I looked particularly at the Will to be sure of it,' he replied. 'A damned, ill-managed business – but I suppose he thought there was no fear the point would arise.'

'He has certainly done his best to thrust me into marriage with the first man who is so obliging as to offer for me!' she said bitterly.

'You are forgetting something, my love!'

She looked mistrustfully at him. 'No! *Your* consent must be obtained!'

'Just so! But make yourself easy! I shan't withhold it unreasonably.'

'You would do anything to spite me!'

'Well, if I do, you will have a very good case against me, and will no doubt be able to break the Trust. Meanwhile, let me give you a piece of advice! If you don't wish to afford the world matter for gossip, assume the appearance at least of complaisance! How you came to make such a ninnyhammer of yourself, for all those fools to gape at, I know not! Rail at me in private if you choose, but in public behave so that the interested may believe you to be very well-satisfied with the arrangement, and see nothing in it but what is natural and comfortable.'

She was obliged to acknowledge the good sense of this advice. 'But for the rest – ! How shall I do? *Can* I support myself on so little, Ivo?'

'You *might* do so on much less, but from what I know of you you would not. But what is all this talk of supporting yourself? You don't mean to set up your establishment, do you? *That* your father never intended!'

'No, I don't – but if I did you could not prevent me! At least I don't have to win your odious consent for anything but marriage!'

'You don't, but if you indulged in any such folly your debts would very soon teach you the unwisdom of flouting my advice,' he retorted.

Her bosom swelled, but she said nothing.

'Well, what *do* you mean to do?' he asked.

'I shall remain with Lady Spenborough,' she answered coldly. She discovered that he was frowning, and raised her brows. 'Pray, have you any objection?'

'No. No, I've no objection. You won't feel yourself straitened, at all events, while you live under her roof, and *she* has been so handsomely provided for that she may well support you. But – here?'

'At the Dower House. I perceive that that displeases you! You must be ingenious indeed if you can hit upon a plausible reason to account for your disapproval!'

'I am not displeased, I don't disapprove, and if you show hackle again without cause, you may expect to have your ears boxed as they never have been yet – more's the pity!' he said savagely. 'Live where you choose! It's all one to me. Have you anything more to say?'

'No, I have not, and I should be very happy to think I need never say another word to you for as long as I live – and of all things in the world there is nothing – *nothing* – so abominable, and contemptible, and cowardly, and ungentlemanly as persons who walk out of the room when one is addressing them!'

He had opened the door, but at that he burst out laughing, and shut it again. 'Very well! But I warn you I shall give as good as I get!'

'You need not tell me that! If you don't disapprove, why did you scowl so?'

'My habitual expression, possibly. It was unintentional, I assure you. The thought in my mind was merely that it would be better for you to remove from this vicinity. To be situated at the Dower House cannot be anything but painful to you, Serena, believe me!'

She said impulsively: 'Oh, I *beg* your pardon! But how could I guess you meant nothing but kindness?'

'A home-thrust!' he interjected.

'No, no! I didn't mean it so! Only, in general – but never mind that! I know it must be painful to remain here, but I think that is the kind of sensibility I ought to overcome. And, you know, Ivo, my cousin is not quite up to the trick!'

'So I should imagine.'

'He is a very good sort of a man in his way, and he wishes to do just as he ought, but although he has always been the heir-at-law he was not *bred* to succeed Papa, and I fancy he never expected that it would come to that, so what with that, and Papa's not liking him above half, he has never been put in the way of things here, and the truth is that he's not *fit to go*!'

'What is that to the purpose?'

'Why, don't you see? I shall be able to help him in a thousand ways, and to school him a little, and to see that all goes on as it should!'

'Good God! Serena, take my word for it, you would be very ill advised to undertake anything of the sort!'

'No, you mistake, Ivo! It was my cousin's own suggestion! He told me that he hoped I would remain at Milverley, and put him in the way of things. Of course I would never do *that*, but I was a good deal touched, and I don't doubt I can be just as useful to him if I live with Fanny, at the Dower House.'

'Nor do I!' he said, with the flash of a wry grin. 'If your cousin wants information, let him seek it of your father's agent!'

'I daresay he will, but although Mr Morley is an excellent person, he was not bred here, as I was! It is not a *part* of him! Oh – ! I express myself so clumsily, but *you* must surely know what I mean!'

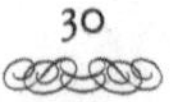

'I do!' he said. 'It is precisely what I meant when I counselled you to remove from this neighbourhood!'

He assured her very kindly that there was not the least need of apology, but she was deeply mortified, knowing herself to have erred in a way that was most likely to cause resentment. She tried to make further amends; he said that he perfectly understood; reiterated his wish that she would always look upon Milverley as her home; and left her with a strong desire to hasten the preparations for her departure.

But even had the Dower House been ready for instant occupation, it would scarcely have been possible for her to have left Milverley. The task of assembling all her own and Fanny's personal belongings proved to be a far more difficult and protracted one than she had anticipated. A thousand unforeseen difficulties arose; and she was constantly being applied to by her cousin for information and advice. She could not but pity him. He was a shy, unassuming man, more painstaking than able, who plainly found the unexpected change in his circumstances overwhelming. That he might succeed his cousin he had never regarded as more than a remote possibility; and since the Earl had shared this view, he had never been granted the opportunity to become familiar with all the details of a great estate. He came to it from a far more modest establishment, where he had been living in quiet content with his wife, and his youthful family, and for many weeks felt crushed by the appalling weight of fortune, lands, and title. In Serena's presence, he had the uncomfortable sensation of being a nonentity, but he was really very grateful to her, and knew that he would have found himself in a worse case without her, since she could always explain the meaning of the mysteries uttered by such persons as agents and bailiffs. With these he had not learnt to be at ease. He knew himself to be under close observation; they assumed that he had knowledge which he lacked; he was afraid to appear contemptible by confessing ignorance; and relied on Serena to make all plain. She thought he would do better when he had his wife beside him, for it appeared, from the many references to Jane's capabilities, that hers was the stronger character. But the new Countess was not coming to Milverley until their London house had been disposed of. She seemed to be very busy, and scarcely a day passed without her writing to know whether she should sell some piece of furniture, or send it to Milverley; what he wished her to do about the new barouche; whether she should employ Pickford's to convey all their heavy cases to Milverley; and a dozen other problems of the same nature.

Serena found that she was obliged to spend several days in London. The preparation of the house in Grosvenor Square for its new owner could not be wholly entrusted to servants. Fanny, whom travel always made unwell, shrank from the journey; so Serena, undertaking to execute all her commissions, set out with no other escort than her maid, and in a hired post-chaise. It was a novel experience, all her previous journeys having been made either in her father's company, or under the direction of a courier, but she was in no way daunted, finding it rather amusing to be paying her own shot at the posting-house in which she spent the night, contracting for the hire of horses and postilions, and ordering her own dinner. But Lady Theresa, whose guest she was, was shocked beyond measure, dared not guess what her father would have said, ascribed it all to her having cried off from her engagement to Rotherham, and recalled with approval her own girlhood, when she had never done so much as walk in the park at Milverley without having her footman in attendance.

It was painful to visit the house in Grosvenor Square under such altered circumstances, and disagreeable to discover that Lady Spenborough had already inspected it from cellars to attics. Serena was thunderstruck when this news was divulged to her by the housekeeper: she had not believed such conduct to be possible. There could be no denying that her ladyship had every right to go to the house, but there was a want of delicacy about the proceeding which gave a disagreeable impression, hard to shake off. It was excused by the Countess herself, who paid a morning-visit at Lady Theresa's house in Park Street for the express purpose of explaining to Serena the peculiar exigency which had made it necessary for her to go to Grosvenor Square. All was glossed over, in a speech beginning with the words: 'I daresay you must have wondered a little…' but although Serena forgave she was unable to forget, and had never been in such sympathy with her aunt as when that lady later described the Countess's behaviour as encroaching, and such as sank her below reproach. But Lady Theresa was not astonished, for she had never liked Jane. From the outset she had detected beneath the insipid formality of her manners a sort of shabby gentility which had quite given her a disgust of the young woman. She dressed badly, too, had no countenance, and grossly indulged her children.

It was not until November that Fanny and Serena were at last installed at the Dower House. So much preparation and bustle had been attached to the arrival at Milverley of Lady Spenborough and her hopeful family, and so many pinpricks had had to be endured, that Serena was able to agree wholeheartedly with Fanny, when she exclaimed, as they sat down to their first dinner in their new home: 'Oh, how comfortable this is!' Wearied out by all the exertions of the past weeks, she believed that she could be happy in her new surroundings, and looked forward with confidence to the future. The sensation of being uncomfortably cooped-up would pass when she grew more accustomed to living in small rooms; it would be amusing to mingle freely with such neighbours as she had previously received only on Public Days; she was sure she should find plenty to do and to be interested in.

Alas for such sanguine hopes! There were more trials to be endured than she had suspected. She had foreseen that the loss of her father's companionship would be hard to bear, but not that she would find herself pining for things she would have voted, a year earlier, a great bore. In her world, winters were enlivened by visits: one expected to spend a week at Badminton, another at Woburn; one presided over shooting-parties, rode to hounds, and entertained a succession of guests. All this was at an end: she had never dreamed that she could miss it so intolerably. She recalled the many occasions on which she had inveighed against the necessity of inviting this or that person to stay at Milverley, but it would not do: that was the life to which she had been bred, and she could not easily relinquish it. Nor could she cross the threshold of Milverley without suffering a pang. Its occupation by her cousins seemed scarcely less deplorable than the invasion of Rome by the Goths. She knew herself to be unreasonable, and for a long time never confided even to Fanny the burning resentment that consumed her every time the new owners departed from some trivial but time-honoured custom. 'We think,' and 'We prefer,' were words too often heard on Jane's tongue, uttered with a calm complacency which was in itself an offence. As for Hartley, it required a real effort for her to maintain friendly relations with anyone so unworthy to succeed her father. She acknowledged his wish to do right, she was aware of the difficulties that confronted him, but when he confessed himself to be no racing man, and divulged that he meant to dispose of his predecessor's string, she could not have been more shocked if he had declared himself to have become a follower of Mahomet. She was not mollified by his considering it to be his duty to hunt a little: his horsemanship, judged by her standards, did him little credit.

Fanny saw how much she was chafed, and grieved over it,

but could not enter into her sentiments. Her changed circumstances exactly suited Fanny. She had never felt herself at home at Milverley; the Dower House was just what she liked. A dining room suitable for the entertainment of no more than six persons, a pretty drawing-room, and a cosy breakfast parlour were infinitely preferable to her than half a dozen huge saloons, leading one out of the other; and the exchange of endless, echoing galleries for two neat halls, one over the other, was to her a gain. To consult with her housekeeper on such questions as how the mutton should be dressed for dinner, or pippins best preserved in jelly; to spend the morning in the stillroom, or in overlooking her linen, was exactly what she liked, and what Serena was no hand at at all. Indeed, Serena knew nothing of such matters. It was natural to her to command; she had reigned over her father's household to admiration, triumphantly confuting the older ladies who had considered her too young to succeed in such a charge; but her notion of housekeeping was to summon the steward, or the groom of the chambers, and to give him a general direction. Had an ill-chosen dinner ever been sent to table, she would have taken instant steps to ensure that such an accident should not be repeated; but had she been required to compose a menu she would have been as hard put to it to do so as to boil an egg, or make up her own bed. As Fanny had been thankful to leave the reins of government at Milverley in her hands, so was she now content to let Fanny manage all the domestic affairs at the Dower House. She could only marvel that she should enjoy the task, and find so much to interest her in such restricted surroundings. But the more brilliant the parties at Milverley had been the more Fanny had dreaded them. Her disposition was retiring, her understanding not powerful, and her marriage had followed so swiftly on her emergence from the schoolroom that she had come to it with little knowledge of her husband's world, and none at all of its personalities. Her grace and gentle dignity had supported her through many ordeals, and only she knew what nerve-racking work it had been, during the first months of marriage, to take part in conversations which bristled with elliptical references to events of which she was ignorant, or to persons whom she had never met. To receive a visit from Mrs Aylsham, from the Grange, or to listen to Jane's anecdotes about her children, suited her very well. Serena could imagine nothing more insipid, and hardly knew how to sit through such sessions without yawning.

The Milverley ladies, though acquainted with most of the neighbouring gentry, had never been intimate with any. The gulf that lay between Milverley and more modest establishments was too great to allow of anything approaching a free exchange of hospitality; and although the 5th Earl had been affable to his neighbours, and Serena meticulous in the observances of civility, it was generally felt that a dinner or an evening party at Milverley called for no reciprocal invitation. On hunting days, if the last point had carried him far from Milverley, it was not unusual for his lordship to take his pot-luck in the house of some hunting-acquaintance. As often as not, he would have his daughter with him, the pair of them muddied to the eyebrows; and no guests, it was agreed, could have been less haughty, or easier to entertain. But after being passed from footman to footman on the way up the Grand Stairway at Milverley, traversing several saloons, being received in the Long Drawing-room by the Lady Serena, and sitting down to his lordship's notion (genially expressed) of 'just a neat, plain dinner,' there were few ladies with minds of so lofty an order that they could contemplate without an inward shudder any formal return of such hospitality.

When the stepmother and daughter took up their residence at the Dower House, a good deal of diffidence was felt by the well-bred; and all but pushing persons of no sensibility waited to see what attitude they would assume towards their neighbours before thrusting upon them civilities which might be unwelcome.

'With the result,' said Serena, fully alive to the scruples operating on the minds of the delicate, 'that we are left to the mercy of the Ibsleys, and that odious Laleham-woman, my dear Fanny! Oh, I must tell you that I came smash up against Mrs Orrell in Quenbury this morning, and taxed her openly with neglect! You know that unaffected way she has! She told me, with *such* a twinkle, that old Lady Orrell had said to her that she hoped she would not be in a hurry to leave cards on us, for *that* would be lowering herself to Lady Laleham's level! You may imagine how I roared!'

'Oh, did you tell her how happy we should be to receive her?'

'To be sure I did! But you would have been shocked, Fanny! We enjoyed a delightful gossip, and made out between us that Lady Laleham's beginnings must have been wholly vulgar! Don't eat me! I know how much you affect her society!'

'Now, Serena – ! You know very well – ! But what is one to do? Sir Walter Laleham's having been a friend of your dear Papa's makes it so impossible for us to snub her! I can't conceive how he came to marry her!'

'Oh, he was all to pieces, and she had a great fortune, or was a great heiress, or some such thing! I pity her daughters: she has them in complete subjection, and, depend upon it, she means them all to contract brilliant marriages! She may succeed with Emily, but I defy her to foist the freckled one on to anything better than a baronet.'

'How can you, Serena?' protested Fanny.

'I'm sure I could *not*!'

'No, pray be serious! I daresay Anne will be quite as pretty as Emily in a year or two, and I do think Emily quite delightfully pretty, don't you? Only I do hope she may not be persuaded into doing anything she doesn't quite like.'

'I'll tell you what, Fanny: I shouldn't wonder at it if all this toad-eating is directed to that end! Lady Laleham hopes to jockey you into sponsoring Emily!'

'Oh, no, surely she could not? Besides, there is no need! She seems to know everyone, and to go everywhere!'

'Franked by the Lalehams! Yes, but she's as shrewd as she can hold together, and knows very well she is only tolerated. She is the kind of person one is obliged to invite to a rout-party, but never to a dinner for one's friends!'

Fanny admitted the truth of this, but said: 'Yet her manners are not at all vulgar, and she doesn't precisely toad-eat one.'

'Her manners have all the tiresome formality of those who dare not unbend for fear of appearing not quite the thing, and her toad-eating is of the most unendurable order of that ancient art! I swear I prefer the truckler to that ridiculous parade of grandeur! "You and I, dear Lady Spenborough…" "A woman of quality's laugh, as we know, Lady Serena…" Ugh!'

'Oh, yes, very bad! quite absurd! But I like Emily, do not you? She is such a lively girl, with such natural, confiding manners!'

'Too easily quelled! It is a study to see her guilt-stricken countenance when Mama's basilisk eyes admonish her! I will allow her to be both natural and beautiful, but if you have discovered more wit in her than may be stowed in your thimble, and leave room to spare, you have remarkable powers of discernment, my dear!'

'Ah, but you are so clever, Serena!' Fanny said simply.

'I?' exclaimed Serena incredulously.

'Oh, yes! Everyone says so, and indeed it is true!'

'My dear Fanny, what in the world are you at? I have not the smallest pretensions to anything more than common sense!'

'But you have! You have a well-informed mind, and you always know what to say to people. Why, when the Castlereaghs were staying with us last year, I was quite lost in admiration at the way you contrived to talk to him! When I could think of nothing to say but the merest commonplace!'

'Good gracious, what nonsense! *That* style of thing, I promise you, is nothing but a trick! You forget how long I have been knocking about the world. When you are as old as I am you will be doing the same.'

'Oh, no! I never shall be able to,' Fanny said, shaking her head. 'I am quite as stupid as Emily Laleham, and I'm sure you must often be quite provoked by me.'

'Never till this moment!' Serena declared, with a slightly heightened colour, but in a rallying tone. 'Good God, if ever I have another suitor I'll take good care to keep him out of your way! You would make him believe me a blue-stocking, and after that, farewell to my chance of contracting even a respectable marriage!'

That made Fanny laugh, and no more was said. But Serena was shocked to realize how truly she had spoken. Much as she loved the gentle creature, she was sometimes provoked by her simplicity, and often longed for the companionship of someone with wits to match her own.

It was hard, too, to accustom herself to what she thought a dawdling way of living, and harder still to abandon her hunting. That, while she was in deep mourning, she must always have done, but she might, had either Fanny or her cousin shared her passion, have enjoyed some gallops. But Fanny was a very nervous horsewoman, willing to amble with her along the lanes, but cast into an agony of apprehension at the mere suggestion of jumping the smallest obstacle; and Hartley regarded horses as nothing more than a means of getting from one place to another.

She had felt herself obliged to send her hunters to Tattersall's, retaining only one little spirting thoroughbred mare, which could be stabled at the Dower House. The stables there had not been built to accommodate more than six horses, and although Hartley had politely begged her to consider the Milverley stables as much her own as they had ever been her pride would not allow her to be so much beholden to him. Fanny, knowing what a grief it must be to her, was aghast, but Serena, who could not bear to have a wound touched, or even noticed, said lightly: 'Oh, fiddle! What's the use of keeping hunters one can't ride? I can't afford to have them eating their heads off, and I know of no reason why my cousin should!'

Shortly before Christmas, they received a visit from Lord Rotherham. One of his estates, not his principal seat, which was situated in quite another part of the country, but a smaller and more favoured residence, was Claycross Abbey, which lay some ten miles beyond Quenbury. He rode over on a damp, cheerless day, and was ushered into the drawing-room to find Serena alone there, engaged, not very expertly, in knotting a fringe. 'Good God, Serena!' he ejaculated, checking on the threshold.

She had never been more glad to see him. Every grudge was forgotten in delight at this visit from one who represented at that moment a lost world. 'Rotherham!' she cried, jumping up, and going to him with her hand held out. 'Of all the charming surprises!'

'My poor girl, you *must* be bored!' he said.

She laughed. 'Witness my occupation! To tears, I assure you! I was so extravagant as to send to London for a parcel of new books, thinking to be kept well entertained for at least a month. But having been so improvident as to swallow *Guy Mannering* almost at one gulp – has it come in your way? I like it better, I think, than *Waverley* – I am left with *The Pastor's Fireside*, which seems sadly flat; a *History of New England*, for which I am not in the correct humour; a most tedious *Life of Napoleon*, written in verse, if you please! and, of all imaginable things, an *Enquiry into Rent*! Fanny has failed miserably to teach me to do tambour-work that doesn't shame the pair of us, so, in desperation, I am knotting a fringe. But sit down, and tell me what has been going on in the world all this time!'

'Nothing that I know of. You must have seen that Wellington and Castlereagh carried it against old Blucher. For the rest, the only *on-dits* which have come in my way are that Sir Hudson Lowe has his eye on a handsome widow, and that the Princess of Wales has now taken to driving about the Italian countryside in a resplendent carriage drawn by cream-coloured ponies. Rehearsing an appearance at Astley's, no doubt. Tell me how you go on!'

'Oh – tolerably well! What has brought you into Gloucestershire? Do you mean to spend your Christmas at Claycross?'

'Yes: an unwilling sacrifice on the altar of duty. My sister comes tomorrow, bringing with her I know not how many of her offspring; and my cousin Cordelia, labouring, apparently, under the mistaken belief that I must be pining for a sight of my wards, brings the whole pack down upon me on Thursday.'

'Good heavens, what a houseful! I wonder you should not rather invite them to Delford!'

'I invited them nowhere. Augusta informed me that I should be delighted to receive them all, and as for taking Cordelia's eldest cub into Leicestershire at this season, no, I thank you! I have more regard for my horses, and should certainly prefer Gerard not to break his neck while under my aegis.'

She frowned, and said, with a touch of asperity: 'It is a pity you cannot be kinder to that boy!'

'I might be, if his mother were less so,' he responded coolly.

'I think it is not in your nature. You have neither patience nor compunction, Ivo.'

'On *your* tongue the stricture sits oddly, my dear Serena!'

She flushed. 'I hope that at least I have compunction.'

'So do I, but I have not seen it!'

Her eyes flashed, but she choked back a retort, saying, after a moment's struggle: 'I beg your pardon! You remind me – very properly! – that your conduct towards your wards is no concern of mine.'

'Good science, Serena!' he said approvingly. 'I am now thrown in the close, and shall make no attempt to come up to time. You are at liberty to censure my conduct towards my wards as much as you please, but why waste these remarks on me? Cordelia will certainly drive over to pay you a visit, and will be delighted to learn your opinion of me: it is identical with her own!'

Fanny entered the room as Serena exclaimed: 'Oh, can we never be for ten minutes together without quarrelling?'

'I believe it has been rather longer than that, so we may plume ourselves upon the improvement,' he replied, rising, and shaking hands with Fanny. 'How do you do? You have no occasion to look dismayed: I came only to pay my respects, and have already stayed too long. I hope you are well?'

She had never known how to reply to such speeches as this, and coloured hotly, stammering that she was so glad – hoped he would stay to dine – they had not expected...

'Thank you, no! I have no business with Spenborough, and paused here only on my way to Milverley.'

'You need not vent your anger on poor Fanny!' Serena said indignantly.

'I have no compunction!' he flung at her. 'My sister spends Christmas at Claycross, Lady Spenborough, and has charged me to discover from you whether you are yet receiving visitors.'

'Oh, yes! We shall be very happy to see Lady Silchester. Pray, assure her – ! It is most kind!'

He bowed, and took his leave of them. Fanny gave a sigh of relief, and said: 'I am so thankful! Mrs Stowe tells me that the turbot had to be thrown away, and to have been obliged to have set an indifferent dinner before Lord Rotherham would have made me feel ready to sink! *How* he would have looked! What has put him out of temper?'

'Must you ask? I did, of course!'

'Dearest Serena, indeed you should not!'

'No, I did mean not to quarrel, only I said something severe – Well! it was true enough, but I never thought it would touch him on the raw! I'm sorry for it, but I daresay if we had not quarrelled over that we should have done so over something else.'

'Oh, dear! But perhaps he won't visit us again!' said Fanny hopefully.

Four

FANNY'S HOPE WAS SOON PROVED TO BE ILL-FOUNDED. Two days later, Serena, who had been walking in the park, returned to the Dower House to find a strange carriage standing in the stableyard. Even as she recognized the crest on the panel, Rotherham came out of the stable, and, after the curtest of greetings, said abruptly: 'That mare of yours is too short in the back.'

'Nonsense!' she replied.

'I never talk nonsense about horseflesh.'

She laughed, putting back the hood from her bright hair. 'I have a wager with myself that I will *once* meet you without quarrelling, so let us agree that the mare is by far too short in the back, has weak hocks as well, and very likely a spavin forming.'

A smile glimmered; he said, in a milder voice: 'Where have you been walking? I should have thought it too dirty a day to lure you out for any other exercise than hunting.'

She stifled a sigh. 'Don't speak of hunting! I believe they met today at Normansholt, and have been thinking that the scent must be running breast-high. How comes it that you are not out?'

'Augusta commanded me to escort her here instead.'

'I pity you! Is she with Fanny? I must go in.'

He began to walk with her towards the house, the long skirt

of his driving-coat of white drab brushing his ankles. 'Do you continue to stable your other horses at Milverley?' he demanded.

She hesitated. 'I might have done so, but no!'

'Where, then?'

'Why, the truth is I've sold 'em!' she said lightly.

He looked thunderstruck. 'Sold them! Good God, am I to understand that your cousin would not house them for you?'

'By no means! He was perfectly willing to do so, but it would be a great piece of nonsense for me to be keeping half a dozen hunters I can't use eating their heads off in the stable; and since Jane doesn't ride I thought it best to be rid of them. Besides, were we not agreed – such an event you cannot have forgotten! – that I cannot, in my present circumstances, afford to maintain a string of hunters?'

He was very much vexed, and said roughly: 'Don't talk that stuff to me! Why the devil didn't you apply to me? If you need money for such a reason as that, you may have it!'

'Out of *your* pocket, Ivo?'

'Nonsense! You are a rich woman!'

She was surprised, and a good deal touched. 'My dear Ivo, I know as well as you do that it is not in your power to contravene the Trust! I am not so bird-witted as you must think me! I had all that out with Mr Perrott long since.'

'Let me tell you, Serena, that these independent ways of yours are not at all becoming!' he said angrily. 'Consulting Perrott – ! There was not the least need!'

She smiled. 'You have convinced me that there was every need! Thank you, Ivo, but I am persuaded you must perceive how improper it would be for you to be franking me!'

'No such thing! If I lend you money, be sure I shall keep strict account of it, and expect to be repaid in due course!'

'Ah, but Papa warned me never to get into the hands of money-lenders!' she retorted, laughing at him. 'No, no! Say no more!

Indeed, I am not ungrateful, but I don't care to be behindhand with the world! As for my horses – why, yes! it cost me a pang to part with them, but that is all done with now, and I promise you I don't repine any more. Pray go in, and tell Lady Silchester that I shall be with her directly! I must not appear in all my dirt!'

She vanished into the house as she spoke; after a scowling moment, he followed her, cast his driving coat and hat on to a chair, and joined his sister and Fanny in the drawing room.

When Serena presently entered the room, she had changed her walking-dress for a robe of clinging black crape, made high to the throat, and relieved only by a little ruff of goffered lawn. The sombre hue seemed to enhance the whiteness of her skin; if Fanny, in her weeds, was ethereally fair, she, with her flaming locks and creamy complexion appeared magnificent.

Lady Silchester, already, though only two years older than her brother, a formidable matron, stared, and exclaimed: 'Upon my word, Serena, I never saw you looking better!'

'Do we take that for praise, or censure?' demanded Rotherham.

'Oh, you need not try to frown me down! Serena knows I always speak my mind! How do you do, Serena? I am glad to find you and Lady Spenborough so comfortable. Though I daresay you are a trifle cramped. How do your cousins go on at Milverley? I suppose I shall be obliged to call. I fancy I never met Hartley's wife. Lady Theresa warns me I shall find her to be no great thing. However, I should not wish to be uncivil!'

'My dear Lady Silchester, if you do not know enough of my aunt at this date – ! Jane is perfectly amiable, I assure you.'

'Well, I am happy to hear you say so. It would be excessively disagreeable for you to be living so close if she were not. Not that I mean to say it is not the horridest thing, whatever she may be like. I shan't enlarge on that head, but I feel for you most sincerely, Serena.'

'Thank you.'

'The stupid way things have been left, too!' pursued the lady. 'Most thoughtless and awkward! I can't think what Spenborough could have been about! If I have been asked once, I have been asked a dozen times if you and Rotherham mean to make it up. You need not fear! I have told everyone there is no question of that. People are so impertinent!'

'As you say!' Rotherham struck in.

'Oh, you mean *I* am, I suppose!' she said, quite unmoved. 'You need not glare at me in that murdering way: I hope I know Serena well enough not to stand on ceremony with her.'

'Certainly you do!' replied Serena, amused. 'Do scotch the rumour! There's not a word of truth in it.'

'So Rotherham has been telling me. I'm very glad to know it. Not that I'm not fond of you, my dear, but it would never have done! You have a great deal too much spirit for Rotherham. Lady Spenborough and I were saying only a few minutes ago that nothing but a meek little mouse will do for him.'

'I am obliged to you both!' said Rotherham.

Scarlet with confusion, Fanny said, 'Oh, no! I didn't – that is, it was Lady Silchester who –'

She was mercifully interrupted by the entrance of a servant, and got up, saying: 'Oh, to be sure – ! Lady Silchester, you'll take a nuncheon! Shall we remove into the breakfast-parlour?'

Serena, who was shaking with laughter, said, as the embarrassing guest was shepherded out of the room: 'I should be sorry for the mouse!'

He grinned ruefully. 'So should I, indeed! Augusta is abominable!'

They joined the other two in the breakfast-parlour, where a noonday repast of cold meat and fruit had been set on the table; but they had hardly taken their seats when the sound of carriage wheels was heard; and in another few minutes the butler came in to inform Fanny that Lady Laleham and Miss Laleham were in the drawing-room.

Fanny was obliged to excuse herself to her guests. She was surprised that Lybster, in general fully to be relied on, should not have denied her; and when he had closed the parlour door behind her, administered a gentle reproof. But it seemed that he had done his best to exclude the unwanted visitors, saying that he believed my lady to be engaged. He had been overborne. Lady Laleham had begged that a message might be carried to my lady: she would not detain her above a minute. With a sinking heart, Fanny entered the drawing-room.

It was as she had foreseen it would be. Lady Laleham, a handsome, fashionably dressed woman, with very correct manners, and an air of great assurance, had plainly no intention of making her visit a brief one. She came forward, full of apologies and protestations. There was a recipe for pickling pears which she had promised quite a fortnight ago to give to dear Lady Spenborough's housekeeper. She dared not guess what Lady Spenborough must have been thinking of her. 'Only, from one cause and another, it went out of my head. I believe you desired to have it immediately, too, which quite covers me with shame! I have it with me here, but felt that a word of explanation was due to you.'

Fanny had no recollection of having expressed a desire to be given the recipe; but she accepted it, with a civil thank-you.

'I so much dislike persons who make promises only to break them. But I must not keep you! I collect you have friends with you. Did I not see the Rotherham carriage in your yard?'

There was nothing for it but to admit it, and to invite the two ladies to join the party in the breakfast parlour. With only a little show of reluctance, Lady Laleham allowed herself to be persuaded. Fanny believed she had come for no other purpose.

Nothing could have exceeded the lady's aplomb when she

reached the parlour. It was quite unnecessary for Fanny to introduce her.

'Yes, indeed I am acquainted with Lady Silchester! How do you do? I believe the last time we met was at the Ormesbys' ball: such a crush, was it not? Ah, Lord Rotherham! Don't disturb yourself, I beg! It is quite shocking to be invading your party in this unconscionable way, but Lady Spenborough *would* have it so! To own the truth, it falls out very fortunately that I should find you here, for I have been wanting to see you.'

'Indeed!' he said, a strong inflexion of surprise in his voice.

'Yes, for my eldest son informs me that Gerard Monksleigh is quite a particular friend of his, and will be staying with you for Christmas. Nothing will do but that I must get up a little party for these flighty young people! I should like so much to ask Mrs Monksleigh if she will not bring her daughters to it, but how this may be done when I have not the pleasure of her acquaintance I know not, unless you will come to my aid, Lord Rotherham!'

He returned a civil answer, but could not take it upon himself to commit his cousin. Lady Silchester said: 'The girls want to go to the Assembly at Quenbury. I don't know how Cordelia Monksleigh likes it for Susan and Margaret, but I'm by no means sure I care to let Caroline go. Serena! What do you think of the scheme? Would you advise it?'

Serena, who had placed Emily Laleham in a chair between her own and Rotherham's, saw the sparkle in the girl's big, pansy-soft eyes as they were turned anxiously towards her, and smiled, saying: 'I never attended the Quenbury Assemblies myself, but I should think there could be no harm in them.'

'A dead bore,' said Rotherham. 'You will meet no one there whom you know, and, unless you have a taste for being toad-eaten, will do better to remain at home.'

'You are too severe,' interposed Serena, with a good deal of meaning in her voice.

'Well, so I would,' said his sister, 'but now the girls have taken the notion into their heads it is very hard to know what to do. It is a great pity they can't dance at Claycross, but with only Elphin and Gerard between the three of them, that won't answer. As long as there are no waltzes or quadrilles I daresay Silchester would not object to Caroline's going. Elphin will be there, after all, and if the company should be too mixed he must dance with his sister.'

'An evening of rare pleasure for both,' commented Rotherham.

A stifled giggle made him glance down at the enchanting face beside him. A look, half of mischief, half of consternation was cast up at him. 'Oh, I beg your pardon!' gasped Emily, in a frightened undervoice.

'Not at all! When I choose to be witty I like to receive just acknowledgment. Do you mean to go to this Assembly?'

'Oh, I don't know! I do *hope* – but I'm not precisely out yet, and perhaps Mama won't permit me.'

'What is the significance of being *precisely* out?'

'Don't quiz her!' said Serena, perceiving that she was at a loss to know how to answer. 'She will be precisely out when she has been presented. When is it to be, Emily?'

'In the spring. Mama will give a ball!' she said, in an awed tone. 'At least,' she added naïvely, 'it is Grandmama really, only she won't come to it, which I think is a great shame.'

Rotherham looked amused, but before he could probe into the mystery of this speech, which Serena feared was his intention, his notice was claimed by Lady Laleham, seated on his left hand.

'What do you say, Lord Rotherham? Your sister and I find that we share the same scruples, but I fancy I have hit on a scheme to make it unobjectionable for our giddy young people to attend the Assembly. Do you not agree that if we make up our own party between us it will solve the problem?'

'Certainly,' he replied.

With this unenthusiastic assent she was satisfied, and began at once to engage Lady Silchester's co-operation.

Rotherham turned again to Emily, and found her face upturned, quite pink with excitement, her eyes sparkling. 'Oh, *thank* you!' she breathed.

'Are you so fond of Assemblies?'

'Yes, indeed! That is to say, I don't know, for I was never at one before.'

'Not being precisely out. Do you live in Quenbury?'

'Oh, no! At Cherrifield Place! Don't you know it? You came by it this morning!'

'Did I?'

'Yes, and Mama knew it must be you, because of the crest. We were at the gate, meaning only to walk into the village, but Mama said we would come here instead, because there was a recipe she wished to give Lady Spenborough.'

'Providential!'

She was puzzled, and, scared by the satirical note in his voice, was stricken to silence. Serena, a trifle unsteadily, said: 'Well, I hope you will enjoy the Assembly, and have a great many partners.'

'Within the limits of exclusiveness,' interpolated Rotherham, meeting her eye.

She frowned at him, knowing him to be quite capable of saying something outrageous enough to be understood by his innocent neighbour. Fortunately, since he met the frown with a bland look she knew well, Lady Laleham, having achieved her object, now judged it to be good tactics to take her leave. Her carriage was called for, and she bore her daughter off, well pleased with the success of her morning's campaign.

'I never meet that woman but I smell the shop,' observed Lady Silchester calmly. 'I wish I may not be her dear Augusta Silchester hereafter!'

'You are well served for having been fool enough to have mentioned the Assembly,' said her brother.

'Very true. I shall have the headache, and send Caroline with Cordelia.'

'I believe she knew you were here, and that is why she came!' declared Fanny, very much ruffled.

'She did!' Serena said, her eyes dancing. 'That absurd child let the secret out in the most innocent fashion imaginable! How I contrived to keep my face I don't know! Well for her Mama was not attending!'

'A pretty little dab of a girl,' said Lady Silchester. 'Not enough countenance, but she'll take very well, I daresay. Dark girls are being much admired just now. Depend upon it, her mother means her to go to the highest bidder. They say Laleham is pretty well at a standstill.'

'What I want to know,' said Rotherham, 'is why Grandmama won't be at the ball which she is to give.'

'I was in dread that you would ask her!' Serena said.

'I shall discover it at the Assembly, when you are not there to spoil sport.'

'You will not go to the Assembly!' she exclaimed incredulously.

'Certainly I shall.'

'Having a taste for being toad-eaten?' she quizzed him.

'No, for Miss Laleham's artless conversation!'

'Ah, she won't gratify you! You have frightened her away!'

'She must be lured back to hand.'

'No, no, it would be too bad of you! You might wake expectations in Mama's bosom, moreover!'

'Irresistible! I shall come out on the side of my niece and my wards, and you will hear next that I am not by half as disagreeable as they had supposed.'

She laughed, but could not believe him to be serious. However, the next visitor to the Dower House was Mrs

Monksleigh, who drove over from Claycross on Christmas Eve, and disclosed that the Assembly scheme was now a settled thing. 'I own, I thought it would come to nothing, and so I warned the girls. I'm sure I was never more astonished than when Rotherham said he saw no harm in it, and as for Susan, she was ready to drop! I expected he would have given her one of his set-downs, but he was perfectly amiable!'

Mrs Monksleigh was the relict of a military man, who had left her with six children and a competence judged by his family to be respectable, and by her, inadequate. She was a very good-natured woman, but having, unfortunately, less than common sense, she had never been able to teach herself habits of economy. There was a want of management in her house which led to a succession of financial crises driving her quite distracted, and never failing to exasperate Rotherham. He was not her cousin, but her husband's; and, in addition to being her Trustee, was joined with her in the guardianship of her children. She could neither understand why her poor husband had made such a choice, nor cease to bewail it. No one could have been more unacceptable to her! He was a man of no sensibility, and impatient temper, and had so little affection for his cousin's children that it was a question whether he knew them apart. His decrees were imperious, and issued without the smallest regard for her wishes; himself a man of huge fortune, he had no comprehension of the difficulties confronting those left to maintain the elegances of life upon a mere pittance. He always thought she should have been able to manage better! It was he who had insisted on Gerard's being sent to school, although her own dear Dr Ryde had pronounced the poor little fellow's constitution to be too delicate for the rigours of Eton. She could not believe that he would have cared if Gerard had died of it. Miraculously, Gerard had survived; and Charlie, of course, had always been very stout, so that she had no fears for him; but now Rotherham was saying that it was time poor little Tom was sent to join his brother. Do as she would, she could not make him understand the shocking expense of having two sons at Eton. There was no end to the calls on her purse: she was sure the fees were the least part of the whole. As for the girls, beyond saying that he saw no reason why Susan should be presented at a Drawing-room, and annihilating Margaret by telling her that when she could address him without prefixing her remarks with a giggle he might attend to her, he never noticed them. Very likely he had forgotten that little Lizzie even existed: he could certainly never remember her name.

The Carlow ladies listened, and sympathized, and agreed that it was a hard case, Fanny rather more sincerely than Serena. Serena could perceive that there might be something to be said in Rotherham's defence. He made too little allowance, she believed, for the difficulties besetting a woman left with six children on her hands; but she, like him, was intolerant of folly, and Mrs Monksleigh was so very foolish! But she thought him less than kind to Gerard, of whom he was contemptuous; and quite indifferent to the younger members of the family. This opinion was shared by Lady Silchester, who excused it, however, by saying that gentlemen always disliked to be plagued by children, and that no one could expect such a thorough sportsman as Rotherham to take to Gerard, who had no taste for sport, a very bad seat, and far too little spirit. But even she could not pretend that her brother had shown the smallest sign of approval when the more robust Charlie, upon the occasion of his only visit to Delford, had given evidence of such spirited behaviour as led him into the performance of every kind of prank, from trying to bestride his guardian's more unmanageable horses to falling off the stable-roof, and breaking his collar-bone. All he had said was that Charlie might think himself fortunate that he had broken his collar-bone, and that he would be damned if ever he saddled himself with the whelp again.

'So Augusta quite mistakes the matter when she says he would like poor Gerard better if he were bolder, and didn't stand so much in awe of him,' complained Mrs Monksleigh. 'I'm sure no boy could be bolder than Charlie, for he is for ever in a scrape, and he never minds a word anyone says to him, but *that* doesn't please Rotherham either! I assure you, Lady Serena, I live in dread of his making Rotherham angry while we are at Claycross, for I know he wouldn't hesitate to use the poor boy with dreadful harshness, which I have told him I utterly forbid. Indeed, I thought all was lost yesterday, when that most disagreeable keeper made such a commotion about Charlie's putting a charge of shot into his leg. Just as though it had not been an accident! Of course, it was wrong of Charlie to take the gun without leave, but the man was only very little hurt, after all! Rotherham said in the most *menacing* way that he would teach Charlie a lesson, and I could feel one of my spasms coming on, only Augusta told Rotherham he was a great fool not to have locked up the gunroom when he had an imp like Charlie to stay, and said surely he could not wish me to fall into strong hysterics, and so it passed off, and I was truly grateful to Augusta.'

Even Fanny could not help laughing at this ingenuous history, although she did not appreciate, as Serena instantly did, the masterly nature of Lady Silchester's strategy. She wondered at Mrs Monksleigh's having dared to leave Charlie to his own devices while she came to the Dower House; but it appeared that Mrs Monksleigh had not dared. She had brought him with her, but she had not wished Fanny to be troubled with him, and had prevailed upon Gerard to take charge of him. The carriage had set them both down at Cherrifield Place. Gerard Monksleigh and Edgar Laleham were up at Cambridge together, in the same year and at the same college. Mrs Monksleigh hoped that Lady Laleham would not object to her having sent Charlie with his brother. Serena did not think that she would object to anything that strengthened the connection with Claycross.

They saw no more of the Claycross party until the night of the Assembly, when, to their surprise, Rotherham walked in on them midway through the evening. His satin knee-breeches and silk stockings made Serena exclaim: 'Then you did go to the Assembly!'

'I did, and am there now, in the card-room – or so I hope Cordelia may believe!'

She raised her brows. 'The bird would not come to hand?'

'On the contrary! But a driven bird, scared into the model of insipid propriety. I stood up for the two first dances with her, and all the conversation I could get out of her was "Oh, Lord Rotherham!" and "Oh, yes, Lord Rotherham!" and once, by way of a change, "Exactly so, Lord Rotherham!" So I tried the effect of telling her she was taking the shine out of all the local beauties, but as that elicited nothing more encouraging than "How can you, Lord Rotherham?" I drew no more coverts, but came instead to take formal leave of you and Lady Spenborough. My party breaks up tomorrow, and I must be in London by the end of the week.'

'Good God, Ivo, do you mean to tell me that Emily is the only girl you have honoured with an invitation to dance? Not even your niece, or Susan, or Margaret?' cried Serena, scandalized.

'They would thank you for that suggestion as little as I do.'

'But it was most improper – quite abominable!' she said hotly. 'Just what sets people's backs up! It would have been bad enough to have danced only with the ladies of your own party. That would have made everyone say merely that you were disagreeably haughty! But to single out one girl, and she not of your own party – Ivo, it is the height of insolence, and a great piece of unkindness to Emily besides!'

'Not at all!' he retorted, with a curling lip. 'Her mother did not think so, I promise you!'

'That is worse than all the rest! You know very well what she is! There are no bounds to her ambition! Depend upon it, you have now raised the most absurd expectations in her breast, turned that unfortunate child into an object of envy and speculation, all for sport! No, Fanny, I will *not* be hushed! There is something so particularly displeasing in the whole business! You may argue it as you will, Rotherham, but it was very ill done! I could name you a dozen girls, all, I daresay, at the Assembly tonight, as worthy of your notice as Emily Laleham! But no! You have been playing the great man; condescending to grace a country Assembly – for anything I can tell, though I should be sorry to think it of you, amused to see what a flutter was caused by your mere presence!'

'You need not think it!' he struck in, his cheeks whitened, and a pulse throbbing beside his thinned mouth.

'Indeed, I believe it to be a kind of unthinking arrogance, but it does you no credit, Rotherham! If you went to a public Assembly, you had no choice but to behave with civility towards all! You might have danced with no one, since your excuse for going there was only to indulge your young guests with a ball, but for a whim to single out one girl and she by far the loveliest! – and then to stroll away, as though you thought yourself above the rest of the company – oh, no, Ivo, how could you? Every feeling is offended!'

'I thank you! You have quite a turn for the high dramatic! No doubt you expect me now to return for the express purpose of conferring upon two or three other damsels the singular honour – if such you do indeed consider it! of standing up with me!'

'It is what my father would have done in such a situation, for he was most truly the gentleman!' she said, a sob rising in her throat. 'I should think the better of you!'

'I care nothing for your opinion of me!' he snapped. 'Lady Spenborough, have you any commissions for me to execute in London? I shall be most happy!'

'Oh, none, thank you!' she said faintly.

'Then I will take my leave! Your most obedient servant, ma'am!'

A formal bow, one scorching glance thrown at Serena, and he was gone.

'Oh, dear!' said Fanny, pressing her hands to her temples. 'I feel quite sick! And, oh, *Serena*, we never thought to offer him so much as a glass of ratafia!'

Five

IT WAS HARDLY TO BE EXPECTED, SERENA THOUGHT, THAT the several ladies of their acquaintance in the neighbouring district would spare her a description of the Boxing Day Assembly, and greatly did she dread being obliged to listen either to animadversions on Rotherham's manners, or to bitter criticisms of Lady Laleham's encroaching ways. But the weather saved her. A week of incessant rain made quagmires of all the roads, and rendered the paying of morning-calls ineligible. They were undisturbed by visitors at the Dower House until Spenborough had himself driven there one afternoon to announce to the ladies Jane's safe delivery of a son.

He was a fond and an excellent father, and could scarcely have been more delighted if the child had been his first son, instead of his fourth. Fanny and Serena tried to say all that was expected of them, and succeeded so well that he found himself very much in charity with them both, and confided to them that the happy event had relieved his mind of considerable anxiety. 'For, you know, with the shock of my cousin's sad death, and all the exertion of disposing of the house, and the bringing of the children to Milverley, there is no saying what might have happened. But Jane is equal to anything!'

They reiterated their congratulations; he beamed, and

thanked, and said: 'Extremely obliging! I knew you would be glad, and determined you should be the first to be informed of the event. We mean the child to be given the name of Francis, and we hope, Lady Spenborough, that you will consent to be one of his sponsors!'

Fanny, quite pink with pleasure, said that she would be most happy; and Serena, seeing that she was really gratified, determined to forgive Jane for cutting up the South Lawn into a formal flower-garden, and even suggested that Hartley should stay to dine at the Dower House. He needed no persuasion; a message was sent to the stables; another to the kitchen; and he sat down in a wing-chair beside the fire to discuss, over several glasses of sherry, the doctor's opinion of Jane's constitution, the midwife's admiration of her fortitude, and the very diverting things the elder children had said upon being informed that God had sent them a new brother.

It was some time before these topics had been talked out, but at last he could think of no more to say on them. He said that he must not go boring on, complimented Fanny on her cook's way of dressing a haunch of venison, and suddenly remarked: 'So Rotherham took his guests to the Assembly on Boxing Day! I wouldn't believe it when Dr Cliffe told me so, but it seems to be true enough. I saw Orrell the other day, and he vouched for it. A queer start, wasn't it?'

'It was a scheme got up for the entertainment of the young people,' said Fanny calmly.

'Ay, so I understand. No harm, of course, but I shouldn't have thought Rotherham the man to condescend so far. I am not particularly acquainted with him, but he has always seemed to me pretty high in the instep: one of your haughty care-for-nobodies! However, Orrell assures me he was very civil and amiable. That Laleham woman was mightily set up by his standing up with her daughter, and not seeming to care for anyone else, but walking off to the card room immediately. Orrell says it was a study to look at the faces of the other mamas! But he came back at tea time, took in his cousin, and afterwards solicited some girl that had no partner to stand up with him, which was thought to be very good-natured in him, and lowered the Laleham crest a trifle! This Rhenish cream is most excellent, Lady Spenborough: a capital dinner! I shall tell Jane I get nothing so good at Milverley!'

Fanny could not help glancing across the table to see whether Serena partook of her own astonishment. She could detect nothing in her face but a look of approval; and when, after Spenborough had left them, she ventured to ask her if she had not been very much surprised, she received a decided negative.

'You were not? I own, I could hardly credit my ears. I had no notion that he cared so much for your opinion!'

'No, indeed, and nor does he!' Serena answered. 'The outcome would have been the same whoever had taken him to task. When he does such things as that it is not from any *conscious* idea of his own consequence, or a contempt for persons of inferior rank, but from a sort of heedless arrogance, as I told him. He had the misfortune to lose his father when he was still a schoolboy: a most estimable man, I believe. Papa was used to say that everyone stood in great awe of him, because he was such a *grand seigneur*, but that pride in *him* didn't lead him to offend people by any careless manners, but to treat everyone with the same punctilious courtesy. *We* should have thought him very stiff, I daresay, for he was held to be old-fashioned even when Papa was a young man. But Lady Rotherham was insufferably proud! You never knew her: I assure you, she was so puffed-up with conceit and consequence that there was no bearing it! She brought up all three of her children, and in particular, of course, Ivo, to believe themselves so superior that they might behave as they chose, since a Barrasford must be beyond the reach of censure! As for considering the feelings of others, such a notion can never have entered her head! Her selfishness was beyond anything, too! Everything, she thought, must give way to *her* whims. One cannot wonder at Ivo's arrogance: the only wonder is that it should be unconscious – not rooted, as it was with her, in conceit! He was never taught to think of anything but his own pleasure, but his disposition is not bad, nor does he mean to offend the sensibilities of others. It is all heedlessness! If he can but be made to see that he has behaved badly, he is sorry for it at once.'

'Oh, Serena! When I am sure he was ready to murder you for having presumed to tell him his conduct was not gentlemanly – !'

'No, no, you are mistaken, Fanny!' Serena said, laughing a little. 'He didn't wish to murder me, but himself! Oh, well, perhaps me, but much more himself! He knew what I said to be true, and that is what wounded his pride, and made him smart so.'

'Do you think so?' Fanny said doubtfully.

'I know it! Don't imagine that he instantly set about mending the matter because his conduct had given *me* an ill opinion of him! He did it because it gave *him* that ill opinion. He has the faults of his mother's temper, but at the bottom he is more his father's son than hers. Papa always held to it that with *that* upbringing, and all the toad-eating and nonsense that surrounded him when he was by far too young to perceive the folly of it, it said a great deal for his character that he grew up to care so little for pomp and dignity, and of all creatures to dislike most those that flatter him. You will never see Ivo in company with any of the odious hangers-on who fawn on great men, administering all the time to their vanity, you know. He holds such stuff in utter contempt. It was otherwise with his brother. If you had but seen Captain Lord Talbot Barrasford – in all the magnificence of silver lace, for he was a Hussar! – plainly thinking how much his regiment was honoured by his having joined it – ! I used to wonder how he contrived to maintain his precious dignity when compelled to quarter himself in some Spanish hovel. Oh, I should not be saying so *now*, I know! He fell in action, very gallantly, I believe, and if he was not much mourned, at least he must be respected. People say that Augusta was very like him, as a girl. But she had the good fortune to marry Silchester, who is a sensible man, and by the time I was old enough to become acquainted with her she was much as you see her today – with a good deal of Ivo's unconcern with what people may be thinking, and quite unaffected. I don't mean to say she does not know her own worth, but it is something she takes for granted, and scarcely thinks about.'

'Oh, yes! She quite frightened me, at first, with her odd, blunt way of talking, but I have always found her perfectly kind, and have never doubted that *she* has a heart!'

Serena smiled. 'None of the Barrasfords has what is generally meant when people speak of *warmheartedness*. If you mean, as I collect you do, that Rotherham's nature is cold, I think I had rather say that it is fiery! He is a hard man, certainly. I shouldn't turn to him for sympathy, but I have known him to be kind.'

'I suppose, when you were betrothed, he must have been, but –'

'Oh, no, not when he fancied himself to be in love with me! Far from it!' Serena interrupted, laughing. 'He would like to be much kinder in the execution of his duty as my Trustee than I could permit!'

'Why, what can you mean? You yourself suspected that the arrangement was made at his instigation!'

'Well, yes, while I was in such a rage, I did,' admitted Serena. 'Only, of course, I soon saw that it could not have been. I'm afraid it was poor Papa's notion of a clever stroke. The match was so much of his making that he could not bear to abandon it.'

'I know it was a splendid one, but did he care for that? It was not like him!'

'Well, I suppose he must have cared a little, but the thing was that he liked Rotherham, and believed we should suit, because he was an honest man, and there was no flummery about either of us! You know what Papa was, when he had taken a notion firmly into his head! I don't think anything could have brought him to believe that Ivo was as thankful to be out of a scrape as I was. I never supposed that the pair of them concerted this infamous scheme because Ivo wished to win me back, and as soon as I was cooler, I knew, of course, that Papa would not have done it to give Ivo an opportunity to be revenged on me.'

'Revenged!'

'Well,' said Serena, reflectively wrinkling her nose, 'he has not a forgiving nature, and there's no denying I did deal his pride the most wounding blow when I cried off. So, when I heard Papa's Will read, I thought – oh, I don't know *what* I thought! I was too angry to think at all. And then I believed that he wouldn't refuse to act because he meant to punish me for that old slight by using the power he had been given in a malicious way. To own the truth, I thought he would be pleased when he discovered that I had been obliged to sell my horses, but I was quite out! He was very much vexed, and tried to make me believe he could increase my allowance. But I had gone into that with Perrott, and I knew better – which vexed him more than ever! He would certainly have given me a larger allowance, and never told me it was his own money, and you will agree that however improper that may have been it was very kind!'

Fanny said in a wondering tone: 'Perhaps he *is* fond of you, Serena!'

'Yes, when he is not disliking me excessively. I never doubted it,' said Serena coolly. 'It is the sort of fondness one has for an old acquaintance, who shares many of one's ideas and tastes. At the moment, however, I expect dislike has the upper hand. He will come about!'

Nothing was heard of Rotherham until the end of January. The weather continued to be dull, and wet, one leaden day succeeding the last, and exercising a depressive influence on the spirits. Fanny contracted a severe chill, and seemed unable wholly to shake off its effects. She continued very languid, complained of rheumatic pains, and found the days intolerably long. The novelty – for such she had felt it to be – of being mistress of her own house had worn off; and the monotony of the life she was leading made her fretful. The only variations that offered were the occasional visits of neighbours with whom she had nothing in common; and her only amusements were playing cribbage or backgammon with Serena, or going up to the great house to play with Jane's children. The Countess always had a kind welcome for her, and she could be merry with the children; but a fatal flaw attached to her visits, and caused them to become less and less frequent. She could never be in Jane's company without being obliged to listen to her complaints of Serena. She knew no way of silencing Jane. 'I wish that you would drop Serena a hint,' were words that always made her heart sink. It was not that Jane undervalued Serena, or was not sincerely attached to her, or was unsympathetic. No one, Jane was careful to assure her, in the calm voice of infallibility which so much exasperated Serena, had a greater regard for her, no one could be more certain of her wish to be of use to her cousin, or could more thoroughly appreciate the painful nature of her feelings, *but* – ! Gentle though she was, Fanny would have leapt to Serena's defence, had she not felt, too often, that Jane had right on her side. As Hartley grew in self-confidence, he naturally depended on his cousin less and less. He inaugurated new customs without consulting her and, since he was inclined to be consequential, he contrived – unwittingly, Fanny believed – to convey the impression that he thought his innovations a vast improvement on anything that had been done by his predecessor. Fanny tried to convince Serena that he did not mean to seem to slight her father, but her attempts at peace-making only drew down the vials of Serena's wrath upon her own head. Serena, fretting quite as much as Fanny at the boredom of her days, found an outlet for her curbed energy in riding about Milverley, detecting changes (none of them acceptable to her), discovering omissions, and chatting with tenants, or discussing improvements with the bailiff just as she had always done, and so rubbing up against her cousin half a dozen times in a week. To make matters worse, she was far more often right than he; and whereas he, lacking the late Earl's geniality, was not much liked, she, inheriting it, was loved.

Serena, having more strength of character than Fanny, did not wilt under the trials that beset her, but tried to overcome boredom by throwing herself even more energetically, and much to her cousin's dismay, into the Milverley affairs. Could she but have found a congenial companion with whom to exchange ideas, she might have refrained, but no such person seemed to exist in the immediate neighbourhood. She became increasingly impatient with Fanny; and the very fact that she seldom allowed her exasperation to appear exacerbated it. There were even days when she felt that she and Fanny conversed in different languages, and that she might almost have preferred to have been cooped up with her aunt. She would have found herself opposed to nearly every one of Lady Theresa's opinions; but Fanny had no opinions. When Lady Theresa, an accomplished and conscientious correspondent, wrote that Lady Waldegrave was dying of water on the chest, Fanny could be interested, and would discuss the sad news at far greater length than Serena thought necessary; but when Lady Theresa informed her niece that retrenchment was all the cry now, and that it was an open secret the Opposition meant to launch an attack on the tax on income which the nation had endured for ten years, some saying that it would be proposed that the two shillings in the pound now exacted should be reduced by as much as half, Fanny had nothing to say beyond a vague: 'Oh!' As for Lavallette's rescue by three British subjects, which, Lady Theresa asserted, was at the moment the only topic to be hotly discussed, she thought an escape very exciting, but never reached the smallest understanding of the wider aspects of the case.

Serena was beginning to think that she could even welcome Rotherham in his most quarrelsome mood when the post brought her a letter from him. It informed her in the curtest terms that Probate having at last been obtained, he should call at the Dower House some time during the following week, when he expected to be at Claycross, to explain to her the arrangements which had been made to enable her to draw her allowance as and when she should require it. He was hers, etc., Rotherham.

'Oh, good God, still in the sullens!' exclaimed Serena disgustedly tossing the single sheet on to the fire. 'And what does he mean by saying coolly that he will call here *some* time next week? If he comes without having the civility first to discover when it will be convenient for us to receive him, Lybster shall say that we are neither of us at home! I will *not* endure his high-handed ways!'

Fanny looked alarmed, but, fortunately for her peace of mind, circumstances made it impossible for this amiable plan to be put into execution. Rotherham drove himself over from Claycross in his curricle, reaching the entrance to the grounds of the Dower House just as Serena, mounted on her mare, approached it from the opposite direction.

Rotherham reined in, and waited for her to come up. She

was looking extremely handsome, in a severe black beaver hat of masculine style, with a high crown and a stiffly curled brim, but the expression on her face was decidedly stormy. Perceiving it, Rotherham instantly said: 'Good-morning, Serena. Who is the latest unfortunate to have incurred your displeasure?'

'My cousin,' she replied curtly. 'It is apparently enough for him to discover that some practice has been the custom at Milverley for years for him to overset it!'

'I pity him!' he said.

Her smouldering eyes, which had been running over the points of the two well-matched bays harnessed to his curricle, lifted to his face, and narrowed. 'Is Lady Spenborough expecting you?' she demanded. 'She has not told me so, and I have had no letter from you since the one you wrote to inform me that you were coming to Claycross.'

'You could hardly have done so, since I have not written another to you.'

'It would have been more civil in you to have discovered when it would be convenient for us to receive you!'

'Accept my apologies! It had not occurred to me that you would so soon be filling your days with engagements.'

'Of course I am not! But –'

'Have no fear! I do not expect to take up many minutes of your time.'

'I hope not, indeed, but I am afraid you will be detained for longer than you may have bargained for. I must change out of my habit before I can attend to you. No doubt Lady Spenborough will be found in the drawing room.'

She wheeled the mare, and rode through the gateway. He followed her at his leisure, and within a few minutes was shaking hands with Fanny. She said something about sending to find Serena, and he interrupted her, saying: 'I met her outside the gate, and the fiend's own temper she was in. I don't envy you!'

She replied, with dignity: 'I am very much attached to Serena, Lord Rotherham.'

'And resent my sympathy?'

'I cannot think that you know – or have ever known – how to value her,' she said, almost trembling at her own boldness.

'Oh, I know her virtues!' he responded. 'She would have been well enough had she ever been broke to bridle.'

She could not trust herself to answer him. A slight pause ensued; he then said, with the abruptness which always disconcerted her: 'Is she at loggerheads with Spenborough?'

She hesitated. He had picked up a book that lay on the table, and was idly flicking over the pages, but he raised his eyes from it, directing a piercing look at her. 'Well?'

She was a little flustered by this compelling glance, and the imperative note in his voice. 'It is often very painful to her. Lord Spenborough means to do right, but he is not always – does not always know how to tell her what he means to do – in a way that won't offend her!'

'I can guess! Spenborough's a fool, and has the misfortune to succeed an excellent landlord.'

'Indeed, he is fully conscious of that, and also I fear that his people do not like him as they like her!'

'Inevitable. I told her at the outset to remove from this neighbourhood.'

'Perhaps she should have done so,' Fanny said sadly. 'She is made to feel sometimes that he holds her Papa's notions cheap. But I am sure he does not mean any such thing!'

'Pretty well for a man who never came to Milverley but as a guest on sufferance! But it won't do to bolster Serena up in such ideas as that!'

'Oh, no, no! Nor would she ever say such a thing to him, or to anyone, except perhaps me! She is most loyal to him. Even when she disapproves of something he has done,

and – and is told of it by one of our people – one of *his* people, I should say –'

'Ay, there's the rub, eh? You need not tell me she gives 'em no encouragement! I know Serena!'

'Perhaps,' said Fanny wistfully, 'she will grow more accustomed to it, in time.'

'She will never do so,' he replied bluntly. 'How do *you* go on with Hartley and his wife, Lady Spenborough?'

'They are always very kind and civil, I assure you.'

'It falls to your lot to keep the peace, does it? You will not succeed, and, I repeat – I don't envy you!'

She said nothing, wishing that Serena would come in, and wondering how to entertain this uncomfortable guest. No topic of conversation occurred to her; after another pause, she said: 'Perhaps I should send someone to find Serena. I am afraid something has detained her, or – or –'

He laughed suddenly. 'No, don't do that, I beg! Having fallen into her black books for not having craved her permission to call here today, I plunged rather deeper by assuring her that my business would not take up more than a few minutes of her time. This, I fancy, led her to suppose that I was in haste, and so she warned me that I should be kept waiting while she changed out of her habit. Do you care to wager any sum on the length of time she will take over that operation? I will lay handsome odds against the chance of her appearing under half an hour.'

'Oh, dear!' she exclaimed, looking more dismayed than amused. 'Oh, *pray* do not quarrel again!'

'Against that chance, I lay no odds at all. Are you moped to death here?'

She jumped nervously, startled by the sudden question. 'Oh – ! No, no! Sometimes, perhaps – the weather has been so inclement! When the spring comes we mean to do great things with the garden. It had been sadly neglected, you know.'

He complimented her upon her show of snowdrops, saying they were more forward than those at Claycross; she was encouraged to pursue the topic; and in the safe discussion of horticulture twenty minutes were successfully spent. The butler then came in to announce that a nuncheon awaited my lady's pleasure; and Fanny, desiring him to have a message carried to Lady Serena, conducted Rotherham to the breakfast-parlour. He continued to converse amiably with her: she thought she had seldom seen him so affably inclined, and was considerably astonished, since nothing, she felt, could have been more calculated to put him out of temper than Serena's continued absence. When Serena did at last sweep into the room, she waited, with a fast-thudding heart, for the expected explosion. But Rotherham, rising, and setting a chair for Serena, said, in the voice of a man agreeably surprised: '*Why*, Serena, already? I had thought it would have taken you longer! You should not have hurried: there was not the least need!'

One look at Serena's face had been enough to tell Fanny that she was in a dangerous mood. She quaked; but after a moment, while the issue trembled in the balance, Serena burst out laughing, and exclaimed: 'Detestable man! Very well! if you are not in quarrelling humour, so be it! What's the news in town?'

The rest of the visit passed without untoward incident: even, Fanny thought, pleasantly. Serena was lively; Rotherham conversable; and neither said anything to provoke the other. They parted on good terms; and Fanny, perceiving how much good the visit had done to Serena's spirits, was even sorry that it would not soon be repeated. Rotherham was returning immediately to London, for the opening of Parliament, and was unlikely to be in Gloucestershire again for some time.

The ladies settled down again to the uneventful existence which was their lot, almost the only alleviation to the monotony being the frequent visits of Emily Laleham. Little though she had known it, Serena had for long been the object of Miss Laleham's awed admiration. As a schoolroom miss, she had had glimpses of her, riding with her father, and had thought that surely no one had ever been more beautiful, or more dashing. She worshipped from afar, wove wonderful stories around her, in which she rescued the goddess from extremely unlikely perils, but never, in her wildest flights, had she imagined herself on terms of quite ordinary friendship with her. But Serena, amused by her ingenuousness, had encouraged her to repeat her visit to the Dower House. She needed no pressing, but thereafter was always finding excuses to call there.

But by the end of February even the mild diversion provided by Emily's visits came to an end, for the Lalehams removed to London, Lady Laleham being quite unable to endure more than three months in the country. Only the schoolroom party remained in Gloucestershire, a house in the best part of town having been hired by Sir Walter for the season. 'For my coming-out!' said Emily proudly.

'Very kind of Papa!' smiled Serena.

'Oh, yes! At least, it is Grandmama's, of course. I wish she could be there to see me in my Court dress!'

'Your grandmama doesn't live in London, I collect?'

'Oh, no, she lives in Bath! And I love her *dearly*!' said Emily, in an oddly defiant voice.

March, coming in like a lion, saw Fanny the victim of neuralgia. Jane came to visit her, but this attention was marred by an air of graciousness which conveyed a strong impression of a great lady condescending to her humbler relations. Jane was beginning to assume consequential manners, and was unwise enough to tell Serena that she did not think it quite the thing for her to ride 'all over the country' with only a groom for companion. Spenborough could not like it. 'I told him I would certainly drop a hint in your ear.'

'Drop one from me in his!' flashed Serena. 'That I am not an attorney's daughter on my preferment!'

The encounter was one of many. Uneasy tension lay between the two houses; there were frequent quarrels; Serena's temper grew brittle, and several times she snapped at Fanny. Then, one wet afternoon, she found Fanny weeping softly beside the fire in her bedroom, and was aghast.

'Fanny! Dearest Fanny, what is it?'

'Oh, nothing, nothing!' Fanny sobbed, trying to hide her face. 'Pray, do not – ! I didn't mean – It is just that I am a little low!'

Serena was on her knees before her, holding her hands comfortingly. 'It is not like you! I'm sure there must be some reason – Oh, Fanny, it is not because I was cross?'

'Oh, no! I never meant to vex you, only I am so stupid!'

Filled with remorse, Serena soothed and petted her back to tranquillity. 'I am the most hateful wretch alive! To turn on you, merely because Hartley had enraged me! I don't know what I deserve!'

Fanny dried her eyes. 'It was silly of me. I know how hard it is for you to endure Hartley. And Jane is growing so conceited! Even I feel it, and it is much worse for you to have her behaving as though she had lived at Milverley all her life! Rotherham told me you ought not to live here, and he is quite right.'

'Much he knows!' said Serena scornfully.

'But he does know, Serena. I have seen how much it rubs you, and it's no wonder! I wish it were possible for us both to go away!'

'But –' Serena stopped suddenly. 'Good God, what a pair of goosecaps we are!' she exclaimed. 'Why – oh, why the *devil* don't we go away? It has been intolerable here ever since Christmas. *You* have been unwell, *I* have been cross, and the plain truth is that we are finding life a dead bore. We *will* go away!'

'But we could not!' gasped Fanny. 'Not to London, while we are in mourning! I know Mama would say I ought not!'

'Not to London, no! We could very well go to Bath, however.'

Fanny's eyes widened. 'Bath?'

'Yes! And not even your mama will think it improper, because you will go there on the advice of Dr Cliffe, to drink the waters! We will hire a house for six months or so, and if we cannot go to the Assemblies, at least there will be the libraries, and the Pump Room, and –'

'Serena!' breathed Fanny, awed.

Serena laughed at her. 'Well? Shall we do it?'

'Oh, Serena, *yes*! Milsom Street – the shops – the London coach coming in – the Sydney Gardens – !'

'And some faces other than our own to look at!'

'Yes, indeed! Oh, what a delightful scheme! Now, *where*,' said Fanny, her woes forgotten, 'should you like to hire a house? And how must we set about it?'

Six

THE REMOVAL TO BATH HAVING BEEN DECIDED UPON, nothing remained but to choose between lodgings there, or a furnished house. Fanny, unaccustomed to arranging such matters, would have wasted weeks in indecision, but it was otherwise with Serena. It was she who entered into all the negotiations, she who knew what would best suit them. Fanny had nothing to do but to agree; and if asked what were her own inclinations she could only say that she would like to do whatever Serena thought most proper. So Serena, remarking that to keep five indoor servants in idleness for several months would be a false economy, discarded all ideas of renting lodgings, and dispatched Lybster to Bath to inspect the various houses recommended by the agent. This resulted in Fanny's signing a contract to hire, for six months, a house in Laura Place, which Lybster pronounced to be the most eligible of all he had seen. By the middle of March all the furniture at the Dower House was shrouded in holland covers, and Spenborough, who had spared no pains to assist the ladies in all the troublesome details of removal (even lending the late Earl's enormous and antiquated travelling coach for the transport of servants and baggage), was able to heave a sigh of rather guilty relief.

Since Milverley lay only some twenty-five miles from Bath,

the ladies accomplished the journey in the barouche. Fanny, fortified on the road by smelling-salts, declared that she had never made a journey more comfortably, and, instead of retiring instantly to bed to nurse a sick headache, was able, on their arrival in Laura Place, not only to inspect the house, but to change her dress for dinner, and to discuss with Serena the exciting news contained in a letter from Lady Theresa, which was found awaiting her. The Princess Charlotte was engaged to Leopold of Saxe-Coburg!

This was just the kind of news which Fanny enjoyed. Nothing could be more interesting than the approaching nuptials of the heiress presumptive to the throne; and when the heiress had already made a considerable stir by breaking her engagement to the Prince of Orange the new contract could not but provide food for a good deal of speculation. Fanny was not acquainted with the Princess, who had been kept very close; but she had met Prince Leopold during the rather premature Peace Celebrations in 1814: indeed, she was sure he had been present at the great rout-party they had given at Spenborough House for so many of the foreign notables. Did not Serena recall a handsome young man in that alarming Grandduchess's train? She was persuaded he must be all that was most amiable; it was no wonder that the Princess should have preferred him to the Prince of Orange. Did not Serena agree that it must be a love-match?

'So my aunt informs us,' said Serena. 'It seems not to be a match of the Prince Regent's seeking, at all events. Indeed, it would be wonderful if it were! It may be very romantic – though I thought the young man a trifle dull, myself! – but a Saxe-Coburg can't be considered any great thing for *such* an heiress! A younger son, too!'

But Fanny insisted that this was even an advantage, since a Prince without a principality would be content to live in England, instead, like the Prince of Orange, of insisting on taking the Princess Charlotte to live for some part of the year in his own domains. As for his being dull, she thought Serena judged too harshly. For her part, she liked his dignified manners, his air of grave reflection; and had felt, on the only occasion when she had met him, that the young Prince of Orange was nothing more than a rattle. And with such an undistinguished face and figure!

To read all the information about Prince Leopold's career and his manifold perfections which was printed in the various newspapers and journals became one of each day's first objects for Fanny. However little she might have to say on the subject of Brougham's extraordinary attack on the Prince Regent, with its disastrous consequences to his Party, she had plenty to say on the shabby nature of the dukedom conferred on Prince Leopold, and perused with painstaking thoroughness all seven Articles of the proposed Marriage Settlement.

Bath was well provided with libraries, and these were considered to be amongst its most agreeable lounges. Most of them provided their subscribers with all the new English and French publications, monthly reviews, and other magazines, all the London papers, and some of the French ones. Fanny divided her patronage between Duffield's, in Milsom Street, and Meyler & Sons, which conveniently adjoined the Great Pump Room. Here, every morning, she dutifully drank the waters, declaring that she derived immense benefit from them. Serena agreed to this, with suitable gravity, but thought privately that the orchestra, which discoursed music there, the shops in the more modish streets, and the constant procession of new faces, were of even greater benefit to her spirits.

Apart from one or two elderly persons, who had been acquainted either with the first Lady Spenborough, or with Lady Claypole, they had no acquaintance in the town. It was no longer a resort of high fashion, though still a very prosperous and genteel watering-place; and the most notable person to be encountered was Madame D'Arblay, who had been residing there all the winter. Fanny once found herself standing beside her at the ribbon counter in a shop on Gay Street, and was very much awed. The celebrated authoress had bought nothing more uncommon than an ell of black sarsenet ribbon; and nobody, Fanny assured Serena, could have supposed from her manners or her appearance that she had ever done anything out of the common way. Fanny had longed for the courage to introduce herself. 'For *Evelina*, you know, was quite my favourite book, and I'm sure I was persuaded I could never love any gentleman one tenth as much as I loved Lord Orville!'

'What a pity you did not tell her so! I daresay she would have been very much pleased,' Serena said.

'Yes, but I thought she might have wished me rather to have spoken about her last book,' said Fanny naïvely. 'Do you recall that author who dined with us once, and was affronted because your dear papa praised his *first* book, and never said a word about his others? And I couldn't have talked to Miss Burney about *The Wanderer*, because it was so tedious I gave it up after the first volume!'

Upon their first coming to Bath, Serena had written both their names in the subscription-books at the Lower and the New Assembly Rooms. Fanny was doubtful of the propriety of this, but the worldly-wise Serena said: 'Depend upon it, my dear, it would be foolish to do otherwise! In such a place as this it never does to offend the susceptibilities of the Masters of Ceremonies. We shan't, of course, go to the balls, or even to the Card Assemblies, but after we have been in mourning for six months we might, I think, go to the concerts, if we wished.'

Fanny submitted, and soon found that her comfort was increased by the good-will of Mr Guynette of the Lower Rooms, and Mr King of the Upper. Neither of these gentlemen delayed to pay a call of ceremony upon the distinguished ladies in Laura Place, and each rivalled the other in civility. Had the Dowager Countess been as old as Mrs Piozzi, Bath's latest resident, the visits would have been made; but the zealous gentlemen might not have felt it to be so incumbent upon them to render her so many little attentions, or to keep her so meticulously informed of any item of Bath news. Any Dowager Countess must command respect: one so touchingly youthful, so angelically fair, and with such gentle, unassuming manners might command devotion.

'Fanny!' said Serena, much amused by the frequent visits of the rival Masters, 'if there should be a Mrs King or a Mrs Guynette, which I'm sure I hope there may not be, I shudder to think of the evil passions you must be arousing in their bosoms!'

'I?' exclaimed Fanny, startled. 'Good God, what can you mean?'

Serena laughed at her. 'Well, how many times have these assiduous gentlemen found it necessary to call in Laura Place? I swear I've lost count! There was Mr King, coming to promise you a secluded place if only you could be brought to attend some lecture or other at the Upper Rooms; there was Mr Guynette, bethinking himself that you might not know which are the best stables for your carriage-horses; there was the occasion when –'

'Serena! Oh, *hush*!' Fanny cried, blushing and aghast. 'I'm sure they have both been very kind, but –'

'Excessively kind! And so attentive! When Mr Guynette ran out of the Pump Room to summon a chair for you on Tuesday, only because three drops of rain had fallen, I began to think that it is you who need a chaperon, not I!'

'Oh, I know you are funning, but indeed I wish you will not!' Fanny said, distressed. 'It would be so very unbecoming in me, and in them, too! And it is all nonsense! They feel it to be their duty to do everything in their power to make *any* visitor's stay in Bath agreeable!' A dreadful thought occurred to her;

she fixed her innocent blue eyes on Serena's face, and gasped: 'Serena! I have not – I have not appeared *fast*?'

'No, no!' Serena said soothingly. 'Just pathetic!' She perceived that Fanny was seriously discomposed, and added: 'Goose! I was only quizzing you!'

'If I thought that I had seemed to be encouraging any gentleman to pay me undue attentions, it would be the most shocking thing, and would destroy all my pleasure in being in Bath!'

Serena reassured her, reflecting, not for the first time, that it was seldom wise to employ a rallying tone with her. The tone of her mind was serious, and she was more prone to be shocked than amused by encounters with more lively spirits. There could be no doubt that her air of youthful helplessness, coupled, as it was, with an ethereal beauty, had awakened chivalry in two middle-aged gentlemen, but Serena refrained from telling her so. Not the most severe critic could suspect her of flirtatiousness; and not for worlds would Serena have destroyed her pleasure in being in Bath.

This was very real. Looking at the shop windows, listening to the orchestra in the Pump Room, walking, on fine days in Sydney Gardens, noting each new face that appeared, speculating on the relationships and identities of the various *habitués* of the Pump Room, seemed to be just what she liked. She was sure the man who always wore a pink flower in his buttonhole must be the brother, and *not* the husband, of the fat woman with the yellow wig. There was a pronounced likeness: did not Serena agree? And had Serena noticed the bonnet with the green feathers which that odd-looking woman who dressed in such an antiquated style was wearing? She had seen it displayed in the window of that milliner's in Milsom Street only last week, and with the most *shocking* price attached! Serena always returned satisfactory answers, but had she told the truth she would have said that she had never noticed the fat woman in the yellow wig, or the odd-looking woman either.

The fact was that the dawdling life in Bath suited Serena no better than life at the Dower House. Mingled with the ache in her heart for the loss of one who had been more a companion than a father, was a restlessness, a yearning for she scarcely knew what, which found its only relief in gallops over the surrounding countryside. Owing to the steepness of its streets, carriages were not much used in Bath, chairmen supplanting coachmen in the task of conveying ladies to balls and concerts. Fanny had entertained serious thoughts of sending home her barouche, and could not understand the impulse which prompted Serena, morning after morning, to escape from Bath, attended only by her devoted but critical groom, Fobbing, to the surrounding hills. She knew that Serena had a great deal of uncomfortable energy, but she never realized that her more protracted expeditions coincided with the arrival in Laura Place of one of Lady Theresa Eaglesham's punctual letters; and certainly never suspected that these letters, which seemed to her to be tiresomely full of dull political news, made Serena feel that she had slipped out of the world. To Fanny, the loss of London dinner-parties where little was talked of but a Government crisis, or a victory over the Opposition, was a gain; and she could not conceive what there was to excite interest in the news that the Grenvilles and the Foxites were splitting, in consequence of Brougham's speech. The fortunes of Whig and Tory were of far less moment to Fanny than the fear that her mama might send her sister Agnes to Bath, to bear her company.

This dread seriously impaired Fanny's peace of mind, until it became apparent that Lady Claypole's anxiety for the well-being of her married daughter was not of so urgent a nature as to prompt her either to go to Bath herself at the beginning of the London season, or to send thither a second daughter of rather more than marriageable age. Lady Claypole, with a third daughter straining at the schoolroom leash, would let no consideration interfere with her determination to achieve a respectable alliance for Agnes. She seemed to have abandoned all thought of a brilliant one, but hinted, in a crossed and double-crossed letter, that she cherished hopes of bringing a very worthy man of tolerable substance up to scratch. Fanny sighed over the letter, but was thankful to be spared Agnes's companionship. An elder and jealous sister, who made up in learning what she lacked in beauty, and might be trusted to keep a censorious eye on her junior, could not add to her comfort. She infinitely preferred the society of her daughter-in-law, however little dependence Mama might place on dear Serena's discretion. Mama could not approve of Serena. She said that she conducted herself as though the protection of a wedding-ring were hers, and had, at once, too great and too little a notion of her own consequence. Mama had seen her hob-nobbing with quite unworthy persons, as though she thought her rank absolved her from the necessity (indispensable to *every* unmarried female) of behaving with reserve. Mama sincerely trusted she might not draw Fanny into some scrape, and ended her letter with an earnest adjuration to her daughter not to forget what her own situation now was, or what respect was due to the relict of an Earl.

Fanny replied dutifully to this missive, but even as her pen assured Lady Claypole that she misjudged dearest Serena, a feeling of guilt made it tremble into a blot. Something told her that Mama would deeply disapprove of Serena's latest friendship. Indeed, it could not be denied that Serena was hob-nobbing with a very ungenteel person.

The acquaintance had been struck up in the Pump Room, and in the oddest way. Upon several occasions, both she and Fanny had been diverted by the startling appearance presented by an elderly female of little height but astonishing girth, who, while she adhered, perhaps wisely, to the fashions of her youth, was not wise enough to resist the lure of bright colours. She had a jolly, masterful countenance, with three chins beneath it, and a profusion of improbable black ringlets above it, imperfectly confined by caps of various designs, worn under hats of amazing opulence. Serena drew giggling protests from Fanny by asserting that she had counted five ostrich plumes, one bunch of grapes, two of cherries, three large roses, and two rosettes on one of these creations. An enquiry elicited from Mr King the information that the lady was the widow of a rich merchant of Bristol – or he might have been a shipowner: Mr King could not take it upon himself to say. No doubt a very good sort of a woman in her way, but (her la'ship would agree) sadly out of place in such a select place as Bath. She was a resident, he was sorry to say, but he had never been more than distantly civil to her. Fabulously wealthy, he believed: for his part he deeply deplored the degeneracy of the times, and was happy to think he could remember the days when mere vulgar wealth would not have made it possible for a Mrs Floore to rub shoulders with my Lady Spenborough.

It might have been this speech, which she listened to with a contemptuous shrug, that inclined Serena to look with an indulgent eye upon Mrs Floore. The widow was a regular visitor to the Pump Room, and often, when not engaged in hailing her acquaintance, and laughing and chatting with them in cheerful but unrefined accents, would sit staring at Serena, in an approving but slightly embarrassing way. Serena, conscious of the fixed regard, at last returned it, her brows a little lifted, and was surprised to see the old lady nodding and smiling at her encouragingly. Considerably amused, she moved gracefully towards her. 'I beg your pardon, ma'am, but I think you wish to speak to me?'

'That's a fact, for so I did!' said Mrs Floore. 'Though whether your ladyship would condescend to speak to me was more than I could tell! Not but what I've been watching you close, and for all you're so tall and high-stepping, my lady, you've a friendly way with you, and you don't look to me to be so haughty you hold your nose up at ordinary folk!'

'Indeed, I hope not!' said Serena, laughing.

Mrs Floore poked a finger into the ribs of a mild-looking man seated in a chair beside her, and said: 'I don't know where *your* wits have gone a-begging, Tom Ramford! Get up, and offer your place to Lady Serena, man!'

In great confusion, Mr Ramford hastily obeyed this sharp command. His apologies and protestations were cut short, Mrs Floore saying kindly, but with decision: 'There, that'll do! You take yourself off now!'

'Poor man!' said Serena, as she seated herself. 'You are very severe, ma'am! Pray, how do you come to know my name?'

'Lord, my dear, everyone knows who *you* are! I'll wager you don't know who I am, though!'

'You would lose, ma'am. You are Mrs Floore, a resident, I believe, of Bath,' Serena retorted.

The old lady chuckled richly, all her chins quivering. 'Ay, so I am, and I'll be bound you know it because you asked someone who the deuce that old fright could be, dressed in a gown with panniers!'

'I did ask who you might be, but I did *not* so describe you!' instantly responded Serena.

'Lord, I wouldn't blame you! I'd look a worse fright if I was to stuff myself into one of these newfangled gowns you all wear nowadays, with a waist under my armpits and a skirt as straight as a candle! All very well for you, my lady, with the lovely slim figure you have, but I'll tell you what I'd look like, and that's a sack of meal, with a string tied round it! Ay, that makes you laugh, and I see that it's quite true about your eyelids, though

I thought it a piece of girl's nonsense when I was told about it: they *do* smile!'

'Good God, who can have told you anything so ridiculous, ma'am?' demanded Serena, colouring faintly.

'Ah, that's just it!' said Mrs Floore. 'I daresay you've been wondering what made me wishful to become acquainted with you. Well, I've got a granddaughter that thinks the world of your ladyship, and by all accounts you've been mighty kind to her.'

'A granddaughter?' Serena repeated, stiffening suddenly in her chair. 'You cannot mean that you are – But, no! Surely Lady Lale – the person who springs to my mind – was a Miss Sebden?'

'So she was,' agreed Mrs Floore affably. 'Sebden was my first, and Sukey's papa. I've had two good husbands, and buried 'em both, which is more than Sukey can boast of, for all the airs she gives herself!'

'Good gracious!' Serena exclaimed, wishing with all her heart that Rotherham could have been present, to share (as he certainly would) her own enjoyment. 'Well, then, I am very happy to know you, Mrs Floore, for I have a sincere regard for little Emily Laleham. She has often taken pity on our dullness this winter, you know. We – Lady Spenborough and I – missed her sadly when she went to London.'

Mrs Floore looked gratified, but said: 'That's just your kindness, my lady, that makes you say so. I don't deny I'm uncommonly partial to Emma, but I ain't a fool, and I can see who it was that took pity, even if Emma hadn't talked so much about you I was in a fair way to hating the sound of your name! Sukey – for Sukey she's always been to me, and always will be, let her say what she likes! – sent her to spend the New Year with me, and it was Lady Serena this, and Lady Serena that till I'd very likely have had a fit of the vapours, if I'd been a fine lady, which I thank God I'm not, nor ever could be!'

'What an infliction!' Serena said, smiling. 'I am astonished you should have wished to become acquainted with me, ma'am! I think, you know, that when she was only a child Emily thought me a very *dashing* female, because I was used to hunt with my father, and do all manner of things which seemed very romantical to her! I hope she may be wiser now that she knows me better. I fear I'm no model for a young female to copy.'

'Well, *that*, begging your pardon, is where you're out, my dear!' said Mrs Floore shrewdly. 'You've done Emma a great deal of good, and I don't scruple to tell you so! She's a good little soul, and as pretty as she can stare, but she hasn't a ha' porth of common sense, and between the pair of them, Sukey, and that piece of walking gentility which calls herself a governess and looks to me more like a dried herring in petticoats, were in a fair way to ruining the poor child! But Emma, admiring your ladyship like she did, had the wit to see the difference between your manners and the ones her ma and that Miss Prawle was trying to teach her! Prawle! *I'd* Prawle her! "Grandma," Emma said to me, "Lady Serena is always quite unaffected, and she is as civil to her servants as to Dukes and Marquises and all, and I mean to behave exactly like her, because she came over with the Conqueror, and is a great lady!" Which,' concluded Mrs Floore, 'I can see for myself, though what this Conqueror has to say to anything I'm sure I don't know!'

'Oh, no! Nor anyone else!' uttered Serena, quite convulsed.

'I promise you, I took no account of *him*,' said Mrs Floore. 'The Quality have their ways, and we have ours, and what may be all very well for high-born ladies don't do for the parson's daughter, as you may say. All I know is that Emma will do better to copy the manners of an Earl's daughter than her ma's, and so I told her!'

Serena could only say: 'Indeed, she need copy no one's manners, ma'am! Her own are very pleasing, and unaffected.'

'Well, to be sure, I think so,' said Mrs Floore, beaming upon her, 'but I'm no judge, though I did marry a gentleman! Oh, yes! Mr Sebden was quite above my touch, and married me in the teeth of his grand relations, as you may say. You might not think it to look at me now, but I was very much admired when I was a girl. Dear me, yes! Such suitors as I had! Only I took a fancy to poor George, and though my Pa didn't like the match above half, George being too idle and gentlemanly for his taste, he never could deny me anything I'd set my heart on, and so we were married, and very happily, too. Of course, his family pretty well cast him off, but he didn't care a button for that, *nor* for turning me into a grand lady. Mind you, when Pa died, and left his whole fortune to me, the Sebdens began to pay me a lot of civilities, which was only to be expected, and which I was glad of, on account of Sukey. Yes, I thought nothing was too good for my Sukey, so pretty as she was, and with her Pa's genteel ways and all! Ah, well! I often think now that her brother wouldn't have grown up to despise his ma, however much money had been spent on sending him to a fashionable school!'

A gusty sigh prompted Serena to say: 'Indeed, I didn't know you had had a son that died! I am so sorry!'

'Well, I didn't, not exactly,' said Mrs Floore. 'Not but what I sometimes feel it just as much as if he had died, for I'm sure he'd have been a good, affectionate boy. The thing was I always longed for a son, but the Lord never blessed us with more than the one child. No. There was only Sukey, and everything that money could buy she had. She went to a grand school in London, and made all manner of fine friends there, I warrant you! So, when poor George died, and the Sebdens offered to bring Sukey out, I let them do it, and the next thing I knew was she was engaged to marry Sir Walter Laleham. Between you and me, my lady, he never seemed to me any great thing, though I'm bound to say I didn't know then what he was going to cost me, first and last! Not that I grudge it, because this I will say: he may be a gamester and he may drink a deal too much, but he ain't ashamed of his ma-in-law, and if it weren't for Sukey I might go to his house, and welcome!'

Staggered by these extremely frank confidences, Serena could think of nothing better to say than: 'I believe Sir Walter is generally very well liked. My father and he were at Eton together, and afterwards at Oxford.'

'Ay, were they so? Oh, well, it's a fine thing for a man to be of the first rank, but it's a better thing to have a bit of sense, if you'll pardon my saying so! And what with offering for Sukey, who, he might ha' known, would rule the roast, even if he'd been a Duke, and never having the wit to back the right horse, he's my notion of a silly noddy! But, there! I shouldn't be saying so, and no more I would have, only that there's something about your ladyship I like, besides knowing you was kind to Emma. What's more, says I to myself, if you've been living in the same place as Sukey it's not likely I could tell you anything you didn't know about her, because it's my belief those airs of hers wouldn't deceive a newborn baby! Now, *would* they?'

'I assure you, ma'am, Lady Laleham is – is everywhere received!'

'I know that well enough, my dear, and many's the time I've enjoyed a laugh over it. For though I don't deny it was marrying Sir Walter that took her into the first circles, it's me that keeps her there!'

Meeting frankness with frankness, Serena said: 'I don't doubt it, ma'am. Even had I not guessed as much from things Emily has said, it is common knowledge that Sir Walter – as the saying goes – married money.'

Mrs Floore chuckled. 'I'll go bail it is! Ah, well! If it weren't for the silly fellow getting knocked into horsenails so often, and him and Sukey not daring to provoke me for fear I might leave my fortune away from them, let alone providing for Emma's coming-out, I daresay I should never see anything of either of 'em, nor my grandchildren neither, so maybe it's all for the best. It suited Sukey very well when I married Ned Floore, because who's to know I'm her ma, unless I tell 'em, which in the general way I don't? What's more, Floore was a very warm man, with never a chick nor child of his own, and every penny he had he left to me, and no strings tied to 'em! So whenever I feel low I tell Sukey I've taken a fancy to pay her a visit in her fine London house. It's as good as a play to see how many excuses she'll make up to put me off, never dreaming that I do it only to tease her! I never had any taste for grand company myself, but Sukey has, and you can say that's my doing, for having sent her to a smart school. So she needn't be afraid! I can't help laughing at her, but I've got no notion of embarrassing her: no, nor Emma either!'

'I am very sure, ma'am, that Emma at least you could not embarrass. She speaks of you with so much affection!'

'Bless her heart!' said Mrs Floore. 'All the same, my lady, it wouldn't do her a bit of good if I was to go around telling everyone I'm her grandma, so I beg you won't mention it. I've been letting my tongue run away with me, like I shouldn't, but you're one of those that can be trusted, *that's* certain!'

'Thank you! If you wish it, I will not mention the relationship to anyone but Lady Spenborough, and her you may also trust.'

'Poor young thing!' remarked Mrs Floore. 'Such a sweet face as she has! It quite goes to my heart to see her in her weeds, and she no more than a baby. There! The General is taking his leave of her, and she'll be looking to see what's become of you. You'd best go, my lady, for I daresay she wouldn't think it a proper thing for you to be sitting chatting to me.'

'Not at all,' said Serena calmly, making a sign to Fanny. 'If you will allow me, I should like to make you known to her, ma'am.'

She smiled at Fanny, as she came up, and said: 'Fanny, I wish to introduce Mrs Floore to you, who is Emily's grandmama.'

Fanny, however astonished she might be, was far too well-bred to betray any other emotions than civil complaisance. She bowed, and held out her hand, which, after heaving herself on to her feet, Mrs Floore shook with great heartiness, saying that she was honoured, and only wished Sukey could see her.

'Which, however, it's just as well she can't. And if ever you should find yourselves in Beaufort Square, that's where I live, and a warm welcome you'd have from me – and no offence taken if you don't choose to come!'

'Thank you, we should like very much to visit you,' replied Serena.

'So kind!' murmured Fanny.

Mrs Floore beamed all over her face. 'Then I'll tell you what you should do, my dears: just you send your footman round to tell me you mean to pay me a call, and if it should happen that there's company with me I'll send 'em packing, because for one thing it wouldn't be seemly for you to be going to parties, and for another my friends ain't just in your style, any more than I am myself, the only difference between us being that I shan't holler at you across the street, or go prating about you all over Bath, which one or two I know *might*!'

With these reassuring words, she shook hands again, blessed Serena's lovely face, and waddled away.

'Serena!' breathed Fanny. 'What an *extraordinary* creature!'

'Yes, but quite delightful, I promise you!'

'But, Serena, she is dreadfully vulgar! You cannot really mean to visit her!'

'Certainly I mean to, and I shall think very poorly of you if you don't accompany me!'

'But, dearest, do you – do you think your papa would have permitted it?' Fanny ventured to say.

That made Serena laugh. 'My dear Fanny, you know very well Papa never interfered with me, or thought himself too grand to rub shoulders with the rest of the world!'

'Oh, no, no, I never meant – only I can't help feeling that everyone would say I ought not to let you become acquainted with vulgar persons, and in particular your Aunt Theresa, though how she thinks I can prevent you from doing exactly as you choose when *she* could not, I'm sure I don't know!' said Fanny despairingly.

Seven

The call was paid, though without the suggested prelude; and the welcome accorded to the ladies was so good-natured and unaffected that Fanny was brought to acknowledge that however vulgar Mrs Floore might be she had a great deal of drollery, and was certainly no toad-eater. She declined a civil invitation to return the visit, saying, with paralysing candour, that it was one thing for their ladyships to visit in Beaufort Square whenever they felt so inclined, and quite another for them to be entertaining her in Laura Place, and very likely making all their acquaintance wonder what kind of company they had got into.

Since this was very much what Fanny had been thinking she instantly turned scarlet, and stammered an inarticulate protest, which made her hostess tell her very kindly that there was no need for her to flush up, because facts were facts, and no getting round them, and in any event she was grown so stout that it was as much as she cared to do to walk to the Pump Room and back. 'And as for calling a chair, I give you my word I never do so without I expect the poor fellows carrying me to drop down dead between the shafts, which would be a very disconcerting thing to happen,' she added.

Serena laughed. 'Very well, ma'am, it shall be as you wish! But pray believe we should be happy to see you in Laura Place!'

This won her a glance of decided approval from their fellow-guest, a gentlemanly-looking young man of some thirty years of age, who had been sitting with Mrs Floore when they were announced. It was to be inferred, since he had not been sent packing, that Mrs Floore considered him worthy to meet her distinguished visitors. She introduced him as Ned Goring, the son of her late husband's business partner, who had ridden over from Bristol to pay his respects to her; and it soon transpired that the redoubtable old lady had inherited, besides two fortunes, considerable interest in her father's soap factory, and her husband's shipyard. Young Mr Goring, a junior partner in the latter, evidently regarded her with respect and affection; and when, in the course of conversation with him, Serena said something about her liking Mrs Floore so much, he replied in his blunt way: 'Everyone must who knows her, I think. I never knew anyone with a kinder heart, or a sounder understanding.'

She warmed to him, knowing the world well enough to realize how many men in his position, having achieved through education a greater gentility than was aspired to by their fathers, would have found it necessary to have excused a friendship with one so frankly vulgar as Mrs Floore. That lady being fully occupied with Fanny, Serena took pains to draw Mr Goring out. She very soon discovered that he had been educated at Rugby and at Cambridge, and liked him the better when he replied, in answer to an enquiry: 'Yes, I am pretty well acquainted with George Alplington, but since I entered my father's business our ways have lain apart. How does he go on? He is an excellent fellow!'

'Very expensively!'

He laughed. 'Ah, I was used to tell him he would end up a Bond Street beau! Then, of course, he would make some opprobrious mention of tar, that being the only commodity to be used in my trade which he knew of, and it was a chance if either of us emerged from the argument without a black eye!'

At this point, Fanny rose to take leave, and the party broke up, Serena shaking hands with her new acquaintance, and expressing the friendly hope that they might meet again. As she walked back to Laura Place beside Fanny, she observed: 'I liked that young man, did not you? There was something particularly pleasing about his manners, which I thought very easy and frank. He has an air of honest manliness, too, which, in these days of fribbles and counter-coxcombs, I own I find refreshing!'

A new terror reared itself in Fanny's head; the weekly letter to Mama was painstakingly inscribed, and contained no reference to Beaufort Square.

However, nothing more was heard of Mr Goring. Serena's friendship with Mrs Floore prospered, but in a mild way that resolved itself into an occasional call, and frequent meetings in the Pump Room, when sometimes conversation was exchanged, and sometimes no more than cordial greetings. The next occurrence to enliven the routine of Bath life was an unexpected visit from Rotherham. Fanny and Serena, coming in one sunny afternoon in April, after walking for an hour in the Sydney Gardens, were greeted with the intelligence that his lordship had been awaiting them in the drawing-room for some twenty minutes or more. Fanny went to take off her bonnet and pelisse, but Serena chose to go immediately to the drawing-room, and entered it, saying: 'Well! This is a surprise! What brings you to Bath, Rotherham?'

He was standing before the small wood-fire, glancing through a newspaper, but he cast this aside, and came forward to shake hands. His expression was forbidding, and the tone in which he answered her decidedly acid. 'I shall be grateful to you, Serena, if you will in future be so good as to inform me of it when you intend to change your habitation. I learned of this start by the merest chance.'

'Good gracious, why should I?' she exclaimed. 'I suppose I need not apply to you for permission to come to Bath.'

'You need not! Responsibility for your movements was spared me. You are free to do as you please, but since I am your Trustee you would save me annoyance, and yourself inconvenience, if you will advertize me when you wish new arrangements made for the payment of your allowance! I imagine it would not suit you to be obliged to send all the way to Gloucester for any monies you might need!'

'No, to be sure it would not!' she agreed. 'It was stupid of me not to have recollected that!'

'Quite featherheaded!'

'Yes, but the thing is that I have a considerable sum by me, and that is how I came to forget the matter. What a fortunate circumstance that you should have put me in mind of it! I must write to ask Mr Perrott to make a new arrangement too, or who knows when I may find myself in the basket?'

'As it is he who collects the larger part of your income, it would certainly be as well.'

'Could you find no one in town with whom to pick a quarrel?' she asked solicitously. 'Poor Ivo! It is too bad!'

'I am not picking a quarrel. It would surprise you, I daresay, if I told you that I rarely quarrel with anyone but yourself.'

'Ah, that's because very few people have the courage to pick up your gauntlet!' she said, smiling.

'An amiable portrait you draw!'

'But a speaking likeness!' she countered, a laughing challenge in her eye.

He shook his head. 'No: I choose rather to prove you wrong. We won't quarrel this time, Serena.'

'As you wish! Will you alter the arrangement for my tiresome allowance, if you please?'

'I have already done so. There is the direction,' he replied, handing her a piece of paper.

'Thank you! That was kind of you. I am sorry to have

been so troublesome. Did you come all the way from town just for that?'

'I had business at Claycross,' he said curtly. 'You seem to be comfortably established here. How do you go on?'

'Very prosperously. It was a relief to escape from Milverley.'

He nodded, but made no comment, merely saying, after a brief, keen scrutiny of her face: 'Are you well? You look a trifle peaked.'

'If I do, it is because black doesn't become me. I mean to lighten my mourning, and have ordered a charming gray gown.'

'You are mistaken.'

'What, in going into half-mourning?'

'No, in thinking black does not become you. Are you sure that Bath agrees with your constitution?'

'Yes, indeed! Now, don't, I beg of you, Rotherham, put it into Fanny's head that I am looking hagged! I think I did become a little out of sorts, but Bath will soon set me to rights.' She glanced at him, and added, with difficulty: 'I have not learned yet not to miss Papa. Don't let us speak of that! You know how it is with me! I don't care to talk of what so much affects me, and making a parade of grief is of all things the most repugnant to me.'

'Yes, I know,' he replied. 'You need not be afraid. I have nothing to say on that subject, for there is nothing to be said. Your aunt, by the by, charged me with all manner of messages to you. I met her at the Irebys' party a couple of nights ago. It is wonderful, Serena, how much she likes you when a hundred miles or so separate you from her!'

She laughed. 'Very true! My love to her, if you please, and tell her that I quite depend upon her letters for the latest *on-dits*. Where are you putting up, Ivo? Do you make a long stay in Bath?'

'At the York House. I return to town tomorrow.'

'How shabby! You will stay to dine with us at least! We keep unmodishly early hours here, I warn you.'

He hesitated. 'I can hardly sit down to dinner with you in my riding-dress, and I brought no other.'

'Ah, so you did mean to pick a quarrel with me!' she rallied him. 'Fanny will pardon your top-boots, and I hope you don't mean to stand on ceremony with *me*!' She turned her head, as Fanny came into the room, and said: 'Here is Rotherham, so full of punctilio he will not dine with us in his riding-dress! Persuade him, Fanny, while I make myself tidy!'

She returned presently to find them apparently in perfect charity with one another, Rotherham having been so obliging as to furnish Fanny with all the latest news of the Royal Marriage preparations. Since it was rarely that he had been known to pander to such feminine curiosity, Serena could only suppose that he was determined on amiability. Nothing occurred during the evening to make her change her mind. He indulged Fanny's taste for gossip, without betraying too much contempt for it; and entertained Serena with a pungent description of what he described as the flutter in the Whig dovecot. Both ladies were pleased, and if an elliptical reference, which made Serena's eyes dance, was incomprehensible to Fanny, or the conversation turned on Mr Canning's journey home from Lisbon, she had her embroidery-frame to occupy her, and was merely glad to see Serena in such spirits. Such phrases as: 'Pretty well to be employing a frigate for one's pleasure!' and: 'Never was there such a job!' put her forcibly in mind of agonizing evenings at Milverley, or in Grosvenor Square, when she had been obliged to strain every nerve in the effort to follow just such conversations. It was no longer her duty to do so, and she could only be thankful.

Her wandering thoughts were reclaimed presently, for the talk seemed to have switched from the despotic behaviour of someone called Ferdinand, to a subject of more interest. Rotherham was asking Serena who was at present visiting Bath.

'My dear Ivo! At the start of the London season? None but dowdies!'

Fanny protested that she was too severe, but Serena laughed, and shook her head. 'General Creake, old Lady Skene, Mrs Piozzi, Madame D'Arblay and her set: Mrs Holroyd, Mrs Frances, Miss Bowdler – need I continue?'

'You need not, indeed! I had hoped you might have found some more enlivening company.'

'I have!' Serena said.

'I mistrust that smile,' Rotherham said dryly. 'Who is it?'

'I'll tell you one day. At present my lips are sealed!' she replied, with an air of mock solemnity.

'That means, I imagine, that you know well I should disapprove.'

'I daresay you might, but very likely you would not, and in any event it doesn't concern you.' She glanced mischievously at Fanny, and added: 'I find the acquaintance excessively enlivening!'

'But Lady Spenborough does not?'

'Fanny has such grand notions! Besides, she is my mama-in-law, and feels it to be her duty to chaperon me very strictly!'

'Now, Serena!'

'I don't envy her *that* task. I shan't gratify you by trying to discover the mystery, but I wish you will take care what you are about.'

'I will. It is not precisely a mystery, only, although I daresay I might safely tell you about it, I believe I ought not, at this present.'

He looked frowningly at her, but said nothing. She began to talk of something else, and the subject was not again mentioned until Rotherham took his leave. Serena having run out of the room to fetch a letter which she desired him to frank, he said abruptly: 'Don't let her run into some scrape! You could not prevent her, I suppose: I know that headstrong temper!'

'Indeed, you are mistaken!' Fanny assured him.

He looked sceptical, but was prevented from saying more by Serena's coming back into the room with her letter.

'There it is,' she said, laying it upon the writing-table, and opening the lid of the standish. 'Cousin Florence will be very much obliged to you for saving her at least sixpence.'

He took the pen she was holding out to him, and dipped it in the ink. 'Shall I carry it to London, and post it there?'

'If you please. I wish you might have stayed longer in Bath, though.'

'Why? To have made the acquaintance of the Unknown?' he said, scrawling his name across the corner of her letter.

She laughed. 'No – though I want very much to present you to the Unknown! To ride with me, merely. You never think a fence too high for me, or beg me to have a care!'

'In the *saddle* I think you very well able to take care of yourself.'

'This is praise indeed!'

He smiled. 'I never denied your horsemanship, Serena. I wish it were possible for me to stay, but it is not. This curst ball looms ahead of me!'

'What ball?'

'Oh, did I not tell you? I am assured it is my duty to lend Rotherham House to Cordelia, so that she may launch Sarah, or Susan, or whatever the girl's name may be, upon the world with as much pomp as possible. I am unconvinced, but when it comes to Augusta adding her trenchant accents to Cordelia's plaintive ones I am against the ropes, and would give a dozen balls only to silence the pair of them.'

'Good God! Upon my word, I think it is amazingly good-natured of you, Ivo!' Serena said, quite astonished.

'Yes, so do I!' he replied.

He departed, and the ladies were left to marvel over this new and unexpected turn, Fanny declaring that she would never have believed he could be brought to do so much for his unfortunate wards, and Serena saying: 'I certainly never thought of his giving a ball for Susan, but I have sometimes suspected that he does a great deal more for them than he chooses to divulge.'

'I'm sure I never thought so! What put it into *your* head?'

'Well, it crossed my mind, when Mrs Monksleigh was complaining of his having insisted on her sending the boys to Eton because it was where their father was educated, that he could not have *compelled* her to do so, which she vows he did, unless it was he, and not she, who was to bear the cost of it. Only consider what that must be! Three of them, Fanny, and Gerard now at Cambridge! I am persuaded Mrs Monksleigh could not have contrived it, even had she had the least notion of management, which she has not!'

Fanny was much struck, and could only say: '*Well!*'

'It is not so wonderful,' Serena said, amused. 'Nor need it make you feel, as I see it does, that you have grievously misjudged him! He is so rich that I daresay he would not notice it if he were paying the school-fees of a dozen children. I shall feel I have misjudged him when I see him showing his wards a little kindness.'

'Well, if he is giving a grand ball for Susan, I call it a great deal of kindness!' said Fanny, with spirit.

Except for various formal notices in the London papers, they heard nothing more of the ball until the arrival of Lady Theresa's next letter to her niece. Lady Theresa had taken her third daughter to the function, but it did not seem as though she had enjoyed it, in spite of the many compliments she had received on Clarissa's beauty, and the gratifying circumstance of her never having lacked a partner. Any pleasure Lady Theresa might have derived from the ball had been destroyed by the sight of Cordelia Monksleigh, in a hideous puce gown, standing at the head of the great stairway to receive the guests. She had been unable to banish the reflection that there, but for her own folly, might have stood Serena, though not, she trusted, in puce. Moreover, had Serena been the hostess it was to be hoped that the company would have been more exclusive. What could have induced Rotherham to have given Cordelia Monksleigh *carte blanche*, as there was no doubt he had done, was a matter passing Lady Theresa's comprehension. Had anyone told her that she would live to see That Laleham Creature storming Rotherham House (heavily underscored), she would have laughed in his face. But so it had been; and if Serena had seen her positively flinging her chit of a daughter at all the eligible bachelors, besides forcing herself on the notice of every distinguished person present, she might, at last, have regretted her own folly, wilfulness, and improvidence.

'Well, well, well!' commented Serena, much appreciating this impassioned missive. 'I wonder what Mrs Floore will have to say about it? For my part, I can't but admire the Laleham-woman's generalship! To have stormed the Rotherham stronghold is something indeed! How angry Lady Silchester must have been! I wish I had been present!'

Mrs Floore, encountered on the following morning in the Pump Room, echoed these sentiments. 'To think of my granddaughter at a party like that, for I've read all the notices, my dear, and there was never anything like it! Lord, Sukey will be as proud as an apothecary and I'm sure I don't blame her! Say what you will, she gets what she's set her heart on, my Sukey! And Emma being solicited to stand up with lords and honourables and I don't know what besides! Depend upon it, Sukey will have got a lord in her eye for Emma already! Well, and if he's a nice, handsome young fellow I hope she may catch him!'

'I expect she will, ma'am,' said Serena, laughing.

'Yes, but I don't trust her,' said Mrs Floore. 'She's a hard, ambitious woman, my dear. Mark my words, if a Duke with one foot in the grave, and cross eyes, and no teeth, was to offer for that child, Sukey would make her accept him!'

'Oh, no!' protested Serena.

'No,' said Mrs Floore. 'She wouldn't, because I should have something to say to it!'

'Very rightly! But I don't think there is such a Duke, ma'am.'

'It'll be as well for him if there isn't,' said Mrs Floore darkly.

Serena left her brooding vengefully, and went off to change a book at Duffield's Library, on Milsom Street. This accomplished, she left the library, almost colliding on the doorstep with a tall man, who fell back instantly, saying: 'I *beg* your pardon!'

Even as she looked quickly up at him he caught his breath on a gasp. She stood gazing almost incredulously into a face she had thought forgotten.

'Serena!' he said, his voice shaking. '*Serena!*'

More than six years slid from her; she put out her hand, saying as unsteadily as he: 'Oh, can it be possible? *Hector!*'

Eight

THEY STOOD HANDFASTED, THE GENTLEMAN VERY PALE, THE lady most delicately flushed, hazel eyes lifted wonderingly to steady blue ones, neither tongue able to utter a word until a testy: 'By your leave, sir! by your leave!' recalled them to a sense of their surroundings, and made Major Kirkby drop the hand he was holding so tightly, and step aside, stammering a confused apology to the impatient citizen whose way he had been blocking.

As though released from a spell, Serena said: 'After all these years! You have not altered in the least! Yes, you have, though: those tiny lines at the corners of your eyes were not there before, I think, and your cheeks were not so lean – but I swear you are as handsome as ever, my dear Hector!'

He smiled at the rallying note in her voice, but his own was perfectly serious as he answered, in a low tone: 'And you are more beautiful even than my memories of you! Serena, Serena – ! Forgive me! I hardly know what I am saying, or where I am!'

She gave an uncertain little laugh, trying for a more commonplace note. 'You are in Milsom Street, sir, wholly blocking the way into Duffield's excellent library! And the spectacle of a gentleman of military aspect, standing petrified with his hat in his hand, is attracting a great deal of attention, let me tell you! Shall we remove from this too public locality?'

He cast a startled glance about him, coloured up, laughed, and set his high-crowned beaver on his fair head again. 'Oh, by God, yes! I am so bemused – ! May I escort you? – Your maid – footman – ?'

'I am alone. You may give me your arm, if you will be so good, but were you not about to go into the library?'

'No – yes! What can that signify? Alone? How comes this about? Surely –'

'My dear Hector, my next birthday, which is not so far distant, will be my twenty-sixth!' she said, placing her hand in his arm, and drawing him gently away from the entrance to the library. 'Did I never go out without a footman in attendance when you knew me before? Perhaps I did not, since I was in my Aunt Theresa's charge! She has the most antiquated notions! How long ago it seems! I was barely nineteen, and you were so proud of your first regimentals! To what exalted heights have you risen? Tell me how I should address you!'

His free hand came up to press her gloved fingers, lying so lightly in the crook of his left arm. 'As you do! The sound of *Hector* on your lips is such music as I never hoped to hear again! There were no exalted heights: I have no more imposing title than that of Major.'

'It sounds very well, I promise you. Are you on furlough? You do not wear regimentals.'

'I sold out at the end of last year. You might not be aware – my elder brother has been dead these three years. I succeeded to the property at the time of Bonaparte's escape from Elba, and but for that circumstance must have sold out two years ago.'

'I did not know – pray forgive me!'

'How should you?' he said simply. 'I never dreamed that I could hold a place in your memory!'

She was struck to the heart, realizing how small a place had been held by him, and said haltingly: 'Or I – that you should recall so clearly – after so – long!'

'You have never been absent from my thoughts. Your face, your smiling eyes, have been with me through every campaign!'

'No, no, how can you be so romantical?' she exclaimed, at once startled and touched.

'It is true! When I read of your engagement to Lord Rotherham – how can I describe to you what I suffered?'

'You saw that notice!'

'I saw it.' He smiled ruefully. 'I was used, whenever a London newspaper came in my way, to search the social columns for the sight of your name! Absurd of me, was it not? The *Morning Post* that included *that* announcement was sent to me by my sister. She knew I had been acquainted with you, and thought I should be interested to learn of your engagement. She little guessed what passions were roused in me! I had prepared myself for your marriage to another; I could have borne it, I hope, with better command over my own sensations had it been any other than Rotherham!'

She looked up in surprise. 'Did you dislike him so much? I had thought you scarcely knew him!'

'It was true: I met him perhaps three times only.' He paused, and she saw his well-moulded lips tighten. After a moment, he said: 'I have always believed that it was *he* who separated us.'

She was startled. 'Oh, no! Indeed, it wasn't so! Why, how could it have been possible?'

'His influence over your father was brought to bear. I knew him for my enemy, Serena, from the outset.'

'No! Recollect how young you were! His manners are not conciliating, and that abrupt way he has, and the frowning look, made you think he disliked you. My father would not countenance the match from worldly reasons. He thought us, besides, too young, and – oh, I suppose he had even then set his heart on my marrying Rotherham!'

'Had he not allowed Rotherham to persuade him into the belief that we were not suited to one another, I cannot think he would have been so adamant! His affection for you was too great to admit of his sacrificing you to mere worldly ambition.'

'Perhaps he did think that, but that Ivo put it into his head I will not allow! Good God, Hector, why should he have done so?'

'When I read the notice of your engagement, I knew the answer to that enigma!'

'Nonsense! That came three years later! Ivo had no thought of marrying me *then*!' She flushed, and added: 'I jilted him, you know.'

'I did know it. For you, it must have been painful indeed; for me – a relief I cannot describe to you! I knew then that your *heart* had not been engaged, that the match was made by your father, *de convenance*!'

She was silent for a moment, but said presently: 'I hardly know how to answer you. Papa most earnestly desired it. He *promoted* it, but no more than that! There was no compulsion no pressure exerted to make me – Hector, if it distresses you, I am sorry for it, but I should be sorrier still to deceive you! I was very willing: I fancied myself in love with Ivo. There! It is out, and you know now that I was not as constant as you.'

He said, in a moved tone: 'It is what I always loved in you – your honesty! that fearless look in your eyes, a frankness so engaging – ! But you *did* not love Rotherham!'

'No – a brief, bitterly fought campaign, that engagement of ours! I behaved shockingly, of course, but you may believe he was as well rid of me as I of him!'

Again he pressed her hand. 'I couldn't believe that. That you were well rid of him, yes! His temper, so peremptory and overbearing –'

'Oh, yes, but my own temper, you know, is very bad!' she said ruefully.

He smiled. 'It is like you say to so, but it is not true, Serena.'

'I'm afraid you don't know me.'

'Don't I? If ever it was bad, there must have been great provocation!'

'I thought so, at all events,' she said, a gleam of fun in her eyes. 'I always think so, whenever I lose it! That was one of the questions on which Rotherham and I could never agree!'

'I cannot bear to think of you subjected, even for so short a time, to that imperious, tyrannical disposition!'

She could not help laughing. 'I wish he might be privileged to hear you! He would think it a gross injustice that you should have no pity for *his* sufferings!'

'I can believe it! Do you ever meet him now?'

'Frequently. There was no estrangement. We are very good friends, except when we are sworn foes! Indeed, he is my Trustee.'

'Your Trustee!' he said, looking as though he found the information shocking. 'I knew how much attached to him Lord Spenborough was, but that he should have placed you in a position of such embarrassment – Forgive me! I should not be speaking to you so!'

'You mistake: I don't find it embarrassing! To be sure, I was in such a passion when I first discovered how it was to be – But there were circumstances enough to enrage me! Never mind that! As for meeting Ivo, in the old way, neither of us has been aware of any awkwardness. It is the popular notion that I should be cast into blushes in Ivo's presence, but either that's a great piece of nonsense, or I am a creature sadly lacking in sensibility! I can't be shy of a man I've known all my life! Since my father's death, too, he seems sometimes to me like a link with –' She broke off. 'But, come! We have talked enough of *me*! Tell me of yourself! I long to hear of all your doings in Spain!'

'I don't think I could ever hear enough of you,' he said seriously. 'Nothing of any consequence has befallen me. Nothing until today! When I saw you, it was as though these six years and more had never been!'

'Oh, hush! I too was conscious of just that feeling, but it is nonsensical! Much has happened to both of us!'

'To *you*! I know well how great a tragedy your father's death must have been to you. To have written to you would have been presumption: I could only *wish* that I had the right to comfort you!'

As always, she was rendered uncomfortable by spoken sympathy. She said: 'Thank you. The shock was severe, and the sense of loss must remain with me for long and long, but you must not think me borne down by it, or out of spirits. I go on very well.'

'I know your indomitable courage!'

Her impulse was to check him. She subdued it, afraid of wounding him, and walked on beside him with downcast eyes while he continued talking of her father. That he truly understood the extent of her loss, and most sincerely entered into her feelings, she could not doubt. He spoke well, and with great tenderness: she would rather he had been silent.

He seemed to realize it, and broke off, saying: 'It is painful for you to talk of it. I will say no more: what I feel – all that I cannot express – you must know!'

'Yes, I – You are very good, very kind! How glad I am I should have chosen to go to Duffield's this very morning! Do you make a long stay in Bath?'

'I came to visit my mother, and arrived only yesterday. There are no calls upon my time, and I had meant to remain with her for a few weeks. Since my father's death, she has resided here. The climate agrees with her constitution, and she derives benefit from the baths. She is a sad invalid, and seldom goes out, or – But are you living here too, Serena!'

'For a few months only, with my mother-in-law.'

'Ah! I knew that Lord Spenborough had married again, and feared that you must have been made unhappy.'

'No, indeed!'

'You live with Lady Spenborough? You like her? She is kind to you?' he said anxiously.

'Very!'

'I am very much relieved to hear you say so. I was afraid it might not be so. To have had a mama thrust upon you at your age cannot have been agreeable. Too often one hears of mamas-in-law domineering over the children of a previous marriage! But if she is *truly* motherly to you I can believe that you may be glad *now* that the marriage took place. Her protection must be a comfort to you.'

Her eyes began to dance, but she said demurely: 'Very true! I look forward to presenting you to her. I hope you will not think her *very* formidable!'

'Will you let me call on you?' he said eagerly. 'She will not object to it?'

'I am sure she will receive you most graciously!'

'There is something quelling in the very word!' he said, smiling. 'As for *dowager*, that conjures up such a picture as might terrify the boldest! If she should wear a turban, I shall shake in my shoes, for it will remind me of a great-aunt of whom, as a boy, I lived in dread! When may I call on her? Where is your direction?'

'In Laura Place.' She looked round her suddenly, and burst out laughing. 'Good God, do you know how far we have walked? Unless my eyes deceive me, we have reached nearly to the end of Great Pulteney Street! If I have at least led you in the right way it must have been by instinct! I have no recollection even of crossing the bridge!'

'Nor I,' he admitted, turning, and beginning to retrace his steps beside her. 'I have been walking in a dream, I think. I could wish we were at the other end of the town, so that I need not part from you so soon. My fear is that when you leave me I shall wake up.'

'Major Kirkby, I begin to think you are turned into an accomplished flirt!'

'I? Ah, you are quizzing me! I never flirted, I think, in my life.'

'Good gracious, will you tell me that there is not *one* beautiful Spaniard left mourning your departure?'

He shook his head. 'Not one, upon my honour!'

'I had no notion life was so dull in Spain!'

'I never saw one whom I thought beautiful,' he said simply.

They walked on, and were soon in Laura Place again. He parted from her at her door, lingering, with her hand in his, to say: 'Tell me when I may call on you!'

'When you wish,' she replied, smiling at him.

His clasp on her hand tightened; he bent to kiss it; and at last released it, and went striding away, as though he dared not trust himself to look back.

A minute later, Fanny was greeting Serena with relief. 'Oh, I am so glad you are come in! I feared some accident had befallen, for you have been away this age and more! Good God, dearest! What has happened? You look as if a fortune had dropped on you from the sky!'

'Not a fortune!' Serena said, her eyes very bright and sparkling, and a smile hovering about her mouth. 'Better than that, and by far more unexpected! I have met – an old acquaintance!'

'*That* would not make you look *so*! Now, be serious, love, I do beg of you!'

'Oh, I cannot be! You must hold me excused! Did you ever

feel yourself a girl again, in your first season? It is the most delightful thing imaginable! I have told him he may call on us: pray be so obliging as to like him! It will be a study to see his face when I present him to you: he pictures you in a turban, Fanny!'

Fanny let her embroidery frame drop. '*He?*' Her face brightened suddenly. 'Not – Oh, Serena, you don't mean you have met that young man again? the man you told me you had loved – the *only* man you had loved?'

'Did I tell you so? Yes, it is he!'

'Oh, *Serena*!' sighed Fanny ecstatically. 'How *very* glad I am! It is exactly like a romance! At least – is he still *single*, dearest?'

'Yes, of course he is! That is to say, I never asked him! But there is no doubt! I wonder how soon he will think it proper to call on us? I fancy it will not be long!'

It was not long. Major Kirkby, in fact, paid his visit of ceremony upon the following day, arriving in Laura Place on the heels of a heavy thunderstorm. Lybster, relieving him of his dripping cloak and hat, sent Fanny's page running to fetch a leather to rub over the Major's smart Hessians, and permitted himself to scrutinize with unusual interest this visitor who was not deterred by inclement weather from paying morning visits. He had been informed that her ladyship was expecting a Major Kirkby to call sometime, but no suspicion had been aroused in his mind that the unknown Major might prove to be a visitor quite out of the common. If he had thought about the matter at all, the picture in his mind's eye would have been of some middle-aged Bath resident; and when he opened the door to a tall, handsome gentleman, nattily attired, and not a day above thirty, if as old, he suffered a severe shock, and instantly drew his own perfectly correct conclusions. While the page wiped the mud from those well-cut boots, and the Major straightened his starched neckcloth, Lybster took a rapid and expert survey, contriving in a matter of seconds to ascertain that the long-tailed blue coat of superfine had come from the hands of one of the first tailors, that the Major had a nice taste in waistcoats, and knew how to arrange a neckcloth with modish precision. He had a fine pair of shoulders on him, and an excellent leg for a skin-tight pantaloon. His countenance, a relatively unimportant matter, came in for no more than a cursory glance, but the butler noted with approval that the features were regular, and the Major's air distinguished. He led the way upstairs to the drawing-room, the Major following him in happy ignorance of the ferment of conjecture his appearance had set up.

A door was opened, his name announced, and he trod into an elegantly furnished apartment, whose sole occupant was a slender little lady, dressed all in black, and seated at the writing-table.

Taken by surprise, Fanny looked up quickly, the pen still held between her fingers. The Major checked on the threshold, staring at her. He beheld a charming countenance, with very large, soft blue eyes, and a mouth trembling into a shy smile, golden ringlets peeping from under a lace cap, and a general air of youth and fragility. Wild thoughts of having entered the wrong house crossed his mind; considerably disconcerted, he stammered: 'I beg your pardon! I thought – I came – I must have mistaken the direction! But I asked your butler if Lady Spenborough – and he led me upstairs!'

Fanny laid the pen down, and rose to her feet, and came forward, blushing and laughing. 'I am Lady Spenborough. How do you do?'

He took her hand, but exclaimed involuntarily: 'The *Dowager* Lady Spenborough? But you cannot be –' He stopped in confusion, began to laugh also, and said: 'Forgive me! I had pictured – well, a very different lady!'

'In a turban! Serena told me so. It is very naughty of her to roast you, Major Kirkby. Do, pray, be seated! Serena will be down directly. She was caught in that dreadful storm, and was obliged to change her dress, which was quite soaked.'

'Walking in this weather! I hope she may not have taken a chill! It was very imprudent.'

'Oh, no! She never does so,' responded Fanny placidly. 'She was used to ride with her Papa in all weathers, you know. She is a famous horsewoman – quite intrepid!'

'Yes, so I believe. I never saw her in the saddle, however. Our – our former acquaintance was in London. You and she now reside here? Or, no! I think she told me you were here only for a visit.'

'Oh, yes! We have been living since Lord Spenborough's death in my Dower House, at Milverley.'

'Ah, then, she has not been obliged quite to leave her home! I remember that she was much attached to it.' He smiled warmly at her. 'When I read of Lord Spenborough's death, I was afraid she might be obliged to live with Lady – with someone, perhaps, not agreeable to her! I am sure she must be happy with you, ma'am!'

'Oh, yes! That is, *I* am very happy,' said Fanny naïvely. 'She is so kind to me! I don't know how I should go on without her.'

At that moment, Serena came into the room, her copper ringlets still damp, and curling wildly. As she closed the door, she said mischievously: 'Now, what an infamous thing it is that you should have come when I wasn't here to present you to my mama-in-law, sir! She has not terrified you, I trust?'

He had jumped up, and strode to meet her, taking her hand, and holding it for a minute. 'What an infamous thing it was that you should have taken me in!' he retorted, smiling down at her with so glowing a look in his eyes that her own sank, and she felt her colour rising.

'It was irresistible! Are you satisfied that she is truly motherly?'

'Serena! You never said so!' cried Fanny indignantly.

'No, not I! It was Major Kirkby's hope!'

He drew her forward to a chair beside the small fire, and placed a cushion behind her as she seated herself. She looked up, to thank him, and he said: 'Do you know that your hair is quite wet?'

'It will soon dry beside this fire.'

'Are you always so reckless? I wish you will take care!'

She smiled. 'Why, do I seem to you invalidish? It's well you didn't see me when I came in, for I don't think there was a dry stitch on me!'

'Then perhaps it is as well. I should certainly have been anxious.'

'Fanny will tell you that I am never ill. Do *you* take cold every time you are caught in the rain?'

'No, indeed! I should not long have survived in Portugal! But that is another matter: you are not a soldier!'

She saw that he would not readily be persuaded that her constitution was not delicate, and was a little amused. It was not unpleasant to find herself an object of solicitude, so she said no more, leading him instead to talk of his experiences in the Peninsula. He stayed for half-an-hour, and then, very correctly, rose to take his leave. Fanny, as she shook hands with him, said, in her pretty, soft voice: 'You know we cannot entertain in any formal style, Major Kirkby, but if you will not think it a bore to dine quietly with us one evening, we should be happy to welcome you.'

'A bore! I should like it of all things!' he said. 'May I indeed do that?'

The engagement was made, and Fanny's hand kissed. 'Thank you!' the Major said, with a twinkle.

There was a good deal of meaning in his voice. Fanny gave a little choke of laughter, and tried to look demure.

He turned from her to Serena. 'I think you are very fortunate in your mama-in-law! Shall I see you, perhaps, in the Pump Room tomorrow? Do you go there?'

'Very frequently – to watch Fanny screwing up her face, and most heroically drinking the water!'

'Ah! Then I shall meet you there!' he said, and pressed her hand, and went away.

Serena glanced almost shyly at Fanny. 'Well?'

'Oh Serena, how *very* charming he is! You did not tell me the half! I think I never saw such kind eyes! He is so much in love with you, too!'

'He does not know me.'

'My dear!'

Serena shook her head. 'Do you think he does? I am so much afraid – You see, he believes me to be oh, so many excellent things which I am not! He has no notion of my shocking temper, or my obstinacy, or –'

'Serena, you goose!' Fanny cried, embracing her. 'He loves you! Oh, and he will take such care of you, and value you as he should, and think nothing too good for you! He is the very man to make you happy!'

'Fanny, Fanny!' Serena protested. 'He has not offered for me yet!'

'How absurd you are! When he can barely take his eyes off you! He will offer for you before the week is out!'

Nine

Fanny was disappointed. It was ten days later before the Major declared himself, and he did it then at her instigation.

That he was head over ears in love no one could doubt. He went about like a man dazzled by strong sunshine, so oblivious of his surroundings or any worldly care that his anxious mother was thrown into great disquiet, convinced at one moment that he no longer held her in affection, and at the next that his restlessness and absence of mind must have its root in some deep-seated disorder. Since the state of her health made her shrink from social intercourse, and her only expeditions from her eyrie in Lansdown Crescent down into the town were to the Abbey Baths, she remained in ignorance of the true state of affairs. Fashionable Bath could have enlightened her, for although the Major retained just enough sense not to haunt Laura Place it seemed not to occur to him that the spectacle of a tall and handsome young man searching the Pump Room every morning for the Lady Serena Carlow might possibly attract attention. The *habitués* of the Pump Room derived considerable entertainment from it, one gentleman asserting that it was now his custom to set his watch by the Major's arrival; and old General Hendy, whose own practice was to steer a gouty and determined course to Fanny's side, saying indignantly that he never saw such a silly, moonstruck fellow, and had a good mind to tell him what a cake he was making of himself. Whenever the Major came bearing down upon Serena, he scowled at him awfully; but as the Major had no eyes for anyone but Serena, this strong hint from a senior officer went unnoticed. General Hendy was not the only person hostile to the courtship. High sticklers viewed it with disapproval, some maintaining that it was improper for the Lady Serena to be encouraging any gentleman to pay his addresses to her while she was in mourning for her father, others considering that such a match would be scandalously unequal.

Had the Major been less besotted he must have perceived the glances, curious, amused, or condemnatory, and have realized that his goddess had become the most talked-of woman in Bath. He would have been aghast. Serena realized it, and laughed. Fanny did not realize it until Mrs Floore shocked her by saying: 'A very pretty beau your daughter-in-law has got for herself, my lady, I do declare! Lord, it's as good as a play to watch him! Morning after morning, in he comes, and if Lady Serena is here he goes plunging across the room to her, never noticing another soul, and if she ain't he goes off like a dog that's lost its tail!'

Dismayed, Fanny exclaimed: 'Oh, how could I be so thoughtless? I never dreamed that people would notice – talk about Lady Serena – !'

'Lord, ma'am, who cares for a bit of gossip?' said Mrs Floore comfortably. 'There's no harm that ever I heard of in a beautiful girl being courted, and if people choose to talk, let 'em!'

Serena said the same. 'My dear Fanny, don't tease yourself! The world began to talk about me when I drove a high-perch phaeton in Hyde Park! I was eighteen then, and much Papa cared for the exclamations of the censorious! When I declared I would no longer be burdened with a duenna hands were upflung in horror; when I jilted Rotherham I was known to be past reclaim! Add to these all my other iniquities, and you must perceive that I've given people so much to talk about that had I cared for their whisperings I must have retired to a nunnery! What's more, didn't my aunt warn you that I am an acknowledged flirt?'

'Serena, do not say so!'

'Well, it's quite true, you know,' said Serena candidly. 'How often have *you* accused me of trifling with some ridiculous creature's sensibilities?'

'Oh, no, no! I never said that! Only that you have so much liveliness, dearest, and so much beauty, that – that gentlemen can't help but fall in love with you, and you are so heedless of your beauty that you don't quite realize it!'

'Fanny, you're a goose!' Serena told her severely. 'Of course I do! If a personable man does me the honour to think me beautiful, alas that there should not be more of them! But my red hair, you know, is a sad blemish! – well, if he *does* admire me, what should I do but reward him with a little elegant dalliance?'

'How can you talk so? If I believed you to be *flirting* with Major Kirkby – Oh, no, Serena, you could not!'

'You are very right! It would be a feat beyond my power. He would be incapable of it!'

'I wish you will be serious!' Fanny said despairingly.

'I can't be! No, no, don't pester me with questions, or lecture me on the proprieties, Fanny! Very likely I have taken leave of my senses – indeed, I sometimes fear I have! – but either I shall come about, or – or – I shall not! And as for the rest of the world, it may go to the devil!'

Fanny could only conclude that she was as much in love as the Major, and wished that he would come to the point. Why he did not do so she was at a loss to understand, and was beginning to wonder if some impediment perhaps existed, when, to her surprise, he was ushered into the drawing-room in Laura Place one afternoon, and said, as he grasped her hand: 'I hoped I might find you at home! Serena is out, I know: it is you I particularly wish to see! You are her guardian – the properest person to be consulted! You know her – I believe you must be aware of the nature of the feelings which I – Lady Spenborough, in the joy of seeing her again, hearing her voice, touching her hand, all other considerations were forgotten! I allowed myself –' He broke off, trying to collect himself, and took a few hasty steps about the room.

Filled with trepidation, she said, after a moment: 'You allowed yourself, Major Kirkby – ?'

'To be happy in a dream! A dream of years, which seemed suddenly to have turned to reality!'

'A dream! I beg your pardon, but why do you call it so?' she asked anxiously.

He turned, and came back to the fireside. 'Should I not? Lady Spenborough, I ask myself that question again and again! I tell myself it could be reality, but I cannot silence the doubt – the scruple – that warns me it *should* not!'

His agitation, the strong emotion under which he was evidently labouring, the oppressed look upon his brow, all awoke her ready compassion. Her disposition was timid; she was always very shy with anyone whom she did not know well; but she felt no shyness upon this occasion. She said, with her pretty smile: 'Will you not be seated, and tell me what it is that is troubling you? You know, I am very stupid, and I don't at all understand what you mean!'

He threw her a grateful look, saying: 'You are so very kind! I am talking like a fool, I suppose! I came to ask you – Lady Spenborough, should I be the most presumptuous dog alive to beg Serena to marry me?'

Astonishment widened her eyes. 'Presumptuous? But – but why?'

'You don't think so? But have you considered? You know, I fancy, that the feelings I entertain are not – are not of recent birth! It is nearly seven years since I first saw her, and from that day those feelings have remained unchanged! She appeared to me then like some heavenly creature descended to earth to make every other woman seem commonplace! Her beauty, her grace, the very music of her voice, I could never forget! They have remained with me, haunted all my dreams –' He stopped, reddening, and tried to laugh. 'I am talking like a fool again!'

'No, no!' she breathed. 'Pray do not think so! Go on, if you please!'

He stared down at his hands, lying clasped between his knees. 'Well! You are aware, I daresay, that I had the temerity to raise my eyes – too high!'

'You should not say so,' she interpolated gently.

'It was true! *Then* I thought otherwise. I was very young! Rank and fortune seemed to me to be of no account when set in the scales against such an attachment as I believed ours to be! I think I never forgave those that parted us until now, when the treasure I had believed unattainable seems to be within my reach, and I see – as any man of honour must! – all the force of the arguments which were advanced against me, seven years ago!'

Again she interrupted him. 'Forgive me! But seven years ago *she* was just come out, and *you* were a younger son, with no prospects! She is her own mistress now, and you are not a boy, just joined, and proud, as Serena once told me, of your first regimentals. *Then*, had she been permitted to marry you, she must have followed the drum; today, it is otherwise, is it not?'

He looked up, fixing his eyes upon her intently. 'I have come into the property which I never thought to inherit, but it is not large. Indeed, in *her* eyes the estate must seem a small one, and brings me what I should rather call an easy competence than a handsome fortune. The *elegances* of life I can command, but not its luxuries! The house to which I should take her, though I have been used to hear it spoken of as commodious, cannot compare with Milverley. I was never at Milverley, but I have visited such places. I have even stayed in one or two, and I know that beside the size and style of such an establishment my poor little manor must be dwarfed indeed. I could afford, I think, to hire a house in town for the Season, but it could not be a mansion, like Spenborough House.'

'Oh!' she cried involuntarily. 'Can you suppose that such considerations as that would weigh with Serena?'

'No! Her mind is too lofty – her disposition too generous! If she gave her heart, she would, I think, be ready to live in a cottage! It is with me that those considerations weigh! They must do so – and the more heavily because *she* would laugh them aside!'

'I don't know what any woman could want more than what you can offer her,' Fanny said wistfully.

'Lady Spenborough, are you sincere? You don't think it would be wrong in me to ask her to be my wife?'

'No, indeed! To be sure, I cannot feel that a *cottage* would do for Serena,' said Fanny, quite unable to picture Serena in such a setting, 'because she doesn't like to feel herself cooped-up. Besides, you could scarcely keep servants in a cottage, and, with all the will in the world, Major Kirkby, she could never manage without!'

He could not help laughing. 'I should think not indeed!'

'You see,' Fanny explained, 'she has always had so many servants to wait upon her that she has never been obliged to attend very much to domestic matters. But I daresay you have a good housekeeper?'

'Of course! I didn't mean that she would have to sweep floors, or cook the dinner, or even tell the maids what they must do. My mother was used to direct the servants, but since she has lived in Bath Mrs Harbury has attended to all such matters, and could very well continue to do so, if Serena wished it.'

'I expect she would wish it,' said Fanny, with lively memories of Serena's unconcern with the domestic arrangements at the Dower House. She added reflectively: 'It is the oddest thing! I am sure Serena never groomed a horse in her life, or swept out a stall, but she would manage a stable far more easily than a house!'

These words brought another scruple to his mind. He said: 'Her hunting! Could she bear to give that up? Even if I could endure to let her risk her neck, my home is in Kent, and that is poor hunting-country – humbug country, I expect she would call it! There are several packs, but I have never been much addicted to the sport. I could become a subscriber, but I doubt – She told me once that she thought nothing equal to the Cottesmore country!'

'Yes,' said Fanny. 'She and her papa were used to visit Lord Lonsdale every year, at Lowther Hall. But for the most part, of course, they hunted with the Duke of Beaufort's pack. I believe – but I have never hunted myself! – that that is very good country too.' She smiled at him, as something very like a groan burst from him. 'Major Kirkby, you are too despondent! It would be a very poor creature who would set such considerations as *that* in the balance!'

'I know she would not! But I should wish her to have everything she desired!'

'Well, if she desired it so very much, perhaps it could be contrived. You might purchase a lodge in the Shires, or –'

'*That* I might do, but maintain a dozen or so first-rate hunters I could not!'

'But Serena has a very large fortune of her own!' said Fanny.

He sprang up, and began to walk about the room again. 'Yes! I have no knowledge – but it was bound to be so! I wish to God it were not! You will understand me, Lady Spenborough, when I say that I had rather by far she were penniless than that there should be so great a disparity – as I fear there must be – between our fortunes!'

'I do understand you,' she replied warmly. 'Such a sentiment cannot but do you honour, but, believe me, it would be most wrong, most foolish, to let such a scruple stand in the way of – perhaps – the happiness of you both!'

He came striding back to her, and caught her hand to his lips. 'I have no words with which to thank you! If I have *your* consent, I care for no other! You know Serena – you love her – and you tell me to go forward!'

'Oh, yes, but I am not her guardian, you know! She is quite her own mistress! At least –' She paused, suddenly struck by an unwelcome thought. 'I had forgot! Oh, dear!'

'She has a guardian? Someone to whom I should apply before approaching her?'

'No, no! Only her fortune is – is strangely tied-up, and perhaps – But I should not be talking of her affairs!'

He pressed her hand slightly. 'Do not! I hope it may be so securely tied-up that I could not touch it if I would! I must go. If I could express to you my gratitude for your kindness, your understanding – !' He smiled down at her with a good deal of archness. 'The word *dowager* will never again have the power to terrify me!'

She laughed, and blushed. He again kissed her hand, and turned to go away, just as the door opened, and Serena, in her walking-dress, came into the room.

'I thought I recognized the modish hat reposing on the table in the hall!' she remarked, drawing off her gloves, and tossing them aside. 'How do you do, Hector?' Her eyes went from him to Fanny, and the smile in them deepened. 'Now, what conspiracy have you been hatching to make you both look so guilty?'

'No conspiracy,' the Major said, going to her, and helping her to take off her pelisse. 'Did you find your very odd acquaintance – Mrs Floore, is it not? – at home? I should think she was very much obliged to you for your visit!'

'I believe you are quite as high in the instep as Fanny, and disapprove of Mrs Floore as heartily!' Serena exclaimed.

'I own I cannot think her a proper friend for you,' he admitted.

'Stuff! I found her at home, and *I* was very much obliged to *her* for the welcome she was kind enough to give me. I must say, Fanny, I wish we were in London, just that we might see with our own eyes the Laleham-woman's triumph!'

'You don't mean to say that she has made up a brilliant match for poor little Emily already?' cried Fanny.

'No, she hasn't done *that*, but, if she's to be believed, she might have her pick of a dozen eligible partis tomorrow, if she chose! Flying at higher game, I conclude! So does Mrs Floore. *She* still holds by her cross-eyed Duke! I am very sceptical about him, but there seems to be no doubt that the Rotherham ball has worked like a charm. I daresay it might help to open *some* doors, but what tactics the Laleham-woman employed to force open some others, and which of the Patronesses she outgeneralled into surrendering vouchers for Almack's, I would give a fortune to know. One can't but admire her!'

'*Odious* woman!' Fanny said. 'I am sorry for Emily.'

'Nonsense! She will be in high feather, enjoying a truly magnificent season.'

'But who is this lady?' asked the Major.

'She is Mrs Floore's daughter, not as engaging as her mama, but quite as redoubtable.'

'She is a hateful, scheming creature!' said Fanny, with unusual asperity. 'Excuse me! – I must speak to Lybster! – Something I forgot to tell him he must do! No, no, pray don't pull the bell, dearest!'

'Good gracious, Fanny, what in the world?' Serena stopped, for the door had closed softly behind Fanny.

'Serena!'

She turned her head, struck by the urgent note in the Major's voice. One look at his face was enough to explain Fanny's surprising behaviour. She felt suddenly breathless, and absurdly shy.

He came towards her, and took her hands. 'It was not conspiracy. I came to ask her, as one who is in some sort your guardian, if I might ask you to marry me.'

'Oh, Hector, how could you be so foolish?' she said, her voice catching on something between a laugh and a sob. 'What has poor Fanny to say to anything? Did she tell you that you might? Must I ask her what I should reply?'

'Not that! But I am aware now, as I never was seven years ago, of the gulf that lies between us!'

She pulled one of her hands away, and pressed her fingers against his mouth. 'Don't say such things! I *forbid* you! Don't think yourself unworthy of me! If you only knew – But you don't, my poor Hector, you don't! It's I who am unworthy! You've no notion how detestable I can be, how headstrong, how obstinate, how *shrewish*!'

He caught her into his arms, saying thickly: 'Do not *you* say such things! My goddess, my queen!'

'Oh, no, no, no!'

He raised his head, smiling a little crookedly down at her. 'Do you dislike to hear yourself called so? There is nothing I would not do to please you, but you cannot help but be my goddess! You have been so these seven years!'

'Only a goddess could dislike it! You see by that how wretchedly short of the mark I fall. I have a little honesty – enough to tell you *now* that you must not worship me.'

He only laughed, and kissed her again. She protested no more, too much a woman not to be deeply moved by such idolatry, and awed by the constancy which, though it might have been to a false image, could not be doubted.

It was not long before he was saying to her much of what he had previously said to Fanny, anxiously laying his circumstances before her, and dwelling so particularly on the disparity between them of rank and fortune, that she interrupted presently to say with mingled amusement and impatience: 'My dearest Hector, I wish you will not talk such nonsense! Why do you set so much store by rank? You are a gentleman, and I hope I am a gentlewoman, and as for fortune, we shall do very well!'

His expression changed; he said: 'I wish to God you had no fortune!'

It was not to be expected that she should understand such a point of view, nor did she. In her world, a poorly dowered girl was an object for compassion. Even a love-match must depend upon the marriage-settlements, and wealthy and besotted indeed must be the suitor who allied himself to a portionless damsel. She looked her astonishment, and repeated, in a blank voice: 'Wish I had no fortune?'

'Yes! I had rather by far you were penniless, than – I daresay – so rich that my own fortune must seem the veriest pittance beside yours!'

Laughter sprang to her eyes. 'Oh, you goose! Do you fear to be taken for a fortune-hunter? Of all the crack-brained ideas to take into your head! No, indeed, Hector, this is being foolish beyond permission!'

'I don't know that I care so much for that – though it is what people will say! – but I must support my wife, not live upon *her* fortune! Serena, surely you must understand this!'

It seemed to her absurdly romantic, but she only said quizzingly: 'Was this thought in your head seven years ago?'

'Seven years ago,' he replied gravely, 'your father was alive, and you were not sole mistress of your fortune. If I thought about the matter at all – but you must remember that I was *then* no more than a green boy! – I imagine I must have supposed that Lord Spenborough, if he countenanced the match, would settle on you a sum comparable to my own means.'

'Or have cut me off without a penny?' she enquired, amused.

'Or have done that,' he agreed, perfectly seriously.

She perceived that he was in earnest, but she could not help saying, with a gurgle of laughter: 'It is too bad that you cannot enact the rôle of Cophetua! I must always possess an independence, which cannot be wrested from me. But take heart! It is by no means certain that I shall ever have more than that. Are you prepared to take me with my wretched seven hundred pounds a year, my ridiculous fortune-hunter? I warn you, it may well be no more!'

'Are you in earnest?' he asked, his brow lightening. 'Lady Spenborough said something about your fortune's being oddly tied-up, but no more than that. Tell me!'

'I will, but if you mean to take it as a piece of excellent good news we are likely to fall out!' she warned him. 'Nothing was ever more infamous! My dear but misguided papa left my fortune – all but what I have from my mother – to Rotherham, in trust for me, with the proviso that he was to allow me no more than the pin-money I had always been given, until I was married – with, mark you! his lordship's consent and approval! In the event of my marrying without that august approval, I may, I suppose, kiss my fingers to my inheritance!'

He was staggered, and his first thoughts agreed exactly with her own. '*What?* You must win Rotherham's consent? Good God, I never in my life heard of anything so iniquitous!'

'Just so!' said Serena, with immense cordiality. 'I hope you will perceive that I was not to be blamed for flying into the worst passion of my career when *that* clause was read to me!'

'I do not wonder at it! Rotherham, of all men alive! Pardon

me, but the indelicacy of such a provision, the – But I must be silent on that head!'

'Abominable, wasn't it? I am heartily of your opinion!'

He sat for a moment or two, with his lips tightly compressed, but as other thoughts came into his mind, his face relaxed, and he presently exclaimed: 'Then if he should refuse his consent, you will have no more than will serve for your gowns, and – and such fripperies!'

'Very true but you need not say it as though you were glad of it!'

'I am glad of it!'

'Well, so am not I!' retorted Serena tartly.

'Serena, all I have is yours to do with as you please!' he said imploringly.

She was touched, but a strong vein of common sense made her say: 'I am very much obliged to you, but what if I should please to spend all you have upon my gowns and such fripperies? My dear, that is very fine talking, but it won't do! Besides, the very thought of Ivo's holding my pursestrings to the day of his death, or mine, is enough to send me into strong convulsions! He shall not do it! And now I come to think of it, I believe he will not be able to. He told me himself that if he withheld his consent unreasonably I might be able to break the Trust. Hector, if you do not instantly wipe from your face that disappointed look, you will have a taste of my temper, and so I warn you!'

He smiled, but said with quiet confidence: 'Rotherham will never give his consent to your marrying *me*!'

'We shall see!'

'And nothing – *nothing!* would prevail upon me to seek it!' said the Major, with suppressed violence.

'Oh, you need not! That at least was not stipulated in Papa's Will! I shall inform him myself of my betrothal – but that will not be until I am out of mourning, in the autumn.'

'The autumn!' He sounded dismayed, but recollected himself immediately, and said: 'You are very right! My own feelings – But it would be quite improper for such an announcement to be made until you are out of black gloves!'

She stretched out her hand to lay it upon one of his. 'Well, I think it would, Hector. In general, I set little store by the proprieties, but in such a case as this – oh, every feeling would be offended! In private we are engaged, but the world shall not know it until October.'

He lifted the hand to his lips. 'You are the only judge: I shall be ruled entirely by your wishes, my queen!'

Ten

THE ENGAGED COUPLE, NEITHER OF WHOM WASTED A moment's thought on what must be the inevitable conclusions arrived at by the interested, admitted only two persons into the secret. One was Fanny, and the other Mrs Kirkby. The Major could not be happy until he had made Serena known to his mother; and since she was reluctant to appear in any way neglectful, it was not long before she was climbing the hill to Lansdown Crescent, escorted by her handsome cavalier.

Had the expedition been left to the Major's management, Serena would have been carried in a sedan-chair, his rooted conviction that no female was capable of exertion making it quite shocking to him to think of her undertaking so strenuous a walk. But Serena had other ideas. 'What, stuff myself into a chair in such bright May weather? Not for the world!' she declared.

'Your carriage, then? My mother goes out so seldom that she has not thought it worth while to keep hers in Bath, or I would –'

'My dear Hector,' she interrupted him, 'you cannot in all seriousness suppose that I would have my own or your mother's horses put to merely to struggle up that steep hill!'

'No, which is why I suggested you should hire a chair. I am afraid you will be tired.'

'On the contrary, I shall enjoy the walk. I feel in Bath as though I were hobbled. Only tell me the exact direction of Mrs Kirkby's house, and I will engage to present myself punctually, and in no need of hartshorn to revive me!'

He smiled, but said: 'I shall fetch you, of course.'

'Well, that will be very agreeable, but I beg you won't put yourself to the trouble if your reason is that you fear for my safety in this excessively respectable town!'

'Not your *safety*, precisely, but I know that you won't take your maid, and I own I cannot like you to go out alone.'

'You would be surprised if you guessed how very well able I am to take care of myself. I was done with young ladyhood some years ago. What is more, my dear, times have changed a trifle since you lived in England before. In London, I might gratify you by taking my maid with me – though it is much more likely that I should prefer to go in my carriage, and alone! – but in Bath it is quite unnecessary.'

'Nevertheless I hope you will allow me to be your escort.'

'Indeed, I shall be glad of your company,' she responded, not choosing to argue the point further, and trusting that time would dull the edge of a solicitude she found a little oppressive.

Certainly the pace she set when they walked up to Lansdown Crescent did not encourage him to suppose that she was less healthy than she looked. She had never lost the rather mannish stride she had acquired in youth, when, to the disapproval of most of her relations, she had been reared more as a boy than as a girl, and she could never shorten it to suit Fanny's demure steps. A walk with Fanny was to Serena a form of dawdling, which she detested; it was a real pleasure to her to be pacing along beside a man again. She would not take the Major's arm, but went up the hill at a swinging rate, and exclaimed, when she was obliged to hold her hat on against the wind: 'Ah, this is famous! One can breathe up here! I wished we might have found a house in Camden Place, or the Royal Crescent, but there were none to be hired that Lybster thought eligible.'

'I myself prefer the heights,' he admitted, 'but there's no doubt Laura Place is a more convenient situation.'

'Oh, yes! And Fanny would not have liked the hill,' she agreed cheerfully. A few minutes later she was making the acquaintance of her future mother-in-law.

Mrs Kirkby, a valetudinarian of retiring habits, and a timid disposition, was quite overpowered by her visitor. She had been flustered at the outset by the intelligence that her only remaining son was betrothed to a lady of title whose various exploits were known even to her. An inveterate reader of the social columns in the journals, she could have told the Major how many parties the Lady Serena had graced with her presence, what was the colour of her dashing phaeton, how many times she had been seen in Hyde Park, mounted on her long-tailed gray, what she had worn at various Drawing-rooms, in whose company she had visited the paddock at Doncaster, and a great many other items of similar interest. Nor was she ignorant of the Lady Serena's predilection for waltzing, and quadrilles; while as for the Lady Serena's previous engagement, so scandalously terminated within so short a distance from the wedding-day, she had marvelled at it, and shaken her head at it, and moralized over it to all her acquaintance. It had therefore come as a severe shock to her to learn that her son was proposing to ally himself to a lady demonstrably unsuited to a quiet Kentish manor and she had not been able to forbear asking him, in a quavering voice: 'Oh, Hector, but is she not very *fast*?'

'She is an angel!' he had replied radiantly.

Mrs Kirkby did not think that Serena looked like an angel. Angels, in her view, were ethereal creatures, and there was nothing at all ethereal about Serena. She was a tall and beautiful young woman of fashion, the picture of vigorous health, and so full of vitality that half an hour in her company left the invalid a prey to headache, palpitations, and nervous spasms. It was not, as Mrs Kirkby faintly assured her elderly companion, that she was loud-voiced, for her voice was particularly musical. It was not that she was talkative, or assertive, or fidgety, for she was none of these things. In fact, Mrs Kirkby had been unable to detect faults; what had prostrated her were the Lady Serena's virtues. 'Anyone can see,' she said, between sniffs at her vinaigrette, 'that she has never moved in any but the first circles! Her manners have that well-bred ease that *shows* she has been used to act as hostess to every sort of person, from Royalty, I daresay, to commoners! Nothing could have been more perfect than her bearing towards me, and what I have ever done to deserve to have such a daughter-in-law thrust upon me I'm sure I don't know!'

Happily, the Major was far too dazzled by his goddess's brilliant good-looks to notice any lack of enthusiasm in his mother's demeanour. It seemed to him that Serena brought light into a sunless room, and it never occurred to him that anyone could find it too strong. So great was his certainty that no one could set eyes on Serena without being captivated, and so complete was his absorption, that he accepted at face value all his mother's acquiescent answers to the eager questions he later put to her. Had she ever seen such striking beauty? No, indeed, she had not. So much countenance, such a complexion! Yes, indeed! Those eyes, too! he had known she could not choose but to be fascinated by them. So changeable, and expressive, and the curve of the lids above them giving them that smiling look! Very true: most remarkable! She must have been pleased, he dared swear, with the perfection of her manners, so easy, so polished, and yet so unaffected! Exactly so! And the grace of her every movement! Oh, yes! most graceful! He did not know how it was, for she never tried to dominate her company, but when she came into a room, her personality seemed to fill it: had his mother been conscious of it? Most conscious of it! Would she think him fanciful if he told her that it seemed to him as though those glorious eyes had some power of witchcraft? He thought they cast a spell over any one on whom they rested! Yes, indeed! Mrs Kirkby (in a failing voice) thought so too.

So the Major was able to tell Serena, in all good faith, that his mother was in transports over her; and such was his infatuation that he would have found nothing to cavil at in Mrs Kirkby's subsequent assertion, to the sympathetic Miss Murthly, that the Lady Serena had bewitched her son.

In his saner moments, slight doubts of his mother's approval of all Serena's actions did cross the Major's mind; and, without being precisely aware of it, he was glad that the seclusion in which she lived made it unlikely that certain freaks would come to her ears. Although herself of respectable lineage, she had never moved in the highest circle of society, and possibly might not appreciate that the code of conduct obtaining there was less strict than any to which she had been accustomed. Great ladies permitted themselves more licence than was the rule amongst the lesser gentry. Their manners were more free; they expressed themselves in language shocking to the old-fashioned; secure in birth and rank, they cared little for appearances, and were far less concerned with the proprieties than were more obscure persons. When he had first encountered Serena, the Major had been struck by the marked difference which existed between her relations with the elders of her family, and those that were the rule in his own family. That she should have lived on terms of unceremonious equality with an indulgent father was not perhaps surprising; but the extremely frank style of her conversations with her formidable aunt had never ceased to astonish him. There was no lack of ceremony about the Lady Theresa Eaglesham, but while, on the one hand, she had not hesitated to censure conduct which she considered unbecoming in her niece, on the other, she had not scrupled to gossip with her, as with a contemporary. Young Hector Kirkby, seven years earlier, had been quite unable to picture any of his aunts informing his sister that Lady M… was big with child, and the wits laying bets on the probable paternity of the unborn infant. Major Hector Kirkby, no longer a green boy, devoutly trusted that Serena would never, in the future, regale these prim spinsters with extracts from Lady Theresa's singularly unrestricted letters. He even refrained from repeating to his mother a very good story Lady Theresa had sent her niece about the Royal Wedding. '*Rumour has it,*' wrote Lady Theresa, '*that the ceremony went off well, except for an* entrave *at the end, when the P. Charlotte was kept waiting for half an hour in the carriage, while Leopold hunted high and low for his greatcoat, which no one could find. The P. Regent,* très benin *until then, hearing the cause of the delay, burst out with "D… his greatcoat!" It is now believed, by the by, that he is* not *dropsical…*'

No: decidedly that was not a story for Mrs Kirkby, quite as inveterate an admirer of Royalty as Fanny.

Nor did the Major inform his parent that her future daughter-in-law, riding out of Bath in his company before breakfast, dispensed with a chaperon on these expeditions. Mrs Kirkby would have been profoundly shocked, and he was himself doubtful of the propriety of it. But Serena laughed at him, accusing him of being frightened of all the quizzy people in Bath, and he stifled his qualms. It was a delight to be alone with her, an agony to be powerless to check her intrepidity. She would brook no hand upon her bridle: he had learnt that, when, in actual fact, he had caught it above the bit, instinctively, when her mare had reared. The white fury in her face had startled him; her eyes were daggers, and the virago-note sounded in her voice when she shot at him, from between clenched teeth:

'Take your hand from my rein!' The dangerous moment passed; his hand had dropped; she got the mare under control, and said quite gently: 'You must never do so again, Hector. Yes, yes, I understand, but when I cannot manage my horses I will sell them, and take to tatting instead!'

He thought her often reckless in the fences she would ride at; all she said, when he expostulated, was: 'Don't be afraid! I never overface my horses. The last time I did so I was twelve, and Papa laid his hunting-crop across my shoulders: an effective cure!'

He said ruefully: 'Can't you tell me some other way I might be able to check your mad career?'

'Alas, none!' she laughed.

He had nightmarish visions of seeing her lying with a broken neck beside some rasper; and, to make it worse, Fanny said to him, with a trustful smile: 'It is so comfortable to know you are with Serena, when she rides out, Major Kirkby! I know she is a splendid horsewoman, but I can never be easy when she has only Fobbing with her, because she is what the hunting people call a *bruising* rider, and for all Fobbing has been her groom since she was a little girl she never will mind him!'

'I wish to God I might induce her to mind *me*!' he ejaculated. 'But she will not, Lady Spenborough, and when I begged her to consider what must be *my* position if she should take a bad toss when in my care, she would do nothing but laugh, and advise me to ride off the instant I saw her fall, and swear I was never with her!'

'Oh, dear!' she sighed. She saw that he was really worried, and added soothingly: 'Never mind! I daresay we are both of us too anxious. Lord Spenborough, you know, was used to tell me there was no need for me to tease myself over her. *He* never did so! If he thought she had been reckless, he sometimes swore at her, but I don't think he was ever really *alarmed*!'

'That, ma'am, I could not do!'

'Oh, no! I know you never would! Though I daresay she would not be in the least offended if you did,' said Fanny reflectively.

The bright May weather was making Serena increasingly impatient of the quiet life she was obliged to lead. At this time, in any other year, she would have been in the thick of the London season, cramming a dozen engagements into a single day. She did not wish herself in London, and would have recoiled from the thought of breakfasts and balls, but Bath provided no outlet for her overflowing energy. Fanny was content to visit the Pump Room each weekday and the Laura Chapel each Sunday, and found a stroll along the fashionable promenades exercise enough for her constitution; Serena could scarcely endure the unvarying pattern of her days, and felt herself caged in so small a town. She said that Bath was stifling in warm weather, sent to Milverley for her phaeton, and commanded the Major to escort her on a tour of the livery stables of Bath, in search of a pair of job horses fit for her to drive.

He was very willing, fully sympathizing with her desire to escape from the confinement of the town, and realizing that to be driven in a barouche by Fanny's staid coachman could only bore her. He thought that the phaeton would provide both ladies with an agreeable and unexceptionable amusement. That was before he saw it. But the vehicle which arrived in Bath was not the safe and comfortable phaeton he had expected to see. Serena had omitted to mention the fact that hers was a high-perch phaeton; and when he set eyes on it, and saw the frail body hung directly over the front axle, its bottom fully five feet from the ground, he gave an exclamation of dismay. 'Serena! You don't mean to drive yourself in *that*?'

'Yes, most certainly I do! But, oh, how much I wish I still had the pair I was used to drive! Match grays, Hector, and such beautiful steppers!'

'Serena – my dearest! I beg you won't! I know you are an excellent whip, but you could not have a more dangerous carriage!'

'No – if I were not an excellent whip!'

'Even nonpareils have been known to overturn these high perch phaetons!'

'To be sure they have!' she agreed, with a mischievous smile. 'The difficulty of driving them is what lends a spice!'

'Yes, but – My love, *you* are the only judge of what it is proper for you to do, but to be driving the most sporting of all carriages – Dearest, do females commonly do so?'

'By no means! Only very dashing females!'

'No, don't joke me about it! Perhaps, in Hyde Park though I own I should have thought – But in Bath – ! You can't have considered! You would set the whole town talking!'

She looked at him with surprise. 'Should I? Yes, very likely! – there is no knowing what people will talk of! But you can't – *surely* you can't expect me to pay the least heed to what they may choose to say of me?'

He was silenced, startled to discover that he did expect this. After a moment, she said coaxingly: 'Will you go with me, and see whether I am to be trusted not to overturn myself? I must try these job horses of mine. From what I can see of them I fancy there can be no fear that they will have the smallest desire to bolt with me!'

'You will give Bath enough to stare at without that!' he replied, in a mortified tone, and left her.

It was as well he did so, for quick anger flashed in her eyes, and he might otherwise have had another taste of her temper. His solicitude for her safety, though it might fret her independent spirit, she could understand, and make a push to bear with patience. Criticism of her conduct was an impertinence she would tolerate no better from him than from her cousin Hartley. She had almost uttered a blistering set-down, when he turned on his heel, and was shocked to realize that she had been within an ace of telling him that whatever might be the creed governing the behaviour of the ladies of his set, *she* was Spenborough's daughter, and profoundly indifferent to the opinion such persons might hold of her.

It was not to be expected that she would, in this instance, think herself at fault. An easy-going father, famed for his eccentricities, had sanctioned, even encouraged, her sporting proclivities. In much the same spirit as he had told her, facing her first jump, to throw her heart over, he had taught her to handle all the most mettlesome teams in his stables. This very high-perch phaeton had been built for her to his order: disapproval of it was disapproval of him. 'Whatever else you may do, my girl,' had said the late Earl, 'don't you be missish!'

The Major having removed himself, Serena's wrath was vented, in some sort, on Fanny. 'Intolerable!' she declared, striding up and down the drawing-room, in her mannishly cut driving-dress. 'I to pander to the prejudices of a parcel of Bath dowds and prudes! If that is what he thinks I must do when we are married the sooner he learns that I shall not the better it will be for him! Pretty well for Major Kirkby to tell a Carlow that her behaviour is unseemly!'

'Surely, dearest, he cannot have said that!' expostulated Fanny mildly.

'Implied it! What, does he think my credit to stand upon so insecure a footing that to be seen driving a sporting carriage must demolish it?'

'You know he does not. Don't be vexed with me, Serena, but it is not only a parcel of Bath dowds who think it a *fast* thing for you to do!' She added hastily, as the blazing eyes turned towards her: 'Yes, yes, it is all nonsense, of course! *You* need not care for it, but I am persuaded that no man could endure to have his wife thought fast!'

'What Papa countenanced need not offend Hector!'

'I am sure it does not. Now, do, *do*, Serena, be calm! Did not what your papa countenanced very frequently offend his own sister?' She saw the irrepressible smile leap to those stormy eyes, the lips quiver ruefully, and was emboldened to continue: 'What *he* permitted must have been right – indeed, how could I feel otherwise? – but, you know, he was not precisely the same as other people!'

'No! The eccentric Lord Spenborough, eh?'

'Do you think that it vexed him to be called that?' asked Fanny, fearing that she had offended.

'On the contrary! He liked it! As I do! Anyone who chooses to say that I am as eccentric as my father may do so with my good will! I don't seek the title, any more than he did: it is what humdrum, insipid provincials say of anyone who does not heed all their tiresome shibboleths! I do what I do because it is what I wish to do, not, believe me, my dear Fanny, to court the notice of the world!'

'I know – oh, I know!'

'You may, but it appears that Hector does not!' Serena flashed. 'His look – the tone in which he spoke his final words to me – ! Intolerable! Upon my word, I am singularly unfortunate in my *prétendants*! First Rotherham –'

'Serena!' Fanny cried, with a heightened colour. 'How can you speak of Rotherham and Major Kirkby in the same breath?'

'Well, at least Rotherham never lectured me on the proprieties!' said Serena pettishly. 'He doesn't give a button for appearances either.'

'It is not to his credit! I know you don't mean what you say when you put yourself into a passion, but to be comparing those two is outrageous – now, isn't it? The one so arrogant, his temper harsh, his disposition tyrannical, his manners abrupt to the point of incivility; and the other so kind, so solicitous for

your comfort, loving you so deeply – Oh, Serena, I beg your pardon, but I am quite shocked that you could talk so!'

'So I apprehend! There is indeed no comparison between them. My opinion of Rotherham you know well. But I must be allowed to give the devil his due, if you please, and credit him with *one* virtue! I collect you don't count it a virtue! We won't argue on that head. My scandalous carriage awaits me, and if we are not to *aborder* one another I'd best leave you, my dear!'

She went away, still simmering with vexation, a circumstance which caused her groom, a privileged person, to say that it was as well she was not driving her famous grays.

'Fobbing, hold your tongue!' she commanded angrily.

He paid no more attention to this than he had paid to the furies of a seven-year-old termagant, but delivered himself of a grumbling monologue, animadverting severely on her headstrong ways and faults of temper; recalling a great many discreditable incidents, embellished with what he had said to his lordship and what his lordship had said to him; and drawing a picture of himself as an ill-used and browbeaten serf, which must have made her laugh, had she been listening to a word he said.

Her rages were never sullen, and by the time she had discovered the peculiarities of her hired horses, this one had quite vanished. Remorse swiftly took its place, and the truth of Fanny's words struck home to her. She saw again the Major's face, as much hurt as mortified, remembered his long devotion, and without knowing that she spoke aloud, exclaimed: 'Oh, I am the greatest beast in nature!'

'Now, that, my lady,' said her henchman, surprised and gratified, 'I never said, nor wouldn't. What I *do* say and, mind, it's what his lordship has told you time and again! – is that to be handling a high-spirited pair when you're in one of your tantrums –'

'Are you scolding still?' interrupted Serena. 'Well, if these commoners are your notion of a high-spirited pair, they are not mine!'

'No, my lady, and it wouldn't make a bit of difference to you if they was prime 'uns on the fret!' said Fobbing, with asperity.

'It would make a great deal of difference to me,' she sighed. 'I wonder who has my grays now?'

'Now, we don't want to have a fit of the dismals!' he said gruffly. 'If you was driving a pair of stumblers, you'd still take the shine out of any other lady on the road, my lady, that I *will* say! It's time you was thinking of turning them, if you don't want to be late back them not being what you might call sixteen mile an hour tits.'

'Yes, we must go back,' she agreed.

He relapsed into silence, and she was free to pursue her own uncomfortable reflections. By the time they had reached Laura Place again, she had beaten herself into a state of repentance which had to find instant expression. Without pausing to divest herself of her hat or her driving-coat, she hurried into the parlour behind the dining-room, stripping off her gloves, and saying over her shoulder to the butler: 'I shall be wanting Thomas almost immediately, to deliver a letter for me in Lansdown Crescent.'

She was affixing a wafer to an impetuous and wildly scrawled apology when she heard the knocker on the front door. A few moments later, she heard the Major's voice saying: 'You need not announce me!' and sprang to her feet just as he came quickly into the room.

He was looking pale, and anxious. He shut the door with a backward thrust of his hand, and spoke her name, in a tense way that showed him to be labouring under strong emotion.

'Oh, Hector, I have been writing to you!' she cried.

He seemed to grow paler. 'Writing to me! Serena, I beg of you – only listen to me!'

She went towards him, saying penitently: 'I was odious! a wretch! Oh, pray forgive me!'

'Forgive you! *I?* Serena, my darling, I came to beg you to forgive me! That I should have presumed to criticize your actions! That I should –'

'No, no, I used you monstrously. Do not you beg my pardon! If you wish me not to drive my phaeton in Bath, I won't! There! Am I forgiven?'

But this, she found, would not do for him at all. His remorse for having presumed to remonstrate with his goddess would be soothed by nothing less than her promising to do exactly as she chose upon all occasions. An attempt to joke him out of his mood of exaggerated self-blame failed to draw a smile from him; and the quarrel ended with his passionately kissing Serena's hands, and engaging himself to drive out with her in the phaeton on the very next day.

Eleven

The Major, reconciled to his goddess, could not be satisfied with setting her back on the pedestal he had built for her: the idealistic trend of his mind demanded that he should convince himself that she had never slipped from it. To have parted with the romantic vision he had himself created would have been so repugnant to him that the instant his vexation had abated, which it very swiftly did, he had set himself to prove to his own satisfaction that not her judgment but his had been faulty. It was impossible that the lady of his dreams could err. What had seemed to him intractability was constancy of purpose; her flouting of convention sprang from loftiness of mind; the levity, which had more than once shocked him, was a social mask concealing more serious thoughts. Even her flashes of impatience, and the dagger-look he had twice seen in her eyes, could be excused. Neither rose from any fault of temper: the one was merely the sign of nerves disordered by the shock of her father's death; the other had been provoked by his own unwarrantable interference.

Not every difference that existed between imagination and reality could be explained away. The Major's character was responsible; he had been an excellent regimental officer, steady in command, always careful of the welfare of his men, and ready to help junior officers seeking his advice in any of the private difficulties besetting young gentlemen fresh from school. His instinct was to serve and to protect, and it could not be other than disconcerting to him to find that the one being above all others whom he wished to guide, comfort, serve, and protect showed as little disposition to lean on him as to confide her anxieties to him. So far from seeking guidance, she was much more prone to impose her will upon her entire entourage. She was as accustomed to command as he, and, from having been motherless from an early age, she had acquired an unusual degree of independence. This, joined as it was to a deep-seated reserve, made the very thought of disclosing grief to another repellent to her. When she felt most she was at her most flippant; any attempt to lavish sympathy upon her made her stiffen, and interpose the shield of her raillery. As for needing protection, it was her boast that she was very well able to take care of herself; and when it came to serving her the chances were that she would say, gratefully, but with decision: 'Thank you! You are a great deal too good to me – but, you know, I always like to attend to such things myself!'

He had not known it. Fanny, understanding his perplexity, tried to explain Serena to him. 'Serena has so much strength of mind, Major Kirkby,' she said gently. 'I think her mind is as strong as her body, and that is very strong indeed. It used to amaze me that I never saw her exhausted by all the things she would do, for it is quite otherwise with me. But nothing is too much for her! It was the same with Lord Spenborough. Not the hardest day's hunting ever made them anything but sleepy, and excessively hungry; and in London I have often marvelled how they could contrive not to be in the least tired by all the parties, and the noise, and the expeditions.' She smiled, and said apologetically: 'I don't know how it is, but if I am obliged to give a breakfast, perhaps, and to attend a ball as well, there is nothing for it but for me to rest all the afternoon.'

He looked as if he did not wonder at it. 'But not Serena?' he asked.

'Oh, no! She never rests during the daytime. That is what makes it so particularly irksome to her to be leading this dawdling life. In London, she would ride in the Park before breakfast, and perhaps do some shopping as well. Then, very often we might give a breakfast, or attend one in the house of one of Lord Spenborough's numerous acquaintances. Then there would be visits to pay, and perhaps a race-meeting, or a picnic, or some such thing. And, in general, a dinner-party in the evening, or the theatre, and three or four balls or assemblies to go to afterwards.'

'Was this your life?' he asked, rather appalled.

'Oh, no! I can't keep it up, you see. I did try very hard to grow accustomed to it, because it was my duty to go with Serena, you know. But when she saw how tired I was, and how often I had the headache, she declared she would not drag me out, or permit my lord to do so either. You can have no notion how kind she has been to me, Major Kirkby! My best, my dearest friend!'

Her eyes filled with tears; he slightly pressed her hand, saying in a moved tone: '*That* I could not doubt!'

'She has a heart of gold!' she told him earnestly. 'If you knew what care she takes of me, how patient she is with me, you would be astonished!'

'Indeed, I should not!' he said, smiling. 'I cannot conceive of anyone's being out of patience with you!'

'Oh, yes!' she assured him. 'Mama and my sisters were often so, for I am quite the stupidest of my family, besides being shy of strange persons, and not liking excessively to go to parties, and a great many other nonsensical things. But Serena, who does everything so well, was never vexed with me! Major Kirkby, if it had not been for her I don't know what I should have done!'

He could readily believe that to such a child as she must have been at the time of her marriage, life in the great Spenborough household must have been bewildering and alarming. He said sympathetically: 'Was it very bad?'

Her reply was involuntary. 'Oh, if I had not had Serena I could not have borne it!' The colour rushed up into her face; she said quickly: 'I mean – I mean – having to entertain so many people – talk to them – be the mistress of that huge house! The political parties, too! They were the worst, for I have not the least understanding of politics, and if Serena had not taken care to tell me what was likely to be talked about at dinner I must have been all at sea! The dreadful way, too, the people of the highest *ton* have of always being related to one another, so that one is for ever getting into a scrape!'

He could not help laughing, but he said: 'I know exactly what you mean!'

'Yes, but, you see, Serena used to explain everybody to me, and so I was able to go on quite prosperously. And it was she who managed everything. She had always done so.' She paused, and then said diffidently: 'When – when perhaps you might sometimes think her wilful, or – or overconfident, you must remember that she has been the mistress of her papa's houses, and his hostess, and that he relied on her to attend to all the things which, in general, an unmarried lady knows nothing about.'

'Yes,' he said heavily. 'He must have been a strange man!' He caught himself up. 'I beg pardon! I should not say that to you!'

'Well, I don't think he was just in the common way,' she agreed. 'He was very good-natured, and easy-going, and so kind that it was no wonder everyone liked him. He was quite as kind to me as Serena, you know.'

'Oh! Yes, of – I mean, I'm sure he must have been!' he stammered, considerably taken aback.

She went on with her stitchery, in sweet unconsciousness of

having said anything to make him think her marriage deplorable. She would have been very much shocked could she have read his mind; quite horrified had she guessed the effect on him of what she had told him of Serena's life and character. Her words bore out too clearly much that he had begun to realize; and with increasing anxiety he wondered whether Serena could ever be content with the life he had to offer her. But when he spoke of this to her, she looked surprised, and said: 'Bored? Dear Hector, what absurdity is in your head now? Depend upon it, I shall find plenty to do in Kent!'

An item of news in the *Courier* made her ask him one day if he had ever had any thoughts of standing for election to Parliament. He assured her that he had not, but before he well knew where he was she was discussing the matter, making plans, sketching a possible career, and reckoning up the various interests at her command. In laughing dismay, he interrupted her, to say: 'But I should dislike it of all things!'

He was relieved to find that she was not, apparently, disappointed, for he had had the sensation of being swept irresistibly down a path of her choosing. 'Would you? Really? Then, of course, you won't stand,' she said cheerfully.

When she talked of her life while he had been in the Peninsula, he was often reminded of Fanny's words: Serena seemed to be related to so many people. 'Some sort of a fifth cousin of mine,' she would say, until it seemed to him that England must be littered with her cousins. He quizzed her about it once, and she replied perfectly seriously: 'Yes, and what a dead bore it is! One has to remember to write on anniversaries, and to ask them to dine, and some of them, I assure you, are the most shocking figures! Only wait until I introduce you to my cousin Speen! Fanny will tell you she sat, *bouche béante*, the first time she ever saw him, at one of our turtle-dinners! He arrived drunk, which, however, he was aware of, and begged her to pardon, informing her as a great secret that he was a jerry-sneak – which the world knows! – and might never be decently bosky when my lady was at home, so that he had determined while she was away never to be less than well to live!'

'An *odious* little man!' said Fanny, with a shudder. 'For shame, Serena! As though you had not better relations than Speen!'

'True! If Hector should not be cast into transports by Speen, I shall take him to stay at Osmansthorpe!' Serena said mischievously. 'Have you a taste for the ceremonious, my love? *There*, his lordship lives *en prince*, and since his disposition is morose and his opinion of his own importance immense, the dinner-table is enlivened only by such conversations as he chooses to inaugurate. The groom of the chambers will warn you before you leave your room, however, what subject his lordship wishes to hear discussed.'

'Serena!' expostulated Fanny. 'Don't heed her, Major Kirkby! It is very formal and dull at Osmansthorpe, but not as bad as that!'

'If it is *half* as bad as that, I would infinitely prefer to make the acquaintance of Cousin Speen!' he retorted. 'Must we really set out on a series of visits to all your relations, Serena?'

'By no means!' she answered promptly. 'Order me to set them all at a distance, and you will be astonished to see with what a good grace I shall obey you! I should not care a button if I never saw most of them again.'

He laughed, but at the back of his mind lurked the fear that these people, deplorable or dull, formed an integral part of the only life she understood, or, perhaps, could be happy in. When he called in Laura Place one day, expecting to find her fretting at the rain, which had been falling steadily since dawn, and discovered her instead to be revelling in a scandalous novel, the conviction grew on him that the placid existence he had planned for them both would never satisfy her.

She gave him her hand, and one of her enchanting smiles, but said: 'Don't expect to hear a word from my lips, love! I have here the most diverting book that ever was written! Have you seen it? The chief characters in it are for the most part easily recognizable, and it is no great task to guess at the identities of the rest. I have not laughed so much for weeks!'

He picked up one of the small, gilt-edged volumes. 'What is it? *Glenarvon* – and by an anonymous writer. Is it so excellent?'

'Good God, no! It is the most absurd farrago of nonsense! But I prophesy it will run through a dozen editions, because none of us will be able to resist searching either for ourselves or our acquaintance in it. Could you have believed it? – Lady Caroline Lamb is the author? The Lambs are all in it, and Lady Holland – very well hit off, I imagine, from all I have ever heard of her, but Papa disliked that set, so that I was never at Holland House – and Lady Oxford, and Lady Jersey, and poor Mr Rogers, whom she calls a yellow hyena! I must say, I think it unjust, don't you? Glenarvon, of course, is Byron, and the whole thing is designed as a sort of vengeance on him for having cried off from his *affaire* with her.'

'Good God!' he exclaimed. 'She must be mad to have done such a thing!'

'I think she is, poor soul! Never more so than when she tumbled head over ears in love with Byron! For my part, I was so unfashionable as to take him in instant aversion. How she could have borne with his insufferable conceit, and the airs he put on to be interesting, I know not – though I daresay if one could bear that dreadful Lamb laugh nothing would daunt one! Not but what I am extremely sorry for William Lamb, laugh as he may! If it is true that he stands by her, I do most sincerely honour him. I fancy she meant to portray him in a kindly way, but some of the things she writes of him may well make him writhe. She is so very obliging as to favour the world with what one can only take to be a description of her own honeymoon – so *warm* as to make poor Fanny blush to the ears! It can't be *pleasant* for William Lamb, but it won't harm him. For she portrays herself, in the character of Calantha, as an innocent child quite dazzled by the world, quite ignorant, wholly trusting in the virtue of every soul she met! Pretty well for a girl brought up in Devonshire House!'

'It sounds to be unedifying, to say the least of it,' the Major said. 'Do you like such stuff?'

'It is the horridest book imaginable!' Fanny broke in. 'And although I never did more than exchange bows with Lord Byron, I am persuaded he never murdered a poor little baby in his life! As for Clara St. Everarde, who followed Glenarvon about, dressed as a page, if *she* is a real person too, and did anything so *grossly* improper, I think it a very good thing she rode over a cliff into the sea – though I am excessively sorry for the horse!'

'Observe!' said Serena, much entertained. 'It is the horridest book imaginable – but she has read all three volumes!'

'Only because you would keep asking me if I did not think Lady Augusta must be meant for Lady Cahir (and I'm sure I don't know!) and laughing so much that I was bound to continue, only to see what amused you so!'

The Major, who had been glancing through the volume he held, laid it down distastefully. 'I think you have wasted your money, Serena.'

'Oh, I did not! Rotherham sent it to me in a parcel by the mail! I never thought to be so much obliged to him! He says nothing else is being talked of in town, which I can well believe.'

'*Rotherham* sent it to you?' he ejaculated, as much astonished as displeased.

'Yes, why not? Oh, are you vexed because he has written me a letter?' Serena rallied him. 'You need not be! Not the most

jealous lover, which I hope you are not, could take exception to this single sheet! He is the worst of letterwriters, for this is all he can find to say to me: *My dear Serena, In case it has not come in your way I send you Lady C. Lamb's latest attempt to set Society by the ears. She succeeds* à merveille. *Nothing else is talked of. The Lambs hoped to be rid of her at last, but W. Lamb stands firm. By the by, if Glenarvon's final letter in this singular effusion is a copy of the original, you will agree I am eclipsed in incivility. I have some thoughts of visiting Claycross, and may possibly come to Bath next week. Yours, etc. Rotherham.* You will agree that there is nothing to rouse your ire in *that*!' Serena said, tossing the letter on to the table. 'Except,' she added thoughtfully, 'that I had as lief he did not come to Bath. He would be bound to discover our secret, my love, and if he should be in one of his disagreeable fits there's no saying how awkward he might not choose to make it for us. I'll fob him off.'

'I could wish that you would not!' he replied. 'For my part, I would choose to admit him into our confidence, if only that I might have the right to inform him that *I* am *not* very much obliged to him for sending you a novel which you describe as "rather warm"!'

'Good God, if that is the humour you are in, I will most certainly fob him off!' she cried. 'How can you be so absurd, Hector? Do you believe *me* to be an innocent Calantha? Rotherham knows better!'

'*What?*' he demanded sharply.

'No, no, pray – !' Fanny interposed, in an imploring tone. 'Major Kirkby, you quite mistake – Serena, consider what you say, dearest! Indeed, your vivacity carries you too far!'

'Very likely! But it will be well if Hector learns not to place the worst construction upon what I say!' Serena retorted, her colour considerably heightened.

He said quickly: 'I beg your pardon! I did not mean – Good

God, how could I possibly – ? If you were *not* an innocent Calantha, as you put it – now, don't eat me! – I am persuaded you would feel as strongly as I do the impropriety of *anyone's* sending you such a book to read! Throw it away, and let us forget it! You cannot like to see your friends libelled, surely!'

'Now, this goes beyond the bounds of what may be tolerated!' declared Serena, between vexation and amusement. '*My* friends? The Melbourne House set! Do you take me for a *Whig*? Oh, I was never so insulted! I don't know what you deserve I should do to you!'

A playful rejoinder would have restored harmony, but the Major's strong sense of propriety had been too much offended for him to make it. He took her up in all seriousness, endeavouring to make her enter into his sentiments. She grew impatient, thinking him prudish, and only the entrance of Lybster, bringing in the letters which had been fetched from the receiving-office, averted a lively quarrel. Serena broke off short, saying coolly: 'Ah! Now, if my aunt has written to me, Fanny, we may learn whether Lord Poulett marries Lady Smith Burgess, or whether it was nothing but an *on-dit*! Good gracious! Between us, we have seven letters, no less!' She handed several of them to Fanny, and glanced at the superscriptions on her own. A gleam of mischief shot into her eyes; she cast a provocative glance at the Major. 'I can guess the subject of most of *my* correspondence! It will be as well if I don't break the wafers until you are gone, I daresay! You will not object, however, to my seeing what my aunt has to say. A great deal, apparently: I'm glad she was able to get a frank, for I should have been ruined else!'

He made no reply, but walked away to the window, looking very much displeased. Suddenly Serena uttered a little crow of laughter. 'Oh, Hector, you are utterly confounded! No, no, don't look so stiff! It is the funniest thing! My aunt writes to

tell me that *she is* sending me *Glenarvon*! She says I shall be *aux anges* over it!'

It was too absurd. In spite of himself, he laughed. She stretched out her hand to him, smiling, and he kissed it, muttering: 'Forgive me!'

Her fingers pressed his. 'Oh, fudge! Such a foolish *tracasserie* as it was! Now, let us see what my aunt has to say to me! Lady Cowper looking hagged and frightened: I don't wonder at it, and shall shed no tears! I believe she has been Lady Caroline's enemy from the start, and think her a false, malicious woman behind those smiles and protestations of hers. Oh, she has been so obliging as to send me a key to the book! Fanny, she thinks Lady Morganet is not wholly a portrait of Lady Bessborough, but has a good deal of the Duchess of Devonshire mixed in it. Well! if one puts one's husband in a novel, I suppose it would be over-nice to exclude one's mama and one's aunt – even if the aunt be dead, and unable to protest!' Her eye ran down the closely written sheets; she gave a gurgle, but folded the letter, and laid it aside. 'The rest is mere town-gossip, and will keep. Hector, where is Stanton-drew? I am told I should not neglect to visit it. Druidical monuments, or some such thing. If I engage to sit primly beside Fanny in the barouche, will you escort us?'

He agreed very readily, promised to discover the exact whereabouts of the place, and soon after took his leave. Serena said, as soon as he had left the house: 'I would not read you the rest of my aunt's letter while Hector was with us, for he is unacquainted with the people she writes of, and I daresay it would have bored him excessively. My dear, where *did* he learn his antiquated notions? From his mother, I should judge – the very picture of provincial respectability! Poor woman! I pity her – but not more than she pities herself, I fancy! It must be a trial to have such a *volage* creature as I am foisted upon her!'

Fanny, her tender heart wrung by the difficulties she clearly perceived to lie in the Major's path, said: 'Indeed, Serena, you did not behave as you ought! I could not but think that his feelings upon this occasion did him honour!'

'Could you not?' Serena said, surprised. 'I thought they showed him to be imbued with some pretty Gothic notions! But never mind that! My aunt writes me an enchanting description of the Laleham-woman's progress – or regress! I don't know which it may be! Only listen!' She picked up Lady Theresa's letter, and read aloud: '*It is now impossible to avoid meeting that Laleham-Creature, who is everywhere to be seen. You would have been diverted to have been a spectator of the comedy enacted last week at Mrs Egerton's party. The Creature was there, with Miss Laleham – who, though well enough, is not, in my opinion, pretty* au fait de beauté *and in high croak. The D. of Devonshire coming in, she took care to place herself in his way, claiming to have made his acquaintance at the Salmesburys' Cotillion-ball, and overwhelming him with simpering civilities. But he, not hearing a word, as you may suppose, favoured her with no more than a bow, and some indifferent response, and passed on. She was obliged to fall back upon a mere Marquis – Rotherham, who was so complaisant as to remain by her for some ten minutes, and to take notice of Miss Laleham. His attention then being claimed by Mrs Martindale, the descent of the Creature down the social ladder was rapid, not a single Earl being present, and the only Viscount Lord Castlereagh, whom she did not attempt,* pour cause. *A handful of paltry barons, all of them married, reduced her to the level of an Esquire, after which, she retired, I must suppose, disconsolate.* A propos, *Cordelia Monksleigh is thrown into rage by the Creature's having dropped her, she says, because her usefulness ended with her procuring for the Creature the invitation-card to the Rotherham ball; but I suspect the cause is farther to seek, Master Gerard having become vastly* épris *during the Easter vacation. Reason enough!* That *connection would by no means suit the Creature's ambition, nor Cordelia's either, if she had but the wit to perceive it.*' Serena lowered the sheet. 'You will own that my aunt, whatever may be her faults, is the most entertaining correspondent, Fanny! What would I not have given to have been at that party – ! You know, if the Laleham-woman should have written to Mrs Floore, boasting of her friendship with Devonshire, I doubt if I shall be able to convince the dear old lady that although his Grace may be as deaf as a post, he is neither cross-eyed nor an octogenarian! As for attempting to persuade her that the Creature might as well lay siege to one of the Royal Dukes as to him, or to Rotherham, for that matter, I shall not do it! It would be too unkind! She believes there does not exist a man who would not fall instantly in love with Emily! Would you not have liked to have seen Rotherham caught in the toils? I think it no more than his just desert, for having attended that Quenbury Assembly!'

Fanny assented to it, but absently. Serena put up the letter, saying: 'I must think of some way of stopping Rotherham's projected visit to us. A pity! After the insipidities of Bath, his caustic tongue would come as a relief. However, in the mood Hector is in, it will not do. I shall be obliged to write an excuse so thin as to put him in a passion.'

She went away, not perceiving the expression of startled reproach in Fanny's face. What, in fact, she wrote to Rotherham she did not disclose; but a few days later she received a brief note from him, read it with raised brows, and said: 'Well! I have succeeded in my object. Rotherham does not come.'

Fanny could almost have believed her to be disappointed. The note was torn up, and Serena began to talk of something else.

Fanny herself was profoundly relieved. If Rotherham should dislike the match, as she feared he would, he would not scruple, she thought, to treat the Major with wounding contempt. Her imagination quailed at the scene; she felt that she could almost have interposed her own shrinking person between the Marquis and his prey; and was thankful that for the present, at any rate, this deed of heroism would not be necessary. She did not know that Fate had another trial in store for her. Her father arrived in Bath, without invitation or advertisement.

He was ushered into the drawing-room in Laura Place when, as ill-luck would have it, Major Kirkby was with her. She was not precisely discomposed, but she was certainly startled, and jumped up with a cry of: 'Papa!'

He embraced her kindly enough, but his countenance was severe, and the glance he cast at the Major repulsive.

'Papa, I had no notion I was to have this pleasure! Oh, is there something amiss at home? Mama? My sisters?'

'All perfectly stout!' he replied. 'I have been spending a few days with my friend, Abberley, at Cheltenham, and while I was in the west I thought I would come to see how you go on.'

'How very much obliged to you I am! Very comfortably, I assure you! Oh, I must introduce Major Kirkby! My father, Sir William Claypole, Major!'

The Major bowed; Sir William nodded, in no very encouraging style, saying briefly: 'How d'ye do?'

'The Major,' said Fanny perseveringly, 'has spent some years in the Peninsula, Papa. Only fancy! He thinks he once met my cousin Harry, when they were both in Lisbon!'

'Ay, did you so? Very likely! Are you on furlough, sir?'

'I've sold out, sir.'

This information appeared to displease Sir William. He said: 'Ha!' and turned to ask Fanny how she liked her situation in Laura Place. She was distressed by his evident dislike of her visitor, and could not forbear looking at the Major, to see whether he was as much offended as she feared he must be. She encountered such a rueful smile, so much amused understanding in his eyes, that she was at once reassured and embarrassed. Within a few minutes, he recollected an engagement, and took his leave, saying in an undervoice, as she gave him her hand: 'It will be better if I don't ride with Serena tomorrow.'

He went away, and she turned to face her father. He broke in immediately upon her enquiries after the other members of her family. 'Fanny, how is this? I promise you I thought the whole tale a Banbury story, but, upon my soul, what do I find but that fellow closeted with you!'

'The whole tale?' she repeated. 'What tale, if you please?'

'Why, that there is some half-pay officer dangling after you, and making you the talk of the town!'

'It is untrue!'

'Very well, very well, it appears he has sold out, but that's mere quibbling!' he said testily.

'He is not dangling after me.'

The quiet dignity of her tone seemed to strike him. She had, indeed, never looked more the great lady. He said, in a milder voice: 'Well, I am happy to receive your assurance on that head, my dear, but I did not expect to find you entertaining a young man tête-à-tête.'

'Papa, I think you must forget my condition! I am not a girl! If my widowhood –'

'The fact is, my dear, your widowhood is no protection!' he interrupted bluntly. 'I don't say, if you were older – But you're little more than a child, and a deal too pretty to rely upon that cap you wear to save you from having advances made to you! I knew how it would be, the instant you informed us you were removing to Bath!'

'Pray, Papa, will you tell me, if you please, who has had the monstrous impertinence to tell such stories about me?'

'I had it from that old fool, Dorrington, and you may suppose I did not enquire who might be his informant. I daresay he may have friends in Bath. I gave him a pretty sharp set-down, and let him see I did not relish his style of humour.'

'Oh, how right Serena is!' she cried, pressing her hands to her hot cheeks. 'Of all the odious people in the world there can be none so detestable as the Bath quizzes! I wonder you have not been told that General Hendy is dangling after me!'

'What, is he staying here? Well, he always had an eye for a pretty female, but as for dangling after you – Good God, Fanny, he must be sixty if he's a day! It's a different matter, my dear, when a young jackanapes like this Major Kirkby of yours throws out lures! Now, don't put yourself in a fuss! I daresay there's no harm done but what may be put right very easily. I told Mama that if you had been indiscreet it must have been all in innocence. The thing is it won't do for you to be living here with no better chaperon than Lady Serena. We must decide what is best to be done.'

In the greatest dismay, she stammered: 'Papa, you are quite, quite mistaken! Major Kirkby does not come here to see me!'

He gave a low whistle. 'You don't mean to tell me Lady Serena is the object of his gallantry?' She nodded. 'Well! So it *was* true! Neither your mama nor I would credit it! I should have thought the young lady too high in the instep to have encouraged the attentions of a mere nobody! She must be the most outrageous flirt!'

'Oh, no, no!' she uttered, almost extinguished.

'Well, I won't argue with you, but I can tell you this, Fanny, if she should get into a scrape you will be blamed for it!'

'Who told you *this* story?' she asked faintly.

'Your Aunt Charlotte had it in a letter from Mrs Holroyd, and told your mama. *She* said your Major was for ever in Laura Place, and careering all over the countryside with Lady Serena besides. I need not tell you that was coming a bit too strong for me, my dear! It made your mama and me disbelieve the whole.'

Fanny sat limply down, and covered her face with her hands. 'Oh, how careless I have been! I should not have allowed – I should have gone with them!'

Sir William regarded her in the liveliest consternation. 'You don't mean to tell me it's true? Upon my word, Fanny!'

'No, no, it is not what you think! Papa, you must not spread it about – Serena does not wish it to be known while she is in mourning – but they are *engaged*!'

'What?' he demanded. 'Lady Serena engaged to a Major Kirkby?'

'Yes!' she said, and, for no very apparent reason, burst into tears.

Twelve

Beyond saying: 'Well, well, there is nothing for you to cry about, my dear!' Sir William paid very little heed to Fanny's sudden spring of tears. Women, in his view, were always bursting into tears for no reason comprehensible to the sterner sex. He was very much taken aback by the news she had confided to him, and, at first, inclined to dislike it almost as much as he would have disliked the news of her own engagement. But Fanny, quickly wiping her eyes, soon contrived to talk him out of his disapproval. He was not much impressed by the touching picture she painted of a seven-year attachment. 'Very fine talking!' he said. 'It may be so with *him*, though I take leave to doubt it! He may *think* he never fancied another female, but all I can say, if he found no little love-bird to entertain him in seven years, is that he must be a nincompoop! No, no, my dear, that's doing it too brown! As for Lady Serena, all this constancy didn't prevent her from becoming engaged to Rotherham! But what you tell me of his having come into property puts a different complexion on the matter. Not that I think the Carlows will take kindly to the match, but that's no concern of mine!'

Guiltily aware of having conveyed to him the impression that the Major's estate was extensive, and his fortune handsome,

Fanny devoutly trusted that he would not question her too closely on the subject. He did ask her in what part of the country the estate was situated, but the timely entrance of Lybster, with wine and glasses on a large silver tray, made it unnecessary for her to say more than: 'In Kent, Papa.' His attention was drawn off; he poured himself a glass of sherry; was agreeably surprised at its quality; and for some minutes was more interested to learn where it had been procured than in the size or whereabouts of the Major's property.

By the time Lybster, after discussing with Sir William the respective merits of Bristol Milk, Oloroso, and Manzanilla, had departed, Sir William had refilled his glass, and was feeling in charity with the world. He told his daughter that she had a good butler; bored her very much by recalling how in his youth Mountain-Malaga had been much drunk; what he had paid for a tun in the '80s; how one was rarely offered it in these degenerate days; and at last came back to the subject of Serena's engagement. The more he thought of it the more he liked it, for if Serena were to be married before the end of the year the way would be clear for Agnes to pay her sister a prolonged visit. 'That is to say, if she doesn't go off this Season, and although your mama is making every effort I need not scruple to tell you, my dear, that I entertain very few hopes. She does not take. It's a pity you cannot give her a little of your beauty! Though to my mind handsome is as handsome does, and a spoonful of honey on her tongue would get her a respectable husband sooner than a bushel of strawberries squashed on her face. Yes, Mama is determined to clear her complexion, and they say strawberries will do the trick. I hope they may, but so far it seems to me a great waste of good fruit. Kitty, now, is another thing. You would be surprised at the improvement in her since you saw her last! She is not unlike what you were at her age, and should go off easily, Mama thinks.'

He continued in this strain for some minutes, so well-pleased with his scheme for foisting an unmarriageable sister on to Fanny that her marked absence of enthusiasm quite escaped his notice. Over his third glass of sherry he once more returned to Serena's engagement, but this time it was to warn Fanny against allowing the Major to be too particular in his attentions. 'It won't do to set tongues wagging, if the engagement is not to be announced until the autumn,' he said. 'Ten to one, it will come to the ears of her family that *one* man is dancing attendance on her. If I were you, Fanny, I would relax a trifle: permit people to call, you know! It is more than six months now since Spenborough died, and although I should not wish you to be leaving off your mourning, or going to public parties, I think there could be no impropriety in your entertaining – quite quietly, of course! – select company in your own house. A card-party, perhaps, or a dinner or two. No doubt there are plenty of other gentlemen in Bath who would be happy to be given the opportunity of dancing attendance on your daughter-in-law, for she's a fine-looking girl, and an heiress besides. I suppose there's no fear of Rotherham's thrusting a spoke into the wheel?'

'We do not know how he will like it, Papa, but he has no power to prevent it.'

'No power! I should call the strings of the purse power enough!'

'Neither Serena nor Major Kirkby would do so, however.'

'More fools they! But it's not my business, after all. What I am concerned with is that there shan't be any more gossip about it, for that must draw *you* in, my dear. A good thing if the young man were to remove from Bath, but I suppose there's no chance of his doing that. The next best thing is to render him less conspicuous, and that you may achieve by allowing others to visit you.'

'If you think it right, Papa,' she said obediently. 'I own, it

would be agreeable if I might go out a little sometimes, and it was on that subject that I was talking to Major Kirkby when you arrived. You must know that the Masters of Ceremonies here have been most civil to us, and in particular have frequently been begging us to go to lectures or concerts. It so happens that there is to be a concert at the Lower Rooms which I should very much like to hear. Mr Guynette came to tell me of it yesterday, and to promise, if we would go, that we should have seats in a retired place. Do you think we might? Major Kirkby sees no harm in it, and if he does not I feel there can be none.'

'None at all,' replied Sir William. 'A concert is not the same thing as a ball, you know. But if the Major means to escort you, take along some other gentleman as well! I daresay you are acquainted with some?'

'Oh, yes!' Fanny said, rather doubtfully.

'You could invite old Hendy!' said Sir William, laughing heartily.

'Yes – except that I don't think he likes the Major very much,' said Fanny.

'Jealous of him, no doubt! Thinks he will be cut out by a fine, upstanding young man!' said Sir William, still much amused, and apparently forgetting his earlier and less flattering description of the Major.

If Fanny felt that her father's scheme was not very likely to achieve his object, she did not say so. She was more concerned to know how Serena would receive the news that her secret had been betrayed. But Serena, when she came in pleasantly refreshed by a seven mile walk with a similarly energetic acquaintance, took it in very good part, merely begging Fanny to adjure Sir William not to mention her engagement to anyone but his wife. She came down to dinner looking so handsome in dove-gray with black ribbons that Sir William was quite captivated. Knowing that it would please Fanny, she laid herself out to amuse him, and succeeded so well that when he took up his candle to go to bed he declared he had seldom enjoyed an evening more. In his own home, no one regaled him with lively conversation, or encouraged him to recount anecdotes of his youth. He would not, in fact, have approved of it had any of his daughters talked in the Lady Serena's racy fashion; and he would certainly not have played piquet with them for penny points, for that, win or lose, could have done him no good at all.

So well pleased with his entertainment was he that he decided to remain in Bath for another night. He told Fanny that it would do no harm for the Major to be seen in his company, and said that he would go with both ladies to the Pump Room, and promenade with them there. It did not seem to Fanny that the sight of her father lending his countenance to the Major would be very likely to allay the suspicions of the Pump Room gossips, but having a strong disposition to think anyone's judgment more to be trusted than her own, and being, besides, still a good deal in awe of him, she made no demur. It was by no means certain that the Major would visit the Pump Room, for ever since the daily rides with Serena had become the rule he had taken care not to go there too often.

But the Major, wishing to discover from Fanny the probable length of Sir William's stay, did visit it, and was considerably taken aback to find himself being shaken warmly by the hand, and greeted in much the same way as he could fancy Sir William greeting a favourite nephew.

And, after all, Fanny perceived, Sir William did not manage so badly. He discovered several acquaintances in the room, and to each one he contrived to convey the impression that Major Kirkby, an old and valued friend, had been devoting himself to Lady Spenborough and her daughter-in-law at his express entreaty. The Major's quickness in following this lead pleased him so much that he began to think him a very good sort of a man, and invited him to dine in Laura Place that evening, and to play a rubber or two of whist afterwards. Fanny, an indifferent cardplayer, was too thankful to have prevailed upon Serena not to introduce her father to Mrs Floore to protest.

At dinner, Sir William continued to be pleased both with the Major and with Fanny's cook, some Spanish fritters earning his special commendation. The port was very tolerable too; and he sat down presently to the card-table in a mood of great good-humour. This, however, did not long endure, for he cut his daughter for partner, and if he was the most skilled of the four players, she was by far the least. The first rubber reduced Fanny almost to tears, so acid and incessant were the criticisms made by her parent of her mistakes. By good fortune, she cut next with the Major, and he smiled at her so reassuringly when she said, with a nervous little laugh, that he was to be pitied, that she quite plucked up courage, and, in consequence, played very much better. Sir William continued to point out her errors to her, but since these were now to his advantage, he did so in a tolerant spirit which did not much discompose her. The Major encouraged her with as much praise as he could, without absurdity, bestow, found ingenious excuses for her blunders, and, when the rubber ended in their defeat, said: 'Lady Spenborough, shall we challenge these expert gamesters to a return? Do let us have our revenge on them!'

She was very willing; and as Serena was a skilled player Sir William raised no objection. Serena was so grateful to the Major for shielding Fanny from assault that she gave him both her hands and her lips at parting, a thing that she was not very prone to do, and said warmly: 'You are quite the kindest man alive, Hector! *Thank you!*'

Sir William went back to London next day, and his daughter did her best to carry out his instructions to her. Rather to her surprise, Serena approved of them. So a very respectable and correspondingly dull gentleman of their acquaintance was invited to accompany them to the concert; and Fanny wrote careful notes to a number of persons, bidding them to a small evening reception. Life settled down into a slightly more variegated pattern, enlivened by morning visitors, and an occasional party. Several expeditions were made to places of historic interest in the vicinity of Bath, and if the Major rode behind the barouche, so too did some other gentleman. There was no difficulty in finding a suitable fourth to these parties: the only difficulty lay in deciding whose turn it was to be honoured with an invitation. Every unattached gentleman who had cudgelled his brains for weeks to hit upon a way of becoming acquainted with the most beautiful woman in Bath no sooner heard that the bereaved ladies were now receiving visitors than he scoured the town for some common acquaintance who could be persuaded to perform the coveted introduction. One or two lost their hearts to Fanny, but these were in the minority, Serena's admirers far outnumbering them, and behaving with an ardency and a devotion which made Fanny fear that the Major might be hurt. He seemed, however, to be rather amused; and whenever one of her flirts contrived to draw Serena away from her mama-in-law, to show her a very fine view, or to conduct her to the top of a ruined keep, he made no attempt to go after the truants, but walked with Fanny instead, concealing whatever chagrin he might have felt.

Fanny, incapable herself of conducting the sort of light flirtation of which Serena was an accomplished exponent, was distressed, and ventured to remonstrate. But Serena only laughed, and said that she was following out the spirit of Sir William's advice. 'The Bath quizzes will *now* say of me that so far from being violently attached to one man I am shockingly *volage*!'

Fanny could only hope that the Major would not share this opinion. She told him once, when she saw Serena positively

encouraging the gallantry of young Mr Nantwich, that Serena had a great deal of vivacity. 'In her set, you know,' she said, trying for an airy note, 'that sort of – of liveliness is quite the thing! It doesn't denote the *least* want of delicacy, or – or unsteadiness!'

He glanced down into her perturbed countenance, smiling a little. 'I am not jealous, I promise you,' he said.

'Oh, no! I am persuaded you could not be!'

His eyes followed Serena and her admirer. 'If all these moon-struck swains flatter themselves that she has any other intention than to enjoy a little sport they must be a set of ninnyhammers,' he remarked. 'I own, it is not a sport I like, but there is no particular harm in it when the lady is as skilled in it as I perceive Serena to be.'

She thought that she could detect a note of reserve in his voice, and said something about funning humours and openness of temper. He agreed to this; and she had the happy thought of adding that by dispensing her favours amongst several Serena was throwing sand in the eyes of those who suspected her of a single attachment. That made him laugh. He said: 'Lady Spenborough, are you trying to bamboozle me, or has Serena been bamboozling you? She is enjoying herself hugely! Don't look so anxious! Do you care to stroll in the wood? May I give you my arm?'

Her conscience told her that it was her duty to follow Serena, but since to do that would entail bringing the Major once more within sight and hearing of what could not (for all his brave words) but give him pain, she yielded to inclination. Nothing was more comfortable than a walk with Major Kirkby! He moderated his pace to hers, handed her carefully over the smallest obstacle, warned her of damp patches, and always chose a smooth path for her to tread. They were on the cosiest of terms, Fanny having very soon lost her shyness, and the Major discovering in her so sympathetic a listener that before very long he had put her in possession of nearly every detail of his

career. In return, she told him all about her home, and her family and how much she dreaded having her sister Agnes sent to live with her. He entered fully into her sentiments upon this; and although she never spoke of Mama except with respect, or mentioned her marriage, it did not take him long to arrive at a pretty fair understanding of why she had accepted the hand of a man old enough to have been her father. His reflections upon this subject he kept to himself.

Nothing occurred to disturb the harmony of these summer days until one morning in June the *Morning Post*, when opened at the only page that interested Fanny, was found to contain a bomb-shell. She had just read aloud to Serena the news of the Princess Charlotte's indisposition, and was about to speculate on the probable nature of the malady, when her eyes alighted on another item of social intelligence. A sharp gasp broke from her, and she cried out impulsively: 'Good God! Oh, *no*! Impossible!'

'Well, what now?' enquired Serena, engaged in arranging roses in a bowl.

'Rotherham!' uttered Fanny, in a strangled voice.

Serena turned quickly to look at her. 'Rotherham? What has happened to him?' she said sharply. 'Is he ill too? Fanny, he's not *dead*?'

'Oh, no, no!' Fanny said. '*Betrothed!*'

'Betrothed!'

'Yes! The most shocking thing! To Emily Laleham!'

'It's not true!'

'It must be, Serena, for here it is, *published*! I don't wonder at your amazement! That poor child! Oh, what a wicked, abominable woman Lady Laleham is! *A marriage has been arranged* – yes, and well do I know who arranged it! – *between Ivo Spencer Barrasford, Marquis of Rotherham, and Emily Mary, eldest daughter of Sir Walter Laleham, Bart* – You see, there *can* be no mistake! Oh, I don't know when I have been more distressed!'

She looked up from the paper to Serena, standing like a stone in the middle of the room, two roses held in her hand, her cheeks perfectly white, and in her eyes an expression of blank horror.

'What have I done?' Serena said, in a queer, hoarse voice. 'O God, what have I done?'

'Dearest, *you* are not to blame!' Fanny cried. 'He met her in my house, not in yours! Not that I feel I am to blame either, for heaven knows I never invited Lady Laleham to visit me on that fatal day! And from all we hear of the horrid, encroaching way she has been thrusting herself into the highest circles, he must have met her somewhere, even if not in *my* house! Though, to be sure, it would not have been in that style, just seated round the table, as we were, conversing without the least formality. Oh, if I had known what would come of it, I would have been *uncivil* to Lady Laleham rather than have admitted her into the breakfast-parlour!' She saw that Serena was staring at her in a fixed, blank way, and then that a trickle of blood was running down one of her fingers. 'Oh, you have scratched your hand with those thorns! Take care you don't smear your gown, dearest!'

Her words seemed to recall Serena to herself. She gave a slight start, and glanced down at her hand. Her fingers unclenched themselves from about the rose-stems; she laid the flowers down, saying quietly: 'So I have! How stupid! Pray, Fanny, attend to these! I must go and wash my hands.'

She went quickly from the room, and was gone for some time. When she returned, it was with some tale of having been obliged to mend the torn gathers of one of the flounces round the hem of her gown. Fanny, who knew that she never set a stitch, might, had her mind not been taken up with the news of Rotherham's engagement, have felt considerable surprise at this unprecedented happening. As it was, she merely said absently: 'How vexing! Have you sent your woman out? You know, Serena, the more I think of it the more I am convinced Lady Laleham had *this* in mind when she forced herself upon us that day!'

'Very likely. I put nothing beyond her!' Serena said lightly.

'I should never have thought Emily the kind of girl to take his fancy!'

'There is no telling what a man will fancy.'

'No, very true! But she is quite as silly as I am, and I thought he held silly females in the greatest contempt! Only think of that impatient, sarcastic way he speaks when one has said something he thinks stupid! He did seem to be amused by the droll things she said, not in the least meaning to be droll, but I thought he was quizzing her, and not very kindly!'

'So did I, but it appears that we were mistaken.'

'Yes, indeed! The Quenbury Assembly, too! *That* was why he chose to take his wards to it! But the way he spoke of Emily that very night, when you quarrelled with him about his having stood up only with her – how could he have done so, if he had felt the smallest *tendre* for her? Do you remember his telling us how he could get nothing out of her but Yes, and No, and so had *drawn no more coverts*, but had come to take his leave of us instead?'

'Very clearly. Also my own words on that occasion! I imagine her behaviour must have piqued him, and what began as an idle amusement became a serious pursuit. I daresay he can never before have tossed his handkerchief and not seen it picked up! I admire Emily very much, I did not think she had it in her to bring the odious Marquis so tamely to heel!'

'Oh, Serena, I am sure such a thought was never in her head! She did not like him! Indeed, I believe she was afraid of him! That is what makes this news so particularly dreadful!'

'If he loves her, she will have nothing to fear,' Serena said, a slight constriction in her throat.

'If – ! I cannot credit it!'

'Whatever else you cannot credit, that at least is sure!' Serena said. 'No other reason can possibly exist for his having asked her to marry him! She has nothing to recommend her, neither birth nor fortune, but a pretty face and the artlessness of a kitten!'

'Then he is infatuated, which is worse than all, for you may depend upon it he will soon recover from that, and grow bored with her, and make her miserable!'

'You take a gloomy view of her prospects!'

'Yes, for I know what a harsh temper he has, and how unfeeling he is, besides being proud and overbearing! And I know she has been forced into this by her hateful mother!'

Serena shrugged her shoulders. 'Why put yourself in this passion, my dear? It is no concern of yours, after all!'

'Oh, no! But if you knew what it means to a girl to be forced into marriage with a man more than twice her age you would not –' She stopped, aghast at her own words. The colour flooded her cheeks; she looked stricken and blurted out, 'I beg your pardon! I didn't mean – I would not for the world – I don't know how I came to say such a thing!'

'There is no need to beg my pardon. I always thought it atrocious, and sincerely pitied you.'

'No, no, don't say so! Your papa – no one could have been kinder – more considerate! You mustn't think that I meant to compare him for one moment with Rotherham!'

'I don't. There, Fanny, don't cry! It is all very sad, but there's no use in becoming agitated over it. We have nothing to do with Emily's troubles.'

Fanny dried her tears, but said: 'I didn't think you could be so unfeeling! It ought to be stopped!'

'Stopped! No, that it cannot be!' Serena said. 'Put that out of your head, Fanny! It has been announced, and must go forward!'

She spoke so sternly that Fanny was quite startled. 'But, Serena, *you* did not think so!' she could not help saying.

'No! I did not, and so the more reason this engagement should not be broken! It will not be: we may trust the Laleham-woman for that!' She paused, and then said: 'Well! I must not delay to send him my felicitations. It had better be done immediately, in fact.'

'Serena, if I ought to do the same, I am sorry, but nothing would prevail upon me to felicitate either of them on an event of which I most deeply disapprove!' Fanny said, with unwonted vehemence.

Serena had already seated herself at the writing table, and spoke without turning her head. 'Unnecessary! I will say on your behalf everything that is proper to the occasion.'

'I wish very much that you would not!' Fanny said.

No answer was vouchsafed to this decidedly pettish remark, but after a moment Serena said: 'After all, it turns out very well for *me*! No moment than this could be better for the announcement I have to make! He will be much too absorbed in his own affairs to cavil at *my* engagement.'

'Yes, indeed!' Fanny said, brightening a little.

Silence fell, broken only by the scratch of Serena's quill. Fanny, seated in the window, and leaning her chin in her hand, remained lost in melancholy thought until her attention was attracted by the sight of an old-fashioned landaulette drawing up immediately beneath the window. The next instant she uttered a sharp exclamation. 'Serena! Mrs Floore! She must be coming to tell you the news! Good gracious, what a figure she is, in that hat! My love, some gentleman is handing her out, and I vow and declare to you the carriage is within an ace of tipping over under her weight! Quick! shall I tell Lybster to say we are gone out?'

'Certainly not! Why should you?' replied Serena shaking the

sand from her letter, and pulling open the little drawer in which Fanny kept her wafers.

'Oh, I don't know, but I wish she had not come here! I shall not know what to say to her!'

'Nonsense! You will say all that is proper.'

'Perhaps she will not be able to mount the stairs!' said Fanny, with a nervous giggle.

But although the performance of this feat took time it proved to be not beyond Mrs Floore's powers. With the aid of the baluster-rail and Mr Goring's stalwart arm she arrived, panting but triumphant, on the first floor, and paused to take breath. Observing that Lybster was about to throw open the door into the drawing-room, she stopped him by the simple expedient of grasping his sleeve. Affronted, he gazed at her with much hauteur, and said in freezing accents: 'Madam!'

'Looby!' enunciated Mrs Floore, between gasps. 'You wait! Trying to push me in – like a landed salmon!'

'One moment, if you please!' said Mr Goring, quite unperturbed either by his old friend's unconventional behaviour or by the butler's evident disgust. He removed the fan from Mrs Floore's clutch, and opened it, and began to ply it briskly.

'Thank you, Ned!' she said presently. 'Lord, how the heat does draw one out!'

Concluding that she now felt ready to meet her hostess, Lybster opened the door, and announced in the voice of one refraining from comment: 'Mrs Floore, Mr Goring, my lady!'

Fanny came forward, with her hand out. 'How do you do? I am so glad you have come to visit us, ma'am: pray, will you not be seated? Lybster, some wine, if you please!'

He bowed, and withdrew; but as his gait was stately he was not gone from the room in time to escape hearing Mrs Floore say gratefully: 'Bless your sweet face! Your butler was all for having me believe he didn't know but what you'd stepped out, for which I'm sure I don't blame him, but, "Lord," I said, "you've no need to be scared! Her ladyship will see me fast enough, take my word for it!" Which he did, so here I am. And I brought Mr Goring along with me, just in case I should be overcome by the heat, which is a thing that happened to me once, right in the middle of the South Parade, and caused as much excitement as if a circus had come to town. Ned! Make your bow to Lady Spenborough!' Mr Goring, who had been shaking hands with Serena, showed no signs of resenting this peremptory command, but turned to greet his hostess. She made him politely welcome, but had scarcely time to offer him her hand before Mrs Floore was again claiming her attention.

'If you've seen the newspapers this morning, my lady, you won't wonder what brings me here!'

'No, indeed: most – most interesting news, ma'am! You must be excessively pleased, I am sure!'

'Well,' said Mrs Floore, 'I don't deny it's a fine thing to be marrying a Marquis, for I daresay they don't grow on every tree, and a very odd sort of a woman I'd be if I didn't feel puffed-up enough at this moment to burst my staylaces. If Emma likes him, I'm very glad he is a Marquis; but if she don't, he might be fifty Marquises, and still I'd say she'd be better off with a plain man she *could* like!'

'We must suppose that she does like him, ma'am,' Serena said smiling.

'Begging your pardon, my dear, we don't have to suppose anything of the kind!' said Mrs Floore bluntly. 'You know that daughter of mine, and so, I'll be bound, does her ladyship! What poor, little Emma might like is the last thing in the world she'd trouble her head about, and that's the truth, small pleasure though it is to me to say such a thing of my own flesh and blood!'

Fortunately, since Fanny knew not what to reply to this

forthright speech, Lybster came back into the room at that moment, so that she was able to create a diversion by supplying her guests with refreshment. Serena said: 'No doubt you have had letters from them, ma'am?'

'I've had one from Sukey, my dear, but Emma's not one for writing letters. And if she had written to me I wouldn't know any more than I do now, because it's my belief that Prawle made her learn off by heart a set of letters out of the *Complete Letter-Writer*, and told her never to use any other ones. As for Sukey, naturally she's in high delight! In fact, anyone would think she was in love with this precious Marquis herself, for she gives him such a character that if I credited the half of what she writes I should very likely think he was an Archangel. So, since Ned, who happened to be with me when Roger came in with the newspaper and the letters, couldn't tell me any more about him than that he was a famous sportsman, I made up my mind I'd come straight round to see *you*, Lady Serena, for, "Mark my words," I said to Ned, "her ladyship will know all about him!" And you needn't mind speaking out in front of him, my dear, any more than if he was my son, which I'm sorry to say he isn't! What's more, he's pretty well acquainted with Emma, for he saw a great deal of her when she was staying with me, and went with us to the Assemblies, and the theatre, and such-like.'

Serena glanced at Mr Goring, but his countenance gave nothing away.

'Yes, Lord Rotherham is very well known in the world of sport, I believe,' Fanny said, in a colourless voice.

Mr Goring raised his eyes from the contemplation of the wine in his glass, and directed a level look at her.

'Well, I don't know that I like the sound of that, to start with!' said Mrs Floore dubiously. 'If he's a racing man, that means betting, and I've got one gamester on my hands already, and I don't want another!'

Fanny was too overcome by the thought of Rotherham's being on Mrs Floore's hands to venture on a response. Serena laughed out, and said: 'Don't be alarmed, ma'am! Rotherham's fortune is extremely large, and he is a great deal more addicted to boxing, and shooting, and hunting than to gaming!'

'Well, I'm glad to hear you say so, my dear. Not that I hold with boxing, because it's low, and not the sort of thing I should expect a Marquis to be fond of. However, Ned tells me it's quite the established mode amongst the smart beaux, and at all events he won't go dragging Emma into boxing-saloons. But if he thinks to make her go out shooting and hunting with him it won't do at all! Why, she'd be frightened to death!'

'I expect, ma'am, that he must be aware that – she doesn't share his tastes in that direction.'

'If he don't know it now he will the very first time he sees her crying her eyes out all because the cat's got hold of a mouse!' said Mrs Floore. She looked piercingly at Serena. 'Tell me this, my dear! How old is he?'

'He is thirty-eight,' replied Serena calmly.

'Thirty-eight! Lord, that's more than twenty years older than she is!' cried Mrs Floore, aghast.

'True. He is not cross-eyed, however,' Serena said, with a faint smile.

'Well, if he isn't, I should like to know how it comes about he wasn't snapped up years ago!' said Mrs Floore tartly. 'He isn't queer in his attic, is he?'

'Far from it! His understanding is excellent, and he does not suffer from any infirmity whatsoever.'

'Come, that's better!' said Mrs Floore, relieved. 'Is he handsome?'

'No. I should rather call him striking, ma'am. Certainly not handsome.'

'Do you know him well, my dear?'

Fanny cast an anxious glance at Serena. After a moment's hesitation, Serena replied: 'Very well. I have known him all my life.'

'There! What did I tell you?' Mrs Floore demanded of her escort. '*I* knew which shop to come to! So now you answer me this, my lady, if you'll be so good, and that I know you are! – Is he the sort of man that'll make my Emma a good husband?'

'Indeed, I hope so, ma'am! He can give her – a great position, wealth, consequence –'

'I know that,' interrupted Mrs Floore grimly. 'And it ain't what I asked you, my dear!'

Aware that not only Mrs Floore's gaze was fixed upon her but Mr Goring's also, Serena said: 'Dear ma'am, you must not question me so closely, if you please! I think you cannot be aware that I was once engaged to Lord Rotherham myself!'

Mr Goring's gaze now became intent; Mrs Floore was so much surprised that she nearly dropped her wineglass. 'You?' she gasped. 'Lord bless my soul! Goodness gracious! Well, I declare! That's *one* thing Sukey didn't see fit to tell me – if she knows it!'

'The engagement – and its termination – were in all the newspapers, ma'am,' Serena replied, her colour heightened.

'Ay, they would be,' nodded Mrs Floore. 'It's a lesson to me to read the Court page, which I don't mind telling you I'm not in the habit of doing. Well, I'm sure I beg your pardon, my dear – not but what if I *had* known of it I'd still have asked you for your opinion of the gentleman, though I wouldn't have done so but in private. Certainly not with Ned Goring sitting in the room, as I hope you'll believe!'

'I don't see that my being in the room makes any difference at all,' said Mr Goring unexpectedly. 'I'll go away, if you like, but, whether I go or whether I stay, don't ask her ladyship any more questions, ma'am!'

'Thank you!' Serena said, smiling at him. 'But it is very natural that Mrs Floore should wish to know why I cried off from the engagement. It was for no reason, ma'am, that precludes him from making some other female a perfectly respectable husband. The truth is that we found we did not suit. Our dispositions were too alike. Each of us, in fact, is autocratic, and neither of us has the sweetest of tempers. But a gentler woman than I am would not provoke Rotherham as I did, and might, I daresay, be very content to be his wife.'

'Yes, and I daresay this carpet is content to be trodden on!' retorted Mrs Floore. 'A man should be master in his own house: I've got nothing to say against that, as long as he don't interfere in what's no business of his! But if I find this Marquis don't know the difference between master and tyrant, not one penny will I settle on Emma, and we'll see what he and Sukey have to say to *that*!'

'I'm afraid, ma'am, that Emily's fortune is a matter of indifference to him.'

'Oh, it is, is it? Well, if Emily's been pushed into this against her will, I'll go up to London, and tell his lordship who I am, and what I mean to do, which is to hire a house in the best part of the town, and set up as his grandma! And we'll see if *that's* a matter of indifference to him!' declared the old lady triumphantly.

Thirteen

A LETTER FROM LADY THERESA FOLLOWED HARD UPON THE announcement in the *Gazette*. It was unfranked, so that Serena was obliged to pay for the privilege of reading two crossed pages of lament and recrimination. Not even his sister could have felt Rotherham's engagement more keenly. Lady Theresa took it as a personal insult, and laid the blame at her niece's door. As for Lady Laleham, no words could describe the shameless vulgarity of her conduct. From the moment of her having brought her chit of a daughter to town, she had lost no opportunity to throw her in Rotherham's way – but who would have supposed that a man of his age would succumb to mere prettiness and an ingenuous tongue? Lady Theresa prophesied disaster for all concerned, and hoped that when Serena was dying an old maid she would remember these words, and be sorry. Meanwhile she remained her affectionate aunt.

Two days later Mrs Floore was the recipient of a letter from London. She met Serena in the Pump Room, her face wreathed in smiles, and pressed upon her a letter from Emily, begging her to read it. 'Bless her heart, I've never had such a letter from her before, never!' she declared. 'So excited as she is – why, she's in downright transports! But you'll see for yourself!'

Serena took the letter with some reluctance, but the old lady was obviously so anxious that she should read it that she made no demur.

It was neither well written nor well expressed, but it owed nothing to any manual: the voice of Emily spoke in every incoherent but ecstatic sentence. Serena thought it the effusion of a child; and could almost have supposed that she was reading a description of a promised treat rather than a girl's account of her betrothal. Although Rotherham's name occurred over and over again, it was always in connection with his rank, his riches, the fine houses he owned, the splendid horses he drove, and the envy the conquest of him had aroused in other ladies' breasts. He had driven with her in the Park, in his curricle, which had made everyone stare, because he was said never to drive females. When he took them to the opera it was like going out with a Prince, because he had his own box in the best place imaginable, and everyone knew him, and there was never any delay in getting into his carriage, because as soon as the lackeys saw him coming they ran out to call to the coachman, and so they had not to wait in the vestibule, or to say who they were. Rotherham House, too! When Grandma saw it, she would be astonished, and wonder to think of her little Emily the mistress of such an establishment, giving parties in it, and standing at the head of the staircase with a tiara on her head. There were *hundreds* of servants, some of them so genteel you would take them for visitors, and all the footmen in black satin knee-breeches. Then there was Delford Park, which she had not yet seen, but she believed it to be grander even than Milverley, and how she would go on in such a place she couldn't think.

So it went on, conveying to Serena the picture of an unsophisticated child, dazzled by riches, breathless at finding herself suddenly the heroine of a fantastic dream, intoxicated by her own staggering success. There was not a word to indicate that she had formed an attachment; she was concerned not with Ivo Barrasford, but with the Marquis of Rotherham.

Serena hardly dared look up from these pages, so clearly did they convey to her the knowledge that affection had played no part in one side at least of this contract. It seemed impossible that Mrs Floore could detect anything in the letter but the excitement of a flattered child; and it was a hard case to know what to say of so disquieting a communication.

'Well?' Mrs Floore said. 'What do you think of *that*, my dear?'

Serena gave her back the folded sheets. 'She is a little carried away, ma'am, which is not to be marvelled at. Perhaps –'

'Ay, that she is!' chuckled Mrs Floore. 'So excited and happy as she is! Lord, he's regularly swept her off her feet, hasn't he? Lord Rotherham this, and Lord Rotherham that till you'd think there wasn't another soul in London! Which you can see there isn't, not in her eyes! Well, I don't know when I've been in higher croak myself, and the relief it is to me, my dear, you wouldn't credit!' She dived into her reticule for her handkerchief, and unashamedly wiped her eyes. 'You see what she writes, my lady, about me visiting her in her grand house! Bless her sweet heart! I shan't do it, but only to know she wants me to makes up for everything!'

Serena said all that was suitable, and left the old lady in a blissful dream of vicarious grandeur. She did not mention the letter to Fanny, and tried to put it out of her own mind. It recurred too often for her comfort; again and again she found herself dwelling upon all its implications, foreseeing nothing but disillusionment in store for such an ill-assorted couple, and wondering, in astonished disgust, how Rotherham could have been fool enough not to have perceived the feather-brain behind a charming face.

It was a week before she received an answer to her letter to him. The London mail reached Bath every morning between the hours of ten and twelve, and the letter was brought up from the receiving-office half an hour after she had set forth on a picnic expedition under the nominal chaperonage of a young matron of her acquaintance. Fanny could not think it proper to make one of a party of merry-makers. She would not go herself, and tried timidly to dissuade Serena. But Serena seemed to be fast recovering the tone of her mind, and was bent on amusement. She might almost have been said to have been in outrageous spirits, gay to dissipation. Fanny lived in dread of her suddenly deciding to go to balls again, and impressed upon Major Kirkby the necessity of his preventing so imprudent a start. He made a hopeless gesture: 'What can I do?'

'She must mind what *you* say!'

He shook his head.

'Oh, yes, yes!' Fanny cried. 'If you were to forbid her –'

'Forbid her! I?' he exclaimed. 'She would most hotly resent it! Indeed, Lady Spenborough, I dare not!'

'She could not resent it from you!'

He flushed, and stammered: 'I have no right – When we are married – Not that I could ever seek to interfere with her pleasure! And surely,' he added, in an imploring tone, 'it cannot be wrong, if she does it?'

She saw that he shrank from arousing Serena's temper, and was too deeply sympathetic to press him further. She could only pray that Serena would stop short of public balls, and beg her to behave with discretion while under Mrs Osborne's casual chaperonage. Serena, setting upon her copper curls the most fetching of flat-crowned villager-hats of white satin-straw with a cluster of white roses, cast her a wicked look out of the corners of her eyes, and said meekly: 'Yes, Mama!'

So Serena, squired by her Major, sallied forth on a picnic expedition; and Fanny, presently glancing through the day's mail and seeing one letter with Rotherham's name on the cover, was obliged to contain her soul in patience until such time as Serena should return to Laura Place. This was not until dinner-time, and then, instead of immediately reading the letter, she put it aside, saying: 'Fanny, have I kept you waiting? I do beg your pardon! Order them to serve dinner immediately: I'll be with you in five minutes!'

'Oh, no! Do read your letters first! I could not but notice that one has Rotherham's frank upon the cover, and you must be anxious to know how he receives the news of your engagement!'

'I am more anxious that you should not be kept waiting another moment for your dinner. I don't think it's of the least consequence whether Rotherham likes it or not: he cannot reasonably refuse his consent to it. I'll read what he has to say after we've dined.'

Fanny could almost have boxed her ears.

But when Serena at last broke the wafer, and spread open the single sheet, the Marquis's message proved to be a disappointment. Fanny watched Serena read it, herself quite breathless with anxiety, and could not forbear saying eagerly: 'Well? What does he say? He does not forbid it?'

'My dear, how should he? He makes no comment upon it, merely that he will be at Claycross next week, and will visit Bath on Thursday, for one night, to discuss with me the winding up of the Trust. We will invite him to dine here, and Hector too.'

'But is that all he has to say?' demanded Fanny incredulously.

'You don't know his style of letter-writing! This is a typical example of it. Oh, he thanks me for my felicitations, of course, and says that it will be proper for him to make the acquaintance of Major Kirkby before giving his formal consent to my marriage.'

'Then at least he doesn't mean to be disagreeable about it!' said Fanny, considerably relieved.

But when, on the following Thursday, Rotherham was ushered into the drawing-room, this comfortable conviction left her. He looked to be in anything but a complaisant mood. The sardonic lines about his mouth were marked, and a frown drew his black brows into a bar across his face. He was dressed with propriety, in an evening coat and knee breeches, but, as usual, there was a hint of carelessness about his appearance, as though the pattern of his waistcoat or the set of his neckcloth was a matter of indifference to him. He greeted her unsmilingly, and turned to meet Serena.

She had chosen to dignify the occasion by arraying herself in a gown which had been made for her by Bath's leading modiste, and never before worn. It was a striking creation, of black figured lace over a robe of white satin, the bodice cut low, and the train long. With it she wore her diamond earrings, and the triple necklace of pearls her father had given her at her coming-of-age. She looked magnificent, but the comment she evoked from the Marquis was scarcely flattering. 'Good God, Serena!' he said, as he briefly shook her hand. 'Setting up as a magpie?'

'Just so! I collect it doesn't find favour with you?' she retorted, a spark in her eye.

He shrugged. 'I know nothing of such matters.'

'No one, my dear Rotherham, having once clapped eyes on you, could doubt *that*!'

With nervous haste, Fanny interrupted this promising start to one of the interchanges she dreaded. 'Lord Rotherham, I must introduce Major Kirkby to you!'

He turned to confront the Major, whom he had not previously seemed to notice. His hard eyes surveyed him unrecognizingly. He put out his hand, saying curtly: 'How do you do?'

Never, thought Fanny, could two men have formed a stronger contrast to each other! They might have served as models for Apollo and Vulcan, the one so tall and graceful, classically featured, and golden-haired, the other swarthy and harsh faced, with massive shoulders, his whole person suggesting power rather than grace. In looks, in deportment, in manners there could be no comparison: the Major far outshone the Marquis.

'We have met before, sir,' the Major said.

'Have we?' said Rotherham, the bar of his brows lifting slightly. 'I've no recollection of it. When, and where?'

'Upon more than one occasion!' replied the Major, steadily meeting that hard stare. 'In London – seven years ago!'

'Indeed? If it is seven years since we met, I must hold that to be a sufficient excuse for having forgotten the circumstance. Did you form one of Serena's court?'

'Yes. I did,' said the Major.

'Ah, no wonder, then! I never disintegrated the mass into its component parts.'

This time it was Serena who intervened. 'I informed you, Rotherham, that the attachment between us was of long-standing date.'

'Certainly you did, but you can hardly have expected me to have known that it was of such long-standing date as that. I had, on the contrary, every reason to suppose otherwise.'

Serena flushed vividly; the Major held his lips firmly compressed over hard-clenched teeth; Fanny flung herself once more into the breach. 'I have not felicitated you yet, Lord Rotherham, upon your engagement. I hope you left Miss Laleham well?'

'Well, and in great beauty,' he replied. 'You remind me that she desired me to convey all sorts of messages to you both. Also that I stand in your debt.'

'In my debt?' she repeated doubtfully.

'So I must think. I owe my first introduction to Miss Laleham to you, and consider myself much obliged to you.'

She could not bring herself to say more than: 'I wish you both very happy.'

'Thank you! You are a notable matchmaker, Lady Spenborough: accept my compliments!'

She had never been more thankful to hear dinner announced.

While the servants were in the room, only indifferent subjects were discussed. It was second nature to Serena to promote conversation, and to set a party going on the right lines. No matter how vexed she might be, she could not fail in her duties as a hostess. Fanny, seated opposite to her, nervous and oppressed, wondered and admired, and did her best to appear at ease. She had never yet been so in Rotherham's presence, however. At his most mellow, he made her feel stupid; when he sparred with Serena for an opening, she felt quite sick with apprehension. The Major saw it, and, chancing to meet her eye, smiled reassuringly at her, and took the earliest opportunity that offered of sliding out of a discussion of the restored King of Spain's despotic conduct, and turned to ask her quietly if she had succeeded in her search for a birthday-present likely to appeal to the taste of her youngest sister. She responded gratefully, feeling herself protected; and Serena, seeing her happily engaged in abusing the Bath shops, and describing her hunt for a certain type of work-box, was content to let drop the subject of Spain, which she had chosen because it was one on which the Major could speak with authority. Rotherham sat for a moment, listening to Fanny but surveying the Major from under his frowning brows; then he turned his head towards Serena, and said: 'I imagine Lady Theresa will have told you of Buckingham's duel with Sir Thomas Hardy? An odd business! The cause is said to be some offensive letters written to and about Lady Hardy. Anonymous, of course, but Hardy held Buckingham to be the author.'

'Persuaded by her ladyship! Of *that* I am in no doubt! I don't credit a word of it! Does anyone?'

'Only the inveterate scandalmongers. The character of a gentleman protects Buckingham, or should.'

'I think so indeed! But tell me, Ivo! how does the *antiquated* courtship progress? My aunt wrote of having seen their Senilities flirting away at some party or other!'

He replied, with a caustic comment which made her burst out laughing; and in another moment they were in the thick of the sort of conversation Fanny had hoped might be averted. Rotherham seemed to have recovered from his ill-humour: he was regaling Serena with a salted anecdote. Names and nicknames were tossed to and fro; it was Rotherham now who had taken charge of the conversation, Fanny thought, and once again she was labouring to keep pace with it. There was something about the Duke of Devonshire dining at Carlton House, and sitting between the Chancellor and Lord Caithness: what was there in that to make Serena exclaim? Ponsonby too idle, Tierney too unwell, Lord George Cavendish too insolent for leadership: what leader-ship?

'I *thought* they had made no way this session!' Serena said.

'The reverse! Brougham threw the cat among the pigeons, of course. By the by, Croker came out admirably over the attack on the Navy Estimates: he was offered a Privy Councillor's office as a result, but declined it.'

'Are you interested in politics, Major Kirkby?' said Fanny despairingly.

'Not in the least!' he replied, in cheerful accents.

'For shame, Hector!' Serena rallied him.

He smiled at her, but shook his head. 'You will have to instruct me!'

'You have been interested in more important matters, Major,' said Rotherham, leaning back in his chair, the fingers of one hand crooked round the stem of his wineglass.

'I don't know that. Certainly politics have not come in my way yet.'

'You must bring him in, Serena. The Party needs new blood.'

'Not I!' she returned lightly. 'How odious it would be of me to try to push him into what he does not care for!'

'You will do it, nevertheless.'

'Do you care to wager on that chance?'

'It would be robbing you. You will never be able to keep your talents buried.' He raised his glass to his lips, and over it looked at the Major. 'Serena was made to be a political hostess, you know. Can you subdue her? I doubt it.'

'She knows I would never try to do so.'

'Good God!' said Rotherham. 'I hope you are not serious! The picture you conjure up is quite horrifying, believe me!'

'And *I* hope that Hector knows that you are talking nonsense!' Serena said, stretching out her hand to the Major, and bestowing her most brilliant smile upon him.

He took the hand, and kissed it. 'Of course I do! And *you* know that whatever you wish me to do I shall like to do!' he said laughingly.

Rotherham sipped his wine, watching this by-play with unexpected approval in his face. The second course had come to an end, and, in obedience to a sign from Serena, the servants had left the room. Fanny picked up her fan, but before she could rise, Serena said: 'Have I your consent and approval, Ivo?'

'Certainly – unless I discover that the Major has a wife in Spain, or some other such trifling impediment. When do you propose to be married?'

'It cannot be until I am out of mourning. I don't feel it would be proper even to announce the engagement at this present.'

'Most improper. It will be as well, however, since the control of your fortune will pass from my hands to his, if I have some talk with him on this subject.'

'Yes, pray do!' she said cordially. 'And I wish you will tell me what I may count on, Ivo! I never made the least enquiry, you know, because to know the precise sum I *might* have enjoyed,

but for that abominable Trust, would have made my situation the more insupportable.'

'About ten thousand a year,' he replied indifferently.

'Ten thousand a *year*?' repeated the Major, in an appalled voice.

Rotherham glanced at him across the table. 'You may call it that. It is not possible to be quite exact. It is derived from several sources, which I shall presently explain to you.'

'But – Good God, how can this be? I knew, of course, that some disparity between our fortunes there must be, but *this*!'

'I own, *I* had not thought it would be as much,' said Serena, mildly surprised.

'But there must have been an entail!' the Major exclaimed, as though snatching at a straw of hope. 'Such an income as that represents –' He broke off, in the throes of calculation.

'Something in the region of two hundred thousand,' supplied Rotherham helpfully. 'All that belongs to the Carlow family naturally goes with the title. This fortune was inherited by the late Earl from his mother, and belonged absolutely to himself.'

'Yes, I knew *that*,' said Serena. 'Papa always told me I should inherit my grandmother's property, but I supposed it to be a comfortable independence merely. I call this a very respectable fortune, don't you, Fanny?'

'I should not know what to do with the half of it!' Fanny said, awed. Rotherham smiled. 'Serena will know. The strongest likelihood is that she will run into debt.'

'I should wish it to be tied up!'

These words, vehemently uttered, made Serena look at the Major in great surprise. 'Why, what can you mean, love? You can't suppose I shall do anything so absurd as to run into debt! I assure you I am not so improvident! Rotherham, I have not the remotest guess why you should laugh in that detestable way! I was never in debt in my life!'

He threw her a glance of mockery. 'You must forgive me,

Serena! I wish you will tell me how you contrived, on the seven hundred pounds a year which I, in my ignorance, thought you spent on your attire, to maintain that expensive stable of yours.'

'You know very well that Papa bought all my horses!' she said.

'Just so,' he agreed. 'Now you will be obliged to buy your own.'

'Which I can well afford to do, and remain excellently mounted!'

'Certainly you can, but you will have to take care, you know! It won't do to be paying nine hundred guineas for some showy-looking bay you are glad to part with on any terms at the end of your first day out on him.'

Wrath flamed in her eyes and her cheeks. 'Were you never taken-in over a horse?' she demanded.

'Yes,' he said reflectively. 'But I can't recall that I ever paid a fancy price for an animal which –'

'Be quiet!' she shot at him. 'All those years ago – when I was still green – ! Only *you* would cast it up at me still, Rotherham! Do I make mistakes now? Do I?'

'Oh, not as bad as that one!' he said. 'I'm prepared to bet a large sum on your having paid too much for that mare I saw at Milverley, but –'

She was on her feet. 'If you dare – if you *dare* tell me again she's too short in the back – !'

'Serena, for heaven's sake!' begged the Major. 'You are distressing Lady Spenborough! What the deuce does it matter if Lord Rotherham chooses to criticize the mare?'

She paid not the slightest heed, but drove home her challenge. 'Well, my lord? Well?'

'Don't try to browbeat me, my girl!' he replied. 'I tell you again, too short in the back!' He looked at her, his eyes glinting. 'And you know it!'

She bit her lip. Her eyes strove with his for a moment or two, but suddenly she burst into laughter, and sat down again. 'Of all the *odious* creatures – ! Perhaps she is a trifle too short in the back – but only a trifle! You need not have been so unhandsome as to provoke me into exposing myself to my betrothed!'

The glint was still in his eyes, but he said: 'The temptation was irresistible to see whether you would take the fly. Console yourself with the reflection that you never look more magnificent than when in a rage!'

'Thank you! I don't admire myself in that state! What were we saying, before we fell into this foolish dispute?'

'Major Kirkby had expressed a desire that your fortune should be tied up. If I am not to provoke you again, I will refrain from applauding so wise a suggestion.'

'You are mistaken,' the Major said. 'There was no thought in my head of keeping Serena out of debt! I should wish it – or the better part of it, at all events! – to be tied up in such a way that neither she nor I can benefit by it!'

'But, my dearest Hector!' cried Serena. 'You must be mad!'

'I am not mad. You haven't considered, my darling! Do you realize that your fortune is almost ten times the size of mine?'

'Is it?' she said. 'Does that signify? Are you afraid that people will say you married me for my money? Why should you care for that, when you know it to be untrue?'

'Not only that! Serena, cannot you see how intolerable my position must be?'

'No, how should it be so? If I used it to alter your way of life, of course it would be quite horrid for you, but I promise you I shall not! It will be in your hands, not in mine, so if I should run mad suddenly, and wish to purchase a palace, or some such thing, it will be out of my power to do so.'

He gave a laugh that had something of a groan in it. 'Oh, my dear, you *don't* see! But Lord Rotherham must!'

'Oh, yes! Shall I refuse my consent to your marriage?'

'I wish to God you would!'

'Well, so do not I!' said Serena. 'Hector, I *do* see, but indeed you are too quixotic! I daresay we shan't spend it – not all of it, I mean – but why should I give it up? Besides, who is to have it if we don't? Rotherham? My cousin? You can't expect me to do anything so crackbrained as to abandon what is my own to them or to anyone!'

'That was not in my head. Of course I would not ask you to give your fortune away! I don't even ask you to tie up the whole. But when it comes to the settlements, could we not create a new Trust, Serena?'

She was puzzled. 'I see no sense in that. What sort of a Trust had you in mind?'

'Not – not an unusual one!' he stammered, thrown off his balance by her entire lack of comprehension. He saw that Fanny was looking at him in innocent enquiry, and said hastily: 'This is not the place – or the occasion! I believe that when I have talked the matter over with Lord Rotherham he will agree as to the propriety of what I have to suggest.'

'But it has nothing whatsoever to do with Rotherham!' Serena said indignantly. 'What *are* you suggesting?'

'Don't be so bird-witted, Serena!' said Rotherham impatiently. 'What I understand Major Kirkby to mean, is that your fortune should be tied up in your children.'

'In my children!' she exclaimed. 'Is that what you indeed meant, Hector? Good gracious, why could you not say so?'

'Because this is neither the place nor the occasion,' said Rotherham. 'He told you so.'

'Well, if it is not, *you* did not seem to think so!'

'No, but that was because I lack delicacy.'

She laughed. 'Or would waste none upon me? You know, Hector, I think I would rather *not* tie up all my fortune in my children.'

'Not all! I'm not so unreasonable as that! But if you kept for yourself a tenth – Serena, could you not be content with that, with what you have now, and what I can give you?' the Major said pleadingly.

She said without hesitation: 'With that, or far less, if I was obliged to, my love! But – but I am *not* obliged to, and I do think that it would be quite ridiculous of us to *choose* to live on a smaller income than we need! Suppose I did get into debt, or that we had a sudden need for a large sum of money? My dear, it would drive us *both* into a frenzy to think we had been so foolish as to put it out of our power to draw upon my fortune!'

Rotherham gave a crack of laughter. 'Admirable common sense, Serena! I trust for both your sakes you will succeed in bringing Major Kirkby round to your way of thinking. You have, after all, several months in which to argue the matter.'

'Oh, yes, let us not talk of it any more tonight!' Fanny begged, getting up from her chair. 'It is so very difficult for you both!'

The Major moved to the door, and opened it. Fanny paused beside him, looking up into his face, and saying with a wistful smile: 'You will find an answer to the problem – I am quite certain that you will!'

His grave face relaxed; he returned the smile, but with an effort. She and Serena went out of the room, and he shut the door behind them, and turned to confront Rotherham.

Fourteen

Rotherham sat down again, and refilled both his own and the Major's glass. The Major returned to his chair, but stood behind it, his hands gripping its back. He said jerkily: 'She must be persuaded to do that!'

'I don't know what your powers of persuasion are,' replied Rotherham, 'but I should doubt whether you will succeed.'

'If she knew that you were in agreement with me –'

'Nothing would more surely set up her back. Moreover, I am not in agreement with you. I fail to see why Serena should be deprived of what she has every right to enjoy.' He picked up his wineglass, and lounged back in his chair, one leg stretched out before him, and his hand thrust into the pocket of his breeches. He surveyed the Major somewhat satirically. 'Serena, my dear sir, is the daughter of an extremely wealthy man, and has lived her whole life, until Spenborough's death, in the first style of affluence. I know of no reason why she should be obliged to spend the rest of it in reduced circumstances. I should doubt very much her ability to do so. However, it is no concern of mine. By all means persuade her, if you think you can do it, and believe yourself able to support her when you have done it!'

There was a long silence. The Major sat down rather heavily, and for some time remained staring blindly at his wineglass, which he kept on twisting round and round, a finger and thumb gripping its stem. At last he drew a long breath, and looked up with an air of resolution. 'Lord Rotherham, when I asked Serena to marry me, it was in the belief that although her fortune might be larger than my own, it was not so immense as to render my proposal an effrontery! I am astonished that you should behave with such – I must call it forbearance! I am well aware in what a light I must appear to anyone not familiar with the circumstances! In justice to myself, I wish to tell you that I have loved her and the memory of her – ever since I first saw her! She, too, formed an attachment. She would have married me then, but my suit was considered to be ineligible – which, indeed, it was! I was a mere lad, a younger son! We were parted. I never hoped to see her again, but forget her I could not! She was to me – an unattainable dream, a beautiful goddess beyond my reach!' He stopped, flushing, and said with some difficulty: 'But I need not try to explain *that* to you, I fancy. I am aware – Serena has told me –'

'If Serena has told you that I ever thought her a goddess, she's either an unconscionable liar, or she's hoaxing you!' interrupted Rotherham tartly.

'She did not – I only thought –'

'Then think it no longer! I collect that when you succeeded to the property you now possess, you decided she was no longer above your touch?'

The Major shook his head. 'It never entered my head. I didn't suppose even that she could remember me. But we met – here in Bath – neither of us dreaming of such a thing.' He raised his eyes fleetingly to that harsh face, and said, colouring as he spoke: 'It was as though the years rolled back – for both of us!'

'I see.' Rotherham smiled slightly. 'Your dream, in fact, had come true.'

'It sounds foolish, I daresay. I had not meant to tell you all this! But what has happened tonight –'

'Not at all. You are singularly fortunate, Major Kirkby. In my experience, the embodiment of such a dream is frequently a severe disappointment. So Serena is just what you had imagined her to be! You must have been far better acquainted with her than I had supposed possible!'

'How could I – how *could* I be disappointed in her?' demanded the Major, with unnecessary violence.

'Evidently you are not.'

'No! Unthinkable!'

'Then we need not think of it. I am obliged to you for honouring me with your confidence, but it was unnecessary. I had not imagined that you wished to marry Serena for the sake of her fortune: she's not such a fool as to be taken in by a fortune-hunter! Nor is she answerable to me for her actions.'

'Was it not – to guard her from just such a fortune hunter as I must appear that her father appointed you to be her Trustee?'

Rotherham's mouth twisted rather wryly. 'No. It was not. No doubt he hoped, at the least, that I should prevent her marriage to some obviously undesirable person. Mere disparity of fortune would not, I fancy, constitute undesirability in the eyes of the Law. She would marry whom she chose, even though I swore she shouldn't touch a penny more than the pin money she now enjoys.' He gave a short laugh. 'And fight me afterwards to the Courts of Appeal!' he added. He got up. 'There is really no more to say. Shall we go?'

'Yes. That is – I must think! Before I knew the size of this appalling fortune, I had qualms that I had no business to – Had it not been for Lady Spenborough, I believe I must have torn myself away!'

Rotherham had strolled towards the door, but he paused, and looked at the Major. 'Did Lady Spenborough encourage you to declare yourself?'

'Yes. I was in miserable uncertainty! I felt she was the most proper person to be consulted!'

'Good God!'

'You are thinking of her youth! But I knew her to be devoted to Serena! Her kindness, her sympathy I can find no words to describe! To lose Serena must be such a blow to her, but I believe she never spares a thought for herself. I think I never knew one so young and so timid to have so much strength of character, so much understanding!'

'An excellent woman,' agreed Rotherham. 'Serena's marriage will no doubt be a sad loss to her. She is really quite unfitted to live alone.'

'Exactly so! One cannot but feel that she needs to be protected from – But I fear she will have her sister thrust upon her, and from all I can discover a more disagreeable, censorious girl never existed!'

'Indeed? A gloomy prospect, certainly. However, I daresay she will marry again.'

'Marry!' The Major sounded thunderstruck, but said quickly, after a blank moment: 'Why, yes! Of course! We must hope she may.'

'I do hope it,' said Rotherham cryptically, and opened the door.

The sound of music met them, as they mounted the stairs. They found Fanny seated by the open window, gazing out into the gathering dusk, and Serena at the piano in the back half of the drawing-room. She stopped playing when she saw that the gentlemen had come in, but the Major went to her, saying: 'Ah, don't get up! You were playing the Haydn sonata I recommended to you!'

'Attempting to play it! It is not fit yet to be heard!'

'Try it once more!' he coaxed her. 'I'll turn for you.'

She allowed herself to be persuaded. Rotherham walked over to the window, and sat down beside Fanny. For a few moments he watched the couple at the far end of the room, his face expressionless. Then he turned his head to look at Fanny. He

said, his voice a little lowered: 'I understand that this marriage has your approval, Lady Spenborough.'

'Yes, I – I feel so sure that he will make Serena happy!'

'Do you?'

'It couldn't be otherwise!' she said wistfully. 'He is so very kind, and – and has loved her so devotedly!'

'So I am informed.'

'Indeed, it is quite true! He worships her: I think there is nothing he would not do to please her!'

'Excellent! Does he quarrel with her?'

'No, no! His temper is of the sweetest, and he is so patient! I cannot but feel that his tenderness and forbearance must put it out of her power to quarrel with him.' She saw the sardonic smile curl his lips, and faltered: 'You do not dislike him, Lord Rotherham?'

He shrugged. 'I see nothing to dislike.'

'I am so glad you have not withheld your consent.'

'It would have been useless.'

She looked anxiously at him, and nerved herself to say: 'I am afraid you are not quite pleased. He is not her equal in rank or fortune, but in worth, I do assure you –'

He interrupted her, in his brusque way. 'On the contrary! I am much better pleased than I expected to be. Had I known –' He broke off. She saw that the smile had quite vanished, and that his brows were lowering again. He sat in a brown study for several minutes. It seemed to her that his face hardened as she watched him. As though he felt her eyes upon him, he came out of his reverie, and turned his head to meet her enquiring look. 'Such persons as you and Major Kirkby are to be envied!' he said abruptly. 'You make mistakes, but you will not make the crass mistakes that spring from a temper never brought under control! I must go. Don't get up!'

She was wholly bewildered, and could only say: 'You will stay for tea!'

'Thank you, no! It is not yet dark, and there will be a full moon presently: I mean to start for London tonight.' He shook hands with her, and strode away to take his leave of Serena and the Major.

'Going so soon!' Serena exclaimed, rising quickly from the piano-stool. 'Good God, have I driven you away by my lamentable performance?'

'I wasn't listening to it. I am sleeping at Marlborough, or Newbury, tonight, and must not stay.'

She smiled, but retained his hand. 'You have not wished me happy.'

There was a moment's silence, while each stared into the other's eyes. 'Have I not? I do wish you happy, Serena.' His grasp on her hand tightened rather painfully for an instant. He released it, and turned to shake hands with the Major. 'I wish you happy too. I fancy you will be.'

A brief goodbye, and he was gone. Serena shut the piano. The Major waited for a moment, watching her, as she gathered her music together. 'No more?' he asked gently.

She looked as though she did not realize what she had been doing. Then she put the music into a cabinet, and replied. 'Not tonight. I must practise it before I play it to you again.' She turned, and laid her hand on his arm, walking with him into the front half of the room. 'Well, that went off pretty tolerably, didn't it? I wish I had not flown into a rage, but he made me do so. Did you hate him?'

'I didn't love him,' he confessed. 'But I thought he treated my pretensions with a degree of kindness I had no right to expect.'

'Your pretensions! I wish you will not talk in that absurd way!' she said impatiently. He was silent, and she pressed his arm, saying, in a lighter tone: 'Do you know I am close on twenty-six years of age? I am very much obliged to you for offering for me! I had quite given up hope of achieving a respectable alliance.'

He smiled, but said: 'It won't do, Serena. You must not try to turn it off! This matter must be seriously discussed between us.'

'Not now! I don't know how it is, but I have the headache. Don't tease me, Hector!'

'My darling! I will rather beg you to go up to bed! You should not have let me keep you at the piano! Have you any fever?'

She pulled her hand away. 'No, no! It's nothing – the heat! Ah, here is the tea-tray at last!'

He looked at her in concern, which was not lessened by Fanny's saying: 'A headache? *You*, dearest? I never knew you to complain of such a thing before! Oh, I hope you may not have a touch of the sun! I wish you will go to bed! Lybster, desire her ladyship's woman to fetch some vinegar to her room directly, if you please!'

'*No!*' almost shrieked Serena. 'For heaven's sake, let me alone! Of all things in the world I most abominate being –' She clipped the word off short, and gave a gasp. 'I beg your pardon!' she said, forcing a smile. 'You are both of you very kind, but pray believe I don't wish to have my temples bathed with vinegar, or to have such a rout made over nothing! I shall be better when I have drunk some tea.'

It seemed as if the Major was going to say something, but even as he opened his mouth to speak Fanny caught his eye, and very slightly shook her head. 'Will you take this cup to Serena, Major?' she said calmly.

But he had first to hover over Serena, while she disposed herself in a wing-chair, to place a cushion behind her head, and a stool at her feet. Her hands gripped the arms of her chair till her knuckles gleamed, and her lips were tightly compressed. But when he set her cup down on a table beside her, she smiled again, and thanked him. Fanny began to talk to him, in her soft voice, distracting his attention from Serena. In a minute or two, Serena sat up, allowing the cushion to slide down behind her, and sipped her tea. When she spoke, it was in her usual manner, but when she had finished the tea in her cup she went away to bed, saying, however, that her headache was gone, and she was merely sleepy.

The Major turned an anxious gaze upon Fanny. 'Do you think her seriously unwell, Lady Spenborough?'

'Oh, I hope not!' she replied. 'I think, perhaps, Lord Rotherham vexed her. If she is not better in the morning, I will try to persuade her to let me send for the doctor. But it never answers to pay any heed if she is not quite well.' She smiled at him consolingly. 'She cannot bear anyone to be in a fuss about her, you see. Indeed, I quite thought she would have flown out at you for trying to make her comfortable. Will you have some more tea?'

'No, thank you. I must go. I shall call tomorrow morning, if I may, to see how she goes on,' he said.

But when he presented himself in Laura Place at ten o'clock next day, he found the ladies breakfasting, Serena in her riding-dress. She greeted him with mock abuse, demanding to be told why he had broken faith with her. 'Ten whole minutes did I wait for you to come trotting over the bridge, and that, let me tell you, is longer than I have waited for any man before! Well for you you did *not* appear by that time, for I should certainly have sworn at you! Fanny, I forbid you to give him that coffee! He has *slighted* me!'

'I never dreamed you would ride this morning!' he exclaimed. 'I came only to see how you did! Are you sure you are quite well? You didn't go alone?'

'No, with Fobbing.'

'It is too hot for riding: I wish you will not!'

'On the contrary, it was delightful. I don't gallop Maid Marian, of course.'

'I was thinking of you, not the mare!'

'Oh, hush!' Fanny said laughing. 'You could not say anything she would think more shocking!'

'No, indeed! And not one word of apology, note!'

'My repentance is too deep to be expressed! You won't go out again, will you? At least not in the heat of the day!'

'Yes, I've persuaded Fanny to forgo the drinking of her horrid waters, and to drive with me instead to Melksham Forest. I hope you give her credit for heroism!'

'What, you don't mean to drive in your phaeton?'

'Most certainly I do!'

'Serena, not alone, I do implore you!'

'You and Fobbing will ride behind us, to protect us from highwaymen, and to set the phaeton on its wheels again when I have overturned it. I won't do so above twice!'

There was nothing but nonsense to be got out of her, then or thereafter. She was in the gayest of moods all day, and at her most affectionate, yet when he parted from her he felt that he had not once come within touching distance of her.

He thought it wisest not to revert immediately to the vexed question of her inheritance, and when, after ten days, he ventured to raise the subject, she surprised him by listening without interruption to his carefully considered arguments, and by saying, when he had done: 'Very well: let it be as you wish, my dear! After all, I don't greatly care. Not enough, at all events, to make you uncomfortable. When the time comes, arrange it as you think proper!'

She would have banished the matter there; he could not. No sooner did she yield than he was torn by doubt. Rotherham's words echoed in his mind: what right had he to insist on her relinquishing the means whereby she might live as she had always done? She listened with what patience she could muster, but exclaimed at last: 'Oh, Hector, what are you at? You told me you cannot bear it if I use my fortune, and I submitted! Now you tell me you cannot bear to deprive me of it!'

'Do I seem absurd? I suppose I must. I don't wish you to *submit*, now or ever! I couldn't do it on such terms as that. Only if you too desired it!'

'No, that is asking too much of me!' she cried. 'I must have less than common sense if I *desired* anything so foolish!'

'Oh, my dear, if it seems foolish to you, how could I let you make a sacrifice to my pride?'

She looked at him strangely. 'Ask yourself how I could let you sacrifice your pride to my extravagant habits. I could tell you how easily I might do that! Don't – don't encourage me to rule you! I shall try to, you know. There! you are warned! Handsome of me, wasn't it? Don't let us speak of this again! Only tell me when you have decided what to do!'

They did not speak of it again. He thought of it continually; she seemed to have put it quite out of her mind. If her indifference was a mask, she never let it slip. She seemed to him to be in the best of health and spirits, so full of unflagging energy that it was he who sometimes felt tired, keeping pace with her. He told Fanny once, half in jest, half in earnest, that he never knew from one moment to the next where she would be, or what she might be doing. 'I think,' Fanny said, 'that it is perhaps because she is very happy. She has always a great deal of energy, but I never saw her so restless before. She can't be still!'

Mrs Floore noticed it, and drew her own conclusions. She bore down upon Fanny one day in the Pump Room, and, ruthlessly ousting young Mr Ryde, her most fervent admirer, from her side, lowered herself into the chair he had been obliged to offer her. 'Well, I don't doubt that's one enemy I've made!' she remarked cheerfully. 'Between you, my lady, you and Lady Serena have got the men in this town so love-lorn that it's a wonder the other young females ain't all gone off into declines!'

Fanny laughed, but shook her head. 'It is Lady Serena they admire, not me, ma'am!'

'I don't deny anyone would take her for a jam-jar, the way all these silly bumble-bees keep buzzing round her,' agreed Mrs Floore, 'but there's some that like you better, if you'll pardon my saying so! As for that young sprig that gave up his chair to me with the worst grace I ever did see, he makes a bigger cake of himself than ever the Major did, when he used to come day after day into this room, looking for her ladyship.'

'Mr Ryde is only a boy, and dreadfully stupid!' Fanny said hastily.

'He's stupid enough, I grant you. Which the Major is not,' said Mrs Floore, cocking a shrewd eye at Fanny. 'What I thought at first, my lady, was that *that* was just a Bath-flirtation. But, lord bless me, Lady Serena wouldn't be in such a fine flow of spirits if that's all it is! When is it to be, that's what I'd like to know?'

Fanny, anything but appreciative of the wink so roguishly bestowed upon her, said as coldly as her tender heart would permit: 'I am afraid I don't know what you mean, ma'am.'

'Keeping it a secret, are they?' Mrs Floore shook with fat chuckles. 'As though it wasn't plain enough for a blind man to see! Well, if that's how it is, I won't ask any questions, my lady. I can't help watching them, and having my own notions, though!'

The very thought of being watched by Mrs Floore was so objectionable to Fanny that she almost summoned up enough resolution to remonstrate with Serena on her imprudence. But before she had quite succeeded in doing so something happened to give the old lady's thoughts another direction. Midway through July she once more had herself driven to Laura Place, announcing on arrival that such a piece of news as she had she couldn't keep to herself, not if she died of it.

'Which I very likely would have done, through going off

pop, like a gingerbeer bottle,' she said. 'Who do you think will be staying with me before I'm more than a day older?'

Neither lady could hazard a guess, though Serena hugely delighted Mrs Floore by saying promptly: 'The Prince Regent!'

'Better than him!' Mrs Floore declared, when she had recovered from the paroxysm into which this sally threw her. 'Emma!'

'Emily!' Serena exclaimed. 'Delightful, indeed! How pleased you must be! The Lalehams are in Gloucestershire again, then?'

'No, that's the best of it!' said Mrs Floore. 'Though heaven knows I shouldn't be saying so, for the other poor little things – three of them, that is – are so full of the measles as never was! So Sukey stayed in London, with Emma, because there wasn't a house to be had in Brighton, which she had a fancy for. Only it seems the Marquis don't care for Brighton, so it was just as well, I daresay. Not that I'd ever want Emma to go and get ill with this nasty influenza that's going about in London, which is what she did do, poor little soul! Not four days after they came back from this place, Delford, which Sukey tells me is the Marquis's country home. Seat, she calls it, and I'm bound to say it don't sound like a *home* to me. Well, it's all according to taste, but you mark my words, my dear, when he gets to be as fat as I am – which I'm sure I hope he won't – this Marquis will wish he hadn't got to walk a quarter of a mile from his bedroom to get to his dinner! I shouldn't wonder at it if that's how poor Emma came to get ill, for she's never been much of a one for long walks.'

'Delford is very large, but Lady Laleham exaggerates a little, ma'am,' Serena said, faintly smiling.

'You can lay your life to that, my dear! Well, the long and the short of it is that she did take ill, and very sick she must have been, because Sukey writes that the doctor says she must go out of London, on account of her being regularly knocked up, and her nerves quite upset besides.'

'I am so sorry!' Fanny said. 'So Lady Laleham is to bring her on a visit to you, ma'am?'

'No!' said Mrs Floore, a smile of delight spreading over her large face. 'Depend upon it, Sukey would have taken her to Jericho rather than come to me! But *she's* got the influenza now, so there's no help for it but for her to send Emma down with her maid tomorrow! She's coming post, of course, and see if I don't have her blooming again in a trice!'

Fifteen

Emily, when encountered a few days later, certainly bore all the appearance of a young lady lately risen from a sickbed. The delicate bloom had faded from her cheeks; she was thinner; and jumped at sudden noises. Mrs Floore ascribed her condition to the rigours of a London season, and told Serena that she could willingly box her daughter's ears for having allowed poor little Emma to become so fagged. Serena thought the explanation reasonable, but Fanny declared that some other cause than late nights must be sought to account for the hunted look in Emily's wide eyes. 'And it is not far to seek!' she added significantly. 'That wicked woman compelled her to accept Rotherham's offer, and she is terrified of him!'

'How can you be so absurd?' said Serena impatiently. 'Rotherham is not an ogre!'

But gentle Fanny for once refused to be overborne. 'Yes, he is,' she asserted. 'I don't scruple to tell you, dearest, that he frightens *me*, and I am not seventeen!'

'I know you are never at ease with him, and a great piece of nonsense that is, Fanny! Pray, what cause has he given you to fear him?'

'Oh, none! It is just – You cannot understand, Serena, because you are not at all shy, and were never afraid of anything in your life, I suppose!'

'Certainly not of Rotherham! You should consider that if there is anything in his manner that makes you nervous he is not in love with you.'

Fanny shuddered. 'Oh, that would be more terrifying than anything!' she exclaimed.

'You are being foolish beyond permission. I daresay the marriage was arranged by the Laleham-woman, and that Emily is in love with Ivo I most strongly doubt; but, after all, such marriages are quite common, and often succeed to admiration. If he loves her, he will very soon teach her to return his sentiments.'

'Serena, I *cannot* believe that he loves her! No two persons could be less suited!'

Serena shrugged her shoulders, saying, in a hard voice: 'Good God, Fanny, how many times has one seen a clever man wedded to a pretty simpleton, and wondered what could have made him choose her? Emily will not dispute with Rotherham; she will be docile; she will think him infallible – and that should suit him perfectly!'

'Him! Very likely, but what of her? If he frightens her now, what will it be when they are married?'

'Let me recommend you, Fanny, not to put yourself into high fidgets over what is nothing but conjecture! You do not know that he has frightened Emily. If she is a little nervous, depend upon it he has been making love to her. He is a man of strong passions, and she is such an innocent baby that I should not marvel at it if she had been scared. She will very soon overcome such prudery, I assure you!' She saw Fanny shake her head, and fold her lips, and said sharply: 'This will not do! If there was any truth in these freakish notions of yours, she need not have accepted his offer!'

Fanny looked up quickly. 'Ah, you cannot know you don't understand, Serena!'

'Oh, you mean that she dare not disobey her mother! Well,

my love, however strictly Lady Laleham may rule her, it is not in her power to force her into a disagreeable marriage. And if she is in such dread of her, she must welcome any chance to escape from her tyranny!'

Fanny gazed at her wonderingly, and then bent over her embroidery again. 'I don't think you would ever understand,' she said mournfully. 'You see, dearest, you grew up under such different circumstances! You never held my lord in awe. Indeed, I was used to think you were his companion rather than his daughter, and I am persuaded neither of you had the least notion of filial obedience! It quite astonished me to hear how he would consult you, and how boldly you maintained your own opinions and went your own way! I should never have dared to have talked so to my parents, you know. Habits of strict obedience, I think, are not readily overcome. It seems impossible to you that Lady Laleham could force Emily into a distasteful marriage, but it is not impossible. To some girls – to most girls, indeed – the thought of setting up one's own will does not even occur.'

'You encourage me to think that Emily will be the very wife for Rotherham!' Serena replied. 'And if you imagine, my dear, that he will give her any reason to be afraid of him, you are doing him an injustice. Though his manners are not conciliatory, he is, I must remind you, a gentleman!'

No more was said; nor did Emily, walking with Serena in the Sydney Gardens, appear to regret her engagement. In the intervals of exclaiming rapturously at the various amenities of this miniature Vauxhall, she chattered about the parties she had been to in London, and seemed to be full of such items of information as that the Queen had smiled at her upon her presentation, and that one of the Princesses had actually spoken to her.

'Did you enjoy yourself?' Serena asked.

'Oh, yes, indeed! And we went several times to Vauxhall Gardens, and to the theatre, and a Review in Hyde Park, and Almack's – oh, I am sure we must have been to everything!' Emily declared.

'No wonder you became so worn out!'

'No, for I am not quite accustomed to so many parties. When one is tired, one doesn't care for anything very much, and – and one gets into stupid humours – Mama says. And I had influenza. Have you ever had it, Lady Serena? It is the horridest thing, for it makes you excessively miserable, so that the least thing makes you cry. But Mama was very kind to me, and she let me come to stay with Grandmama, and, oh, it is so comfortable!'

'I hope you are making a long stay with her?'

At this, the frightened look returned. Emily stammered: 'Oh, I wish – I don't know – Mama said…'

'Your Mama will be thinking of your bride-clothes soon, no doubt,' Serena said lightly.

'Yes. I mean – Oh, not *yet*!'

'When is the wedding-date to be?'

'I – we – it is not decided! Lord Rotherham spoke of September, but – but I would like not to be married until I am eighteen! I shall be eighteen in November, you know, and I shall know how to go on better, don't you think?'

'What, because you are eighteen?' Serena laughed. 'Will it make such a difference to you?'

'I don't know. It is only that I seem not to know the things I should, to be a Marchioness, and I think I should try to learn how to be a great lady, and – and if I am not married till November perhaps I may do so.'

'I cannot suppose that Lord Rotherham desires you to be in any way other than you are now, my dear Emily.'

There was no reply to this. Glancing at her, Serena saw that

Emily was deeply flushed, her eyes downcast. She said, after a pause: 'Do you expect to see Lord Rotherham in Bath?'

The eyes were quickly raised; the colour receded. 'In Bath! Oh, *no*! The doctor said I must not be excited! Mama said she would explain to him. Besides – he must not meet Grandmama!'

'Indeed!' Serena said dryly. 'May I ask if he is never to meet Mrs Floore?'

'No, no! I could not *endure* it!'

'I don't wish to seem to criticize your mama, Emily, but you are making a mistake. You must not despise your grandmama.'

Emily burst into tears. Fortunately, one of the shady arbours with which the gardens were liberally provided was close at hand, and unoccupied. Having no desire to walk through a public place in company with a gustily sobbing girl, Serena guided Emily into the arbour, commanding her, in stringent accents, to compose herself. It was a little time before she could do this, and when her tears ceased to flow they left her face so much blotched that Serena kept her sitting in the arbour until these traces of emotion had faded. By way of diverting her mind, she asked her if she had enjoyed her visit to Delford. From the disjointed account Emily gave her of this, she gathered that it had not been wholly delightful. Emily seemed to waver between a glorious vision of herself ruling over the vast pile, and terror of its servants. She was sure that the housekeeper held her in contempt; she would never dare to give an order to the steward; and she had mistaken Lady Silchester's dresser for a fellow-guest, which had made Mama cross. Yes, Lady Silchester had been acting as hostess for her brother. She was very proud, wasn't she? There had been a great many people staying at Delford: dreadfully alarming people, who all looked at her, and all knew one another. There had been a huge dinner-party, too: over forty persons invited, and so many courses that she had lost count of them.

Lord Rotherham had said that when next such a dinner-party was held at Delford she would be the hostess.

This was said with so frightened a look up into Serena's face, the pansy-brown eyes dilating a little, that Serena was satisfied that it was not her bridegroom but his circumstances which had thrown Emily into such alarm. She wondered that Rotherham should not have realized that to introduce this inexperienced child to Delford under such conditions must make her miserably aware of her shortcomings. What could have induced him to have filled his house with exalted guests? He might have guessed that he was subjecting her to a severe ordeal; while as for summoning, apparently, half the county to a state dinner-party, and then telling the poor girl that in future she would be expected to preside over just such gatherings, Serena could think of nothing so ill-judged. Plainly, he had wanted to show off his chosen bride, but he should have known better than to have done it in such a way.

She found that Mrs Floore shared this opinion. She was hugely gratified to know that his lordship was so proud of her little Emma, but thought him a zany not to have realized how shy and retiring she was. Mrs Floore was in a triumphant mood, having routed her daughter in one swift engagement. Unfortunately for Lady Laleham, who wished to remove Emily from her grandmother's charge as soon as she herself was restored to health, Sir Walter had suffered severe reverses, and these, coupled with the accumulated bills for her own and Emily's expensive gowns, had made it necessary for her to apply to her mother for relief. Mrs Floore was perfectly ready to send her as much money as she wanted, but she made it a condition that Emily should be left in her charge until her own doctor pronounced her to be perfectly well again. Lady Laleham was obliged to accede to these terms, and Emily's spirits immediately improved. A suggestion, put forward by her ladyship, that she should join her daughter in Beaufort Square was so bluntly vetoed by Mrs Floore that she did not repeat it.

'Which I knew she wouldn't,' Mrs Floore told Serena. 'She's welcome to play off her airs in her own house, but I won't have her doing it in mine, and so she knows! Well, my dear, I don't deny Sukey's been a rare disappointment to me, to put it no higher, but there's a bright side to everything, and at least I have the whip hand of her. Offend me, she daren't, for fear I might stop paying her the allowance I do, let alone cut her out of my Will. So now we must think how to put Emma in spirits again! I'll take her to the Dress Ball on Monday, at the New Assembly Rooms, and Ned Goring shall gallant us to it. There'll be nothing for Sukey to take exception to in that, nor his lordship neither, even if they was to know of it, which there's no reason they should, because there's no waltzing, you know, and not even a cotillion on the Monday night balls.'

'But I thought Emily was to be very quiet!' said Serena, laughing. 'Was she not knocked up by balls in London?'

'Ay, so she was, but it's one thing to be going to them night after night, and never in bed till two or three in the morning, and quite another to be going to one of the Assemblies here now and then! Why, they never go on beyond eleven o'clock at the New Rooms, my dear, and only till midnight at the Lower Rooms, on Tuesdays! What's more, it won't do the poor little soul any good to be hipped, and to sit moping here with only me for company!

'I'll take her to the next Gala night at the Sydney Gardens, too, which is a thing I've never done yet, because this is the first time she's visited me during the summer. I'll be bound she'll enjoy watching the fireworks, and so I shall myself.'

Serena, looking at that fat, jolly countenance, did not doubt it. Mrs Floore was in a rollicking humour, determined to make the most of her beloved granddaughter's visit. 'For it's not likely she'll ever stay with me again,' she said, with a sigh. 'However, she shall do what the doctor tells her she should, never fear! And one thing he says is that she mustn't sit cooped up within doors this lovely weather, so if you would let her go walking with you sometimes, my lady, it would be a great kindness, and what she'd like a deal better than driving in the landaulet with me, I daresay, for that's mighty dull work for a girl.'

'Certainly: I shall be glad of her company,' Serena replied. 'Perhaps she would like to ride with me.'

This suggestion found instant favour with Mrs Floore, who at once made plans for the hire of a quiet hack. Emily herself was torn between gratification at being asked to ride with such a horsewoman as Lady Serena, and fear that she might be expected to leap all sorts of obstacles, or find herself mounted on a refractory horse. However, the animal provided for her proved to be of placid, not to say sluggish, disposition, and Serena, knowing her limitations, took her for just the sort of expeditions that would have suited Fanny. Whenever opportunity offered, she did her best to instruct Emily in the duties of the mistress of a noble household; but the questions shyly put to her by the girl, and the dismay which many of her answers provoked, did not augur very well for the future. She supposed that Rotherham, himself careless of appearances, disliking the formality that still obtained in many families of *ton*, was indifferent to Emily's ignorance of so much that any girl of his own rank would have known from her birth.

August came, and still Emily remained in Bath. To any impartial observer, she seemed quite to have regained her bloom, but Mrs Floore, looking her physician firmly in the eye, said that she was still far from well. He was so obliging as to agree with her; and upon Emily's happening to give a little cough, shook his head, spoke of the unwisdom of neglecting coughs, and prescribed magnesia and breadpudding as a cure.

Major Kirkby, finding that he was frequently expected to squire Emily as well as Serena, told Fanny that he was in a puzzle to discover what there was in the girl to endear her to Serena. A pretty little creature, he acknowledged, but gooseish. Fanny explained that it was all kindness: Emily had always looked up to Serena, and that was why Serena took pity on her. But the Major was not satisfied. 'That is all very well,' he objected, 'but she seems to believe herself to be in some sort responsible for Miss Laleham! She is for ever telling her how she should conduct herself in this or that circumstance!'

'I wish she would not!' Fanny said impulsively. 'I would like Emily to conduct herself so awkwardly as to give Lord Rotherham a disgust of her, for I am persuaded she will be miserable if she marries him! How Serena can fail to see that, I know not!'

'I don't think Serena cares for that,' he said slowly. 'She appears to me to be wholly bent on training Miss Laleham to make Rotherham a conformable wife. I can tell you this, Lady Spenborough: she does not mean *this* engagement of his to be broken off.'

'But what concern is it of hers?' cried Fanny. 'Surely you must be mistaken!'

'I asked her very much that question myself. She replied that it had been no very pleasant thing for him when she jilted him, and she would not for the world have him subjected to another such slight.'

Fanny looked very much surprised, but when she had thought it over for a minute, she said: 'She has known him all her life, of course, and no matter how bitterly they quarrel they always seem to contrive to remain on terms with each other. But it is very wrong of her to interfere in this! I don't believe Emily wants to marry Rotherham. She would not dare to tell Serena so, I daresay, and Serena takes care not to leave her alone with me, because she knows what my feelings are on that head.'

He smiled. 'So if Serena interferes in one direction, you would be happy to do so in the other?'

'Oh, no, no! Only if Emily confided in me – if she should ask my advice – I would counsel her most strongly not to marry a man for whom she feels no decided preference! A man, too, so much older than herself, and of such a harsh disposition! She cannot be aware – even if he were as kind, as considerate as –' Her voice failed; she turned away her head, colouring painfully.

Unconsciously, he placed his hand over hers, as it lay on the arm of her chair, and pressed it reassuringly. It seemed to flutter under his. After a moment, it was gently withdrawn, and Fanny said, a little breathlessly: 'I should not have spoken so. I don't wish you to think that I was not most sincerely attached to Lord Spenborough. My memories of him must always be grateful, and affectionate.'

'You need say no more,' he replied, in a low voice. 'I understand you perfectly.' There was a brief pause; then he said, with a resumption of his usual manner: 'I am afraid you must sometimes be lonely now that Serena is so often with her tiresome protégée. I have a very good mind to give her a scold for neglecting you!'

'Indeed, you must do no such thing! I assure you, she doesn't neglect me, and I am not at all lonely.'

It was true. Since she had emerged from her strict seclusion she had never lacked for company, and had by this time many acquaintances in Bath. She received and returned morning visits, attended one or two concerts, dined out several times, and even consented to appear at a few select rout-parties. She felt herself adventurous indeed, for she had never before gone alone into society. Before her marriage, she had dwelt in her mother's shadow; after it, in her husband's, or her stepdaughter's. She was too well-accustomed to every sort of social gathering to feel the want of support, and only one circumstance marred her quiet enjoyment of Bath's mild social life. Protected as she had been, she had never learnt how to hold her many admirers at a distance. She was not naturally flirtatious, and an elderly and fond husband, who knew his world, had taken care not to expose her to the temptations of fashionable London. Would-be cicisbeos, throwing out lures, had made haste to seek easier game after encountering one look from my Lord Spenborough; and Fanny had continued in serene unconsciousness that she was either sought or guarded. But so young and so divinely fair a widow exercised a powerful fascination over the susceptible, and she soon found herself in small difficulties. A shocked look was enough to check the advances of her more elderly admirers, but several love-lorn youths seriously discomposed her by the assiduity of their attentions, and their apparent determination to make her and themselves conspicuous. Serena would have known just how to depress pretensions, but Fanny lacked her lightness of touch, and, moreover, could never bring herself to snub a young gentleman who bashfully presented her with an elegant posy, or ran all over town to procure for her some elusive commodity which she had been heard to express a wish to possess. She believed that her circumstances protected her from receiving unwanted proposals, and comforted herself with the thought that the more violent of her adorers were too young to nourish serious intentions. It came as a severe shock to her, therefore, when Mr Augustus Ryde, the son of an old acquaintance of her mother's, so far forgot himself as to cast himself at her feet, and to utter an impassioned declaration.

He had gained admittance to her drawing-room by offering to be the bearer to Fanny of a note from his gratified parent. He found Fanny alone, looking so pretty and so fairy-like in her clinging black robe and veil, that he lost his head. Fanny, having read Mrs Ryde's note, said: 'Excuse me, if you please, while I write an answer to Mrs Ryde's kind invitation! Perhaps you will be so obliging as to deliver it to her.' She made as if to rise from her chair, but was prevented by Mr Ryde's throwing himself on to his knees before her, and imploring her to hear him.

Startled, Fanny stammered: 'Mr Ryde! I beg you – get up! You forget yourself! Oh, *pray* – !'

It was to no avail. Her hands were seized, and covered with kisses, and upon her outraged ears fell a tumultuous torrent of words. Desperate attempts to check this outpouring were unheeded, possibly unheard. Mr Ryde, not content with laying his heart at her feet, gave her an incoherent account of his present circumstances and future expectations, swore eternal devotion, and declared his intention of plunging into the Avon if denied hope. Perceiving that she shrank back in alarm, shocked tears in her eyes, he begged her not to be frightened, and contrived to get an arm round her slim waist.

Into this ridiculous scene walked Major Kirkby, unannounced. He checked on the threshold, considerably astonished. One glance sufficed to put him in tolerably accurate possession of the facts. He trod briskly across the floor, as the disconcerted lover turned a startled face towards him, and Fanny gave a thankful cry. A hand grasping his coat-collar assisted Mr Ryde to rise swiftly to his feet. 'You had best beg Lady Spenborough's pardon before you go,' said the Major cheerfully. 'And another time don't come to pay a morning visit when you're foxed!'

Confused, and indignant, Mr Ryde hotly refuted this suggestion, and tried somewhat incoherently to assure both Fanny and the Major of the honourable nature of his proposal. But Fanny merely hid her scarlet face in her hands, and the Major propelled him to the door, saying: 'When you are five years older you may make proposals, and by that time you will know better than to force your attentions upon a lady whose circumstances should be enough to protect her from annoyance. Take yourself off! If you oblige me to escort you downstairs, I shall do so in a way you won't care for.'

With these damping words, he pushed Mr Ryde out of the room, and shut the door upon him. 'Stupid young coxcomb!' he remarked, turning again into the room. When he saw that Fanny was by no means inclined to laugh the matter off, but was, in fact, excessively distressed and agitated, and he went quickly towards her, exclaiming in concern: 'You must not take it so to heart! The devil! I wish I *had* kicked him downstairs!'

She tried to overcome her emotion, but as fast as she wiped the tears from her cheeks her eyes filled again. The novelty of the experience had upset her as much as its impropriety. She was trembling pitiably, and as pale as she had before been red. 'How could he? How *could* he insult me so?' she sobbed.

'It was very bad, but he didn't mean to insult you!' the Major assured her. 'To be sure, he deserves to be flogged for impertinence, but it was nothing more than a silly boy's infatuation!'

'Oh, what must *my* conduct have been to have allowed him to suppose that such *dreadful* advances could be welcome to me?' wept Fanny. 'Not one year widowed, and this – I never dreamed – it never occurred to me – !'

'No, no, of course it did not!' said the Major soothingly, dropping on one knee in precisely the spot vacated by Mr Ryde, and taking the widow's hand in a comforting clasp. '*You* are not to be blamed! Your conduct has been irreproachable! Don't – ! I can't bear to see you so unhappy, my – Lady Spenborough!'

'I beg your pardon – it is very silly!' Fanny choked, making heroic efforts to compose herself, and succeeding only in uttering a stifled sob. 'I didn't know how to stop him, and he kept on kissing my hands, and saying such things, and frightening me so! Indeed, I am very sorry to be so foolish! I am s-so very m-much obliged to you for s-sending him away! I can't think w-what I should have done if you had not c-come in, for he – oh,

Major Kirkby, he actually put his arm round me! I am so much ashamed, but *indeed* I never gave him the least encouragement!'

At this point, the Major, going one better than Mr Ryde, put both his own arms round the drooping figure, cradling it protectively, and saying involuntarily: 'Fanny, Fanny! There, my darling, there, then! Don't cry! I'll see to it the young cub doesn't come near you again! There's nothing now to be frightened of!'

Quite how it happened, neither knew. The outraged widow, finding an inviting shoulder so close, sank instinctively against it, and the next instant was locked in a far more alarming embrace than she had been subjected to by the unlucky Mr Ryde. The impropriety of it did not seem to strike her. Her heart leaped in her bosom; she clung tightly to the Major; and put up her face to receive his kiss.

For a long moment they stayed thus, then, as though realization dawned simultaneously on each of them, Fanny made a convulsive movement to free herself, and the Major's arms dropped from about her, and he sprang up, exclaiming: 'Fanny! Oh, my God, my God, what have I done?'

They stared at one another, pale as death, horror in their faces. 'I – I beg your pardon!' the Major stammered. 'I didn't mean – Oh, my darling, what are we to do?'

The colour came rushing back to her cheeks; so tender a glow shone in her eyes that it was all he could do not to take her back into his arms. But she said in a constricted voice: 'You were only trying to comfort me. I know you did not mean –'

'Fanny, Fanny, don't say it! We could not help ourselves!' he interrupted, striding over to the window, as though he dared not trust himself to look at her. 'The fool that I have been!'

Such bitter anguish throbbed in his voice that she winced, and bowed her head to hide a fresh spring of tears. A long silence fell. Fanny surreptitiously wiped her eyes, and said faintly: 'It was my fault. You must forget – how silly I was. I don't regard it. I know you cannot have meant it.'

'I think I must have loved you from the moment I saw you.'

'Oh, no, no! Hector, think what you are saying! You love Serena! All these years you have loved her!'

'I have loved a dream. A sickly, sentimental dream which only a moonstruck fool could have created! The vision I cherished, it was not of Serena! She was never like it!'

'No, not like your dream, but better by far!' she said quickly.

'Yes, better by far! She is a grand creature! I admire her, I honour her, I think her the most beautiful woman I ever beheld – but I do not love her!'

She pressed a hand to her temple. 'How can this be? Oh, no it is not possible! It *could* not be!'

'Do you believe me to be mad?' he asked, coming away from the window. 'How can I make you understand?' He sat down opposite to her, and dropped his head into his hands. 'It wasn't madness, but folly! When I knew her first – oh, I was head over ears in love with her! as ridiculous an object, I suppose, as that wretched boy I found with you just now! Separated from her, joining my regiment, as I did, in the Peninsula, seeing no women other than camp-followers and Spanish peasants for months, there was nothing to banish Serena's image from my memory. It was not enough to remember her: insensibly I laid coat upon coat of new and more dazzling paint upon my image! Her face I could not alter; her *self* I did! Perhaps I never knew it!' He looked up, a painful smile twisting his lips. 'Were you ever given laudanum for an aching tooth, Fanny? Enough to make you believe your dreams were real? That was what Serena's image was to me. Then – I met her again.' He paused, and sank his head in his hands again, and groaned. 'Her face, more lovely even than I remembered it! her smiling eyelids, the music in her voice, her witchery, the very grace of her every movement – all, all as I had remembered them! I was in love again, but still in that insane dream! The woman beneath what blinded my eyes was a stranger to me. My image I had endowed with my own thoughts, my own tastes: Serena and I have scarcely a thought in common, and our tastes –' He broke off, with a mirthless laugh. 'Well, you must know how widely divergent they are!'

'I know that you have sometimes been surprised – even disappointed, but you have been happy! Surely you have been happy?' Fanny said imploringly.

'I have been happy because of *you*,' he replied. 'Today I know that. I did not before. I was like a man dazzled by strong sunlight, and when my eyes grew accustomed, and I saw a landscape less perfect than I had imagined it, I shut them. I didn't think it possible that my feeling for Serena could change. That *you* were the woman I loved I never knew until I had you in my arms, and realized that to let you go would be to tear the heart out of my chest.'

She rose quickly, and knelt beside him, putting her arms round him. 'And mine! Oh, Hector, Hector, and mine! Oh, how wicked I have been! For I knew how much I loved you!'

They clung together, her head on his shoulder, his hand holding it there. Her tears fell silently; when she spoke again her voice had a resolute calm. 'It cannot be, my dearest.'

'No. I know it. Well for you to be saved from such a contemptible clodpole as I have proved myself to be!' he said bitterly.

She drew his hand from her cheek, and held it. 'You must not talk so. Or speak to me of what might have been. We must neither of us think of that ever again. Hector, we *could* not – !'

'You need not tell me so. In me, it would be infamous!'

'You will learn to be happy with Serena – indeed, you will, dearest! Just now it seems as though – but we shall grow accustomed, both of us! Where there is no question of *dislike*, one does, you see. I-I *know* that. Serena must never so much as suspect this!'

'No,' he said hopelessly.

She could not forbear to put her hand up, lightly stroking his waving fair hair. 'There is so much in Serena that is true, not a part of your image! Her courage, and her kindness, and her generosity – oh, a thousand things!' She tried to smile. 'You will forget you were ever so foolish as to love me, even a little. Serena is cleverer than I am, and so much more beautiful!'

He took her face between his hands, and looked deep into her eyes. 'Cleverer, and more beautiful, but so much less dear!' he said, in an aching voice. He let her go. 'Don't be afraid! I have been a fool, but I hope I am a man of honour.'

'I know, oh, I know! You have been a little shocked to find that Serena is not quite what you thought her, but you will recover, and you will wonder at yourself for not having perceived at once how much more worth loving she is than that stupid image you made! And she loves you, Hector!'

He was silent for a moment, staring at his clenched hands, but presently he raised his eyes to Fanny's again, in a searching, questioning look. 'Does she?' he asked.

She was amazed. 'But, Hector – ! Oh, how can you doubt it, when she has even said she will relinquish her fortune only to please you?'

He sighed. 'Yes. I was forgetting. But it has sometimes seemed to me – Fanny, are you sure it is not Rotherham whom she really loves?'

'Rotherham?' The blankest incredulity sounded in Fanny's voice. 'Good God, what makes you think such a thing?'

'I didn't think it. But when he came here – afterwards – the suspicion crossed my mind that it was so.'

'No, no, she could not! Oh, if you had ever heard what she

says of her engagement to him you would not entertain such thoughts! They cannot meet without falling out! And he! Did you think he loved her still?'

'No,' he said heavily. 'I saw no sign – it did not occur to me. He made no attempt to prevent our engagement. On the contrary! He behaved to me with a forbearance, indeed, a kindness, which I neither expected nor felt that I deserved! And his own engagement was announced before he knew of Serena's.'

There was another long silence. Fanny rose to her feet. 'She doesn't care for him. Oh, I am sure she could not! It is the feeling for a man who was her father's friend! If it were so – and you too – !'

He too rose. 'She shall never, God helping me, know the truth! I must go. How I am to face her I know not! Fanny, I cannot do it immediately! There is some business at home which I should have attended to long since. I'll go away. Inform her that I called to tell her I had a letter from my agent, that I mean to leave by the mail-coach this afternoon!' He glanced at the gilded clock on the mantelshelf. 'It leaves Bath at five o'clock, does it not? I have just time to pack my portmanteau, and to catch it.'

'It will not do!' she cried. 'If you go away like this, what must she think?'

'I shall come back. Tell her that it is only for a few days! I must have time to collect myself! Just at this moment –' He broke off, caught her hands, and kissed them passionately, uttering: 'My darling, my darling! *Forgive* me!' Then, without another word, or a backward look, he strode quickly out of the room.

Sixteen

When Serena returned to Laura Place, it was nearly three hours later, and Fanny had had time to compose herself. She had fled to the security of her bedchamber as soon as she had heard the front door slam behind the Major, and had given way to uncontrollable despair. The violence of her feelings left her so exhausted that even in the midst of her agitating reflections, she fell asleep. She awoke not much refreshed, but calm, and if her spirits could not be other than low and oppressed and her cheeks wan, there were no longer signs to be seen in her face of a prolonged bout of crying.

Serena came in to find her seated in the window-embrasure, with a book lying open on her knee. 'Fanny, have you been picturing me kidnapped, or lost, or dead on the road? I am filled with remorse, and why I ever consented to go to Wells with that stupid party I cannot imagine! I might have known it would be too far for comfort or enjoyment! Indeed, I did know it, and allowed myself *and* you to be victimized merely because Emily wanted to go, and could not unless I took her. Or so I thought, but, upon my soul, I fancy Mrs Beaulieu would have accepted her with complaisance even though she had met her but once before in her life! Her good-nature is really excessive: such a parcel of ramshackle people as she had permitted to join the party I never companied with in my life before! I assure you, Fanny, that with the exception of her own family, the Aylshams, young Thormanby, and myself, Mr Goring was the most creditable member of the expedition!'

'Good heavens, did *he* go with you?'

'He did, upon Mrs Floore's suggestion. It was out of my power to refuse to sponsor him, and by the time I had run my eye over the rest of the party I was glad of it! He is not, perhaps, the most enlivening of companions, but he may be depended upon to maintain a stolid sobriety, and his joining us enabled me to dispense with Fobbing's escort, for which I was thankful! I should have been in disgrace with Fobbing for a week, had he seen our cavalcade! I am well served, you will tell me, for not attending to Hector! He told me how it would be – though I *don't* think he foresaw that I should spend the better part of my time in Wells in giving set-downs to one dashing blade, and foiling the attempts of another to withdraw me from the rest of the party!'

'Dearest, how disagreeable it must have been! I *wish* you had not gone!'

'Yes, so did I! It was a dead bore. We didn't reach Wells until noon, for in spite of all the fine tales I was told it is a three-hour drive; and we spent four interminable hours there, resting the horses, eating a nuncheon, looking at the Cathedral, and dawdling about the town. And, that nothing might be lacking to crown my day, I allowed Emily to drive to Wells in a landaulet with the young Aylshams and no chaperon to check the sort of high spirits that inevitably attack a party of children of whom not one is over eighteen years of age! By the time she had reached Wells she was by far too full of liveliness for propriety, and ready to maintain an *à suivre* flirtation with the court-card who had ridden close to the landaulet all the way to Wells.'

'Serena, you did not permit it? For *either* of you to be in a chain with such vulgar persons is shocking!'

'Exactly so! I formed an instant alliance with the respectable Mr Goring, and between us we kept her under close guard. To do her justice, once away from the wilder members of the party she soon became sober again. But I gave her a tremendous scold on the way home, I promise you!'

'Did you consider what Lord Rotherham would say to all this?' Fanny asked, glancing fleetingly at her.

'It was unnecessary: I knew! *That* was the gist of my scold, and it brought upon me a flood of tears, and entreaties not to tell him, or Mama.'

'Tears and entreaties! Do you still say that she is not afraid of him, Serena?'

'No, she is a good deal in awe of him, and I fancy he has frightened her,' Serena replied coolly.

'If he has done that, you will scarcely persist in believing that he loves her!'

Serena turned away to pick up her gloves. 'I have every reason to believe, my dear Fanny, that he loves her *à corps perdu*,' she said, in a dry voice. 'Unless I much mistake the matter, it is the violence of his passion which has put her in a fright, not his withering tongue! Of *that* she stands in awe merely, and it is as well she should, for she is too giddy, and too often betrayed into some piece of hoydenish conduct. She was not thrown into a panic by rebuke, I'll swear! She is too well-accustomed to it. For a man of experience, Rotherham has handled her very ill. If I did not suspect that he has realized it already, I should be strongly tempted to tell him so.'

'*Serena!*' Fanny protested, quite scandalized.

'Don't distress yourself! I fancy that is why he has not come to Bath to see Emily. No doubt Lady Laleham hinted him away: she at least is clever enough to know that with such a shy little innocent as Emily it would be fatal to set too hot a pace to courtship. I wonder she ever left them alone together except that I collect he was at first careful not to alarm a filly he must have known was as shy as she could stare, ready to bolt at one false move.' Her lip curled. 'He's impatient, but I never knew him to be so on the box or in the saddle. I own, I am astonished that a man with such fine, light hands could have blundered so!'

'Serena, I do beseech you not to talk in that horrid way!' broke in Fanny. 'Emily is not a *horse*!'

'Filly, my love, filly!'

'*No*, Serena! And whatever you may choose to imagine, it's my belief he hasn't come to Bath because he doesn't know Emily is here. Recollect that Lady Laleham would not let him set eyes on Mrs Floore for the world! Depend upon it, she has fobbed him off – if it was necessary, which I don't at all believe! – with some lie.'

'Rotherham is well aware of Emily's direction. She received a letter from him yesterday, written from Claycross,' replied Serena. 'Lady Laleham found another means of keeping him away from Bath, you see. I don't doubt he will handle Emily with far more discretion when he meets her again – though I cannot think it wise of him to write, pressing for an early marriage, before he has soothed her maidenly fears. However, I trust I have to some extent performed that office for him.'

'He is pressing for an early marriage?' Fanny repeated.

'Yes, why not?' Serena said evenly. 'He is very right, though he had better have seen her first. Once she is his wife, he will very soon teach her not to shrink from his embraces.'

'How can you? Oh, how can you?' Fanny exclaimed, shuddering. 'When you know that she neither loves nor trusts him!'

'She will rapidly do both. She is amazingly persuadable I assure you!' Serena retorted. She glanced at the clock. 'Do we dine at eight? How *tonnish* we become! I must go and make myself tidy. Does Hector dine with us tonight, or is he vexed with me for having flouted his extremely wise advice?'

'You know he is never vexed,' Fanny said. 'But he doesn't come to us tonight. He called this afternoon, to desire me to tell you that he was obliged to go into Kent for a few days, and meant to catch the mail, at five o'clock.'

'Good heavens, what a sudden start! Has some disaster befallen?'

'Oh, no! That is, I did not question him, naturally! But he said something about business which he had neglected, and his agent's having written to tell him that it had become most urgent.'

'Oh, I see! Very likely, I daresay. I recall that he told me once that he had come to Bath for a few weeks only. The weeks have turned into months! I hope he will despatch his business swiftly: how moped we shall be without him!'

'Yes, indeed!' Fanny agreed. Her voice sounded hollow in her own ears; she fancied Serena had noticed it, and made haste to change the subject. 'Serena, if Rotherham comes to see Emily – and if he is now at Claycross you cannot doubt that he will! –'

'I doubt it very much,' Serena interrupted. 'I understand he has been there for a fortnight, or more! He has neither visited Emily, nor suggested to her that he should. If you won't allow my first answer to that riddle to be correct, perhaps he is trying to pique her. How good for him to be kept champing at the bit! I wish I might see it!'

'Can it be that he has guests staying with him?' said Fanny.

'I have not the remotest conjecture, my dear!' replied Serena. 'Perhaps, since Lady Laleham is at Cherrifield Place again, he finds her company sufficiently amusing!'

But his lordship, although alone at Claycross, showed no disposition to fraternize with his future mother-in-law. He even omitted to pay her the compliment of leaving cards at Cherrifield Place, a circumstance which made her so uneasy that she bullied Sir Walter into riding over to Claycross to discover whether Rotherham had taken offence at Emily's prolonged stay in Bath, and to reassure him if he had.

Sir Walter was a man of placid temperament, but he was also strongly opposed to any form of activity that seemed likely to cast the least rub in the way of his quite remarkable hedonism, and he resented this effort to compel him to enter into his wife's matrimonial schemes. It was his practice to abandon home and children entirely to her management, partly because he was indifferent to both, and partly because argument was abhorrent to him. Having long outlived his fondness for his wife, he spent as little time in her vicinity as was possible, and was inclined to be aggrieved that his only reward for being so obliging as to spend a week under his own roof was to be hunted out on an embarrassing errand.

'I sometimes wonder,' declared Lady Laleham acidly, 'whether you have a spark of affection for your children, Sir Walter!'

He was stung by the injustice of this speech, and replied indignantly: 'Very pretty talking, upon my soul, when I've let you drag me down to this damned lazar-house! If coming to see the brats when they're covered all over with spots isn't being affectionate, I should like to know what is!'

'Have you *no* desire to see your eldest daughter creditably established?' she demanded.

'Yes, I have!' he retorted. 'It's a damned expense, puffing her off all over town, and the sooner she's off my hands the better pleased I shall be.'

'Expense!' she gasped. '*Your* hands! And who, pray, paid the London bills?'

'Your mother did, and that's what I complain of. I'm not unreasonable, and if you choose to persuade the old lady to fritter away a fortune on presentation-gowns, and balls, and the rest of it, I'm not surprised she hasn't sent me that draft.'

'Mama has promised to send it when Emily is well again,' Lady Laleham said, controlling herself with some difficulty.

'Yes, provided you don't take the girl away from her! A rare bargain, that! I shouldn't be surprised if Emily never does get well, and then where shall we be?'

'What nonsense!' she said scornfully. 'Emily shall come home the instant we are rid of these vexatious measles. Mama cannot withhold our daughter from us for ever!'

'No, but she can withhold her money, which is a deal more to the point! If you weren't stuffed so full of senseless ambition, Susan, you'd see whether the old lady wouldn't be prepared to pay us a handsome sum to let her keep Emily for good!'

'Emily,' said his wife coldly, 'will return to us precisely when I desire her to, and she will be married as soon afterwards as Rotherham chooses.'

'Well, the odds are he won't choose to marry her at all, if I get a clap on the shoulder, so take care you don't out-jockey yourself, my lady!' said Sir Walter.

'You will not be arrested for debt, if that is what you mean, while your daughter is known to be betrothed to one of the richest peers in the land,' she replied. 'If the engagement were to be declared off, it would be another matter, no doubt. You will oblige me, therefore, by going to Claycross, and setting Rotherham's mind at ease – if any suspicion lurks in it that Emily is reluctant to marry him!'

'I don't mind going to Claycross, because Rotherham has a devilish good sherry in his cellars; but if Emily bolted to your mother because she didn't want to marry Rotherham it stands to reason she'll come home if he cries off, and as soon as she does that the old lady will hand over the blunt. Which will be all the same to me. In fact, if she don't like him, I'd as lief she didn't marry him, for I've nothing against her, and I don't like him myself.'

'She does like him!' Lady Laleham said swiftly. 'She is very young, however, and his ardour frightened her. It was nothing but a piece of nonsense, I assure you! I blame myself for having allowed them out of my sight: it shan't happen again.'

'Well, you can make yourself easy on one count: Rotherham won't cry off.'

'I wish I might be certain of that!'

Sir Walter shook his head. 'Ah, it's one of the things I never could teach you!' he said regretfully. 'You will just have to take my word for it: a gentleman, my dear, doesn't cry off from a betrothal.'

She bit her lip, but refrained from speech. Sir Walter was so much pleased with his triumph that he rode over to Claycross the very next day.

He was ushered into Rotherham's library twenty minutes after Lord Spenborough, paying a ceremonial visit, had left it: a circumstance which possibly accounted for the expression of impatient boredom on his host's face. He was accorded a civil, if unenthusiastic, welcome, and for half an hour sat talking of sporting events. Since this was his favourite subject, he might have continued to discuss for the remainder of his visit the form of various race-horses, and the respective chances of Scroggins, and Church, a reputedly tiresome customer, in a forthcoming encounter at Moulseyhurst. But when Rotherham rose to refill the glasses he said: 'What news have you to give me of Miss Laleham?'

Reminded of his errand, Sir Walter replied: 'Oh, tol-lol, you know! Better: decidedly better! In fact, she's fretting to come home.'

'What prevents her?'

'Measles. Can't have the poor girl coming out in spots! However, it won't be long now! There aren't any more of them to catch 'em. William was the last – no, not William!

Wilfred? Well, I've no head for names, but the youngest of them, at all events.'

'Is Miss Laleham well enough to receive a visit from me?' asked Rotherham.

'Nothing she'd like better, I daresay, but the deuce is in it that her grandmother's not well. Not receiving visitors at present. Well, she can't: she's in bed,' said Sir Walter, surprising himself by his own inventiveness.

He found to his discomfort that his host was looking at him in a disagreeably piercing way. 'Tell me, Laleham!' said Rotherham. 'Is Miss Laleham regretting her engagement to me? The truth, if you please!'

This, thought Sir Walter bitterly, was just the sort of thing that made one dislike Rotherham. Flinging damned abrupt questions at one's head, no matter whether one happened to be swallowing sherry at the moment, or not! No manners, not a particle of proper feeling! 'God bless my soul!' he ejaculated, still choking a little. 'Of course she isn't! Nothing of the sort, Marquis, nothing of the sort! Lord, what a notion to take into your head! Regretting it, indeed!'

He laughed heartily, but saw that there was not so much as the flicker of a smile on Rotherham's somewhat grim mouth. His curiously brilliant eyes had narrowed, in a measuring look, and he kept them fixed on his visitor's face for much longer than Sir Walter thought necessary or mannerly.

'Talks of nothing but her bride clothes!' produced Sir Walter, feeling impelled to say something.

'Gratifying!'

Sir Walter decided that his visit had lasted long enough.

Returning from attending his guest to where his horse was being held for him, Rotherham walked into the house, a heavy frown on his face. His butler, waiting by the front-door, observed this with a sinking heart. He had cherished hopes that a visit from his prospective father-in-law might alleviate his lordship's distemper, but it was evident that it had not done so. More up in the boughs than ever! thought Mr Peaslake, his countenance wholly impassive.

Rotherham stopped. Peaslake, enduring that disconcerting stare, rapidly searched his conscience, found it clean, and registered a silent vow to send the new footman packing if he had dared yet again to alter the position of so much as a pen on my lord's desk.

'Peaslake!'

'My lord?'

'If anyone else should come to visit me while I remain under this roof, I have ridden out, and you don't know when I mean to return!'

'Very good, my lord!' said Peaslake, not betraying by the faintest quiver of a muscle his heartfelt relief.

There was never anything at all equivocal about his lordship's orders, and no one in his employment would have dreamt of deviating from them by a hairsbreadth, but this particular order cast the household, two days later, into a quandary. After a good deal of argument, some maintaining that it was not meant to apply to the unexpected visitor left by the head footman to cool his heels in one of the saloons, and others asserting that it most certainly was, Peaslake fixed the head footman with a commanding eye, and recommended him to go and discover what his lordship's pleasure might be.

'Not me, Mr Peaslake!' said Charles emphatically.

'You heard me!' said Peaslake awfully.

'I won't do it! I don't mind hearing you, and I'm sorry to be disobliging, but what I don't want to hear is *him* asking me if I'm deaf, or can't understand plain English, thanking you all the same! And it ain't right for you to tell Robert to go,' he added, as the butler's eye fell on his colleague, 'not after what happened this morning!'

'I will ask Mr Wilton's advice,' said Peaslake.

This announcement met with unanimous approval. If any member of the establishment could expect to come off scatheless when his lordship was in raging ill-humour, that one was his steward, who had come to Claycross before his lordship had been born.

He listened to the problem, and said, after a moment's thought: 'I fear he will not be pleased, but I am of the opinion that he should be told of it.'

'Yes, Mr Wilton. Such is my own view,' agreed Peaslake. He added dispassionately: 'Except that he said he did not wish to be disturbed.'

'I see,' said Mr Wilton, carefully laying his pen down in the tray provided for it. 'In that case, I will myself carry the message to him, if you would prefer it?'

'Thank you, Mr Wilton, I would!' said Peaslake gratefully, following him out of his office, and watching with respect his intrepid advance upon the library.

Rotherham was seated at his desk, a litter of papers round him. When the door opened, he spoke without raising his eyes from the document he was perusing. 'When I say I don't wish to be disturbed, I mean exactly that! Out!' he snapped.

'I beg your lordship's pardon,' said the steward, with unshaken calm. Rotherham looked up, his scowl lifting a little. 'Oh, it's you, Wilton! What is it?'

'I came to inform you, my lord, that Mr Monksleigh wishes to see you.'

'Write and tell him I'm ruralizing, and will see no one.'

'Mr Monksleigh is already here, my lord.'

Rotherham flung down the paper he was holding. 'Oh, hell and the devil confound it!' he exclaimed. '*Now* what?'

Mr Wilton did not reply, but waited placidly.

'I shall have to see him, I suppose,' Rotherham said irritably.

'Tell him to come in! – and warn him he isn't staying here more than one night!'

Mr Wilton bowed, and turned to leave the room.

'One moment!' said Rotherham, struck by a sudden thought. 'Why the devil are you being employed to announce visitors, Wilton? I keep a butler and four footmen in this house, and I fail to see why it should be necessary for you to perform their duties! Where's Peaslake?'

'He is here, my lord,' responded Mr Wilton calmly.

'Then why didn't he come to inform me of Mr Monksleigh's arrival?'

Mr Wilton neither blenched at the dangerous note in that harsh voice, nor answered the question. He merely looked at his master very steadily.

Suddenly a twisted grin dawned. 'Pigeon-hearted imbecile! No, I don't mean you, and you know I don't! Wilton, I'm blue-devilled!'

'Yes, my lord. It has been noticed that you are a trifle out of sorts.'

Rotherham burst out laughing. 'Why don't you say as sulky as a bear, and be done with it? I give you leave! *You* don't exasperate me by shaking like a blancmanger merely because I look at you!'

'Oh, no, my lord! But, then, I have known you for a very long time, and have become quite accustomed to your fits of the sullens,' said Mr Wilton reassuringly.

Rotherham's eyes gleamed appreciation. 'Wilton, are you *never* out of temper?'

'In my position, my lord, one is obliged to master one's ill-humour,' said Mr Wilton.

Rotherham flung up a hand. '*Touché! Damn you*, how dare you?'

Mr Wilton smiled at him. 'Shall I bring Mr Monksleigh to you here, my lord?'

'No, certainly not! Send Peaslake to do so! You can tell him I won't snap his nose off, if you like!'

'Very well, my lord,' said Mr Wilton, and withdrew.

A few minutes later, the butler opened the door, and announced Mr Monksleigh, and Rotherham's eldest ward strode resolutely into the room.

A slender young gentleman, dressed in the extreme of fashion, with skin-tight pantaloons of bright yellow, and starched shirt-points so high that they obscured his cheek-bones, he was plainly struggling with conflicting emotions. Wrath sparkled in his eyes, but trepidation had caused his cheeks to assume a somewhat pallid hue. He came to a halt in the middle of the room, gulped, drew an audible breath, and uttered explosively: 'Cousin Rotherham! I must and will speak to you!'

'Where the *devil* did you get that abominable waistcoat?' demanded Rotherham.

Seventeen

Since Mr Monksleigh had occupied himself, while left to wait in the Green Saloon, in composing and silently rehearsing his opening speech, this entirely unexpected question threw him off his balance. He blinked, and stammered: 'It isn't ab-bominable! It's all the c-crack!'

'Don't let me see it again! What do you want?'

Mr Monksleigh, touched on the raw, hesitated. On the one hand, he was strongly tempted to defend his taste in waistcoats; on the other, he had been given the cue for his opening speech. He decided to respond to it, drew another deep breath, and said, in rather too highpitched a voice, and much more rapidly than he had intended: 'Cousin Rotherham! Little though you may relish my visit, little though you may like what I have to say, reluctant though you may be to reply to me, I will not submit to being turned away from your door! It is imperative –'

'You haven't been turned away from my door.'

'It is imperative that I should have speech with you!' said Mr Monksleigh.

'You are having speech with me – a vast deal of speech! How much?'

Choking with indignation, Mr Monksleigh said: 'I didn't come to ask you for money! I don't want any money!'

'Good God! Aren't you in debt?'

'No, I am not! Well, nothing to signify!' he amended. 'And if I hadn't had to come all the way to Claycross to find you I should be quite plump in the pocket, what's more! Naturally, I didn't bargain for that! There's no way of living economically if one is obliged to dash all over the country, but that wasn't my fault! First there was the hack, to carry me to Aldersgate; then there was my ticket on the mail coach; and the tip to the guard; and another to the coachman, of course; and then I had to hire a chaise-and-pair to bring me here from Gloucester; and as a matter of fact I *shall* have to ask you to for an advance on next quarter's allowance, unless you prefer to *lend* me some blunt. I daresay you think I ought to have travelled on the stage, but –'

'Have I said so?'

'No, but –'

'Then wait until I do! What have you come to say to me?'

'Cousin Rotherham!' began Mr Monksleigh again.

'I'm not a public meeting!' said Rotherham irascibly. 'Don't say *Cousin Rotherham!* every time you open your mouth! Say what you have to say like a reasonable being! And sit down!'

Mr Monksleigh flushed scarlet, and obeyed, biting his over-sensitive lip. He stared resentfully at his guardian, lounging behind his desk, and watching him with faint scorn in his eyes. He had arrived at Claycross so burning with the sense of his wrongs that had Rotherham met him on the doorstep he felt sure that he could have discharged his errand with fluency, dignity, and forcefulness. But first he had been kept waiting for twenty minutes; next he had been obliged to suspend his oratory to admit that a monetary advance would be welcome, indeed necessary, if the post-boys were to be paid; and now he had been sharply called to order as though he had been a schoolboy. All these things had a damping effect upon him, but, as he stared at Rotherham, every ill he had suffered at his hands, every malicious spoke that had been thrust into his ambitions, and every cruel set-down he had received, came into his mind, and a sense of injury gave him courage to speak. 'It is of a piece with all the rest!' he said suddenly, kneading his hands together between his knees.

'What is?'

'You know very well! Perhaps you thought I shouldn't dare speak to you! But –'

'If I thought that, I've learnt my mistake!' interpolated Rotherham. 'What the devil are you accusing me of?' He perceived that his ward was labouring under strong emotion, and said, with a good deal of authority in his voice, but much less asperity: 'Come, Gerard, don't be a gudgeon! What am I supposed to have done?'

'Everything you could, to blight every ambition I ever had!' Gerard replied, with suppressed violence.

Rotherham looked considerably taken aback. 'Comprehensive!' he said dryly.

'It's true! You never liked me! Just because I didn't wish to hunt, or box, or play cricket, or shoot, or – or any of the things you like, except fishing, and it's no thanks to you I *do* like fishing, because you forbade me to borrow your rods, as though I had *intended* to break it – I mean –'

'What you mean,' said Rotherham ruthlessly, 'is that I taught you in one sharp lesson not to take my rods without leave! If this is a sample of the various ways in which I have blighted your ambition –'

'Well, it isn't! I only – Well, anyway, I shouldn't care for that if it weren't for all the rest! It has been one thing after another! When I was at Eton, and had the chance to spend the summer holidays sailing with friends, could I prevail upon you to give your consent? No! You sent me to that miserable grinder, just because my tutor told you I shouldn't pass Little-Go. Much he knew about it! But of course you chose to believe him, and not me, because you have always taken a – a malicious delight in thwarting me! Ay! and when you *knew* that I wanted to go up to Oxford, with my particular friends, you sent me to Cambridge! If that was not malice, *what* was it?'

Rotherham, who had stretched both legs out, was lying back in his chair, with his ankles crossed, and his hands in the pockets of his buckskin breeches, regarding his incensed ward with a look of sardonic amusement. He said: 'A desire to separate you from your particular friends. Go on!'

This answer not unnaturally fanned the flames of Mr Monksleigh's fury. 'You *admit* it! I guessed as much! All of a piece! Yes, and you refused to lend me the money to get my poems published, and not content with that, you insulted me!'

'Did I?' said Rotherham, faintly surprised.

'You know you did! You said you liked better security for your investments!'

'That was certainly unkind. You must blame my unfortunate manner! I've never had the least finesse, I fear. However, I can't feel that I blighted *that* ambition. You'll be of age in little more than a year, and then you can pay to have the poems published yourself.'

'And I shall do so! And also,' said Gerard belligerently, 'I shall choose what friends I like, and go where I like, and do what I like!'

'Rake's Progress. Have I chosen any friends for you, by the way?'

'No, you haven't! All you do is to *object* to my friends! Would you permit me to visit Brighton, that time, when Lord Grosmont asked me to go along with him? No, you would not! But that wasn't the worst! Last year! When I came down in the middle of term, after Boney escaped from Elba, and *begged* you to give me permission to enrol as a volunteer! Did you listen

to a word I said? Did you *consider* the matter? Did you give me permission? Did –'

'No,' interrupted Rotherham unexpectedly. 'I did not.'

Disconcerted by this sudden answer to his rhetorical questions Gerard glared at him. 'And very poor-spirited I thought you, to submit so tamely to my decree,' Rotherham added.

A vivid flush rose to Gerard's face. He said hotly: 'I was forced to submit! You have always had the whip hand! I have been obliged to do as you ordered me, because *you* paid for my education, and for my brothers', and Cambridge too, and if ever I had dared to –'

'Stop!' Such molten rage sounded in the one rapped-out word that Gerard quailed. Rotherham was no longer lounging in his chair, and there was no vestige of amusement in his face. It wore instead so unpleasant an expression that Gerard's heart began to thud violently, and he felt rather sick. Rotherham was leaning forward, one hand on his desk, and clenched hard. 'Have I ever held that threat over your head?' he demanded. 'Answer me!'

'No!' Gerard said, his voice jumping nervously. 'No, but – but I knew it was you who sent me to Eton, and now Ch-Charlie as well, and –'

'Did I tell you so?'

'No,' Gerard muttered, quite unable to meet those brilliant, angry eyes. 'My mother…'

'Then how *dare* you speak to me like that, you insufferable cub?' Rotherham said sternly.

Scarlet-faced, Gerard faltered: 'I – I beg your pardon! didn't mean – Of course, I am excessively grateful to you, C-Cousin Rotherham!'

'If I had wanted your damned gratitude I should have told you that I had taken upon myself the charge of your education! I don't want it!'

Gerard cast a fleeting look up at him. 'I'm glad you don't! To know that I'm beholden to you – *now*!'

'Make yourself easy! You owe me nothing – any of you! I have done nothing for you!' Gerard looked up again, startled. 'That surprises you, does it? Do you imagine that I cared the snap of my fingers how or where you were educated? You were wonderfully wrong! All I cared for was that your father's sons should be educated as he was, and as he would have wished them to be! Anything I've chosen to do has been for him, not for you!'

Crestfallen, and considerably shaken, Gerard stammered: 'I – I didn't know! I beg your pardon! I didn't mean to say – to say what I *did* say, precisely!'

'Very well,' Rotherham said curtly.

'I didn't really think you would –'

'Oh, that will do, that will do!'

'Yes, but I lost my temper! I shouldn't have –'

Rotherham gave a short laugh. 'Well, I must be the last man alive not to pardon you for that! Have you come to the end of your catalogue of my past crimes? What is my present offence?'

Mr Monksleigh, having been obliged to offer his guardian an apology, now found it extremely difficult to hurl his culminating accusation at him with anything approaching the passion requisite to convince him of the magnitude of the charge, and of his own desperate sincerity. He had been forced into a position of disadvantage, and the knowledge of this filled him with annoyance rather than with noble rage. He said sulkily: 'You have ruined my life!'

It had sounded better, when he had uttered it in the Green Saloon. If Rotherham had been privileged to have heard it then, it would have shocked him out of his scornful indifference, and might even have penetrated his marble heart, and touched him with remorse. It certainly would not have amused

him, which was the only effect it appeared now to have upon him. Venturing to steal a glance at him, Gerard saw that he was faintly smiling. The relaxing of his face from its appalling grimness, the quenching of the menacing glitter in his eyes, enabled Gerard to breathe much more easily, but did nothing to endear his guardian to him. Flushing angrily, he said: 'You think that ridiculous, I daresay!'

'Damned ridiculous!'

'Yes! Because you have no more sensibility yourself than – than a stone, you think others have none!'

'On the contrary! I am continually being sickened by the excessive sensibility displayed by so many persons of my acquaintance. But that is beside the point! Don't keep me in suspense! How have I so unexpectedly achieved what you are persuaded has been my object for years?'

'I never said that! I daresay you may not have intended to destroy all my hopes! I can readily believe you never so much as thought of what must be *my* sensations when I heard when I discovered –'

'Do try to cultivate a more orderly mind!' interposed Rotherham. 'The very fact that I take a malicious pleasure in thwarting you shows intention. I ought to have sent you to Oxford, after all. Clearly, they don't make you study Logic at Cambridge.'

'Oh, *damn* you, be quiet!' exclaimed Gerard. 'You think me a child, to be roasted and sneered at, but I am not!' His underlip quivered; angry tears sprang to his eyes. He brushed them away, saying in a breaking voice: 'You did not even *tell* me – ! You left me to discover it, *weeks* afterwards, when you must have known – you *must* have known the shock – the c-crushing blow – it would be to me!' His pent-up emotions choked him. He gave a gasp, and buried his face in his hands.

Rotherham's brows snapped together. He stared at Gerard for

a moment, and then rose, and walked across the room to where a side-table stood, bearing upon it several decanters and glasses. He filled two of the glasses, and returned with them, setting one down upon his desk. He dropped a hand on Gerard's shoulder, gripping it not unkindly. 'Enough! Come, now! I've told you I don't like an excess of sensibility! No, I am not roasting you: I see that things are more serious than I had supposed. Here's some wine for you! Drink it, and then tell me without any more nonsense what it is that I have done to upset you so much!'

The words were scarcely sympathetic, but the voice, although unemotional, was no longer derisive. Gerard said thickly: 'I don't want it! I –'

'Do as I bid you!'

The voice had sharpened. Gerard responded to it involuntarily, starting a little. He took the glass in his unsteady hand, and gulped down some of its contents. Rotherham retired again to his chair behind the large desk, and picked up his own glass. 'Now, in as few words as possible, what is it?'

'You know what it is,' Gerard said bitterly. 'You used your rank – and your wealth – to steal from me the only girl I could *ever* care for!' He perceived that Rotherham was staring at him with sudden intentness, and added: 'Miss Laleham!'

'Good God!'

The ejaculation held blank astonishment, but Gerard said: 'You knew very well – must have known! – that I – that she –'

'No doubt! – had I half the interest in your affairs with which you credit me! As it is, I did not know.' He paused, and sipped his wine, looking at Gerard over the rim of the glass, his brows frowning again, the eyes beneath them narrowed, very hard and bright. 'It would have made no difference, except that I should have informed you of the event. I am sorry, if the news came as a blow to you, but at your age you will very speedily recover from it.'

This speech, uttered, as it was, in a cold voice, was anything but soothing to a young gentleman suffering the pangs of his first love-affair. It was evident that Rotherham thought his passion a thing of very little account; and his suggestion that it would soon be forgotten, instead of consoling Gerard, made his bosom swell with indignation.

'So that is all you have to say! I might have known how it would be! *Recover* from it!'

'Yes, recover from it,' said Rotherham. His lips curled. 'I should be more impressed by these tragedy-airs if it had not taken you so long to make up your mind to enact me an affecting scene! I know not how many weeks it is since the engagement was announced, but –'

'I came into Gloucestershire the instant I knew of it!' Gerard said, half starting from his chair. 'I never saw the announcement! When I'm up at Cambridge, very often I don't look at a newspaper for days on end! No one told me until only the other day, when Mrs Maldon asked me – asked *me*! – if I was acquainted with the future Lady Rotherham! I was astonished, as may be supposed, to learn that you were engaged, but that was as nothing to the – the horror and stupefaction which held me s-speechless, when Em – Miss Laleham's name was disclosed!'

'I wish to God you were still suffering from horror and stupefaction, if that is the effect such feelings have upon you!' broke in Rotherham. 'Be damned to these periods of yours! If you would play-act less, I might believe more! As it is – !' He shrugged. 'You came down at the beginning of June, it is now August, your mother is well aware of my engagement, and you say you heard no mention of it until a few days ago? Coming it too strong, Gerard! The truth is that you've talked yourself into this fine frenzy – putting on airs to be interesting!'

Gerard was on his feet, colour flaming in his cheeks. 'You shall unsay that! How dare you give me the lie? I have not seen my mother, that is I had not done so until yesterday! I went with the Maldons to Scarborough! When I learned of the engagement, I posted south immediately!'

'What the devil for?'

'To put a stop to it!' Gerard said fiercely.

'To do *what*?'

'Yes! It did not occur to you that *I* might thrust a spoke into *your* wheel, did it?'

'No, and it still does not.'

'We shall see! I know, as surely as I stand here –'

'Which won't be very surely, if I have to listen to much more of this rodomontade!'

'You cannot silence me by threats, my lord!'

'It seems improbable that you could be silenced by anything short of a gag. And don't call me *my lord*! It makes you appear even more absurd than you do already.'

'I care nothing for what you may think of me, or for your jibes! Emily does not love you – *cannot* love you! You have forced her into this horrible engagement! You and her mother between you! And I say it shall not be!'

Rotherham was once more lying back in his chair, the derisive smile on his lips. 'Indeed? And how do you propose to stop it?'

'I am going to see Emily!'

'Oh, no, you are not!'

'Nothing – *nothing* will prevent me! I know well how the business was accomplished! *I* was out of the way, *she*, *so* gentle, so timid, so friendless, a dove, fluttering unavailingly in – in the clutches of a *vulture* (for so I think of Lady Laleham, curse her!) and of a – a *wolf*! She, I say –' He broke off, for Rotherham had given a shout of laughter.

'Oh, I don't think the dove would do much fluttering in such a situation as that!' he said.

Gerard, white with fury, hammered his fist on the desk

between them. 'Ay, a splendid jest, isn't it? Almost as droll as to lead to the altar a girl whose heart you know to be given to another! But you will not do it!'

'I probably shouldn't. Are you asking me to believe that her heart has been given to you?'

'It is true, for all your sneers! From the moment I first saw her, at the Assembly, last Christmas, we became attached!'

'Very likely. *She* is a beautiful girl, and *you* were the first young man to come in her way. You both enjoyed an agreeable flirtation. I've no objection.'

'It was not a flirtation! It endured! When she came to London, before *you* had cast your – your predatory eye in her direction, the attachment between us had been confirmed! Had it not been for the odious pretensions of her mother, who would not listen to my offer, it would not have been your engagement that was announced, but mine!'

'Rid your mind of that illusion at least! I should not have permitted you to become engaged to Miss Laleham, or to anyone else.'

'I can believe it! But I do not admit your right to interfere in what concerns me so nearly!'

'What you admit doesn't signify. Until you come of age, I have rights over you of which you don't appear to have the smallest conception. I have not chosen to exercise very many of these, but I will tell you now that I shall allow you neither to entangle yourself in an engagement, nor to embarrass my affianced wife by obtruding yourself upon her.'

'Obtruding – ! Ha! So you fancy she would be embarrassed, do you, cousin?'

'If you subjected her to such a scene as this, I imagine she would be thrown into a fever. She is recovering from a severe attack of influenza.'

'Is she?' said Gerard, with awful sarcasm. 'Or was it a severe

attack of the Marquis of Rotherham? I know that she has been hidden from me: *that* I learned at Cherrifield Place, this very day! From Lady Laleham I expected to hear nothing of Emily's present whereabouts! She would take good care not to let me come near Emily! Now it appears that you too are afraid to disclose her direction! That tells its own tale, Cousin Rotherham!'

'I have not the smallest objection to disclosing her direction,' replied Rotherham. 'She is visiting her grandmother, in Bath.'

'In Bath!' cried Gerard, his face lighting up.

'Yes, in Bath. But you, my dear Gerard, will not go to Bath. When you leave this house, you will return to London, or to Scarborough, if you like: that's all one to me!'

'Oh, no, I shall not!' countered Gerard. 'It is not in your power to compel me! You have told me where I may find Emily, and find her I will! She must tell me with her own lips that her feelings have undergone a change, that she is happy in her engagement, before I will believe it! I tell you this because I scorn to deceive you! You shall never say that I went without informing you of my intention!'

'I shall never say that you went at all,' said Rotherham, thrusting back his chair, and rising suddenly to his feet. 'And I will tell you why, cockerel! You dare not! For just so long as I will bear with you, you crow a puny defiance! But when my patience cracks, you have done with crowing! Beneath all this bombast, you are so much afraid of me that one look is enough make you cringe!' He gave a bark of laughter. '*You* disobey my commands! I wish I may see it! You haven't enough spirit to do so much as keep your knees from knocking together when I comb you down! I know exactly what you will do in this case. You will boast of what you have a very good mind to do, play the broken-hearted lover to gain the sympathy of the credulous, whine to your mother about my tyranny, and give as an excuse for your chickenheartedness the fear that if you failed to respond

to my hand on your bridle I should wreak my vengeance on your brothers! What you will not say is that you fear my spurs! But that is the truth!'

He paused, scanning his ward. Gerard was as white as his preposterous shirt-points, trembling a little, and breathing jerkily, but his burning eyes were fixed on Rotherham's face, and did not flinch from the piercing challenge of those contemptuous gray ones. His hands were clenched at his sides; he whispered: 'I would like to *kill* you!'

'I don't doubt it. You would probably like to hit me too, but you won't do it. Nor will you treat me to any more of your heroics. You may remain here tonight, but tomorrow you will return whence you came.'

'I wouldn't remain another instant under your roof for anything you might offer me!' Gerard gasped.

'Gerard, I said I would have no more heroics!'

'I am leaving Claycross *now*!' Gerard spat at him, and plunged towards the door.

'Not so fast! You are forgetting something!' Gerard paused, and looked over his shoulder. 'You told me that your pockets were to let, which is not surprising, after all this posting about the country. How much do you want?'

Gerard stood irresolute. To spurn this offer would be a splendid gesture, and one which he longed to make; on the other hand, there were the post-charges to be paid, and more than a month to be lived through before he received the next quarter's allowance. His sense of dramatic value was outraged by what he perceived to be an anticlimax of a particularly galling nature, and it was in anything but a grateful tone that he said: 'I shall be obliged to you if you will advance me fifty pounds, cousin!'

'Oh, you will, will you? And what shall I be expected to advance midway through the next quarter?'

'Rest assured that I shall not ask you to advance me a penny!' said Gerard grandly.

'You wouldn't dare to, would you?' said Rotherham, opening a court-cupboard at the end of the room, and taking from it a strong-box. 'You would apply to your mother. Well, since it appears to be entirely my fault that you are at a standstill, I'll let you have your fifty pounds. Next time you wish to upbraid me, do it by letter!'

'If you refuse to advance me my own money, I will only accept *yours* as a loan!' declared Gerard. 'I shall repay you the instant I come of age!'

'As you please,' shrugged Rotherham, unlocking the strong-box.

'And I will give you my note-of-hand!'

'By all means. You'll find a pen on my desk.'

Gerard cast him a look of acute loathing, snatched up a quill, dragged a sheet of paper at random from a sheaf, and in trembling haste wrote a promise to pay. He then flung the quill down, and said: 'I shall meet that on the day I gain possession of my principal at latest! And, if I can contrive it, much sooner! I'm obliged to you! Goodbye!'

He then crammed the bills held out to him into his pocket, and hurried out of the room, slamming the door behind him. Rotherham put his strong-box away, and walked slowly back to his desk. He picked up the note-of-hand, and began, abstractedly, to tear it into small shreds, his brows lowering, and his lips compressed. The door opened again, and he glanced up quickly.

It was his steward who had entered, and who said in a quiet but resolute voice: 'My lord, you will please allow me to have speech with you!'

'Well?'

'I saw Mr Gerard as he left the house, my lord. It is not for

me to remonstrate with you, but since there is no one else to do it, I must! You must not let him go like that!'

'I'm damned glad he has gone. My temper will stand no more of him!'

'My lord, this will not do! He is your ward, remember! I have never seen such a look on his face before. What did you do to him, to make him as white as his shirt?'

'What the devil do you suppose I did to a whey-faced weakling I could control with my right hand tied behind me?' demanded Rotherham wrathfully.

'Not that you used your strength, my lord, but your tongue!'

'Yes, I used that to some purpose,' said Rotherham, with a grim smile.

'My lord, whatever he may have done –'

'He has done nothing. I doubt if he has the spirit to do anything but nauseate me with his gasconades and his fustian theatrics!'

'Let me fetch him back!' Wilton begged. 'You should not frighten him so!'

'I should not be able to frighten him so!'

'You frighten many people, my lord. It has sometimes seemed to me that when your black mood is on you it is your wish to frighten people. But I am sure I don't know why, for you can never tolerate anyone who fears you.'

Rotherham looked up quickly, a reluctant laugh escaping him. 'True!'

'It is not too late: let me fetch Mr Gerard back!'

'No. I should not have flayed him, I acknowledge, but the temptation to do so was irresistible. It will do him no harm, and may do him a great deal of good.'

'My lord – !'

'Wilton, I have a considerable regard for you, but you have not the power to make me change my mind!'

'I know that, my lord,' Wilton said. 'There was only one person who ever had that power.'

Danger flickered in Rotherham's eyes, but he did not speak. The steward looked steadily at him for a moment, and then turned, and walked out of the room.

Eighteen

Mr Monksleigh reached Bath after dark, and in a Thrasonical mood. When he had given the order to the post-boy to take the Bath road, he had done so in the white heat of his rage, but with a quake of fear in his heart. The experience he had passed through had set every nerve in his slight body quivering, for although he had been stung to fury by the lash of Rotherham's tongue only pride had kept him from breaking down, and betraying the terror beneath his bravado. He was both timid and abnormally sensitive; and from having a keen and often morbid imagination was apt to fancy that persons who, in fact, never gave him a thought were criticizing him unkindly. Anticipation was more dreadful to him than performance; and to be harshly rated turned him sick. A wish to appear to be of consequence was unhappily allied to a lack of self-confidence which he tried to conceal under a boastful manner; and nothing could more surely have won for him the contempt of his guardian. There was never a more ill-assorted pair; and if Gerard was the last boy alive to appeal to Rotherham, no worse guardian than Rotherham could well have been found for a boy compact of timidity and vainglory. A much younger Gerard, at once anxious to impress an almost unknown guardian and afraid that he would be despised by him, encountered a look from those hard, bright eyes, and wilted under it. It was neither angry nor disdainful; it was almost incurious, but it utterly disconcerted Gerard. He had the feeling that it pierced right into his mind, and saw everything that he most wished to hide; and he never recovered from that first, disastrous meeting. Rotherham indifferent made him feel ill-at-ease; when, later, he saw Rotherham angry, he was terrified. A natural abruptness he mistook for a sign of dislike; he read a threat into every curt command; and if he was reprimanded, he was always sure that the brief but shattering scold was but the prelude to hideous retribution. The fact that on the only occasion when condign retribution had fallen upon him it was neither hideous nor even particularly severe quite irrationally failed to reassure him. He thought it a miracle that he had been let off lightly, just as he was convinced, every time he annoyed Rotherham, that he had escaped chastisement by no more than a hairsbreadth.

It was doubtful if Rotherham, with his nerves of steel, his tireless strength, and his impatience of weakness, would ever have felt much liking for so delicate and nervous a boy as Gerard; but he would not have been intolerant of him had it not been for Gerard's unfortunate tendency to brag about himself. In the early days of his guardianship, he had frequently invited him to one or other of his country seats, feeling that however great a nuisance a schoolboy might be to him it was clearly his duty to take an interest in him, giving him a day's hunting, teaching him how to handle a gun, or cast a line, and how to keep a straight left. He very soon realized that Gerard, so far from being grateful, regarded these benefits in the light of severe ordeals,and would have become merely bored had he not heard Gerard, after an ignominious day in the saddle, during the course of which he had contrived to evade all but the easiest of jumps, boasting to one of the servants of the regular raspers he had taken. Rotherham, caring nothing for anyone's admiration or disapproval, and contemptuous of shams, was violently exasperated, and thereafter regarded his ward not with indifference but with scorn. Even Gerard's docility irritated him. He preferred the more resilient Charles, whose predilection for getting into all the more damaging and perilous forms of mischief had made him declare that never again would he have the whelp to stay with him. But as soon as Charles had outgrown his destructive puppyhood he had every intention of opening his doors to him, and of taking him in hand. Charles provoked him to anger, but never to contempt. Severely castigated for setting a booby trap for the butler, which resulted in a splendid breakage of crockery, the chances were that he would bounce into the room not half an hour later, announcing in conscience-stricken accents that he feared he had killed one of the peacocks with his bow and arrow. He found nothing unnerving in the look that made his elder brother shake in his shoes; and when threatened with frightful penalties he grinned. He was outrageously mischievous, maddeningly obstinate, and wholly averse from respecting prohibitions; and since these characteristics never failed to rouse his guardian to wrath neither Gerard nor Mrs Monksleigh could understand why he was quite unafraid of Rotherham, or why Rotherham, however angry, never withered him with the remarks which made Gerard writhe.

'Cousin Rotherham likes people who square up to him,' said Charles. 'He's a great gun!'

But Rotherham today had shown no signs of liking it, thought Gerard bitterly, unable to perceive the gulf that lay between his rehearsed defiance, and his graceless brother's innate pugnacity. It had angered him into uttering words so scathing that for several stark minutes Gerard had been thrown into such a storm of shocked fury that he was jerked out of his shams, and hurled his defiance at Rotherham without the smallest thought of impressing him. He was angry, and frightened, and deeply mortified; and for quite some time continued in this frame of mind. But as the distance increased between himself and Claycross the tone of his mind became gradually restored, and from quaking at the realization that he was flatly disobeying Rotherham, and wondering what the result would be, he began to believe that he had acquitted himself well in his distressing interview with him. From thinking of all the retorts he might have made was a very short step to imagining that he really had made them; and by the time he reached Bath he was almost set up again in his own conceit, and much inclined to think that he had taught Rotherham a lesson.

Since nothing would be more disagreeable than to be obliged to apply to Rotherham for more funds, he prudently sought out a modest hostelry in the less fashionable part of the town, and installed himself there with every intention of discovering Emily's whereabouts on the following morning. In the event, it was not until two days later that he saw her entering the Pump Room with her grandmother, and was at last able to approach her. The task of locating the house of a lady whose name he had never been told had proved to be unexpectedly difficult.

Emily was very much surprised to see him, and accorded him an ingenuously delighted welcome. He was a pretty youth, with pleasing manners, and such an air of fashion that his company could not but add to her consequence. His passion for her, moreover, was expressed with the greatest decorum, and took the form of humble worship, which was quite unalarming. Upon her first going to London, he had been assiduous in his attentions, and she had enjoyed with him her first flirtation. Not a profound thinker, if she remembered the vows she had exchanged with him, she supposed that he had meant them no more seriously than she had. She did recollect that she had felt very low for quite a week after Mama had forbidden him to visit them again, but Mama had assured her that she would soon recover from her disappointment, which, in fact, she had. Amongst the crowd of Pinks, Tulips, Blades, Beaux, and High Sticklers with whom she rapidly became acquainted, Gerard was to a great extent forgotten.

But she liked him very well, and was happy to meet him again, and at once presented him to Mrs Floore.

Mrs Floore came as a shock to him, for although he had frequently heard his mama stigmatize Lady Laleham as a vulgar creature he had paid very little heed to a stricture he had heard often before, and which generally denoted merely that Mrs Monksleigh had quarrelled with whichever lady was in question. He had expected nothing as unrefined as Mrs Floore, who was arrayed in a gown of such a powerful shade of purple that he almost blinked. However, he had very good manners, and he quickly concealed his astonishment, and made her a civil bow.

Mrs Floore was inclined to favour him. She liked young persons, and Gerard struck her as a pretty-behaved beau, dressed as fine as fivepence, and plainly of the first respectability. But her shrewd gaze had not failed to perceive the ardour in his face when he had come hurrying up to Emily, and she determined not to encourage him. It would never do, she thought, for him to be dangling after Emily in a love-lorn way calculated to set Bath tongues wagging. There was no saying but what Emily's grand Marquis might not like it above half, if it came to his ears. So when she heard him asking Emily if she would be at the Lower Rooms that evening, she interposed, saying that Emily must stay at home to recruit her strength for the Gala night at the Sydney Gardens on the following evening. Gerard, on his guard from the instant he realized this amazing old lady's relationship to his adored, took this with perfect propriety. It was Emily who exclaimed against the prohibition, but so much more in the manner of a child denied a treat than in that of a damsel bent on flirting with a personable admirer, that Mrs Floore relented a little, and said that they would see. It naturally did not occur to her that Emily could have a *tendre* for any other man than her betrothed, but she was well aware that Emily was apt (in the most innocent way) to give rather more encouragement than was seemly in her situation to her admirers. It was all very well for the chit to talk in that misleadingly confiding way of hers to a steady young fellow like Ned Goring, whom one could trust to take no liberties; quite another for her to be giving this smart town sprig to think that she would welcome a flirtation.

But when, after Gerard had escorted the two ladies back to Beaufort Square, very politely giving Mrs Floore his arm, she told Emily that it would not do for her to be too friendly with such a handsome young beau, Emily looked surprised, and said: 'But he is such a splendid dancer, Grandmama! Must I not stand up with him? Why ought I not? He is quite the thing, you know!'

'I daresay he's of the first stare, pet, but would his lordship like it? That's what you ought to think of, only you're such a flighty little puss – well, there!'

'Oh, but Lord Rotherham could have not the least objection!' Emily assured her. 'Gerard is his ward. They are cousins.'

That, of course, put a very different complexion on the matter, and made Mrs Floore exclaim against Emily for not having told her so in time for her to have invited Mr Monksleigh to dine with them. But that was soon rectified. She took Emily to the ball, and there was Mr Monksleigh, nattier than ever in evening dress, his ordered locks glistening with Russia Oil, and the many swathes of his neckcloth obliging him to hold his head very much up. Several young ladies watched his progress across the room with approval, most of the gentlemen with tolerant amusement, and Mr Guynette, who had attempted unavailingly to present him to a lady lacking a partner for the boulanger, with strong disapprobation.

Gerard was in no mood for dancing, but since there seemed to be no other way of detaching Emily from her grandmother, he led her into the set that was just forming, saying urgently: 'I must see you alone! How may it be contrived?'

She shook her head wonderingly. 'Grandmama would not like it! Besides, everyone would stare!'

'Not here! But we must meet! Emily, I have only just learnt of this – this engagement you have entered into! Have been forced into! I know you cannot – I have come all the way from Scarborough to see you! Quickly, where may we meet?'

Her hand trembled in his; she whispered: 'Oh – ! I don't know! It is so dreadful! I am very unhappy!'

He caught his breath. 'I knew it!'

There was no time for more; they were obliged to take their places in the set; to school their countenances; and to exchange such conversation as was suitable to the occasion. When the movement of the dance brought them together, Gerard said: 'Will your grandmama permit me to visit her?'

'Yes, but pray take care! She said I must not be too friendly, only then I told her you were Lord Rotherham's ward, and so she will ask you to dine with us, and go to the Sydney Gardens tomorrow. Oh, Gerard, I do not know what to do!'

He squeezed her fingers. 'I have come to save you!'

She found nothing to smile at in this announcement, but threw him a look brimful of gratitude and admiration as they parted again, and waited hopefully to know how her rescue was to be accomplished.

She had to remain in suspense until the following evening; and when he was at last able to disclose his plans to her, she found them disappointing.

After dining in Beaufort Square, and taking immense pains to ingratiate himself with Mrs Floore, Gerard accompanied the ladies to the Sydney Gardens, where various entertainments, ranging from illuminations to dancing, were provided for Bath's visitors. Here, by great good fortune, a crony of Mrs Floore's was encountered, who had been staying at Lyme Regis for some weeks. The two ladies naturally had much gossip to exchange; and when they were fairly launched in intimate conversation, Gerard seized the opportunity to beg permission to take Emily to look at the waterfalls, which had all been illuminated for the occasion. 'I will take good care of her, ma'am!' he promised.

Mrs Floore nodded indulgently. She still thought him an agreeable youth, but he would have been affronted had he known how swiftly and how accurately she had summed him up. He was, in her estimation, a harmless boy, scarcely fledged as yet, but anxious to convince everyone that he was a buck of the first head. She had been much amused, at dinner, by the carelessness with which he related anecdotes of *ton*; and when, encouraged by a good-nature which he mistook for respect, he played off a few of the airs of an exquisite, her eyes twinkled appreciatively, and she decided that however much pride and sensibility the Marquis might have he could scarcely take exception to Emily's accepting the escort of so callow a young gentleman.

Since two or three thousand persons were in the Gardens, it was some little time before Gerard could find a vacant and sufficiently secluded nook to appropriate. All his mind was concentrated on this, but Emily, who possessed the faculty of living only in the immediate present, kept on stopping to exclaim at Merlin grottoes, or cascades, or festoons of coloured lanterns. However, he eventually discovered a discreet arbour, persuaded her to enter it, and to sit down upon the rustic bench there. Seating himself beside her, he clasped her mittened hand, and uttered: 'Tell me the whole!'

She was not articulate, and found this command hard to obey. Her account of her engagement was neither fluent nor coherent, but by dint of frequently interpolated questions he was able to piece the story together, if not entirely to understand the circumstances which had induced her to enter into an engagement with a man for whom she felt not a scrap of affection. He believed that her mother's tyranny accounted for all, and failed to perceive that the prospect of becoming a Marchioness had strongly attracted her. Nor had he the smallest suspicion that her sentiments towards himself had undergone a change.

She had been taken quite by surprise. She had had no notion that Rotherham had a decided preference for her, for although he had been her host at the Rotherham House ball, it had been Mrs Monksleigh whose name had figured on the invitation-card, and she had quite thought that he had had nothing to say in the matter.

'He never troubled himself at all, *that* you may be sure of!' said Gerard. 'I made Mama invite you!'

'Oh, did you? How *very* kind that was of you! I never enjoyed anything half as much, did you? It was a *magnificent* ball! I had no notion how grand Rotherham House is! So many handsome saloons, and *hundreds* of footmen, and that huge crystal chandelier in the ballroom, sparkling like diamonds, and your Mama standing at the head of the great staircase –'

'Yes, yes, I know!' Gerard said, a trifle impatiently. 'But Rotherham didn't even solicit you to dance, did he?'

'Oh, no! He only said how do you do to me, and of course I had no expectation of his asking me to stand up with him, with so many grand people there! In fact, until we – we became engaged, I never did dance with him, except that once, at Quenbury. We were for ever meeting, at parties, you know, and he was always very civil to me, and sometimes he paid me a compliment, only – only I don't know how it is, but when he says a thing that sounds pretty, he does so in a way that – well, in a way that makes one feel that he is being satirical!'

'You need not tell *me* that!' said Gerard, with a darkling look. 'When did he commence making up to you?'

'Oh, never! In fact, I had no notion he was disposed to like me, for whenever he talked to me it was in a quizzing way, which put me quite out of countenance. So you may imagine my astonishment when Mama told me had offered for me! Mama says he behaved with the greatest propriety, exactly as he ought.'

'Behaved with the greatest propriety?' echoed Gerard incredulously. '*Cousin Rotherham?* Why, he doesn't give a groat for such stuff! He always does just as he chooses, and doesn't care for ceremony, or for having distinguished manners, or for showing people proper observance, or any thing like that!'

'Oh, yes, Gerard, he does!' Emily said earnestly, raising her eyes to his face. 'He becomes dreadfully vexed if one does not behave just as he says one ought, or – or if one is shy, and does not know how to talk to people! He says very cutting things, d-doesn't he? If one angers him!'

'So he has treated you to his devilish ill-humour already, has he?' demanded Gerard, his eyes kindling. 'Pretty conduct towards his betrothed, upon my word! It is just as I thought! He does not love you! I believe he wishes to marry you only to spite me!'

She shook her head, turning away her face. 'No, no! He *does* love me, only – Oh, I don't want to be married to him!'

'Good God, you shall not be!' he said vehemently, seizing her hand, and kissing it. 'I cannot think how you could have consented! That he should have behaved to you in such a way – !'

'Oh, no! Not *then*!' she explained. 'How could I say I would not, when Mama had arranged it, and was so pleased with me? It is *very* wrong not to obey one's parents, and even Papa was pleased, too, for he said that after all I was not such a complete zero as he had thought. And Mama said I should learn to love

Lord Rotherham, and he would give me everything I could possibly desire, besides making me a great lady, with all those houses, and my own carriage, and a Marchioness's robes, if there should happen to be a Coronation, which, of course, there must be, mustn't there? Because the poor King –'

'But, Emily, all that is *nothing*!' protested Gerard. 'You would not sell yourself for a Marchioness's coronet!'

'No,' agreed Emily, rather doubtfully. 'I did think at first that perhaps – But that was when Lord Rotherham was behaving with propriety.'

Aghast, and quite thunderstruck, Gerard demanded: 'Do you mean to tell me that Rotherham – that Rotherham used you *improperly*? It is worse even than I guessed! Good God, I would never have believed –'

'No, no!' stammered Emily, blushing fierily, and hanging down her head. 'It was only that he is a man of strong passions! Mama explained it to me, and she said I must be flattered by – by the violence of his feelings. But – I don't like to be k-kissed so roughly, and that m-makes him angry, and – Oh, Gerard, I am *afraid* of him!'

'He is the greatest beast in nature!' Gerard said, his voice shaking with indignation. 'You must tell him at once that you cannot marry him!'

Her eyes widened in startled dismay. '*C-cry off?* I can't! M-mama would not allow me to!'

'Emily, dearest Emily, she cannot compel you to marry *anyone* against your will! You have only to be firm!'

Anything less firm than the appearance Emily presented as she listened to these brave words would have been hard to find. Her face was as pale as it had a moment earlier been red, her eyes charged with apprehension, and her whole frame trembling. Nothing that he could urge seemed to convince her that it would be possible to withstand the combined assault of her mother and Lord Rotherham. The very thought of being forced to confront two such formidable persons made her feel faint and sick. Moreover, the alternative to marriage, little though Gerard might think it, was almost worse, since it would carry with it no such alleviations as coronets and consequence. Mama had said that ladies who cried off from engagements were left to wear the willow all their days, and she was quite right, for only think of Lady Serena, so beautiful and clever, and still single! She would have to live at home, with Miss Prawle and the children, and be in disgrace, and see her sisters all married, and going to parties, and – oh no, impossible! Gerard did not understand!

But Gerard assured her that none of these ills would come to pass – or, at any rate, only for a short time. For Gerard had evolved a cunning scheme, and he rather fancied that when he had explained it to her his adored Emily would perceive that nothing could better have served their ends than her engagement to Rotherham and its rupture. 'For if you had not become engaged, dear love, your Mama would continue scheming to marry you to some man of rank and fortune, and I daresay she could never have been brought to listen to my suit. But when you have declared off with Rotherham, she will think it useless to persist, and she will very likely bring out Anne next season, and leave you in Gloucestershire.'

'Anne?' exclaimed Anne's elder sister indignantly. 'She will only be sixteen, and I could not *endure* it!'

'Yes, yes, only listen!' begged Gerard, alight with eagerness. 'I come of age in November of 1817 – very little more than a year from now! *Then* Rotherham will be obliged to put me in possession of my fortune – well, it is not precisely a *fortune*, but it brings me close on three hundred pounds a year, which is an independence, at least. I am not perfectly sure whether Rotherham would be obliged to pay it to me *now*, if I left Cambridge, because my father left it to me – well, to Cousin

Rotherham in trust for me, until I am twenty-one – so that it should provide for my schooling and maintenance. Only Rotherham gives it to me for my allowance, and chose to pay for my education himself. *I* did not ask him to, and, in fact, I would liefer he did not because to be under an obligation to him is of all things what I most dislike! I daresay he sent me to Eton just to get me into his power! However, never mind that! The thing is that I fear he can compel me to finish my time at Cambridge – and, you know, I do think perhaps I should, because I mean to embrace a political career, and to get my degree would be helpful, I expect. One of my particular friends is related to Lord Liverpool, and has interest with him, and he is very ready to oblige me. So you see that I have excellent prospects *besides* my poetry! Rotherham may not think that writing poetry is a gainful occupation, but only consider Lord Byron! Why, he must have made a fortune, Emily, and if he could do so, why should not I?'

Emily, a little dazed by all this eloquence, could think of no reason why he should not, and shook her head wonderingly.

'No! Well, we shall see!' said Gerard. 'I do not count upon it, mind, for public taste is so bad – But we needn't concern ourselves with that at this present! This is what we must do! *You* must cry off from this *wicked* engagement: that's certain! I will go up to Cambridge for my Third Year, and the instant I come down, which will be next June, I shall seek an introduction to Liverpool – there will be no difficulty about *that*! and establish myself in the way to a successful career. *Then*, in November, when I come of age, and your Mama has despaired of finding what *she* thinks an eligible husband for you – only, if you *should* receive an offer, you must be resolute in declining it, you know! – I shall offer for you again, and she will be only too thankful! What do you think of *that*, dearest?'

She did not tell him. She was a very softhearted girl, besides being almost wholly deficient in moral courage, and she shrank from giving him her opinion of a scheme which in no way recommended itself to her. She perceived that he entertained no doubts that her sentiments towards him were the same as they had been in the spring; and to break it to him that although she still liked him very well she had no desire to marry him seemed to her to be an impossible task. She sought refuge in evasions, talked of filial duty, and said that Lady Serena had told her that she was a goose to be afraid of Lord Rotherham.

'Lady Serena!' he ejaculated. 'Pray, why did *she* jilt him? I should very much like to ask her that same question!'

'Well, she is residing in Laura Place, with Lady Spenborough,' said Emily doubtfully, 'but do you think you ought? She might think it an impertinence. Besides, she told me herself that she cried off because she and Lord Rotherham didn't suit. They quarrelled so frequently that she became quite exhausted, but I can't think she was afraid of him! She is afraid of *nothing*!'

'Lady Serena in Bath?' said Gerard, in a tone of considerably less elation. 'Lord, I wish she were not!'

'Don't you like her?' asked Emily, shocked.

'Oh, yes! Well – yes, I like her well enough! I wish she may not tell Rotherham I am here, though! You know, for all she jilted him they are still wondrous great, and there's no telling what she might take it into her head to do, for I am sure she is very odd and unaccountable. On no account, Emily, must you divulge to her the attachment between us!'

'Oh, no!' she said, glad to be able to accede to one at least of his demands.

'If I should chance to meet her, I shall say that I came to Bath to visit a friend of mine. The only thing is, Cousin Rotherham forbade me to come here, so –'

'He forbade you?' she cried, cast into renewed dismay. 'You have not seen him, surely?'

'Certainly I have seen him!' he replied, throwing out his chest a little. 'When Lady Laleham refused to disclose your whereabouts –'

She interrupted with a tiny shriek. 'You have been to Cherrifield Place? Oh, Gerard, how *could* you? Whatever shall I do? If Mama knew –'

'Well, it can't be helped,' he said, rather sulkily. 'How else was I to find you? And if I leave Bath immediately – as soon as we are agreed upon what we should both do, I mean – very likely she won't think anything of my visit. If she does, I think you should tell her that you would not listen to my suit, and that will make all right.'

'Does Lord Rotherham know that you are here?' she asked anxiously.

'Well, I told him that I *should* come here, but ten to one he didn't believe I should dare to disobey him. Indeed, I know he did not! He is so set up in conceit of himself – But I fancy I have shown him that he cannot browbeat *me*! I'm not afraid of him! Though I should wish not to be in Bath, if he should take it into his head to visit you,' said Gerard, with perfect sincerity. 'I don't mean, of course, that I shouldn't prefer to face him *now*, man to man, but the thing is that it would very likely ruin all if I did,' he added, lapsing slightly.

Emily, both hands to her cheeks in a distracted gesture, paid very little heed to this. 'Oh, heavens, what shall I do? Oh, how could you, Gerard?'

'But I have *told* you what you must do!' he pointed out. 'You have only to be resolute in refusing to continue in the engagement, and, although it may be a trifle unpleasant at first, I daresay, there is nothing either your mama or Rotherham can do to compel you to yield, recollect! Of course, it would not do, if you were to disclose that you are betrothed to me. It is the shabbiest thing that I'm not of age! If I *were*, and Rotherham had no legal power over me, I need not tell you that I should remain at your side, and see to it you were not scolded or bullied! But it is only for a little time, dearest, and then we shall be married!'

But Emily, deriving no comfort from this prospect, merely begged him to take her back to her grandmother, and declared herself to be incapable of deciding, without reflection, upon any course of action. She was so much agitated that Gerard saw that it would be useless to press her for an immediate promise. He could perceive no flaw in his plan, but he knew that females were easily alarmed by anything unexpected, besides not being possessed of superior intellects capable of grappling in a flash with all the aspects of a problem. So he said soothingly that she must consider all he had said, and tell him the result of her lucubrations on the following day. Where should they meet?

Emily was at first inclined to think that they ought not to meet at all, but since he persisted in his determination, she said at last: 'Oh, dear! I'm sure I shan't – Oh, I don't know how it may be contrived, unless Grandmama will let me go to Meyler's Library, while she is in the Pump Room, which I frequently do, because it adjoins it, you know, and –'

'But we can't talk in a crowded library!' objected Gerard. 'I'll tell you what, Emily! You must pretend that you wish to change your book, but instead slip away to the Abbey! I shall be there, and it is only a very little way!'

Nineteen

Emily kept the appointment, but little was gained by the clandestine interview. She arrived at the Abbey doors in a flutter, because she had caught sight of one of Mrs Floore's acquaintances on the way, and could not be sure that she had not herself been seen. It was in vain that Gerard assured her that the sight of an unattended damsel traversing the short distance between the Pump Room and the Abbey would not shock the most prudish person: Emily could not be easy. He drew her into the Abbey, but, as might have been foreseen, this was found to be over-full of visitors, wandering about it, and looking at its beauties and antiquities. Even Gerard could not feel that he had chosen an ideal spot for the assignation; and as for Emily, she could lend him no more than half an ear, so much occupied was she in keeping a look-out for any more of Mrs Floore's friends. In any event, it was only too plain that she was still in a state of miserable indecision, and the end of it was that they parted with nothing settled but that they should meet again that evening at the theatre. Mr Goring was coming to Bath later in the day, and had invited Mrs Floore and Emily to go with him to the box he had procured. This was just the sort of evening's entertainment which exactly suited Mrs Floore, for not only did she enjoy any kind of spectacle, but the New Theatre being situated on the south side of Beaufort Square, she could go to it without being obliged to order out her carriage. When people marvelled at her choosing to live in Beaufort Square, she pointed this advantage out to them, adding that on such evenings as she was alone she was able to sit in the window of her drawing-room, and watch who was attending the theatre, and thus avoid being moped to death.

Emily acquiesced in Gerard's suggestion that he should obtain a seat in the house, but she showed no enthusiasm at the prospect of being again urged to make up her mind. It was an exercise to which she was not at all accustomed. However, Gerard was insistent, and she gave way, reflecting that it was unlikely that he would find an opportunity to be private with her.

She then sped back to the Pump Room, and Gerard, who had not journeyed into the west country prepared to make a prolonged stay, went off to purchase a shirt, and some additional neckcloths. It would have been too much to have said that his inamorata had disappointed him, but she had certainly disconcerted him. When he was himself behaving with what he considered to be amazing resolution, it was a little hard to find that the person for whom he had made his brilliant plan showed so Laodicean a spirit. Moreover, he had hoped to have left Bath by midday, and to be kept kicking his heels indefinitely in such a dangerous locality was not at all what he liked. At any moment, Rotherham, suspicious of his intentions, might take it into his head to come to Bath, just to make sure he was not there; and then, thought Gerard, where would they be?

It was as he emerged from a shop in Bond Street that he had the misfortune to encounter one of the perils which beset him. He heard himself hailed, in surprised accents, and looked round to see Lady Serena, escorted by a tall man of very upright bearing, waving to him. There was nothing for it but to cross the street towards her, summoning to his lips what he hoped was a delighted smile.

'Why, Gerard, how comes this about?' Serena said, giving him her hand. 'What brings you to Bath?'

'A friend – a college friend of mine, ma'am!' he replied. 'Has been begging me for ever to pay him a visit! He lives here, you see, with his family. At least, not here, but just beyond the town!'

'Indeed! Do you mean to make a long stay?' she asked kindly.

'No, oh, no! In fact, I am going back to London tomorrow.' He then thought that she must wonder at his having come over a hundred miles only to spend a couple of days with his friends, and at once created another friend, living in Wiltshire, with whom he said he had been staying for several weeks.

Serena, taking only a casual interest in this, introduced him to Major Kirkby. They all three walked on to the end of the street, where Gerard took his leave, saying that he was pledged to meet his host in Westgate Street. He then walked quickly away down Parsonage Lane, and the Major and Serena, turning to the left, strolled along in the direction of Bridge Street.

'And who is that young fribble?' enquired the Major.

She laughed. 'Rotherham's eldest ward. He is guardian to all his cousin's children, and a very bad guardian, too! He takes not the least interest in them, and *this* boy he holds in contempt, and is often, I think, very unkind to him. For there is no harm in Gerard, even if, in his efforts to be taken for a Bond Street beau, he does contrive to look very like a counter-coxcomb. I can see you thought him one!'

'Oh, no!' said the Major. 'I have seen too many boys of his age trying to come the dandy! Most of them outgrow it quite speedily. He wasn't at all glad to meet you, was he?'

'Did you think he was not?' she said. 'He's very shy, you know. I daresay you overawed him with your height and your grave countenance!'

'My grave countenance!' he repeated, a tinge of red creeping into it. 'Is it so grave?'

'It has been grave since you returned to Bath,' she told him. 'Did you find something amiss at home?'

'Not exactly amiss – some tiresome business, too long neglected! My mother is rather unwell!' said the Major, snatching at this excuse, and thankful for the first time in his life that his parent's chief diversion was to detect in herself unmistakable symptoms of some deep-seated disorder.

'I am so sorry!' Serena said, with quick sympathy. 'I hope no serious illness?'

'No, I believe – that is, I trust not! The doctor was to visit her this morning.'

'I shouldn't wonder at it if Bath is to blame. It was tolerable in the spring, but I know of no more enervating town to be in during the summer. It does not agree with Fanny, I know. Have you noticed how hagged she is looking? She says this heavy, windless weather we've endured now for a week makes her feel stuffed to death. I know exactly what she means, don't you? I am conscious of it myself. Everything seems to be an abominable fag, and one becomes languid in spirit, and rather cross. That is to say, I become rather cross! Fanny was never cross in her life.'

'Cross you may be, but not languid in spirit!' he said, smiling.

'Hipped, then, and on the fidgets!' She glanced up at him as she spoke, and saw that he was regarding her with a little trouble in his eyes. She slid her hand in his arm, and said, in her funning voice: 'You may take that as a compliment, if you please! Five days you were away! The only marvel is that I did not fall into a lethargy. I daresay I must have done so, had I not been occupied in thinking how shabbily I was used, and how best I should punish you!'

'Did you miss me?' he asked.

'Very much: it was a dreadful bore! I hope you missed me: it would be too bad if I were the only sufferer!'

He responded in kind; and spent the rest of the walk to Laura Place in telling her of the alterations to his house he meant to put in hand. He parted from her on her doorstep. She invited him to come in, and to partake of a nuncheon, but although he longed to see Fanny he knew that he must see her as seldom as possible, and he declined, saying that he had promised his mother to come home within the hour.

'I won't press you, then. Pray, give my love to Mrs Kirkby, and tell her how sorry I am to hear that she is out of sorts!'

'Thank you, I will. Do we ride tomorrow, Serena?'

'Yes, indeed! Will you – Oh, confound it! Is not tomorrow Wednesday? Then I cannot. I promised I would ride with Emily to Farley Castle. Drive with me instead, later in the day!'

'Willingly! At what time?'

'A little before three o'clock? That is, if Mrs Kirkby will spare you to me.'

'Of course she will. I shall be here!' he promised.

She went into the house, and up the stairs to the drawing room, where Fanny was seated, with her embroidery frame in front of her. She looked up, and smiled, as Serena came in, but her eyes were heavy, and her cheeks rather wan. Serena said quickly: 'Fanny, have you the headache again?'

'It's nothing! Only a very little headache. I shall lie down presently, and soon be quite cured of it.'

Serena stood looking down at her in some concern. 'You look worn to a bone! Tell me, my dear, wouldn't you like to go away from Bath? I don't know how anyone can escape being invalidish here, it is so oppressive! Shall we go back to the Dower House?'

'No, no!' Fanny said. 'Indeed, I'm not ill, dearest! I daresay if the sun would but shine I should be in a capital way again. I don't know how it is, but these hot, dull days always give me the headache.'

'We only hired this house until the end of August,' persisted Serena. 'Why not leave it now? Do you say no because you think I don't wish to leave Hector? Tell me truthfully, Fanny! I'll go with you tomorrow, if you would like it.'

'Dear, dear Serena!' Fanny said, catching Serena's hand, and nursing it to her cheek. 'So good to me! so *very* good to me!'

'Now, what in the world is this?' Serena rallied her. 'I begin to think that you must be more sickly than I had guessed! I warn you, if you talk to me of my *goodness* – and in such a melancholy voice! – I shall send for a doctor. Or shall it be the Dower House?'

'It shall be neither,' Fanny said, with determined cheerfulness. 'I don't at all wish to leave Bath before I must. Don't let us prose about my health! Next you will be telling me I look hagged and *ridée*! Did you hear any news in the town?'

'No news, but I saw a new face: Gerard Monksleigh's! I wish you might have seen him! Very much the Pink of the *Ton*, with shirt-points serving as blinkers, and a very dashing waistcoat!'

'Good gracious, I wonder what brings him here? Is Mrs Monksleigh here too?'

'No, he said he was staying with friends in the neighbourhood. Hector thought he wasn't pleased to see me, but *my* guess is that –' She broke off suddenly, and a laugh sprang to her eyes. 'Oh, I wonder if Hector was right after all? Fanny, do you recall my aunt's writing to me once that Gerard had been very much smitten with Emily? Can it be that the foolish boy has come here to dangle after her?'

'He would be a more suitable match for her than Lord Rotherham,' said Fanny.

'He would be the worst possible match for her, my dear, for, setting aside the fact that he has no fortune, he is very

nearly as silly as she is, and has not yet outgrown the schoolboy. However, it is not all likely that he will be a danger to Ivo, even if he has come to Bath in a love-lorn state. I notice that Emily's flirtations are always with men a good deal older than herself: her youthful admirers she considers stupid. It won't do, of course, if Gerard makes a cake of himself by enacting the disappointed lover for the entertainment of the Bath quizzes. I do wonder whether he was telling me a whisker when he said he was visiting friends, or whether he is lurking somewhere in Bath. It will be well, perhaps, if I drop a hint to Emily not to encourage him to dangle after her. She is riding to Farley Castle with me tomorrow.'

She spoke lightly, unaware of the fact that all recollection of this engagement had been banished from Emily's mind. The four o'clock mail had brought her shocking tidings. Lady Laleham and Lord Rotherham were coming to Bath.

Lady Laleham was so obliging as to disclose the day of her arrival; Lord Rotherham, more alarmingly still, wrote at the end of a brief letter which all too clearly showed impatience, gathering wrath, and a determination to claim his reluctant bride, merely that he proposed to come to Bath immediately, and expected to find Emily not only ready to receive him, but prepared to come to a point. He made no mention of Mr Monksleigh; Lady Laleham, on the other hand, telling her daughter of Gerard's abortive call at Cherrifield Place, warned her that if, by some chance, he had succeeded in discovering her direction, and was even now in Bath, he must be sent instantly to the rightabout. If Lord Rotherham were to find out that although he had been refused permission to visit his betrothed Mr Monksleigh (who appeared to think himself a rival) was making up to her, he would be very (heavily underscored) and justifiably angry. So, too, would be Emily's affectionate Mama.

The combined effect of these two missives was to throw

Emily into a fever of apprehension. Converging upon her, each filled with rage and determination, were two dread figures, one of whom would certainly arrive on the following afternoon, the other perhaps even sooner. Between them she would inevitably be crushed. She saw herself being dragged by her mother to the altar, and there delivered into the power of one who by this time figured in her distorted imagination as a merciless ogre. That her grandmother might intervene to save her from this hideous fate never occurred to her, partly because Mrs Floore, not unnaturally, had refrained from expressing to her her opinion of her only daughter; and partly because it was incredible to Emily that her vulgar, good-natured grandmama could exercise the smallest influence over the far more formidable Lady Laleham. Her only hope of support seemed to lie in Mr Monksleigh's slender person. Terrifying under any circumstances though the approaching ordeal must be, she felt that if he would only remain at her side to protect her there might be a very faint chance of her surviving it. Or he might be able to think of a way of escape. It was true that the only plan he had so far evolved would not serve the purpose at all, since it depended for its success on the resolution she was well aware that she lacked; but when he learned of the imminent peril in which she stood he might, perhaps, be inspired with further schemes.

Her hope was not misplaced. After looking round the theatre, and perceiving, with a start of surprise, that Mrs Floore was in one of the boxes, Gerard hurried upstairs in the first interval, encountering Mr Goring's party on their way to the foyer. He received a friendly greeting from Mrs Floore, a slight bow from Mr Goring, and from Emily a look so full of meaning that he at once realized that something of an appalling nature must have happened since the morning. Mr Goring being occupied in guiding Mrs Floore to a seat against the wall, it was an easy matter for Gerard to whisk Emily to the other end of the foyer, where in an urgent undervoice she told him of the letters she had received, and besought his counsel and support.

He showed no tendency to minimize the danger. Indeed, he was more inclined to magnify it. The intelligence that his guardian was coming, like Nemesis, to Bath, transfixed him with dismay, and set his wits working faster than ever before in his life. Emily's timid suggestion that he should come to Beaufort Square to confront Rotherham at her side, he dismissed hastily, saying with great vehemence: 'Useless!'

Emily wrung her hands. 'They will make me do just as they say, then! I can't – I *can't* tell them I w-won't, Gerard! Oh, do you think Mama and Lady Serena may be right, and it won't be so very dreadful to be married to Lord Rotherham?'

'No,' said Gerard positively. 'It would be far worse than you dream of! I tell you this, Emily, Rotherham is a tyrant! He will make you wholly subservient to his will. I have cause to know! *You* cannot yet have seen him in one of his rages, my poor darling! They are quite ungoverned! His servants are all terrified of him, and with good cause!' He saw that her face was perfectly white, and pressed home his advantage. 'You must not meet him! All will be lost, if you come within reach of that – that ruthless despotism! Emily, we must elope!'

It was not to be expected that she would instantly perceive the advantages of this course. She was, in fact, shocked by such a suggestion, but by the time Gerard had regaled her with an account of his own sufferings at Rotherham's hands, and some liberal prophecies of the horrors in store for her; and had declared himself to be incapable of imagining the extent or effects of the Marquis's wrath, when he discovered – as discover he would – what had been going on in Bath, she was ready to consent to any measure that would rescue her from her Andromeda-like plight. People were beginning to leave the foyer; Gerard had only time, before Mrs Floore bore down upon them, to warn her not to breathe a word to her, but to meet him in Queen's Square at ten o'clock on the following morning. 'Leave everything to me!' he ordered. 'Once in my care you are safe!'

These somewhat grandiloquent words were music to her ears. Naturally dependent, she was only too thankful to be able to cast her cares on to his shoulders; and now that he had ceased to counsel her to face her tyrants with resolution she began to think that she might like him very well as a husband. At least he was kind, and gentle, and loved her very much; and although he was not her ideal she supposed that they might live very contentedly together.

Her mind relieved of its paramount dread, she was able to listen to the rest of the play with tolerable enjoyment, but she did not recover her vivacity, her attitude being languid and listless enough to make Mrs Floore say, as soon as Mr Goring had escorted them home: 'Now, Emma-love, you just tell Grandma what's the matter, and no nonsense! If you're looking like a drowned mouse all because your ma is coming to stay with me tomorrow, you're a goosecap! Now, ain't you?'

'I-I am afraid Mama means to take me away from you, Grandmama!' faltered Emily.

'Bless your sweet heart!' exclaimed Mrs Floore, planting a smacking kiss upon her cheek. 'So you don't want to leave your grandma! Well, I don't deny I love to hear you say so, my pet, but there's reason in all things, and I can't say that I'm surprised your ma's got to be a trifle impatient. I'll be bound she's got her head full of your bride-clothes by this time – and so will you have before you are very much older! Lord, how I do look forward to reading all about you when you're a Marchioness! You think about what's before you, pet, and never mind about your old grandma!'

This bracing speech, excellent in intention though it was, shut the door on confidence. Grandmama, as much as Mama, wished to see Emily a Marchioness. Emily kissed her, and went upstairs to bed, planning her escape on the morrow, praying that it might not be frustrated by the arrival of her betrothed, and wondering where Gerard meant to take her.

Twenty

Serena, arriving in Beaufort Square at eleven o'clock on the following morning, mounted on her good-looking mare, and attended by her groom, was a little surprised not to see a livery horse waiting outside Mrs Floore's house. Fully alive to the honour of being invited to ride with so noted a horsewoman, Emily had formed the practice, on these occasions, of ordering her hired hack to be brought round quite twenty minutes too soon, and of running out of the house, the instant she saw, from her look-out in the dining-room window, that neat figure rounding the corner of the square.

'You had better knock on the door, Fobbing,' Serena said, holding out her hand for his bridle.

He gave it to her, but before he had reached the front door, it opened, and Mr Goring stepped out. He came up to the mare, and, looking gravely into the beautiful face above him, said: 'Lady Serena, Mrs Floore desires me to ask you if you will be so good as to come into the house for a moment.'

Her brows rose swiftly. 'I will do so, certainly. Is anything amiss?'

'I am afraid very much amiss,' he replied, in a heavy tone. He held up his hand. 'May I assist you to –'

'No, I thank you.' One deft, practised movement, and her

voluminous skirt was clear of the pommels. The next instant she was on the ground, and giving her bridle into Fobbing's hand. She caught up her skirt, swinging it over her arm, and went with Mr Goring into the house. 'Is Emily ill?' she asked.

'No, not ill. It will be better, I daresay, if you learn from Mrs Floore what has occurred. I myself arrived here only a short time ago, and – But I will take you up to Mrs Floore! I should warn you that you will find her in considerable distress, Lady Serena.'

'Good God, what can have happened?' she exclaimed, hurrying towards the stairs, her whip still in her hand.

He followed close on her booted heels, and on the first floor slid in front of her, to open the door into the drawing-room. Serena went in, with her free stride, but checked in astonished dismay at the spectacle that met her eyes. The redoubtable Mrs Floore, still attired in her dressing-gown, was lying back in a deep wing-chair, her housekeeper holding burnt feathers to her nose, and her maid kneeling before her and chafing her hands.

'My dear ma'am – ! For heaven's sake, what dreadful accident has befallen?' Serena demanded.

The housekeeper, shedding tears, sobbed: 'It's her poor heart, my lady! The shock gave her such palpitations as was like to have carried her off! Years ago, the doctor told me she should take care, and now see what's come of it! Oh, my lady, what a serpent's tooth she has nourished in her bosom!'

The maid, much moved, began to sob in sympathy. Mrs Floore, whose usually rubicund countenance Serena saw to have assumed an alarmingly gray tinge, opened her eyes, and said faintly: 'Oh, my dear! What shall I do? Why didn't she *tell* me? Oh, what a silly, blind fool I have been! I thought – What am I to do?'

Serena, casting her whip on to the table, and stripping off her elegant gauntlets, said, in her authoritative way: 'You shall remain perfectly quiet, dear ma'am, until you are a little restored.

Get up off the floor, woman, and fetch some hartshorn, or a cordial, to your mistress immediately! And take those feathers away, you idiot! Mr Goring, be so good as to help me move her on to the sofa!'

He was very willing, but a little doubtful, and said in a low voice: 'I had better call up the butler: she is too heavy for you, ma'am!'

Serena, who had quickly arranged some cushions at the head of the sofa, merely replied briefly: 'Take her shoulders, and do not talk nonsense!'

Once disposed at full length on the sofa, Mrs Floore moaned, but soon began to look less gray. She tried to speak, but Serena hushed her, saying: 'Presently, ma'am!' When the maid came back, bearing a glass containing a dose of some cordial in her trembling hand, Serena took it from her, and, raising the sufferer's head, obliged her to swallow it. In a very short space of time the colour began to come back into Mrs Floore's cheeks, and her breathing became more regular. The housekeeper, bereft of her evil-smelling feathers, waved a vinaigrette about under her nose, and her maid, still much affected, fanned her with a copy of the *Morning Post.*

Serena moved away to the window, where Mr Goring was standing. 'The less she tries to talk the better it will be for her,' she said, in an undervoice. 'Now, tell me, if you please, what has happened to overset her like this?'

'Emily – Miss Laleham I should say, has left the house,' he responded, still in that heavy tone. He saw that she was staring at him with knit brows, and added: 'She has run away, ma'am. Leaving behind her a letter for her grandmother.'

'Good heavens! Where is it?'

'Give it to her, Ned!' commanded Mrs Floore, struggling to sit up. 'Drat you, Stoke, don't keep pushing me back! Give me those smelling-salts, and go away, do! I don't need you any more,

nor you neither, Betsey, crying all over me! No, don't you go, Ned! If there's anything to be done, there's no one else to do it for me, for I can't go careering all over the country – not that it would do a mite of good if I could, for who's to say where she's gone to? Oh, Emma, why ever didn't you tell your grandma?'

Mr Goring had picked up a sheet of paper from the table, and had in silence handed it to Serena.

Dearest Grandmama, it began, in Emily's unformed writing, *I am so very sorry and I do not like to grieve you but I cannot bear it and I cannot marry Lord R. in spite of coronets, because he frightens me, and I did not tell you but he has written me a dreadful letter and is coming here and he and Mama will make me do just what they want, and indeed I cannot bear it, though I hate excessively to leave you without saying goodbye. Pray do not be angry with me, my dear, dearest Grandmama. Your loving Emma. P.S. Pray, pray do not tell Mama or Lord R. where I have gone.*

'You would certainly be in a puzzle to do so!' said Serena, reaching the postscript. 'Of all the bird-witted little idiots – ! My dear ma'am, I beg your pardon, but she deserves to be slapped for such folly! What the *devil* does she mean by writing such stuff? Rotherham write her a "dreadful letter"? What nonsense! If he has grown impatient, it is not to be wondered at, but to write of him as though he were an ogre is quite abominable!'

'But she is afraid of him, Lady Serena,' said Mr Goring.

'I ought to have known it was Sukey's doing!' said Mrs Floore, in an agony of remorse. 'Right at the start, didn't I suspect it? Only then Emma wrote me such a letter, so happy it seemed to me, that I thought – Poor little lamb, if I'd only had the sense to tell her what I think of Sukey, which I never did, not thinking it seemly, she wouldn't have been afraid to tell me! And now there's Sukey coming here this very day, and how to face her I don't know, for there's no denying I haven't taken proper care of Emma. Not that I care a fig for Sukey, and so I shall tell her! And as for this precious Marquis, let him dare show his face here! Let him dare, that's all I ask! Scaring the dear little soul out of her senses, which nobody can tell me he hasn't done, because I know better! And last night – Oh, Ned, I thought she was moped because she didn't want Sukey to take her away from me, and all I did was to tell her to think about her bride-clothes, so I daresay she took it into her head I was as set on this nasty marriage as her ma! And now what am I to do? When I think of my little Emma, running off all alone, to hide herself heaven knows where –'

'You may be certain of one thing at least, ma'am!' interrupted Serena. 'She has not run away alone!'

Mr Goring directed a steady look at her. 'Is there an attachment between her and young Monksleigh, ma'am?'

She shrugged. 'On her side, I should very much doubt it; on his, evidently! I shall be sorry for him if it ever comes to Rotherham's ears that he persuaded Emily into this escapade! It is the most disgraceful thing to have done, and if he comes off with a whole skin he may think himself fortunate! Mrs Floore, pray don't cry! The matter is not past mending, I assure you. I collect that Gerard came to Bath to see Emily, not to stay with friends: has he been to this house? Had you no suspicion of what was in the wind?'

'No, my dear, because Emma said he was the Marquis's ward, which made it seem right to me, and besides which I thought he was such a twiddle-poop there wasn't the least harm in letting him go with us to the Gala night, which I did.'

Serena smiled, but said: 'Depend upon it, this dramatic flight was his notion, not Emily's, ma'am! What is more, I would wager my pearls all this nonsense about Rotherham was put into her silly head by him! But let us not waste time in discussing that! What we have to do is to get her back. Mr Goring, I shall need your help!'

'I shall be happy to do everything in my power, Lady Serena, to restore Miss Laleham to Mrs Floore, but I will have no hand in forcing her into marriage with a man whom she fears,' he replied bluntly.

'Let me see anyone dare!' said Mrs Floore. 'Only fetch her back to me, and trust me to send this Marquis to the rightabout, and Sukey too!'

'There is no question of forcing her to marry Rotherham,' said Serena. 'When she meets him again, I fancy she will discover that the extremely unamiable portrait she has painted of him is wide of the mark. Is it known when she left the house?'

'No, because no one saw her go, only she wasn't gone before ten o'clock, that Betsey swears to, for she heard her moving about in her bedroom when she passed the door. And she ate a bite of bread and butter, and drank a cup of coffee, before she went, and Stoke says the tray was taken up to her at a quarter to ten, just as usual. For I don't get up to breakfast myself, so Emma has hers in bed too.'

'Come, this is much better!' said Serena. 'I feared she might have left overnight, in which case we should have had something to do indeed. Mr Goring, have you met Gerard Monksleigh?'

'I met him at the theatre last night, ma'am.'

'Then you will be able to describe him,' said Serena briskly. 'We may be sure of this: they are not lurking in Bath! I do Gerard the justice to think that he means to marry Emily though how he imagines he may do so, when each of them is under age, is more than I can tell! It would be in keeping with all the rest if he is bearing her off to Gretna Green, but where he found the money for such a journey is again more than I can tell! He may, of course, be taking her to London, with some hopeful notion of procuring a special licence there.'

'Oh, my dear, supposing he has it in his pocket already?' exclaimed Mrs Floore. 'Supposing he went to Wells, or Bristol, and has married her? Oh, I don't want her to go throwing herself away on that young fellow!'

'Don't distress yourself, ma'am! He would find it difficult to induce anyone to believe he is of age.'

'Lady Serena is right, ma'am,' interpolated Mr Goring. 'He would be required to bring proof of his age, for he looks a stripling. What do you wish me to do, Lady Serena?'

'To visit the posting-houses here, of course. I imagine you must know them well. Discover if Gerard hired a chaise, and where it was to take him. Did you ride here from Bristol? Is your horse in Bath?'

'I drove here, ma'am, in my curricle. If I should be able to discover the road they took, I can have the horses put to in a trice,' he replied. 'I'll set out immediately.'

'Ned Goring, I'll go all the way to Land's End for Emma, but I'll do it decently!' declared Mrs Floore. 'Don't you think to hoist me into any nasty, open carriage! A chaise-and-four, that's what you'll hire!'

'My dear ma'am, you are going to remain quietly here,' said Serena. 'It would be quite unfit for you to be rocked and jolted for heaven knows how many hours! Moreover, if this exploit is to be kept secret, it is most necessary that you should be here. If Rotherham is indeed on his way to Bath, he will have to be fobbed off, you know. Whatever be the issue between him and Emily, you cannot wish him to know how scandalously she is behaving – or Lady Laleham either, for that matter! You must tell them both that Emily has gone with a party on an expedition of pleasure. And as for your curricle, Mr Goring, leave it where it is! We shall catch our runaways very much more speedily if we ride, and we shan't advertise to every pike-keeper, and every chance traveller, that we are racing in pursuit of someone. That is a thing we should do our best to avoid.'

He stared at her. 'You do not mean to go, ma'am!'

'Of course I mean to go!' she replied impatiently. 'How in the world do you think you could manage without me? You are quite unrelated to Emily; you cannot compel her to return with you! All that would happen, I dare swear, is that you and Gerard would be fighting it out, with the post-boys as seconds, and then there *would* be the devil to pay!'

He was too much surprised to hear such an expression on her lips to smile at the absurdity of the picture she conjured up. 'But you will not ride, ma'am? You cannot have considered! They must be many miles ahead of us already! It would not do for you: you would be fatigued to death!'

'Mr Goring, have you ever hunted with the Cottesmore?' she demanded.

'No, ma'am, I have not, but –'

'Well, I have done so every year!' she said. 'There is no country like it for long and fast runs. It is said to be the wildest and the roughest of the Shires, you know. So don't waste solicitude on me, I beg of you! My mare was bred to stay, and she's as fresh as she can stare. The only difficulty will be *your* mount.'

His sense of decorum, which was strong, was shocked by the thought of a lady's setting out, quite unchaperoned, on a chase that might lead her many miles from Bath, but he attempted no further remonstrance. He was conscious of the same sensation which had more than once assailed Major Kirkby, of being swept along irresistibly by an impetuous, vigorous will, against which it was impossible to fight. It was plain to him that the Lady Serena was going to assume the control of the chase. He wondered whether she had considered the possibility of finding herself, at nightfall, out of reach of her home, unprovided with so much as a hairbrush, and escorted by a single gentleman, but he did not venture to put

the question to her. He said instead: 'I know where I may procure a good horse, Lady Serena.'

'Excellent! Then will you go now, and see what you can discover? Inform my groom, if you please, that my plans have been altered. I am going with Miss Laleham to join a picnic party, and since we do not set out immediately he must walk the mare a little, till I am ready for her.'

'You will not take him with you?' he suggested tentatively.

'No, certainly not: he would be a confounded nuisance, for ever trying to persuade me to turn back! I had rather have your escort, Mr Goring!' she replied, with the flash of a smile.

He stammered that he would be honoured to serve her, and went away to obey her various commands.

Mrs Floore, who had been sitting limply on the sofa, listening to this exchange, a gleam of hope in her eyes, but the lines on her face deeply carven all at once, said, with an effort: 'I ought not to let you go, my lady. I know I ought not. Whatever will Lady Spenborough say to me?'

Serena laughed. 'Why, nothing, ma'am! I am going to write to her, and Fobbing shall take the letter to her. I must tell her what has taken me away, I am afraid, but you may rest assured the story is safe with her. May I write at your desk?'

'Oh, yes, my lady!' Mrs Floore answered mechanically. She sat plucking restlessly at a fold of her dressing-gown, and suddenly demanded: 'What did he do to her? Why did he scare her out of her senses? Why did he want to offer for her, if he didn't love her?'

'Exactly!' said Serena dryly. 'An unanswerable question, is it not? I believe the truth is, ma'am, that he is more in love with her than she can as yet understand. She is very young – quite childish, in fact! – and not, I think, of a passionate disposition. It is otherwise with him, and that, unless I much mistake the matter, is what alarmed her. What can she have known of love, after all? A few discreet flirtations, the homage of a boy like Gerard, protestations, compliments, respectful hand kissings! She would not get such tepid stuff from Rotherham! No doubt her shrinking provoked him! I can believe that he let her see that he is not a man to be trifled with, but as for giving her cause to fly from him, in this outrageous fashion, stuff and nonsense! Of course he should have guessed that it would be necessary to handle her at first with the greatest gentleness! It is unfortunate that he did not, but we may suppose that he has learnt his lesson. He has been careful to keep away from her: another mistake, but from what she has told me I collect he has allowed himself to be ruled in this by Lady Laleham. He would have done better to have visited Emily long since. She would not then have built up this ridiculous picture of him! However, if he is indeed coming here, he will very soon set matters to rights. He has only to show her tenderness, and she will wonder how she came to be such a goose.'

'There's a great deal in what you say, my dear,' agreed Mrs Floore. 'But it's as plain as a pikestaff she don't love him!'

'She loves no one else,' Serena replied. 'It is not unusual, ma'am, for a bride to start with no more than liking.'

'Well, it don't appear she likes him either!' said Mrs Floore, reviving a little. 'What's more, my dear, those ways may do very well for *tonnish* people, but they don't do for me! If Emma don't love him, she shan't marry him!'

Serena looked up from the letter she was writing. 'It would not be well for her to cry off, ma'am, believe me!'

'*You* did so!' Mrs Floore pointed out.

'Yes, I did,' agreed Serena, dipping the pen in the standish again.

Mrs Floore digested this. 'Sukey and her dratted ambition!' she said, suddenly and bitterly. 'You needn't tell me, my dear! *I* know the world! *You* could cry off, and no one to say more than that you were rid of a bad bargain; but if Emma did it, there'd

be plenty to say that, if the truth was known, it was him, and not her, that really did the crying off!'

'I did not say it was well for me either, ma'am,' Serena replied quietly.

Mrs Floore heaved a large sigh. 'I don't know what to do for the best, and that's a fact! If you're right, my lady, and Emma finds she likes him after all, I wouldn't want to spoil her chances, because there's no doubt she has got a fancy to be a Marchioness. At the same time – Well, one thing is certain, and that's that I'm not letting the Marquis into the house until I have Emma safe and sound here again! The servants shall tell him she's gone off for a picnic, and very likely won't be home till late – Oh, lor', whatever's to be done if you and Ned don't find them today? If they go putting up at a posting-house for the night, it'll be no use finding them at all!'

'If I know Gerard,' retorted Serena, 'he will insist on driving through the night, ma'am! He will wish to put as much ground as possible between himself and Rotherham – and with good reason! But if Mr Goring can discover the road they took, I have no doubt we shall catch them long before nightfall.'

Mr Goring returned to Beaufort Square just before twelve o'clock, and came running up the stairs, with a look of triumph on his face. Serena said, as soon as he entered the drawing-room: 'You have found out where they went! My compliments, Mr Goring! You have been very much quicker than I had dared to hope.'

'It was just a piece of good luck,' he said, colouring. 'I might as well have gone to half a dozen houses before hitting upon the right one. As it chanced, I got certain news at the second one I visited. There seems to be no doubt that it was Monksleigh who hired a post-chaise early this morning, and ordered it to be in Queen's Square at ten o'clock. A yellow-bodied chaise, drawn by a single pair of horses.'

'Well, I must say!' exclaimed Mrs Floore indignantly. 'If he had to make off with poor little Emma, he might have done it stylishly! One pair of horses only! I call it downright shabby!'

'I fancy Master Gerard is none too plump in the pocket, ma'am,' said Serena, amused.

'Then he's got no business to elope with my granddaughter!' said Mrs Floore.

'Very true! Where are they off to, Mr Goring?'

'The chaise was booked to Wolverhampton, ma'am, which makes it seem as though your guess was correct.'

'*Wolverhampton?*' demanded Mrs Floore. 'Why, that's where all the locks and keys come from! Very good they are, too, but what maggot's got into the boy's head to take Emma there? It's all of a piece! Whoever heard of going to a manufacturing town for a wedding trip?'

'No, no, ma'am, I don't think you need fear that!' Serena said, laughing. 'It's as I told you: Gerard is husbanding his resources! Depend upon it, they mean to go on by stagecoach, or perhaps mail, to the Border. Never mind!' she added soothingly, seeing signs of gathering wrath in Mrs Floore's countenance. 'They are not going to reach Wolverhampton, or any place near it, ma'am.'

Mr Goring, who had spread open a map upon the table, said: 'I bought this, for although I know the country here-abouts pretty well, if we are obliged to ride much beyond Gloucester I might find myself at a loss.'

'Very well done of you!' Serena approved, going to his side, and leaning one hand on the table, while she studied the map. 'They will have taken the Bristol pike road, though it's longer. We came into Bath from Milverley by way of Nailsworth, but the road is very bad: brings the horses down to a walk in places. How far is it to Bristol?'

'Twelve and a half miles. They should have reached it in an

hour. Bristol to Gloucester is about thirty-four miles: a good pike-road. They must change horses ten miles out of Bristol, at the Ship Inn, or go on to Falfield, fifteen miles out.'

'They won't do that, travelling with one pair.'

'No. The next change, then, will be at the Cambridge Inn, here, about a mile short of the Church End turnpike, and ten miles from Gloucester. If we knew when they set out from Bath – !'

'We have a fair notion. Gerard ordered the chaise to be in Queen's Square at ten, and at ten Emily was still in her bedroom which one can't but feel is precisely what would happen in such an absurd adventure as this. When did you know that she was missing, ma'am?'

Mrs Floore shook her head helplessly, but Mr Goring, thinking the matter over, said: 'I arrived here about a quarter of an hour before you rode up, Lady Serena, and it had been known then for several minutes, I think.'

'Then we may take it that they started between – ten or fifteen minutes after ten, and half past ten. My dear sir, we are only an hour and a half behind them! What I wish to do is to overtake them before they reach Gloucester. We can't but run true on the line up to that point, but once in Gloucester we might be obliged to make several casts. We will take the Nailsworth road as far as Badminton, and the ride cross-country to Dursley – a nice point, that! – and join the Bristol–Gloucester Road *here*!'

He nodded. 'Ay, the road comes out at the Cambridge Inn.'

'Where the scent should be hot!' she said, her eyes dancing. 'Come, let's be off!'

'I am ready, but – it will be a twenty-five mile ride, Lady Serena! Do you think –'

'Oh, the mare will do it!' she said cheerfully, pulling on her gauntlets. 'All we have to do now is to get rid of Fobbing! The worst of a groom who ran beside one on one's first pony is that he can't be ordered off without explanation. I'll tell him our picnic party doesn't assemble until half past twelve, but that I want my letter carried to Lady Spenborough at once, in case she should be uneasy. Mrs Floore, you will have Emma under your wing again before nightfall, I promise you! Pray don't tease yourself any more!'

Mr Goring opened the door, and held it for her, but before he followed her out of the room, he looked at Mrs Floore and said: 'I'll do my best to bring her back, ma'am, but – don't let them push her into marriage with Lord Rotherham!'

'You may depend upon it I won't!' said Mrs Floore grimly.

'She isn't old enough to marry anyone yet!' he said, and hesitated, as though he would have said more. Then he seemed to think better of it, bade Mrs Floore a curt goodbye, and departed in Serena's wake.

Twenty-one

THE START TO THE ELOPEMENT WAS NOT ALTOGETHER auspicious, for the bride was tardy, and the groom harassed. What had seemed to Gerard, after watching the first act of a romantic drama, a splendid scheme, he found, upon more sober reflection, to present several disagreeable aspects to his view. For one thing, he had no idea whether the marriage of two minors was any more legal in Scotland than in England, or whether it would be possible for it to be set aside. He told himself that once the knot was tied neither Rotherham nor his mother would choose to cause a scandal by intervening; and tried to think no more of the possibility. Instead, he reckoned up his resources, made a vague guess at the distance to be travelled, totted up post-charges, and, at the end of all these calculations, decided to sell his watch. Elopements to Gretna Green, he realized bitterly, were luxuries to be afforded only by men of substance, for not merely was one obliged to journey over three hundred miles to reach the Border: one was obliged to come all the way back again. This reflection brought another difficulty before him: how, if his pockets were to let, was he to support a wife during the month that must elapse before he received the following quarter's allowance? The only solution that presented itself to him was that he should convey Emily to his mother's house, and he could not but see that, fond parent though she was, his mother might not accord his clandestine bride a very warm welcome. And if Rotherham (out of revenge) insisted on his spending another year at Cambridge, Emily would have to remain under his mother's roof until he came down for good, and it was just possible that she might not like such an arrangement. He wondered if he could install her in rooms in Cambridge, and decided that if he exercised the most stringent economy it could be managed.

These problems nagged at him, but they were for the future, which he was much in the habit of leaving to take care of itself. A far more pressing anxiety was the fear that Rotherham, arriving in Bath to find Emily gone, might guess her destination, and follow her. He had warned her not to tell anyone of her flight, and he could not think that he had given Mrs Floore the least cause to suspect him of being implicated in it; but if she mentioned his name Rotherham would know at once that the flight was an elopement. And then what would he do? Perhaps he would be too proud to chase after an unwilling bride. Gerard could picture his look of contempt, the curl of his lip, the shrug of his powerful shoulders. Unfortunately he could even more clearly picture his look of blazing anger; and when he at last fell asleep his dreams were haunted by the sound of hooves, relentlessly drawing nearer and ever nearer, and by lurid, muddled scenes, in which he was always looking down the barrel of a duelling-pistol. Waking in a sweat, it was a little time before he could throw off the impression of the dream, and realize that whatever else Rotherham might do, he would not challenge his ward to a duel. But Rotherham was a boxer, and whether he would consider himself debarred by his guardianship from wreaking a pugilistic vengeance on his ward was a question to which Gerard could find no answer. Of the two fates he thought he would prefer to be shot.

That Rotherham would be very angry with him, he had no doubt; that Rotherham (and, indeed, several other interested persons) would have every right to be angry, scarcely occurred to him. In general, of course, elopements were condemned; in his case, only an insensate person could fail to perceive the purity of his motive. The thing was not so much an elopement as a rescue. Indeed, only as a last resort had he planned it, when he had failed to induce Emily to be resolute.

He was up betimes in the morning, for he had much to do. The sale of his watch was disappointing; he was obliged, regretfully, to part with his second-best fob, and a very pretty tie-pin as well; and even when these sacrifices had been made the hire of a chaise-and-four to the Border was quite out of the reach of his purse. With post-charges as high as one shilling and twopence per mile for each horse, the hire of a chaise-and-pair only for a journey of over three hundred miles would, he realized, leave him in extremely straitened circumstances. Like Mrs Floore, he felt that to elope in anything less than a chaise and four was odiously shabby, but there was no help for it. Then it occurred to him that to pay off the chaise at some point along the road, and to continue by stage, or mail, would not only be a vast saving, but would throw Rotherham (if he pursued them) off the scent. So he booked a chaise to Wolverhampton, and began to think that in so doing he had performed a masterly stroke.

This mood of elation was of brief duration. He and the yellow-bodied chaise arrived in Queen's Square precisely at five minutes to ten, in case Emily should be early, which meant that for twenty-five tense minutes he had nothing to do but walk up and down one side of the square, in fretting impatience, a prey to every gloomy foreboding. And when Emily did appear, carrying two bandboxes, and looking perfectly distracted, she exclaimed breathlessly, and in total disregard of the post-boy: 'Oh, I am so sorry! I could not escape before, because Betsey was for ever in and out of Grandmama's room, and she must have seen me! Pray don't be vexed! Indeed, it was not my fault!'

Nothing could have been more unfortunate, as Gerard was immediately to discover. The postilion, ejecting the straw from his mouth, indicated in unmistakable terms that, being possessed of strong scruples, he could not bring himself, unless greased in the fist, to assist in a runaway marriage. His manner was amiability itself, and a broad grin adorned his homely countenance, but Gerard, grinding his teeth, thought it well to comply with his suggestion, and to untie the strings of his purse. Amongst the incidental expenses of the journey he had not foreseen the need to bribe the post-boys, so it was not surprising that his first words to Emily, when he climbed up into the chaise, and sat down beside her, were more aggrieved than lover-like. 'What in thunder made you say all that in that fellow's hearing?' he demanded. 'When I had taken care to tell them at the stables that you were my sister! Of course, if you mean to blurt out the truth in that fashion, I shall have no money left to pay the post-boys, or the tolls, or anything!'

'Oh, I am sorry! Oh, don't be vexed!' she replied imploringly.

'No, no!' he assured her. 'Good God, how could I be vexed with you, dearest, sweetest Emily? I only said – well, you must own it was the most totty-headed thing to do!'

Her lip trembled. '*Oh* – !'

'No, not that!' Gerard said hastily, slipping his arm round her waist. 'Just a dear little goose! But do take care, my darling! Setting aside all else, if it were known along the road that we were eloping, we should be easily traced, and we don't want that, do we?'

No, decidedly Emily did not want that. The mere thought of being pursued made her shiver, and turn saucer-like eyes towards him. 'D-do you suppose M-mama will come after me?' she faltered.

'Good God!' he ejaculated. 'I had not thought of that! Yes, very likely she might, only I daresay she will not find it convenient to drop as much blunt as a chaise-and-four would need, because you told me yourself your papa don't often find himself with the dibs in tune, and you've no notion what it costs to hire four horses, Emily! You may depend upon it she'd hire a pair only!'

'Yes, but Grandmama has a great deal of money!'

'Well, it doesn't signify. If she isn't expected to arrive in Bath until the afternoon, we shall have several hours' start of her. She'd never catch us – even if she knew the way we had gone, which she won't. The person I was thinking of is Rotherham.'

'Oh, no! Oh, Gerard, no!'

He patted her shoulder soothingly. 'Don't be afraid! Even if he did catch us, I shall not permit him to alarm you,' he said stoutly. 'The only thing is that I'd as lief he didn't come up with us, because of this dashed business of my being his ward. It's bound to make things awkward. However, there's no reason to suppose he means to come to Bath today, and in any event I've got a precious good scheme for throwing him off the scent! If he's devilish clever, he might be able to follow us as far as to Wolverhampton, but I flatter myself he'll throw-up there, because I've provided him with a regular stopper! We shall pay off the chaise, Emily, and go on by stage-coach! Depend upon it, he will never think of *that*, particularly as we shall have to change stages at one or two places. I think there are no stages running direct from there to Carlisle, which is where I thought we should change into a chaise again.'

'But it is horridly uncomfortable on the stage!' objected Emily.

She was still unconvinced that she would find a complicated journey by stage-coach entertaining when they reached Bristol, and changed horses for the first time. Gerard kept a sharp eye on the extortionate post-boy, alighting from the chaise, and engaging him in talk to prevent his passing the word to the new postilion that he was helping an eloping couple to reach the Border. Meanwhile, the ostlers, adjured to fig out two lively ones, poled up the two most lethargic animals in the stables, and assured Gerard (with a wink at the post-boy) that they would be found to be prime steppers. After a very short distance, it became obvious that they were prime stumblers, and Gerard, letting down the window in the front of the chaise, angrily scolded the postilion, who at once pulled up, and, slewing himself round in the saddle, hotly defended himself. Emily tugged at Gerard's sleeve, begging him not to argue with the man, and pointing out, very sensibly, that since there was no possibility of changing the undesirable steeds until the next posting-house was reached, it was wasting precious time to quarrel with the postilion. Gerard sat back again, fuming with wrath, and the chaise was set in motion with a sudden jerk that almost flung the passengers on to its floor.

To persons anxious to put as much space between themselves and Bath as possible, and in the shortest time, the slow progress over the next nine miles was agonizing. Emily soon became a prey to agitating reflections. Against all reason, she fancied that they were already being pursued, and every time an imperative blast on a horn gave notice that some faster vehicle was about to pass the chaise, she clutched Gerard's arm, and uttered a shriek. However, at the Ship Inn they fared better, being supplied with two strengthy beasts, and a youthful post-boy, who, on being urged to spring 'em a bit, obeyed with such enthusiasm that the body of the chaise rocked and lurched so violently that Emily began to feel sick. Gerard had to request the post-boy to abate the pace, but he felt that a good deal of lost time had been made up, and applied himself to the task of assuaging Emily's fears, and directing her thoughts towards a halcyon future. By dint of skimming lightly over the next year or two, and dwelling on the time when he should have become an important member of Lord Liverpool's administration, he succeeded pretty well. By the time the Cambridge Inn was reached, twenty-three miles out of Bristol, Emily had temporarily forgotten her fears in discussing the rival merits of Green Street and Grosvenor Square as possible localities for the house of a rising politician.

A couple of miles farther on, a slight contretemps occurred, at the Church End turnpike, where the pike-keeper made a spirited attempt to overcharge one whom he took to be a greenhorn. But from this encounter Gerard came off triumphant, which pleased him so much that he began to feel more confident; and for the next four miles boasted to Emily of all the occasions when ugly customers, trying to cheat him, had found themselves powerfully set down.

It was at about this time that Serena and Mr Goring, after a splendid cross-country gallop, dropped into a narrow lane, leading to the village of Dursley from the Bristol to Gloucester pike-road.

'By Jove, Lady Serena, you're a devil to go!' Mr Goring exclaimed, in involuntary admiration.

She laughed, leaning forward to pat the mare's steaming neck. 'I like a slapping pace, don't you?'

'I should have called it a *splitting* pace!' he retorted. 'Neck or nothing! My heart was in my mouth when you rode straight for that drop fence!'

'Was it indeed? It didn't seem to me that you were precisely hanging back, Mr Goring!'

He smiled. 'Why, if *you* chose to take the fence, what could I do but follow?'

'Very true! Pitting that peacocky bay of yours against my mare, you could do nothing else – but you did your best to get ahead of me, I thought!' she said, throwing him a quizzical look. 'Confess that you enjoyed that last point as much as I did! For myself, I could almost forgive Gerard and Emily their iniquities: I haven't liked anything so well since I came to Bath. What is the time?'

He pulled out his watch. 'Twenty minutes to two. We should come up with them before they reach Gloucester, I think.'

In another few minutes they were on the pike-road, and with the Cambridge Inn in sight. Here, Serena permitted Mr Goring, who knew the house well, to make the necessary enquiries. He returned to her presently with the intelligence that the yellow chaise had changed horses there about twenty minutes previously. 'They were sweating badly,' he added, as he hoisted himself into the saddle again, 'so no doubt young Monksleigh is making the best speed he can.'

'In that case, we won't jaunter along either,' said Serena.

'What do you mean to do when we sight the chaise?' asked Mr Goring. 'Am I to hold it up?'

'Good God, no! We want no dramatic scenes upon the high-road! We shall follow discreetly behind, to see which inn they mean to patronize. Leave it to me, then! I know Gloucester as you know Bristol. I shall be better able to carry it off smoothly than you. Yes, I know you would like to have a turn-up with Gerard, but it's my ambition to emerge from this imbroglio without kicking up any dust!'

Thus it was that Gerard, jumping down from the chaise at the Bell Inn, Gloucester, to inspect the horses that were being led out, received an extremely unpleasant shock. 'How glad I am to have caught you!' said an affable voice. 'You need not have the horses put to!'

Gerard spun round, hardly believing his ears. But they had not deceived him: it was the Lady Serena who had spoken. She was standing just behind him, a pleasant smile on her lips, but her eyes glinting. His own eyes starting at her, he stood transfixed, and could only stammer: 'L-Lady Serena!'

'I knew you would be surprised!' she said, still with that horrid affability. 'It is not necessary, after all, for Emily to hurry north: her brother is very much better! Famous news, isn't it? The letter came too late for anyone to be able to stop you before you left Bath, so I told her grandmother I would ride after you. Mr Goring – do you know Mr Goring? – was so obliging as to give me his escort, and here we are!'

He uttered in a choked voice: 'It's no concern of yours, ma'am! I –'

'Oh, no, but I was happy to be of service!' She nodded smilingly at the elderly ostler, who was touching his forelock to her. 'Good-day to you, Runcorn! It is some time since you stabled my horses for me, isn't it? I am glad you are still here, for I want you to take charge of my mare, and Mr Goring's horse too. Ah, I see Emily staring at me! I must instantly tell her the good news, Gerard! Do you go into the house, and bespeak refreshment for us all! Tell the landlord it is for me, and that I should like a private parlour!'

'Lady Serena!' he said furiously. 'I must make it plain to you –'

'Indeed, yes! We have so much to say to one another! I in particular! But not, do you think, in the courtyard?'

She turned away, and walked towards the chaise, where Mr Goring, having relinquished the bridles he had been holding into the ostler's hands, was already persuading Emily to alight. She seemed to be on the point of bursting into tears, but he took her hand in a firm clasp, and said gravely, but with great kindness: 'Come, Miss Laleham! There is nothing to be afraid of: you must not go any farther! Let me help you down, and then we will talk the matter over sensibly, shall we?'

'You don't understand!' she said, trying to pull her hand away. 'I can't – I won't –'

'Yes, I do understand, but you are making a mistake you would bitterly regret, my child. Rest assured that your grandmama won't permit anyone to compel you to do what you don't like!'

She looked unconvinced, but his tone, which was much that of a man bent on soothing a frightened baby, calmed her a little, and made her feel a sense of protection. She stopped trying to free her hand, and only made a faint protest when he lifted her down from the chaise. She found herself confronting Serena, and hung her head guiltily, not daring to look up into her face.

'That's right!' said Serena, in a heartening voice. 'Now, before we go home again, we'll drink some coffee, my dear. Mr Goring, I shall leave it to you to see that the horses are properly bestowed. Tell old Runcorn that Fobbing will ride over to fetch home my mare in a couple of days' time, if you please, and arrange for four good horses to be put to half-an-hour from now. I know I may safely depend upon you.'

She then swept Emily irresistibly into the inn, encountering Gerard in the doorway, and saying: 'Well, have you done as I bade you?'

This question, calculated as it was to reduce Mr Monksleigh to the status of a schoolboy, made him flush angrily, and say in a sulky voice: 'I am willing to break our journey for a few minutes, ma'am, but pray do not imagine that I shall permit you to dictate to me, or to tyrannize over Miss Laleham! In future, Miss Laleham's welfare –'

He stopped, not because he was interrupted, but because it was abundantly plain that she was not attending to him. The landlord was bustling up, and she walked past Gerard to meet him, saying, in her friendly way: 'Well, Shere, and how are you?'

'Pretty stout, my lady, I thank you! And how is your ladyship? And my Lady Spenborough? Now, if I had but known we was to have the honour of serving your ladyship with a nuncheon today – !'

'Just some coffee and cold meat will do excellently for us. I daresay Mr Monksleigh will have told you that he was escorting Miss Laleham here on what was feared to be a sad errand. One of her brothers took ill suddenly, and the worst was apprehended, so that nothing would do but she must post to Wolverhampton, where he is staying. However, better tidings have been received, I am happy to say, and so I have come galloping after her, to save her a tedious and most anxious journey! Dear Emily, you are still quite overset, and I am sure it is not to be wondered at! You shall rest quietly for a while, before returning to Bath.'

The landlord at once, and in the most solicitous fashion, begged them both to come into his best private parlour; and Emily, dazed by Serena's eloquence, and incapable of resisting her, allowed herself to be shepherded into the parlour, and tenderly deposited in a chair. Mr Monksleigh brought up the rear, not knowing what else to do. Self-confidence was rapidly deserting him, but as soon as the landlord had bowed himself out of the room, he made another attempt to assert himself, saying, in a blustering voice: 'Let it be understood, ma'am, that we are not to be turned from our purpose! You do not know the circumstances which have led to our taking what no doubt seems to you a rash step! Not that it signifies in the least! Upon my word, I shall be interested to learn by what right you –'

The speech ended here somewhat abruptly, for Serena rounded on him, an alarming flash in her eyes. 'Are you out of your senses?' she demanded. 'What the *deuce* do you mean by daring to address me in such terms?'

He blenched, but muttered: 'Well, I don't see what business it is of yours! You need not think –'

'Let me remind you, Gerard, that you are not talking to one of your college friends!' she interrupted. 'I don't take that tone from anyone alive, and least of all from a cub of your age! I have previously thought that Rotherham was too severe with you, but I am fast reaching the conclusion he has been too easy! What you need, and what I am strongly tempted to see that you receive, is a sharp lesson in civility! Do not stand there glowering at me in that stupid, ill-bred style! And do not waste your time talking fustian to me about the circumstances which led you to take what you call a rash step, but which you know very well to be a disgraceful and a dishonourable prank!'

Mr Goring, who had entered the room at the start of this masterly trimming, and had listened to it with deep appreciation, said very politely: 'I shall be happy to be of service to you, Lady Serena.'

Her eyes twinkled. 'I don't doubt it – or that you are an excellent teacher, sir! but I hope not to put you to so much trouble.'

'It would be a pleasure, ma'am.'

Mr Monksleigh, finding himself between an avenging goddess on the one hand, and a stocky and determined gentleman on the other, thought it prudent to retreat from his dangerous position. He begged pardon, and said that he had not meant to be uncivil. The landlord, accompanied by a waiter, then came back into the room, to set the table, a mundane business which seemed to Gerard quite out of keeping with the romantic nature of his escapade. And when they were alone again, Lady Serena sat down at the head of the table, and began to pour out the coffee, commanding the star-crossed lovers to come and take their places, as though she were presiding over a nursery meal.

'Oh, I could not swallow anything!' Emily said, in lachrymose accents.

'I daresay you will find, when you make the attempt, that you are mistaken,' replied Serena. 'For my part, I am excessively hungry, and so, I don't doubt, is Mr Goring. So come and sit down to the table, if you please! Mr Goring, if you will take the foot, and carve the ham, Gerard may sit on my other hand, and so we shall be comfortable.'

Anything less comfortable than the attitudes assumed by the lovers could scarcely have been imagined. Mr Goring, glancing up from his task, was hard put to it not to laugh.

'I won't go back! I *won't*!' Emily declared, tearfully. 'Oh, no one was ever so unhappy as I am!'

'Well, you know, I think you deserve to be unhappy,' said Serena. 'You have caused Mr Goring and me a great deal of trouble; you have behaved in a way that must, if ever it were to be known, sink you quite beneath reproach; and, which is worst of all, you have made your grandmama ill. Really, Emily, you are quite old enough to know better than to be so outrageously thoughtless! When I arrived in Beaufort Square this morning, it was to find Mrs Floore recovering from a heart attack, and in such distress that I don't know when I have been more shocked.'

Emily burst into tears. 'Lady Serena, it is useless to seek to interfere!' said Gerard. 'This step has not been lightly taken! And as for being dishonourable, it's no such thing! If you think I acted behind Rotherham's back, you are much mistaken! Before ever I came to Bath I went to Claycross, and told my cousin what I should do!'

Lady Serena lowered her cup. 'You told Rotherham you were going to elope with Emily?' she repeated.

He reddened. 'No, not that! Well, I didn't mean *then* to elope! I told him I should go to Bath, *whatever* he said, and if he didn't choose to believe me, I'm sure it was not my fault!'

'Are we to understand that Rotherham, in fact, forbade you to approach Emily?' asked Serena. 'My poor Gerard! What a fortunate thing it is that I was able to catch you! We must *hope* that this escapade doesn't reach his ears, but there's no saying that it won't, and I am strongly of the opinion that you should book yourself a seat on the next London-bound coach.'

'*I'm* not afraid of Rotherham!' stated Gerard.

'Then I know just what you should do!' said Serena cordially. 'Take the bull by the horns, my dear Gerard! You know what Rotherham is! Seek him out, and make a clean breast of it, and he won't be *nearly* as angry!'

He cast her a look of intense dislike. 'I've no desire to see him at all, ma'am!'

Serena spread mustard on a mouthful of ham, and said thoughtfully: 'Well, I can't but feel that if I stood in your shoes I had rather seek him than have him seek me. However, that is quite your own affair! But put this absurd Gretna Green idea out of your head, I do beg of you! If I fail to persuade you to abandon your project, I shall have no choice but to inform Rotherham immediately, and then you will see him somewhere on the road to Scotland. I shan't envy you *that* meeting.'

Emily shrieked: 'You would not! Oh, you would not do so cruel a thing!'

'Of course I should! It would be far more cruel to let you ruin yourself in Gerard's company. And talking of ruin, pray how did you come by the money to pay for this trip, Gerard?'

'I suppose you think I stole it!' he said furiously. 'If you must know, I borrowed it!'

'Who in the world was fool enough to lend you enough money to get to Gretna Green and back?' she demanded, quite astonished.

'I shall pay it back on the day I come of age! In fact, he holds my note-of-hand!'

'Who does? You know, this becomes more and more serious!' Serena said. 'I fear Rotherham will be quite out of patience with you.'

'Well, he will not, because it was he who lent me the money!' retorted Gerard.

Mr Goring choked over a mouthful of bread and butter; Serena, after gazing in an awed way at Gerard for a few moments, said unsteadily: 'You borrowed money from Rotherham to enable you to elope with the girl to whom he is betrothed? No doubt he gave you his blessing as well!'

'No, he did not! Of course I didn't tell him I wanted it for – Well, I *didn't* want it for that! I mean, I hadn't thought of eloping then, or I shouldn't have – though it isn't as if I asked him to give me the money, after all!' he added defensively.

Mr Goring, listening to him in grim amusement, remarked dispassionately: 'You're certainly an original, Monksleigh!'

'Oh, Gerard, how could you?' said Emily. 'Oh, dear, how dreadful everything is! I'm sure it would be *very* wrong of us to let Lord Rotherham pay for my marriage to *you*! Now I shall have to go back to Bath, and I wish I were *dead*!'

Gerard, who, to do him justice, had not until now considered this particular aspect of his exploit, flushed scarlet, and said in a deeply mortified voice: 'Well, if it was wrong, at least I did it for your sake!'

Serena refilled her cup. 'I daresay it may prove to be a blessing,' she observed. 'His worst enemy never said of Rotherham that he had no sense of humour, and the chances are he would laugh so much that he would forget to be angry with you, Gerard.'

He did not appear to derive much comfort from this, but before he could speak, Emily said, tightly clasping her hands: 'Lady Serena, I don't want to marry Lord Rotherham! Oh, pray do not try to persuade me! I cannot love him!'

'Then I suggest that you tell him so,' replied Serena calmly.

'T-tell him so – ?' repeated Emily, her eyes widening in horror.

'Yes, tell him so,' said Serena. 'When a gentleman, my dear Emily, does you the honour to offer for your hand, and you accept his offer, the barest civility demands that if you should afterwards wish to cry off you must at least inform him of the alteration in your sentiments.'

Emily began to cry again. Mr Goring said: 'Miss Laleham,

pray don't distress yourself! What Lady Serena says is true, but she should have told you also that you have nothing to fear in returning to Mrs Floore's house! I can assure you that you will find in her a stout supporter! Had you informed her of your dislike of Rotherham, this unfortunate affair need never have been!'

She raised her wet eyes to his face in an incredulous look. 'Oh, but Mama – !'

'Believe me,' he said earnestly, 'Mrs Floore is more than a match for your mama! Indeed, my poor child, you must return with us! You have allowed the irritation of your nerves to overset your judgment: I have never met Lord Rotherham, but it is inconceivable to me that he, or any other man, could wish to marry a lady who held him in such aversion!'

'Mr Goring,' said Serena, 'it is a happiness to have become acquainted with you! Your common sense is admirable! I can think of no one more unlikely than Rotherham to hold a reluctant female to her engagement to him, and you will own that I have reason to know what I am talking about!' A murmur from Emily caused her to whip round, saying sharply: 'If you bleat "Mama" just once more, Emily, you will find that I have a temper quite as much to be dreaded as Rotherham's! Why, you little ninnyhammer, if it is Mama you fear, marry Rotherham tomorrow! You could not have found any man more capable of protecting you from her! Or, I dare swear, more willing to do so! Yes, you may stare! That had not occurred to you, had it? There is another thing that has not occurred to you! We have heard a great deal from you about the terror with which he has inspired you, but I have yet to hear you acknowledge that he has treated you during these weeks you have skulked in Bath with a forbearance of which I did not believe a man of his temper to have been capable! Why he should love such a sapskull as you, I know not, but it is clearly seen that he does! His reward is that when he at last tells you that it is time you came to a point, rather than summon up the courage to face him, and to tell him the truth, you elope with a silly schoolboy for whom you do not care the snap of your fingers! His own ward, too! Did you plan it, between the pair of you, to make him appear ridiculous? Of you, Gerard, I can believe it! After this day's disclosures, it is not in your power to surprise me! You are an ill-conditioned puppy, without gratitude, without propriety, without a thought in your head for anything but what may happen to suit your pleasure!' Her scorching gaze swept to Emily's horrified countenance. 'You I acquit of all but childish folly, but I will tell you this, my girl: but for that saving grace – if grace you call it! – I should think you the most contemptible and vulgar of jilts!'

These flaming words not unnaturally left both the persons to whom they were addressed speechless and shaken. Gerard was red to the roots of his hair, Emily paper-white, and almost cowering in her chair. Mr Goring rose, and went to her, laying a hand on her shoulder. Over her head he spoke to Serena. 'No more, ma'am, I beg of you! You have said enough! She has indeed behaved ill, but you forget what you yourself have said! – She is the merest child: one, moreover, who is timid, and has felt herself to be alone, and has never known the sympathy and support which girls more fortunately circumstanced than herself enjoy!'

'Yes!' burst in Gerard. 'But when I rescue her, and try to protect her –'

'If you have the slightest regard for your skin, be silent!' interrupted Mr Goring, his voice losing some of its deliberate calm. 'No man who wishes to *protect* an ignorant girl persuades her into taking a step that must expose her to the censure and the contempt of the world!'

The storm vanished from Serena's face, and she gave an involuntary laugh. 'You set us all to rights, Mr Goring! There is really no more to be said, and if we are to be in Bath again by dinner-time we should set forward immediately. You need not look so scared, Emily! I shan't scold you any more – and I hope you will not, because I once lost my temper with you, imagine me to be an ogress!'

'Oh, no, no!' Emily stammered. 'How *could* I? I never meant – I didn't think –'

'But you have turned Rotherham into an ogre, have you not?' Serena said, arching her brows. 'Come! I think you would do well to wait until you have seen him again before you decide to jilt him, my dear. It may be, you know, that you will find that the picture you have painted is a false one. If he still seems terrible to you, why, then, tell him you wish to cry off!' She held out her hand, but spoke to Mr Goring. 'Do you come with us, sir?'

'I shall ride behind the chaise, ma'am.'

'Emily!' exclaimed Gerard. 'Will you permit yourself to be dragged from my side?'

'I am so very sorry!' she said, trembling. 'Pray forgive me! I didn't mean to behave so wickedly!'

'My dear Gerard, if you wish to remain at Emily's side, you have only to hire a horse!' said Serena. 'Then, when Rotherham comes to Bath, you may confront him together.'

'No, no!' cried Emily, clutching her arm. 'Oh, don't let him! Lord Rotherham and Mama would know what I did, and I couldn't *bear* it!'

'If my love means so little to you, go!' said Gerard nobly. 'I see that the coronet has won!'

Twenty-two

When Major Kirkby rode over the Bridge into Laura Place shortly before three o'clock, he was surprised not to see Fobbing waiting there with Serena's phaeton, and still more surprised to be informed by Lybster that the Lady Serena had gone off on a picnic expedition. Lady Spenborough, added Lybster, was in the drawing-room, and had desired him to show the Major upstairs. He observed that the Major had hitched his horse's bridle over the railings, and said that he would send my lady's footman to take charge of the animal.

He then led the Major upstairs, announced him, and went away, shaking his head. In his view, there was something smoky going on, some undergame of which he could not approve.

Fanny jumped up from the sofa, as the door shut behind Lybster, and moved impulsively towards the Major, exclaiming: 'Oh, Hector, I am so glad you have come! I am in the most dreadful worry!'

'My dear, what is it?' he asked quickly, catching her hands. 'Fanny, you are trembling! My darling – !'

She gave a gasp, and disengaged her hands, casting an imploring look up at him. 'Hector – no! You must not – I should not have – ! Oh, my love, – *remember*!'

He walked away to the window, and stood staring out.

'Yes, I beg your pardon! What has happened to distress you, my dear?'

She blew her nose, and said rather huskily: 'It's Serena. She has quite taken leave of her senses, Hector!'

He turned his head. 'Good heavens, what has she done? Where is she?'

'That,' said Fanny distractedly, 'is what is so agitating, for I don't know! I mean, *anything* might have happened to her, and if she has not been murdered by footpads, or kidnapped by Mr Goring – for what, after all, do we know of him? she may be halfway to Wolverhampton by this time!'

'Halfway to *Wolverhampton*?' he repeated, startled. 'Fanny, for heaven's sake – ! Why should Serena go to Wolverhampton? Who is Mr Goring?'

'Oh, he is Mrs Floore's godson, or some such thing! I daresay a very worthy young man, but so *very* dull and respectable!'

He could not help laughing. 'Well, if he is dull and respectable, he will hardly have kidnapped Serena!'

'No, I don't suppose it is as bad as that, but what if she *doesn't* catch them before they reach Gloucester? She can't ride all night, and there she will be, miles and miles from Bath, and no luggage, but only Mr Goring, and her reputation quite lost! You had better read her letter!'

'Indeed, I think I had!' he said.

She dragged it from her reticule, and gave it to him. 'She says I am to tell you what has happened, so you may as well see just what she says. Hector, I am quite *vexed* with Serena!'

He had unfolded the sheet of paper, and was rapidly running his eyes down it. 'Emily – Gerard – Gretna Green! Good God! What's this? Oh, I see! Monksleigh hired the chaise to take him to Wolverhampton. My dear, Serena doesn't say *she* means to go there!'

'She is equal to anything!' said Fanny despairingly.

He went on reading the letter, frowning a little. When he reached the end of it, he folded it, and gave it back to Fanny without a word.

'What am I to do?' she asked. 'What *can* I do?'

'I don't think either of us can do anything,' he replied. 'If I thought it would be of the least use, I would ride after her, but either she is already on her way back, or she must be far beyond my reach. Fanny, does she *often* do things like this?'

'Oh, thank goodness, no! In fact, I've never before known her to ride off with a strange man – well, the merest acquaintance, at all events! and not even take Fobbing with her! Of course, it is very wrong of Gerard and Emily to elope, but it is not Serena's business to take care of Emily! And, I must say, if the wretched girl fears that her odious mother will push her into marrying Lord Rotherham unless she runs away with Gerard, I cannot wholly blame her! How Serena can believe that Emily could ever be happy with such a man as Rotherham is something that quite baffles me, Hector!'

'Do you think that Serena is greatly concerned with Emily's happiness?' he asked slowly. 'It seems to me that it is *Rotherham's* happiness which interests her.' He took the letter out of her hand, and unfolded it again. '*I can't and I won't allow them to serve Ivo such a trick! It is unthinkable that he should be twice jilted, and this time for such a Bartholomew baby as Gerard – a silly boy that is half flash and half foolish, and his own ward besides!*' He lowered the paper, and looked at Fanny. 'If you ask me, my love, Emily might have eloped with Serena's blessing had Rotherham not been in question! Lord, what a tangle!'

She stared up at him. 'But, Hector, it isn't possible! She told me months before she met you again that she had only once cared for anyone, and that it was you! And when you met – oh, Hector, you cannot doubt that she was in love with you again on that instant!'

He said ruefully: 'I did not doubt it any more than I doubted my own feelings, Fanny.'

'Hector, I am persuaded you are mistaken! She *could* not love Rotherham! As for him, I have never seen a sign that he regretted the breaking of the engagement: indeed, far otherwise! He doesn't care the snap of his fingers for her – well, has he not shown that he doesn't, if we had needed showing? He has no tenderness for her, not even solicitude! He –'

'Do you think that Serena desires to be treated with solicitude, Fanny?' he asked. 'It has sometimes seemed to me that nothing vexes her more.'

'Oh, no, no!' she protested. 'Not *vexes* her! She doesn't like one to *cosset* her, but –' She stopped uncertainly. 'Well, perhaps – But Rotherham does not even admire her beauty! Do you recall what he said when he dined here, and she was looking quite ravishing? He said she looked like a magpie and that is precisely the sort of thing he always does say to her! Indeed, I am sure you are refining too much upon what she has written in that letter! Though she does not regret it, I believe she thinks that she didn't use him well, which is why she must feel it so particularly, now that it seems as though he will be jilted a second time. For, of course, it *was* quite shocking to have cried off almost at the last moment. I can't think how she had the courage to do it!'

'She doesn't lack courage, Fanny,' he replied. He glanced at Serena's letter again, and then laid it down on the table at Fanny's elbow. 'I suppose she will bring that foolish girl back. If they outwit her – I wonder? But they won't! To own the truth, I can't imagine her being outwitted by anyone!' He sighed faintly, but said with determined cheerfulness: 'There is nothing to be done, my dear. We can only trust to this man, Goring, to take care of her. I had better leave you. If she returns in time for dinner, as she promises, will you send me word by your footman? If she does not –'

'If she does not,' said Fanny resolutely, 'I shall set out myself!'

'Fanny, Fanny!' he said, half laughing. 'No, my darling, you will not!'

'I must!' said Fanny tragically. 'It is my duty, Hector! I know I shan't find Serena, but as long as I am not in this house, I can *prevaricate*, and say I was with her! And I beg of you, Hector, don't leave me here alone! I *know* Lord Rotherham will come here, and even when there is *nothing* on my conscience he puts me in a flutter! He will fix his eyes on my face, and ask me the most stabbing questions, and I shall betray all!'

'But, Fanny – !'

'Don't – *don't*, I implore you, say that I have only to decide what I shall tell him!' Fanny begged. 'You must know that I am not at all clever, and when Rotherham bends that *look* upon me I become utterly bird-witted! Hector, I cannot be your wife, but I shall be your mother-in-law, and you *cannot* leave me to Rotherham's mercy!'

He dropped on his knees beside her chair, gathering her hands in his, and kissing them again and again. 'Fanny, Fanny, don't!' he said unsteadily. 'If you look at me like that, how can I – ? Dearest, most foolish Fanny, there is no reason to think Rotherham will come to Bath today! I ought not to remain! Besides, I can't keep your footman walking my horse up and down outside for the rest of the day!'

'Tell John to take him back to the stables!' she urged him. 'Pray, love, don't take away your support! If I must remain alone here, wondering what has become of Serena, and thinking every knock on the door to be Rotherham's, my senses will become wholly disordered!'

He was not proof against such an appeal. He thought it not very likely that Rotherham would arrive in Bath that day, but he remained with Fanny, with a backgammon-board as chaperon.

And Fanny was quite right. Not very long after five o'clock,

Lybster opened the drawing room door, and announced Lord Rotherham.

Fanny was taken by surprise, neither she nor the Major having heard a knock on the street-door. She had just lifted a pile of backgammon pieces, and she gave such a violent start that she dropped them, and they went rolling over the floor in several directions. The Major met her agonized look with a reassuring smile, and was near to bursting into laughter, so comical was her expression of dismay.

Rotherham, pausing halfway across the room, glanced keenly from one to the other of them, bent to pick up a piece that had come to rest against his foot, and said: 'How do you do? I am afraid I have startled you, Lady Spenborough!'

'No – oh, no!' Fanny said, blushing, and rising to her feet. 'That is, yes! I wasn't expecting to see you! Oh, pray don't trouble about those stupid pieces!'

He dropped three of them on to the board, and shook hands. 'I understand Serena is out,' he said, turning to offer his hand to the Major. 'When does she return?'

The look Fanny cast at the Major was eloquent. *I told you so!* said her eyes. He came at once to the rescue. 'It would be a bold man who would dare to prophesy!' he said smilingly. 'She has gone off on an expedition, with a party of her friends, and there's no saying when they will get back to Bath.'

'Where has she gone to?'

To Fanny's deep admiration, the Major replied without hesitation: 'I believe there was some notion of trying to get as far as to the Wookey Hole.'

'I wonder you let her.'

This remark, though it sounded more of a comment than a criticism, shook the Major slightly. Fanny sprang loyally into the breach. 'She will be sorry to have missed you. What a pity you did not advise us of your coming to Bath!'

'Oh, she won't miss me!' said Rotherham. 'I'll wait for her – if I shall not be in your way?'

'No, no, not at all!' said Fanny, in a hollow voice. 'Pray, won't you sit down?'

'Thank you.' He chose a chair opposite to the sofa. 'Don't let me interrupt your game!'

'We had just finished. Do you – do you make a long stay in Bath?'

'I can't tell. Has Miss Laleham also gone to the Wookey Hole?'

'I don't know – that is, I forget whether – Oh, I expect she has!' said Fanny, feeling herself being driven into a corner. She knew that that unnerving gaze was fixed on her, and began with slightly trembling hands to put the backgammon pieces into their box.

'By the by, has my eldest ward been seen in Bath?' asked Rotherham abruptly.

The Major was just in time to catch one of the pieces which, slipping from between Fanny's fingers, rolled across the board to the edge. 'Oh, thank you! So clumsy! G-Gerard, Lord Rotherham? *I* haven't seen him. Did you expect to find him here?'

'I wasn't sure. That's why I asked you.'

Fanny found herself obliged to look up, and was lost. The compelling eyes held hers, but they were not frowning, she noticed. A rather mocking smile lurked in them. 'I accept without question that you haven't seen him, Lady Spenborough. Has anyone?'

'Are you talking of a boy called Monksleigh?' interposed the Major. 'Yes, I've seen him. Serena introduced him to me. He said he was staying with friends outside the town.'

'He lied, then. Has he too gone to the Wookey Hole?'

'No, indeed he hasn't!' Fanny said quickly. 'He – he has left Bath, I believe!'

'Oh, my God, why did I never thrust some jumping powder down his throat while there was still time to cure him of cowheartedness?' exclaimed Rotherham, in accents of extreme exasperation. He got up abruptly. 'He heard I was coming, and fled, did he? I wish you will stop fencing with me, Lady Spenborough! Sooner or later I am bound to discover what has been going on here, and I'd as lief it was sooner! I've already been refused admittance in Beaufort Square, where I learned that Miss Laleham will not be in until late this evening, that Mrs Floore is out, visiting friends, and that Lady Laleham is expected in Bath this afternoon. Now I find that Serena too is not expected back until late, and that that ward of mine has taken himself off in a hurry, which makes nonsense of the whole! Having had the spirit to come here, why the devil couldn't he –' He stopped suddenly, his brows snapping together: 'Good God, did she send him packing?'

Fanny cast another of her imploring looks at the Major, but he too had risen, and his eyes were on Rotherham's face. 'Am I to understand that you knew young Monksleigh to be in love with Miss Laleham?' he asked bluntly.

'Knew it?' Rotherham gave a short laugh, and strode over to the window. 'What can one *know* of a bag of wind? He enacted me a ranting tragedy, but as to discovering whether there is one grain of sincerity amongst the fustian, you might as well try to milk a pigeon! Just playing off his tricks, was he?' He shrugged. 'I should have guessed it!'

'No,' said the Major deliberately. 'Far from it!'

'*Hector!*' The cry was startled out of Fanny.

Rotherham swung round. One swift glance at Fanny's horrified face, and his eyes went to the Major's, in a hard, questioning stare. 'Well? Out with it!'

Fanny sprang up, with a rustle of silken skirts, and clasped her hands about the Major's arm. 'Hector, you must not! Oh, pray – !'

He laid his hand over her clutching fingers. 'But I think I should,' he said gently. 'Haven't you said from the outset that nothing but misery could come of the marriage? Your ward, Marquis, according to our information, eloped this morning with your betrothed.'

'*What?*' Rotherham thundered, making Fanny wince. 'Are you trying to hoax me?'

'On *such* a subject? Certainly not! They set out in a chaise and pair, and were bound, it is presumed, for Gretna Green.'

'By God, I've wronged that boy!' exclaimed Rotherham. 'So that's why I wasn't permitted to enter Mrs Floore's house! Gretna Green, indeed!' His brows drew together again. 'Good God, they will never get there! I'll swear all the money the young fool had was the fifty pounds I gave him! Why the devil couldn't he have asked me for a hundred while he was about it? Of all the addle-brained cawkers – ! *Now* he'll find himself aground before he reaches Carlisle!'

Fanny's hands fell from the Major's arm. Fascinated, she stared at Rotherham.

'He appears only to have booked the chaise as far as to Wolverhampton,' said the Major, contriving by a superhuman effort to preserve his countenance. 'Possibly – he has foreseen that he might find himself without a feather to fly with, and means to proceed thence by stage-coach.'

'God grant me patience!' ejaculated Rotherham wrathfully. 'If ever I knew such a slow top – ! Does he know no better than to take a girl to Wolverhampton – *Wolverhampton*, my God! – and then to push her into a stage-coach? And I don't doubt I shall be blamed for it, if all comes to ruin! How the devil could I guess he was such a cod's head that he wouldn't know better unless I told him?'

'Perhaps,' said the Major, who had sat down again, and was giving way to his emotion, 'he f-felt there might be a little – awkwardness in applying to you for instruction!'

One of his sharp cracks of laughter broke from Rotherham. 'He might, of course!' he acknowledged. Another thought brought back the frown to his brow. 'What's Serena doing in this?' he demanded. 'You're not going to tell me she has gone along to chaperon Emily?'

'No: to bring her back!' said the Major. 'She has ridden in pursuit of them.'

'*And you let her?*'

'It was not in my power to attempt to stop her. I only learned of it this afternoon. It was far too late to try to catch her. I can only trust she'll come to no harm.'

'Serena?' Rotherham's lip curled. 'You needn't be anxious on her account! It isn't she who will come to harm. So she means to bring Emily back, does she? I am obliged to her!'

He came slowly away from the window, a brooding look in his harsh face, his lips tightly gripped together. He saw that Fanny was watching him, and said curtly: 'No doubt she will be home presently. I shouldn't tease yourself about her, Lady Spenborough, if I were you: she's very well able to take care of herself. I won't wait to see her.'

He held out his hand, but before she could take it the Major had risen, and picked up from the table Serena's letter. 'You had better read what she wrote to Lady Spenborough,' he said. 'I fancy it makes the matter tolerably plain.'

Rotherham took the paper from him, directing a searching glance at him from under his brows. Then he bent his gaze upon the letter, and began to read it, his face very grim. But he had not proceeded far before his expression changed. The set look disappeared, to be succeeded by one of mingled wrath and astonishment. He did not speak, until he came to the end, but he seemed to find it difficult to control himself. At last he looked up, and Fanny's heart instantly jumped into her mouth, such a blaze of anger was there in his eyes. 'I *will* wait to see Serena!'

he said. 'I must certainly thank her in person! So busy as she has been on my behalf!' He rounded suddenly on the Major: 'And who the devil is this Goring she writes of?' he demanded.

'I have never met him, but Lady Spenborough tells me he is Mrs Floore's godson, and a most – er – sober and respectable young man,' replied the Major. 'We must depend on him to bring her safely back.'

'Oh, we must, must we?' said Rotherham savagely. 'She is a great deal more likely to bring him back – on a hurdle! Any man who lets Serena lead him into one of her damned May Games can't be other than a bottlehead!' He broke off, jerking up his head, his eyes going swiftly to the window. The clop of a horse's hooves, which had been growing steadily louder, ceased suddenly. Two quick strides took Rotherham back to the window. He flung it up, and looked down at the vehicle drawn up outside the house. There was a tense pause; then Rotherham said, leaning his hands on the window-sill, Serena's letter crushed in one of them: 'Her ladyship – in a hired hack!'

He shut the window with a slam, and turned. Fanny sprang up. 'Serena? Oh, thank God! Oh, what a relief!'

She then shrank instinctively towards the Major, for the look Rotherham turned on her was bright and menacing. 'Don't thank God too soon, Lady Spenborough! Serena is in a great deal more danger now than she has been all day, believe me!'

'No, no, stop!' she cried. 'What are you going to do to her?'

'Murder her!' he said, through shut teeth, and went hastily out of the room.

Fanny started forward, but the Major caught her arm. 'No, my dear! Let be!'

'Hector, go after him!' she said urgently. 'His face – Oh, he looked like a *fiend*! Heaven only knows what he may do in such a wicked passion! You *must* do something! Hector, it is your duty to protect Serena!'

'So I might, if I thought she stood in peril of her life,' he replied, laughing. 'What I do think is that I should make a very bad third in *that* quarrel!'

Meanwhile, Rotherham, running down the stairs, reached the entrance floor just as Serena walked past Lybster into the house. Under the stiff, curling brim of her tall hat, her face was a little pale, and her eyes frowning in a look of fatigue. She laid her whip down on the table, and began to strip off her gauntlets. 'Is her ladyship in, Lybster?'

'In the drawing-room, my lady. Also –'

'Ridden that short-backed mare of yours to a standstill, Serena?'

She looked round quickly. 'Ivo! You here?'

'Yes, Serena, as you see!' he said, advancing upon her. 'Not only here, but extremely anxious to have a few words with you!'

'Dear me, in the sullens again?' she asked, her voice light, but her eyes watchful. 'Are you vexed because Emily did not abandon our expedition on the chance that you might arrive in Bath today? How absurd of you!'

'My girl,' said Rotherham dangerously, 'it will be just as well for you if you stop thinking me a bleater, whom you can gull by pitching me your damned gammon! Come in here!' He pushed open the door into the dining-room, and to Lybster's intense disappointment pulled Serena into the room, and shut the door in the butler's face. 'Now, Serena! *Now!*' he said. 'What the *devil* have you been doing? Don't lie to me! I know what expedition yours was!' He unclenched his left hand, and showed her the crushed letter. 'Do you recognize that? Then tell me the truth!'

She said indignantly: 'So, not content with browbeating Emily, you have bullied Fanny into giving you my letter, have you? Well, if I find you've upset her, you will very speedily wish you had remembered with whom you would have to deal, if you came raging into this house! I am not a wretched schoolgirl, wilting under your frown!'

'You are a meddlesome vixen!' he told her angrily.

Her eyes flashed, but she choked back a pungent retort, struggled for a moment with herself, and finally said, in a voice of determined calm: 'No. This is no moment for a turn-up, Rotherham. If you have read my letter, it may be for the best. Of course you are angry – though why you should make *me* your scapegoat God knows! Never mind that! I can stand a knock or two. Ivo, what a *fool* you have been! You may blame yourself for what happened today! Don't vent your wrath on Gerard! I've sent him back to London with such a flea in his ear as he will not soon forget, I assure you!'

'You have, have you? How much – how *very* much – I am obliged to you! Go on!'

'You are more obliged to me than you know! You may dismiss Gerard from your mind: Emily is no more in love with him than I am! Had you had enough sense to have come to Bath, without heralding your arrival in a letter anyone but an *idiot* would have known must scare the child out of what little wit – out of her wits! – she would never have spared Gerard a thought! She seized on him merely as a means of escape. Really, Ivo, you have handled this like the veriest whipster! *You!* You have the vilest temper in creation, but I've never known you lose it with a nervous young 'un! Couldn't you guess that if you let Emily see it, she would behave exactly as would a filly you had spurred? She turned you into a positive ogre – and you could have made her adore you! Instead, you frightened her – and the devil's own task I have had, all the way from Gloucester, to convince her she has been a goose! I can't tell whether I've succeeded, but I can't do any more! The rest is with you! Be gentle with her, and I think all may be well!'

'*O God!*' uttered Rotherham, in a strangled voice. 'What have I ever done to be cursed with such a marplot as you,

Serena? So you've convinced her that I'm not such a devil as I made her think! I thank you! And I thought that if there was *one* person I could depend upon to urge the wretched girl on no account to marry me, it was you! I might have guessed you would bullfinch me if you could!'

'*Rotherham!*' exclaimed Serena, grasping a chairback. 'Are you telling me – are you *daring* to tell me – you *meant* to scare Emily into jilting you?'

'Of course I meant it!' he said furiously. 'You think I'm clever in the saddle, do you? Much obliged to you! A pity you didn't remember it earlier! Good God, Serena, you can't have supposed that I wanted to marry that hen-witted girl?'

'Then why the *devil* did you offer for her?' she demanded.

'It only needed that!' he said. 'Serena, I could break your damned neck!'

She stared at him in bewilderment. 'Why? How was I to guess you had run mad? Anyone would think it was *my* fault you lost your head over a pretty face!'

'I never lost my head over any but *one* face, God help me! My temper, yes – once too often! I offered for Emily because *you* had become engaged to Kirkby! And if you were not a paperskull, you would have guessed it!'

'It's a lie! I only wrote to tell you of my engagement after the notice of yours had appeared in the *Gazette*!' she said swiftly.

'And you thought that because you hadn't told me of it I didn't know? Well, I did know! You cannot live in a man's pocket here, my girl, without setting tongues wagging! From three separate sources did I hear of your doings!'

'If you choose to listen to gossip –'

'No, I didn't listen to it – until I knew who it was who had appeared in Bath! *Then* I did more than listen! I got the truth out of Claypole!'

'You didn't so much as remember Hector!' she stammered.

'Of course I remembered him!' he said scornfully. 'I remembered something else too! – that unknown person whose name you refused to divulge, when I first visited you here!'

'Unknown person?' she repeated blankly. 'Oh, good God! Mrs Floore! I had not *seen* Hector then! Ivo, what a *fool* you were!'

'I was a fool,' he said grimly, 'but not in believing that Claypole spoke the truth!'

'And you became engaged to Emily merely because *I* – Ivo, it is beyond words! To use a child very nearly young enough to be your daughter as a weapon of revenge on me – I wonder that you dare to stand there and tell me of such an *iniquity*!' Serena said hotly.

'It wasn't as bad as that!' he said, flushing. 'I meant *then* to marry her! If that curst Adonis of yours had won you, what did it signify whom I married? I must marry *someone*, and Emily was as good as another – better! I knew I could mould her into whatever shape I pleased; I knew she would be happy enough with what I could give her; I knew the Laleham-harpy would jump at my offer. And I knew you would hate it, Serena! Oh, yes, infamous, wasn't it? I did it because I was mad with anger – but I never meant to play the child false!'

'And what, most noble Marquis,' enquired Serena scathingly, 'made you change your mind, and decide instead to be rid of her?'

He set his hands on her shoulders, and gripped them, holding her eyes with his. 'Years ago, Serena, you fancied yourself head over ears in love with a devilish handsome lad! I didn't think then that he was the man for you – and when I saw you both together here, I was even more certain of it! But when I heard of his reappearance, and of the reception he got from you, I was shaken as I never was before, and hope to God I never shall be again! But the instant I saw the pair of you I knew that

I had rolled myself up to no purpose at all! I don't know what madness seized you, but I do know that you don't love Kirkby, and never did, or will!'

She wrenched herself away. 'Did you? Did you, indeed? Perhaps you thought I loved you!'

'No – but I knew that I still loved you! I could see you would break with Kirkby – Lord, Serena, if I hadn't been in such a damned tangle myself I should have laughed myself into stitches! My poor girl, did you really think you could be happy with a man that would let you walk rough-shod over him? For how long did you enjoy having your own, undisputed way? When did you begin to feel bored?'

'Let me tell you this, Rotherham!' she flung at him. 'Hector is worth a dozen of you!'

'Oh, probably two or three dozen! What has that to say to anything?'

'It has this to say! I am pledged to him, and I shall marry him, so let me recommend you to lose no time in reinstating yourself in Emily's good graces! How *dare* you talk to me like this? And to think I didn't believe the things Emily poured out to me today!' She paused, almost choking. 'You deliberately tried to make that girl cry off!'

'Well, how the devil else was I to get out of a marriage that was going to wreck the pair of us – and Emily, too, for that matter?'

'*You* made your bed –'

'– and we could all of us lie on it, I suppose?' he interjected witheringly.

She drew a breath. 'Good God, had you no compunction? You had offered her a great position, a –'

'Yes, I had! And if you fancy that her mother forced her to accept my offer, you're out, my girl! I never tampered with her affections: don't think it! Had I thought she cared one jot for me it would have been a different story, but she didn't! She wanted nothing from me but rank and fortune, and she made that abundantly plain!'

'Ivo, did you, or did you not make violent love to her, and tell her that if she played the coquette with you after you were married it would be very much the worse for her?' Serena demanded.

'Oh, not then!' he replied coolly. 'That was later! God knows what she thought I had in store for her, little fool!'

'Oh, how I wish she had slapped your face!' raged Serena.

'So did I wish it!' he retorted. 'Lord, Serena, I even made her think I should be such a jealous husband that she would do better to marry a Bluebeard! I ran the gamut of impatience, jealousy, intemperate passion, veiled threats, and nothing I could do or say outweighed my coronet!'

'In her mother's eyes!'

'Oh, yes! I don't deny that woman had a good deal to do with it! But make no mistake about it, Serena! – until I convinced Emily that she would not enjoy all that stuff by half as much as she had thought she would, I could have been as brutal as I chose, and she would still have married me!'

She gave a gasp. 'Delford! Ivo, you – you *fiend*! When she told me about that visit – the pomp and the ceremony you overwhelmed her with – the *people* you filled the house with – the formality you insisted on – I thought that either she was exaggerating to impress me, or that you had run mad!'

He grinned at her. 'You never saw such a party! I had the state apartments opened, and shut my own rooms up, and dug out the gold plate, and –'

'How you can stand there and *boast* to me – ! No wonder Emily stared at me when I told her you had no turn for ceremony!'

'Grandeur she wanted, and grandeur I gave her – full measure, and brimming over! Lady Laleham revelled in it, but Emily didn't. That was when I saw the scales begin to tip. Then she was ill – by the bye, Serena, that was the best thing I've ever heard Gerard say! I told him Emily had been suffering from an attack of influenza, and damme if he didn't rip back at me that it was more likely an attack of the Marquis of Rotherham! I never thought the boy had it in him to land me such a doubler!'

'Or to elope with Emily?' she demanded. 'Was that your doing too? I can believe you capable even of that!'

'No, it never entered my head that he had enough spirit for such a stroke as that. All I did was to try whether I could sting him into coming here, and enacting his tragedy to Emily. He prated about the attachment that had existed between them, and for anything I knew it might have been true. If it was true, and he had enough courage to come here in defiance of me, I thought he might be the very thing that was wanted to weigh the scales completely down against that damned coronet. I gave him a couple of day's grace, and then sent Emily a letter, calculated – as you so correctly pointed out to me, my clever one! – to scare her out of her wits. I can't say I expected an elopement, though.'

'And if you had? Do you expect me to believe that you would not still have used the wretched boy in that unprincipled way?'

To her seething anger, he appeared to consider this quite dispassionately for a moment or two. 'No, I couldn't have helped him to a Gretna Green marriage,' he decided.

'This is something indeed! No doubt, if I had not frustrated that crazy scheme, *you* would now be posting north to do it yourself!'

'What I should be doing at this moment, if you had not wrecked everything with your damned meddling, would be thanking God for deliverance!' he returned trenchantly. 'What I *thought* to find here was Emily playing Juliet to Gerard's Romeo! His heroics may not appeal to me, but they are just the thing to put a little spirit into her! All she needed to make her cry off by the time her mother sent her here, was someone to support her! The fool that I was, I believed I could rely on *you* to scotch what you must have seen was the worst marriage ever planned! Very free you are with your condemnations of what *I* did, you shrew! Reserve some of your censure for your own behaviour! Instead of telling the chit she had better go hang herself than cling like a damned limpet to a man you knew would make her a hellish husband, you did all you could to persuade her I had all the amiable qualities which no one knows better than you I have *not*! By the time Gerard burst in on me, I knew you were failing me, but that you were ranged on the side of the Laleham-harpy I never dreamed! What was in that red head of yours, my sweetest scold? Spite?'

Quick as a flash she struck at him, but he was quicker still, and caught her wrist in mid-air. 'Oh, no, you don't! You'll hit me when I choose to let you, and at no other time, Serena! Why did you try to push me into that marriage? Answer me, *damn* you!'

'I never pushed you into anything!' she replied pantingly. 'Wiser men than you have fallen in love with pretty feather heads! You to talk to *me* of spite! It never entered my head that you had offered for Emily because you wanted to be revenged on me, and hoped I should be hurt! You have gone your length, Rotherham! I may be every one of the things you are so obliging as to call me, but the only thought I had was to save you from the humiliation of being twice jilted! You may let me go: I would not *touch* you, any more than I would touch a toad!'

He laughed. 'Wouldn't you? We'll see that! Now, you listen to me, my girl! There's nothing I should like better than to continue quarrelling with you, but thanks to your well-meant but corkbrained efforts on my behalf the tangle is now past unravelling, and must be cut! When I've done that, I'll come back, and you may revile me to your heart's content!'

'Don't you dare set foot inside this house again!' she said.

'Try if you can keep me out!' he advised her, and let her wrist go, and strode out of the room, a little too quickly for Lybster, hovering in a disinterested fashion in the narrow hall. 'What a rare day's entertainment for you!' he said sardonically.

'I beg your lordship's pardon?' said Lybster, the picture of bewildered dignity.

'You may well! Inform Lady Spenborough that I shall be dining here tonight!'

'Yes, my lord.'

Serena was in the doorway, her eyes flashing green fire. 'You will on no account admit Lord Rotherham into this house, Lybster!'

'No, my lady,' said Lybster, moving to the street door, and opening it for Rotherham.

Serena turned towards the stairs. Fanny, on the first landing, whisked herself back into the drawing-room, and softly closed the door. 'There! You heard what she said!' she whispered to Major Kirkby.

'Yes, and I heard what he said,' he replied.

Serena's hasty steps sounded outside. Fanny looked anxiously towards the door, but Serena passed on, and up the next flight. 'Oh, dear, I fear she is in one of her rages!' said Fanny. 'What shall I do? Oh, what a dreadful day this is!'

He smiled. 'No, I think not, love. If I were you, I would do what I am going to do: retire to change for dinner!'

'Hector, you don't mean to leave me to dine with those two?' she cried, aghast.

'Not I! Do you think I have no interest in the outcome of this battle? I too am dining with you, my love!' he said.

Twenty-three

Admitted into Mrs Floore's house, Rotherham had barely time to hand his hat to the butler before a door opened at the back of the hall, and Lady Laleham came out, dressed in all the elegance of figured silk and lace, and wreathed in smiles. 'Ah, dear Lord Rotherham!' she pronounced. 'I knew you might be depended upon to call again! Such a sad mischance that you should have found no one at home when you came this afternoon! But you must not blame us, you know, for you forgot to tell Emily which day you meant to arrive in Bath! I hope I see you well?'

'My health, I thank you, ma'am, is excellent. I cannot, however, say as much for my temper, which has been exasperated beyond anything which I am prepared to endure!' he replied, in his harshest voice.

She laid the tips of her fingers on his arm, in a fleeting gesture of sympathy. 'I know,' she said, considerably to his surprise. 'Will you come into the morning-room? You will, I know, forgive my mother for not receiving you: she is elderly, and, alas, not capable of exertion!'

'The person I wish to see, Lady Laleham, is not your mother, but your daughter!'

'Exactly so!' she smiled, preceding him into the morning room. 'And here she is!'

He strode into the room, and paused, looking grimly at his prospective bride. She was standing beside a large wing chair, one trembling hand resting on its back, her eyes huge in her white face, and her breathing uneven. She looked very young, very pretty, and very apprehensive, and she showed no disposition to come forward to greet her betrothed until her mother said, in a voice of honeyed reproof: 'Emily-dear!' After that, she advanced, and said: 'How do you do?' putting out her hand.

'Effusive!' said Rotherham. 'You must not behave as though I were your whole dependence and delight, you know!'

'She is a little tired,' explained Lady Laleham, 'and she has been a very silly, naughty child, which she knows she must confess to you.'

His eyes went to her face, an arrested expression in them.

'L-Lady Serena said I n-need not t-tell, Mama!'

'We are very much indebted to Lady Serena, my love,' Lady Laleham returned smoothly, 'but you will allow Mama to know best what you should do.' She met Rotherham's fierce stare with perfect coolness, a faint smile on her painted lips. 'The poor child is afraid that you will be very angry with her, Lord Rotherham, but I have assured her that where there is full confession there must always be forgiveness, particularly when it is accompanied by deep repentance.'

The wretched Emily, perceiving that her betrothed was looking like a thundercloud, began to feel faint. But Rotherham was not thinking about her. He was seeing the ground being cut from beneath his feet by a stratagem which he recognized, in a cold fury, to be masterly. And he could think of no way to prevent Emily from casting herself upon his mercy. Out it all came, in halting, shamefaced sentences from Emily, skilfully embroidered by her mother. She had thought he was very angry with her, when she had received his letter; he had stayed away from her for so long that she feared he no longer loved her; Gerard had told her such dreadful things that she had taken fright. But Lady Serena had come to the rescue just when she was wishing she had not done such a wicked thing; and Lady Serena had assured her that she had nothing to fear from Lord Rotherham. So she had come home and had been crying her eyes out ever since because she was so very, very sorry. Finally, would he forgive her, and believe that she would never do it again?

He became aware that she had finished speaking, and saw that her eyes were fixed on his face in a look of painful enquiry. He said abruptly: 'Emily, do you love Gerard?'

'Oh, *no*!' she said, and there was no mistaking the sincerity in her voice.

No way of escape there. There was only one way out, and that was to play the outraged lover, and repudiate the engagement. It could not be done. To push her into flinging that handsome diamond ring he had given her in his face was one thing; to push her into eloping with his ward, and then to round on her, was quite another. He wondered what pressure her mother had brought to bear to make her so anxious to marry him. She was no longer thinking of riches and position. If he could get rid of Lady Laleham, he might be able to reach an understanding with Emily – if she was capable of understanding anything, which she did not look to be.

'I think it would be as well if we talked this over alone,' he said.

Lady Laleham had no intention of allowing this. Unfortunately, Emily's terror of him was greater than her dread of her mother, and she gave him no support, but shrank towards Lady Laleham.

At which moment the door opened, and a startling vision surged into the room. 'I thought as much!' said Mrs Floore ominously. 'And who gave you leave to entertain guests in my house, Sukey?' She retained her clutch on Mr Goring's supporting arm, and added: 'No, you stay here, Ned! There's nothing that's happened here this day you don't know, and a true friend you've been, like your father would have been before you!'

Rotherham, with difficulty withdrawing his eyes from the magnificence before him, glanced at Lady Laleham. What he saw in her face afforded him considerable solace. Fury and chagrin were writ large in it, and beneath these emotions, unless he much mistook the matter, fear. So this was the mysterious grandmother about whom he had quizzed Emily on his first meeting with her! He bent his penetrating stare upon her again, as she settled herself in the chair of her choice, and directed Mr Goring to pull forward a footstool.

Mrs Floore was doing justice to the occasion in a staggering gown of lustring, with tobine stripes of a rich ruby, and a quantity of floss trimming. This splendid robe was draped over panniers, fashionable in her youth, and was worn over an underdress of satin. A medley of brooches adorned the low-cut corsage, and round her short neck she had clasped several strings of remarkably large pearls. A turban of ruby silk and tinsel was embellished with a cluster of ostrich plumes, and from the lobes of her ears hung two large rubies.

'That's right,' nodded Mrs Floore, shifting the position of the stool a trifle with one red heeled and buckled shoe. 'Now let me take a look at this precious Marquis I've heard so much about!'

Lady Laleham, with an unconvincing smile pinned to her mouth, murmured to Rotherham: 'Dear Mama is quite an eccentric!'

'I'm not an eccentric, and I'm not deaf!' said her dear Mama sharply. 'I'm a plain woman that came of good merchant stock, which, though I may not have your fine-lady airs and graces, my dear, I've got more sense than to be ashamed of! And another thing I'll tell you is that you'd do better to introduce this Marquis to me than to stand there biting your lips, and wondering what he must be thinking of your ma! He can think what he likes, and if Emma means to marry him – which, however, isn't by any means a settled thing! – the sooner he gets used to her grandma the better it will be for him!'

'How do you do?' said Rotherham, slightly bowing, his tone indifferent, but his eyes keenly surveying this amazing old lady.

She gave him back stare for stare, taking him in from the heels of his boots to the crown of his black locks. 'Good gracious, you're a regular blackamoor!' she exclaimed. 'Well, they say handsome is as handsome does, but from all I can make out, my lord, you haven't done very handsome yet.'

'You must not mind Mama: she is so droll!' said Lady Laleham.

'It'll be more to the point if I don't mind him,' observed Mrs Floore, who was clearly in a belligerent mood. 'You must excuse me staring at you, my lord, but I never did see such peculiar eyebrows! Now, I shouldn't wonder at it, Emma, my pet, if half the time you thought he was scowling at you it was nothing but the way his eyebrows grow, which he can't help, though, of course, it's a pity.'

Rotherham kept his countenance set in its forbidding lines. At any other moment, he would have exerted himself to please Mrs Floore, for he was strongly attracted to her, but since her attitude appeared to be hostile he saw in her his one hope of salvation, and began to consider how best to annoy her.

'Dear Mama, you know that Emily wished to see Lord Rotherham in private!' said Lady Laleham. 'Don't you think, perhaps –'

'No, I don't,' replied Mrs Floore bluntly. 'What's more, it wasn't Emma that wanted to be private with him, and if she had done, I don't see much privacy for her with you standing over her, Sukey!'

'You forget, Mama, that I am her mother.'

'Well, and if I do, whose fault is that?' demanded Mrs Floore. 'You act motherly, and maybe I *won't* forget! From the look on poor little Emma's face, you've been bullying her, the pair of you. That's right, Ned, you give her a chair, and don't you be afraid, my pet, because you haven't any need to be!'

'None at all!' said Lady Laleham. 'Lord Rotherham has been most forbearing, just as I knew he would be, and has not uttered one word of censure, has he, Emily?'

'No, Mama,' said Emily, in a small, scared voice.

'It's to be hoped he hasn't!' said Mrs Floore, her eyes snapping. 'That's not to say he won't hear a word of censure from me – in fact, a good many words! Yes, it's all very well to be high in the instep, my lord, and to look at me as though I was a spider, and very likely you're thinking I'm just a vulgar old woman, but what I say is that if anyone's to blame for what's happened it's you!'

'I've no objection to vulgarity,' replied Rotherham. 'What, however, I do not tolerate is interference. That had better be understood immediately.'

Mrs Floore seemed to swell. 'Ho! So when I tell you I won't have my granddaughter made miserable, that's interference, is it.'

'If Emily is made miserable by me, the remedy is in her own hands.'

'Mama, pray be quiet!' cried Lady Laleham. 'Such nonsense! As though she has not every reason to be the happiest girl alive!'

'You may toad-eat his lordship as much as you like, Sukey, but don't you run away with the idea you can tell me to be quiet, or you and me will fall out, which would *not* suit your book! Ever since Emma got herself engaged to this Marquis, she's looked downright seedy, and she's been no more her merry self –'

'My dear Mama, I have told you a score of times that London, and all the gaieties she enjoyed, were too much for her!'

'Then there is no need for you to feel any further anxiety about her health,' said Rotherham. 'We are not going to live in London.'

This pronouncement, uttered as it was in a curt, matter-of-fact voice, surprised Emily into uplifting her voice: 'Not going to live in London?' she repeated.

'No.'

'Dear child, Lord Rotherham means that you will mostly be at Delford, or at Claycross!' interposed Lady Laleham. 'Naturally, you will be in London for a few months during the spring!'

'I mean nothing of the sort,' said Rotherham, without heat, but with finality. 'I am closing Rotherham House.'

'Closing Rotherham House?' exclaimed Lady Laleham, as though she could not believe her ears. 'But – but why?'

He shrugged. 'I dislike living in town, and abominate *ton* parties.'

Emily's eyes darkened in dismay. 'N-no parties at all?' she asked.

He glanced down at her. 'We shall entertain at Delford, of course.'

'Oh, no!' she said involuntarily. 'I-I couldn't!' She flushed, and added pleadingly: 'I would rather live in London! At least, *some* part of the year! Delford is so very big, and – and – I don't like it!'

'I am afraid, since it is my home, you will have to overcome your dislike of it.'

'Of course she will!' said Lady Laleham. 'But surely you cannot mean to keep her there throughout the year!'

'Why not?'

'I'll soon tell you why not!' interrupted Mrs Floore, who had been listening in gathering wrath. 'If Delford is the place where poor little Emma had to walk half a mile from her bedroom to the dining-room, it isn't the kind of house that'll suit her at all! Besides, from what she tells me, it's stuck right out in the country, and she's had enough of that kind of thing at Cherrifield Place! What's she going to do with herself all day long?'

'She will find plenty to do, I imagine. She will have first to learn what is expected of Lady Rotherham, which is likely to keep her pretty fully occupied for some months. She will hunt, of course –'

'Hunt?' cried Emily. 'Oh, no, please! I never do so!'

'You will,' he said.

'J-jump over those *dreadful* fences you showed me?' Emily said, horror in her voice. 'I *couldn't*!'

'We shall see!'

'Well, if ever I heard anything to equal it!' gasped Mrs Floore. 'First, she's to learn a lot of lessons, and next she's to be made to break her neck!'

'Oh, she won't break her neck!' said Rotherham. 'A few tumbles won't hurt her! I shall have some fairly easy jumps put up, and school her over them.'

'*No!*' almost shrieked Emily. 'I won't, I won't!'

'No more you shall, lovey!' hotly declared Mrs Floore.

'It will be as well, Emily, if you realize that when you are Lady Rotherham I shall expect obedience from you. I warn you, it will not do if you say "I won't" to me.'

Mr Goring, who had been seated rather in the background got up, and said in his level tone: 'We've heard a great deal of what *you* expect, and what *you* like, my lord, but we haven't yet heard you ask Miss Laleham what *she* would like!'

'She'll learn to like what I like – if she's wise! I did not choose a bride out of the schoolroom, sir, to have her setting up her will against mine!'

Mr Goring's jaw was becoming momentarily more aggressive. 'It seems to me, Lord Rotherham, that what you want is a slave, not a wife!'

Mrs Floore, unable to contain herself another instant, said forcefully: 'And he's not getting a slave in my Emma! Why, the man's a downright monster! A fine husband you caught for Emma, Sukey! I wonder you aren't ashamed to look me in the face! If I didn't say to Lady Serena that it wouldn't matter to you if a man was cross-eyed, and had one foot in the grave! Not so long as he was a Duke, which is all you care for! And this Choctaw Indian here isn't even a Duke!'

There was the faintest tremor at the corners of Rotherham's mouth, but it went unnoticed. Lady Laleham said: 'I cannot believe that Lord Rotherham means all he says! I am sure he means to make Emily very happy!'

'Certainly,' said Rotherham, bored. 'She has only to adapt herself to my wishes, and I see no reason why she should not be perfectly happy.'

Suddenly Emily sprang up, and fled to her grandmother's chair. 'I can't, I can't! I don't care if I am ruined! I *can't*! Oh, Grandmama, don't let Mama make me!'

'Emily!' There was a red spot on each of Lady Laleham's cheeks. 'How dare you say such a thing? As though I should dream –'

'You keep your distance, Sukey!' commanded Mrs Floore.

Mr Goring, stepping up to Rotherham, his chin now well out-thrust, said: 'Perhaps your lordship will do me the favour of stepping outside for a few minutes!'

'No, you fool!' said Rotherham, very softly.

'Emily, think what you are doing!' Lady Laleham was saying urgently. 'You'll never get a husband, if you play the jilt! Particularly after your folly today! The whole world will think it was *you* who were jilted! You'll have to stay at home, for I shan't take you to town again, and you'll end your days an old maid –'

'You're wrong, ma'am!' said Mr Goring. 'There's time and to spare before she need think of being married, but you needn't fear she won't get another offer, because I can tell you that she will!'

'You can lay your life she will!' said Mrs Floore. 'Now, don't you cry, my pretty, because your ma isn't going to make you do anything!'

'What shall I do?' sobbed Emily. 'I don't w-want to go home in d-disgrace, and I don't w-want to have n-no reputation!'

'Emma, would you like to stay with your old grandma? Now, think, lovey! It ain't very lively, living here, and nothing but the Assemblies, and the Sydney Gardens, and if it's the *ton* parties you want, I can't give them to you, because if I was to take you to London I couldn't chaperon you, my pet, because there's no getting round it, I'm not a fine lady, and I never will be! Myself, I think you'd be a deal happier if you was to forget all these Marquises and things, but it's for you to say.'

'Live with you *always*?' Emily cried, lifting a flushed, tear-stained face from Mrs Floore's lap. 'Oh, *Grandmama*!'

'Bless you, my precious!' said Mrs Floore, giving her a smacking kiss.

'Have you taken leave of your senses?' demanded Lady Laleham. 'I'll have you know Emily is *my* daughter, Mama!'

'And I'll have you know, Sukey, that if I have one more word out of you, you can pay your own bills from now on, and so can Sir Walter!'

There was a pregnant silence. Mrs Floore patted Emily's shoulder. 'You dry your eyes, love, and give the Marquis back his ring!'

'When you see your sisters all married before you, I hope you will remember this day, Emily!' said Lady Laleham. 'For my part, I wash my hands of you!'

'And a very good thing too,' commented Mrs Floore. 'Go on, love! The sooner we're rid of this Marquis of yours the sooner we can have our dinner, which I'm sure we all need!'

The door shut with a slam behind Lady Laleham. Emily shyly held out the ring to Rotherham. 'If you please – I beg your pardon, – but we should not *suit*!'

'Thank you,' he said, taking the ring. 'You have no need to beg my pardon: I will beg yours instead. The truth is that we both made a mistake. I wish you extremely happy, and I feel sure you will be – but Mr Goring is quite right: there's plenty of time before you need think of marriage. As for your reputation, and your sisters, and all the rest of that nonsense, you needn't regard it!' He glanced at the ring in his hand, and said: 'I think you had better keep this – but wear it on another finger!'

'Oh, *thank* you!' gasped Emily naïvely.

He turned from her, to confront Mrs Floore, who had heaved herself up out of her chair, and was eyeing him with sharp suspicion. He grinned at her. 'Don't worry, ma'am! All that you would like to say to me, and a great deal more, has already been hurled at my head, and I fancy there is more to come. I am delighted to have made your acquaintance, and I trust that – next year, perhaps – I shall have the pleasure of entertaining you, and Emily, of course, at Rotherham House! By the way, don't send a notice to the papers! I shall be sending one that will obviate the necessity, and will convince the world that I have treated Emily abominably – which, I own, I have!'

'So that's it, is it?' said Mrs Floore. 'Of all the impudence! Well, I'm sorry for her, that's all! And I hope with all my heart that she'll lead you such a dance as will put you in your place once and for all!'

'She will do her best. Pay me a visit when you come to town, Goring, and we'll put the gloves on. You shall tell me, too, how you enjoyed taking care of Lady Serena: you have my sympathy!'

A brief bow, and he was gone. Half an hour later, he was being admitted to the house in Laura Place by Fanny's footman.

He found the butler in the drawing-room, engaged in lighting the candles in the wall-sconces. 'Masterly, Lybster!' he said. 'Go and tell the Lady Serena that although you did not let me in I am nevertheless here, and should like to see her immediately!'

'Her ladyship, my lord,' said Lybster, with an apologetic cough, 'informed me that if your lordship *should* happen to cross the threshold, she would partake of dinner in her bedchamber.'

'Did she, by God? Go and tell her ladyship that if she does not come down to me, I shall go up to her!'

'Yes, my lord – if your lordship insists!' said Lybster, and departed.

He did not return, but within five minutes Serena swept into the room, her cheeks flushed, and her eyes far too fierce to suit the dove gray gown she was wearing. 'How – *dare* – you send me insolent messages by my own servants?' she demanded.

'I thought that would fetch you down,' he remarked, walking forward.

'Yes, and you will be shortly extremely sorry that it did! If you think, Ivo –'

This speech ended abruptly. Not only was she roughly jerked into Rotherham's arms, but her mouth was crushed under his. For a moment or two, she strained every muscle to break free, and then, quite suddenly, the fight went out of her, and she seemed to melt into his embrace. It tightened ruthlessly, and only relaxed sufficiently to allow her to get her breath when Rotherham at last raised his head, and looked down into her eyes. 'Well, you beautiful, bad-tempered thorn in my flesh? Well? Have you done scolding yet?'

She lay against his arm, her head flung back on his shoulder her eyes glinting at him under their curved lids. 'Detestable creature! Mannerless, conscienceless, overbearing, selfish, arrogant – oh, how much I dislike you!' she sighed. 'And how much you dislike me! I'd as lief be mauled by a tiger! You're mad, too. Never were you more thankful to be rid of anything than of me! Own it! All these years – !'

'Never!' he assented fervently. 'I swore then that never again would I put it in your power to drive me to the brink of insanity with your obstinate, headstrong, wilful, *intolerable* conduct! But it's no use, Serena! don't you *know* that? I thought I had torn you out of my heart – I thought you were nothing to me but an old friend's daughter – until – What made you do it, Serena? What crazy folly made you do it?'

The smile vanished from her eyes. 'O God, I don't know! I *meant* it, Ivo! When I saw him again – oh, I felt I was a girl – a nineteen-year-old! Perhaps it was because I was so lonely, perhaps because he still loved me so much, thought me a goddess, flattered me – oh, Ivo, *worshipped* me as you never did, I'll swear!'

'No, I don't worship you,' he said, mocking her. 'I know you for what you are, you enchanting termagant! And what you are I can't exist without! I saw him worshipping you, poor devil, and shutting his eyes to your imperfections! I pitied him, but I held him in contempt as well, because what is most admirable in you he liked least! *I'll* open no gates for you, my girl! you'll take any fence I take, and we'll clear it neck and neck!' He felt the response in the quiver that ran through her, and laughed, and kissed her again. 'You may set the county alight, if you choose, but ride rough-shod over me you will not, if we fight from cockcrow to sundown!'

'Ivo, Ivo!' she whispered, turning her face into his shoulder. She seemed to struggle with herself, and looked up at last, to say: 'I cannot – I must not! It is too base – and oh, what would Papa say to me for behaving *ungentlemanly*? Ivo, I have been Hector's *dream*!'

'It's a dream he has awakened from, believe me!' he said dryly. 'Lord, Serena, the clever fool that you are! Stop mouthing fustian to me, or I'll shake some sense into you! Haven't you

seen what has been going on under your nose? Your calf-love doesn't want to be your husband! He is hoping to God he may become your father-in-law!'

She stared at him with knit brows; then she began to laugh. He kissed her again, heard a slight sound, and looked over her head towards the door. Major Kirkby, quietly entering the room, was standing with one hand on the door, watching them.

'I don't beg your pardon, Kirkby,' Rotherham said. 'I am reclaiming my own property.'

Serena pulled herself out of his arms, and went towards the Major, her hands held out: 'Hector, forgive me! I have used you so shamefully: I think I must be the most fickle wretch alive!'

He took her hands and kissed them. 'Not as fickle as I! Nor such a crass fool! My dear, I wish you happy with all my heart! You are a grander creature than any I ever dreamed of.'

She smiled. 'Only I am not your dear. And you are the kindest and best of men, but not my love!'

He was still holding her hands, rather flushed, a rueful look in his eye. 'There is something – I don't know how to tell you! I must appear worse than a fool!'

'I've told her already,' interposed Rotherham. 'I see no need to wish you happy: you will both be extremely happy!' He held out his hand, and gripped the Major's, saying, with his derisive smile: 'Do you own at last that I was right, when I told Spenborough seven years ago that you and Serena would never suit? When I met you again, in this house, I came prepared to dislike you profoundly: I ended the evening most sincerely pitying you! You are too good a man for such a termagant, Kirkby!'

'How like you – how *very* like you!' Serena said. Her eyes went to the door. 'Fanny! Oh, foolish Fanny, why didn't you tell me to take my claws out of Hector weeks ago? My dear, you were made for one another!'

'Oh, Serena, I feel a traitress!' Fanny said, her eyes brimming over.

'No, why should you? I'm afraid you will be shocked, my dear, but I am going to marry the odious Marquis after all!'

'Hector said it would be so,' Fanny said, sighing. 'I do so much *hope* that you will be happy, dearest!'

'You don't depend upon it, however, Lady Spenborough?'

She blushed rosily. 'Oh, no, no! I mean, yes! Only it has always seemed to me that you held one another in positive aversion!'

'Acute of you!'

She had never known how to take his abrupt, incomprehensible remarks, and was always flurried by them. She said quickly: 'I am so very glad you have made up your differences! My lord would have been so happy!' She saw Serena's face quiver, and added at once: 'Only, how very awkward it will be for you! How shall you advertise it? For you will be dreadfully roasted, you know, if you announce your engagement for the *second* time!'

Serena turned laughing eyes towards Rotherham. 'Fanny is perfectly right! Shall we say that the engagement between the Marquis of Rotherham and the Lady Serena Carlow has been *resumed*?'

'No, intolerable! I will never be engaged to you again, Serena! The advertisement which I propose to send to the *Gazette* will state that the marriage between the Marquis of Rotherham and the Lady Serena Carlow took place, privately, at Bath.'

Her eyes lit, but she said: 'Ivo, how can I? It is not yet a year.'

'No, it is not a year, but even your Aunt Theresa will not think it improper if I add to the notice the information that we are spending our honeymoon abroad, and do not expect to be in England again until November. There will be no wedding festivities, and no bride-visits. What we may choose to do while touring the Continent will offend no one.' He stretched out his hand imperatively, and she laid hers in it. His fingers closed on hers. 'We will do better this time, Serena.'

'Yes,' she said, holding tightly to his hand. 'We will do better, Ivo!'

BY JANE AIKEN HODGE

An internationally bestselling phenomenon and queen of the Regency romance, Georgette Heyer is one of the most beloved historical novelists of our time. She wrote more than fifty novels, yet her private life was inaccessible to any but her nearest friends and relatives.

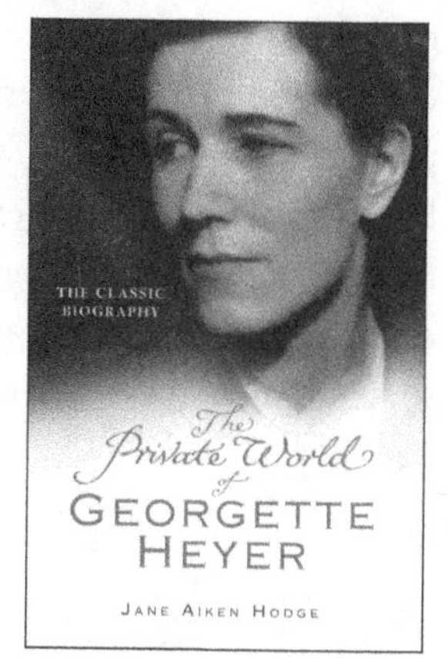

Lavishly illustrated and with access to private papers, correspondence and family archives, this classic biography opens a window into Georgette Heyer's world and that of her most memorable characters, revealing a formidable, energetic woman with an impeccable sense of style and, beyond everything, a love for all things Regency.

"The Georgette Heyer bible... This is a must-have book for any Georgette Heyer lover."

—HISTORICALLY OBSESSED

978-1-4022-5192-4 • $14.99 U.S.

About the Author

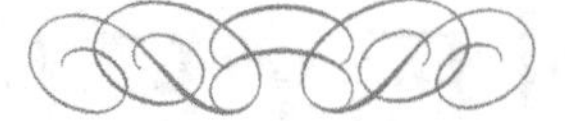

Author of over fifty books, Georgette Heyer is one of the best-known and best-loved of all historical novelists, making the Regency period her own. Her first novel, *The Black Moth*, published in 1921, was written at the age of seventeen to amuse her convalescent brother; her last was *My Lord John*. Although most famous for her historical novels, she also wrote twelve detective stories. Georgette Heyer died in 1974 at the age of seventy-one.